I0585369

CHILD OF PARADISE

BOOK FOUR OF THE PARADISE SERIES

IVANA L. TRUGLIO

JONQUIL
PRESS

First published in Australia in 2019
by Jonquil Press
ABN: 99871403756

A catalogue record for this
book is available from the
National Library of Australia

ISBN: 978-0-6483416-2-8 (paperback)

Cover illustration by Gabriel T. Marques

Typeset in Minion Pro 9.2pt/10.5pt

For Chris,
who supports me every step of the way
even when I ask him to roleplay scenes with swords

ABOUT THE AUTHOR

Ivana lives in Sydney, Australia. She devotes most, if not all, of her spare time to writing.

She studied aviation, archaeology and ancient history at university. During her studies, it was rumoured that she lived in the university library. She holds a private pilot licence, rides a motorbike and is attempting to learn the violin.

Ivana is married and has two young children who reap the benefits of having a mother with a wild imagination. She has been writing since she was a child and the characters in the Paradise Series have been living in her head for over 20 years.

ACKNOWLEDGEMENTS

This book has been a long time coming and I thank everyone for not getting angry with how long it's taken to finish. I want you to know that the reason for this is that I wanted to make it as good as I could. It's the last book in a series that I have been writing on and off since high school. Plots that started over twenty years ago needed to be resolved and that took time to get right.

I think it's important to thank my family – they never seem to mind just how much time I spend writing my stories. They don't make me feel guilty for basically ignoring them while they're in the same room by putting my headphones on and typing away.

I've been through a few editors with this series and can honestly say that *Child of Paradise* would not be the book it is without my current and favourite editor, Anicee Dowling. She makes the editing experience that much less painful, while still providing constructive criticism.

Though most of them only got to read the first half of the book, I thank my writing group for all their comments and support when I felt (like every author feels at some point) that it just wasn't worth the effort.

As some of you already know, I have a new cover illustrator this time around. Thanks to everyone who voted for the designs from my DesignCrowd choices. I love the artwork that Gabriel T. Marques did for me and how easy it was to work with him.

Finally, I'd like to thank everyone who has read my books. You're not the reason I write, but you *are* the reason I publish. Every time someone reviews or rates my books online, it makes me smile so much my cheeks hurt! I love finding out what you think of my books, and it's a great way to help other people to decide if they should read them. The power is in your hands.

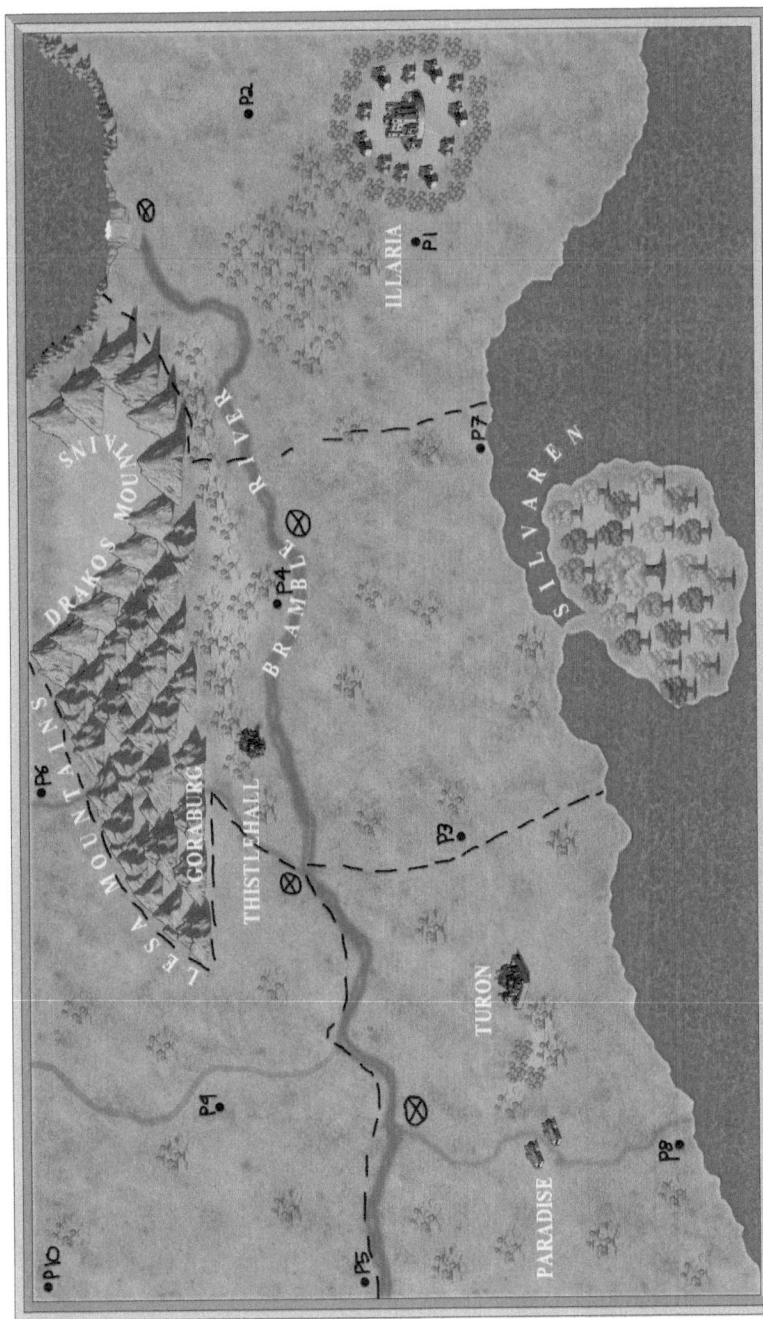

Chapter One – Not A Word

"He's not dead. He's not dead," Rilla mumbled over and over.

Shuut looked at her sister as she sat rocking herself back and forth. Aislen was not much better. Shuut could feel the hopelessness cascading off her.

"Do something," Shuut angrily instructed Kayte.

"What do you expect of me?" Mistress Kayte replied evenly.

"Stop your princess before she drowns the whole castle in her misery."

There was a pounding at the door.

"Open the door!"

Shuut rushed to let King Lukys in. He immediately ran to Aislen and roughly grabbed her wrists. Shuut began to protest until she realised her feelings were her own again. Whatever his methods, Lukys had just fixed Aislen.

"What happened? What's wrong with *that one*?"

Shuut took offence to the way Lukys spoke about her sister. This was not Rilla's fault. Why did they always assume everything was her fault? A guilty thought trickled through her mind – she had been prone to doing that herself not so very long ago.

"*That one* just helped save your cousin's life. You might want to thank her for it."

Shuut stared at Lukys coldly. She knew he didn't believe her, not really. Aislen got to her feet.

"It's true, Father. Uncle Aaron is gravely injured. Eliséo and Rilla came up with a plan to save him."

Shuut appreciated Aislen's discretion about the precise nature of the wound. It would surely only make Lukys more unreasonable than he already was.

"And they woke me up for it. If you don't mind, I'd like to get some more rest before my morning lessons."

Mistress Kayte took a step towards the door, but Shuut slammed it closed and stood in front of it.

"Not yet. Who's going to help my sister?"

"Your sister is in shock. My skills cannot help her. I'm sure Princess Aislen is more than capable of bringing her out of her situation."

Shuut glared angrily at Mistress Kayte. It was no wonder Rilla found herself at odds with the healing mistress so often. Such arrogance did not go down well with either of them.

"I ... don't think I can," Aislen said in a trembling voice. "If I lose control of my feelings again, it will only make Rilla worse."

Mistress Kayte stood, hands on hips, glaring at Shuut.

"I cannot help her. She is afraid of what is happening out there, and nothing I do can change that. I can't fly us to her elf and Lord Aaron to heal them myself."

"Shuut, let her go."

Shuut looked around Mistress Kayte to Lukys. He rubbed his temples with his fingers. His face was haggard and worn.

"I'm sure between the two of us we can help Rilla. Mistress Kayte is right – she needs to rest for her classes."

Grudgingly, Shuut stood aside to allow the healing mistress to leave. There was an air of hostility around her that Shuut was glad to feel leave the room. Shuut walked over to Rilla and dropped down on the floor by her side. She didn't know what else to do, so she put an arm around Rilla's shoulders. That, at least, stopped the rocking.

"He's not dead. He's not dead."

"That's right, Rilla," Shuut said quietly, hugging her sister. "Eliséo's not dead. And he likely just saved Lord Aaron's life."

"Can someone please tell me what's happened?" Lukys asked in a strained voice.

Shuut knew how close both Aislen and Lukys were with Aaron. They were surely more concerned about him than Eliséo, but Shuut knew it was the reverse for Rilla. If Rilla knew he wasn't dead, then that meant Elessa could still feel him. The fact that she couldn't talk to him, however, must have meant that he was gravely injured.

"We don't know how it happened, but Uncle Aaron was injured," Aislen explained.

"I should never have allowed him to go to Goraburg," Lukys growled.

Shuut snorted. "I doubt you had a choice. Aaron seems to be about as stubborn as the rest of his family, myself included."

Her remark only earned her a glowering scowl. She shrugged indifferently and went back to trying to soothe Rilla.

"He'll be fine," she whispered to Rilla. "With a few days of rest, he'll be up and about. I'm sure of it."

Rilla looked at her with haunted eyes. Shuut drew her close, not wanting to see the look in those eyes.

"We have to help them," Rilla said, suddenly breaking free of her hold. "We have to go there and help them!"

"Where is *there*?" Lukys asked.

Rilla's eyes glowed a bright shade of green.

"They're in the Lesa Mountains, near the Yoswen Stream."

Lukys shook his head.

"It would take days, possibly even a week to ride there. Surely Lord Ilya will send out karliki to look for them when they don't return."

"But ... but that could take days as well," Rilla protested.

"Rilla, we cannot do anything from here," Lukys pointed out. Shuut saw his fists clenched at his side. "I would appreciate if you all keep this information to yourselves until we learn something new. I must insist you stick to your normal routine. I do not want widespread panic without due cause."

"Without due cause?" Shuut found herself asking. "Your cousin, our *grandfather*, and Eliséo could be dying out there!"

Lukys sighed heavily. "I know. But there is nothing we can do about it for now. At the very least, we should spare our pain from as many people as possible. Unless you *want* all of Illaria to feel as worried as you do."

Shuut tapped her teeth together, thinking. He was right. She knew he was. But it didn't make her feel any better it. She thought it was unfair to keep this information a secret, especially from Kora and Plyke.

"Not a word, not even to the rest of your family."

Shuut checked her mental walls. They were firmly guarded. Lukys had not read her mind, but that didn't stop him from knowing what she was thinking.

"Fine," she said angrily. "We won't tell anyone, will we Rilla?"

Rilla looked up at her, a mixture of confusion and fear in her eyes. Shuut tried to smile at her but failed.

"Rilla?"

Her sister nodded but said nothing. Shuut knew that was the most she could expect from Rilla right now. She showed Lukys and Aislen out of her room and closed the door behind them. Left alone with Rilla, Shuut helped her sister off the floor and back to her bed. For the first time since they had been given two separate beds, Shuut crawled into Rilla's bed and lay beside her.

* * *

"Idiot," Anya muttered under her breath as she watched Eliséo fall beside the stricken Aaron. Not trusting skin contact with either of them, she found a sturdy stick to disentangle the elf's hands from the lintep's.

"What happened?" Ermolai asked in confusion.

"I don't know," Anya replied angrily. "But Eliséo now shares a wound just like the lintep and Lord Aaron is breathing more steadily now. All I can guess is that the elf somehow made the lintep heal himself faster than usual by taking on some of the injury himself.

"A fine mess they've made of things. We can't possibly leave them behind, and we can't bring the two of them and the rebels back to Goraburg alone."

"So, what, we just wait?" Rufina asked irritably. "Demyan's family will not be pleased to hear that his body lay in the cold open air while we sat and waited."

"We have no choice, Rufina," Anya pointed out. "Unless you want to walk back to the tunnels alone, then we wait."

"At least we can bring them in from the cold." Ermolai looked at the snow which had just begun to fall. "The first snow of the season could be mild, but I don't want to take the chance and be stuck outside in a blizzard."

Working together, all three being cautious not to allow any skin contact with the lintep, they moved Lord Aaron, Eliséo, and the unconscious rebel into the makeshift hut the rebels had been hiding out in. Without ceremony, they dragged the dead rebel karliki out into the fresh layer of snow on the forest floor.

"You're just going to leave me here?" Vladimir yelled out at them as they retreated to the hut. "You're executing my death sentence by freezing me!"

Anya looked back at the karlik who would have been their clan leader had he only been content to wait his turn. Eliséo had somehow encased his feet in earth, making it impossible for Vladimir to move. Anya didn't know if they really could dig him out, and she did not want to risk being in close quarters with the rebel as he was angry enough to kill them all at the first chance he got.

"Well, Vladimir, think of it this way, if you don't survive the blizzard, at least you won't have the shame of meeting your brother in his new position as clan leader." Anya smiled cruelly at him. She ignored the insults hurled at her as she closed the door of the hut behind her and left the rebel to freeze.

* * *

Aaron opened his eyes groggily. His head was pounding. He could barely see. He tried to move his head but was blinded by pain. Groaning, he sent a small spark of heat into the air, creating a floating flame. Even that small amount of concentration was exhausting, but it gave him all the information he needed before he snuffed it out. He was inside the hut.

Lying still, he tried to remember what had happened.

We found the rebel hideout. Eliséo landed us on the bank of the Yoswen Stream. My job was to subdue the karliki inside before the others went in to kill them. I did that ... and then?

"Lord Aaron?" a familiar voice hesitantly called out. "Are you awake? Ermolai, light a candle."

"What happened?" Aaron asked, as Anya crouched over him, shielding what little light the candle provided. "Where's Eliséo?"

"Beside you," she said. "No! Don't move your head again. He's beside you, with a gash in his head the size of my fist. What did you do to him?"

Memories slowly fought their way through the fog in his mind. Aislen had been there. She had pulled him into consciousness briefly so he could steal enough energy to heal himself. How had Aislen been in his mind?

"Aaron, the elf is dying." Anya brought him back to the present. Eliséo had sacrificed himself in the hopes of saving him.

"Are any of the rebels still alive?" he asked weakly.

Ermolai nodded. "The one who attacked you is unconscious, but alive. We also have Vladimir, but Eliséo bound him outside."

"Bring my assailant here," he ordered hoarsely. Without questioning him, Ermolai, Anya and Rufina dragged the unconscious karlik over. His head still throbbing with pain, Aaron hurriedly searched through the karlik's memories of the rebels. Finding nothing of importance, he took a deep, ragged breath. He'd never tried this before, but he knew it was possible. It would almost certainly spell the karlik's death, but he had been told time and again that her life was forfeit – all rebels' lives were forfeit.

He placed one hand on the fallen karlik's head and felt around until he found Eliséo. Anya, clearly understanding what he was about to attempt, placed his hand gently over the elf's open wound. As soon as she was clear, Aaron drew out all of the rebel's energy. Carefully, he passed it to Eliséo, concentrating it around the wound. Using that energy, he passed a modicum of his own healing power into the elf. The healing power took hold of the extra energy, stealing its strength to heal him. It was a dangerous and delicate procedure. Aaron took great care to ensure the wound healed itself properly. It took longer than he expected but, eventually, the wound grew smaller. Aaron let his hands drop from the elf and the karlik before succumbing to darkness.

* * *

"This is ridiculous," Anya fumed, as Eliséo and Aaron both stirred momentarily and lapsed back into unconsciousness. "We'll be here for days at this rate!"

"What do you suggest?" asked Rufina, irritably. "As you said, we can't bring them back to Goraburg by ourselves, so we're stuck here until they're fit to travel."

"Not necessarily," she thought aloud. "We have a few choices. The first, quite obviously, is to wait here until they are fit to travel. The second is to execute Vladimir, build something to transport the elf, the lintep and Demyan and return to Goraburg. The third is for two of us to travel to Goraburg and get help while the other stays behind to guard these two idiots and make sure Vladimir doesn't somehow escape."

"Kill Vladimir ourselves?" Ermolai gasped.

"His life was always forfeit." Anya shrugged. "What difference does it make if we kill him now? If we'd killed him in the course of defending ourselves, we wouldn't even be having this conversation."

"Don't you think Lord Ilya would want to publicly put him to death if he has the chance?" Ermolai insisted.

"I think Lord Ilya would be angrier with us for somehow allowing him to escape while we tried to transport him back than he would be if we simply killed him now," Anya pointed out.

Rufina had been quiet as she tended to the potatoes.

"Who do you propose will kill him?" she asked, keeping her eyes firmly on her task. Anya didn't answer immediately. As Rufina had suspected, Anya wasn't overly keen to kill Vladimir herself, no matter what she said.

"It's not worth discussing if that isn't the option we're taking." Anya tried to delay the inevitable.

"I saw a broken wagon on the side of this hideaway. If I can fix it, that would help us transport people," Rufina told them. "The worst of the storm is over now. I'll go and see what I can do about it. That will give you time to consider our options more carefully."

* * *

Rilla opened her eyes to the weak winter light creeping in through the gaps of her curtains. She lay there, motionless. Shuut's arm was wrapped around her. Usually, Rilla would have wriggled away from the skin contact, but today she just didn't care.

He's alive, Rilla, Elessa spoke softly through their bond. *Take heart in that.*

Rilla did not respond, nor did she bother to block out Elessa.

"So, he's still alive," Shuut said as she got out of bed. "That's something at least."

Rilla closed her eyes and drew the covers up to her chin. The blankets were ripped away from her. She turned angrily to see Shuut holding them in one hand.

"Snap out of it, Rilla. He's alive. Be happy with that. We can't do anything more for him right now. What you *can* do is get on with your day. I've got the day free, but Lukys wants you in class, so that's exactly what you'll do. We can have breakfast up here if you want, but then it's on with our day."

"No."

Shuut threw a change of clothes on the bed.

"You don't have a choice. Moping around up here won't help anyone, least of all you. All it will do is make you think of the worst possible scenarios. Trust me when I tell you that keeping yourself busy today is the best thing you can do."

Rilla knew Shuut would not leave her be. It was the only reason she got out of bed.

Chapter Two – Seers and Prophecies

Arishen walked silently alongside his guardian, Master Reuben, through the streets of Illaria. As they reached the bridge to the castle, Arishen felt his stomach tighten. His hands were frozen and clammy. He tried to clear his mind of all thoughts before Master Reuben took his hand to escort him past the invisible barrier around the castle. It wasn't enough. He knew the master lintep would be able to sense everything with that one touch. His fear that the students would pry, that they would see things he didn't want them to, that he couldn't control.

As they walked through to the outer courtyard, Master Reuben guided him to a more secluded part of the gardens.

"Arishen, would it make you more comfortable if I accompany you today?" Master Reuben placed a gentle hand on his shoulder. "Mistress Emeline had no right to offer you up as a prize for her students without asking your permission first. Had I known what she was planning, I might have been able to talk her out of it. As it stands, she has already promised this to her students. The most I can do now is offer my assistance."

"You have lessons to teach." Arishen dragged the toes of his shoes through the pebbles on the ground.

"I do, but I could try to shuffle things around. Perhaps I could allow Tommaso to teach the beginner students today."

"If Tommaso is free, maybe he could come with me." Arishen looked at his guardian with raised eyebrows.

Master Reuben smiled. "I didn't realise how well the two of you were getting along. Of course, he can accompany you this morning. It would have the appearance of normality, considering recent circumstances, wouldn't it?"

Arishen grinned and nodded. Master Reuben pursed his lips and his cheeks puffed out, but Arishen could not hear a sound. He knew that the lintep whistle could travel over longer distances than most lintep could communicate with just their minds. Master Reuben stood still for a moment, then cocked his head as though listening intently.

"Tommaso should meet us in Mistress Emeline's classroom," Master Reuben said as they walked towards the castle. "Keep your mind clear. Think only of the visions you want to show them. Anything else could bring in other memories or thoughts that you don't want them to see."

Arishen cringed at the memory of that exact thing happening with Rilla. "Keep my mind on my visions and nothing else. I know."

Master Reuben clapped him on the shoulder. "You'll be fine, Arishen. Tommaso will help focus your thoughts if you need him to. Just don't let those students bully you."

Arishen sat patiently in the hall as it filled with students, some of whom stared at him in open fascination. He was glad for Master Reuben's presence. It would stop them from trying to talk to him. All except Miette. Arishen saw her brown eyes widen as she spotted him. Her cheeks flushed as she ran over.

"Arishen, what are you doing here?" she asked excitedly. "I mean, not that you can't be here. It's nice to see you again, actually, but I don't often see you in the castle is all."

"Hello Miette." Arishen smiled.

"Good morning, Miette," Master Reuben chuckled. "I see you've met my young seer before."

"Oh yes!" Miette clapped her hands in front of her chest. "We met at Pér's performance in the market square a few nights ago. He's quite a fascinating person."

"Yes, that's your favourite word to describe Arishen," Kalydron said, as he jostled Miette's shoulder from behind. "You've barely stopped talking about the *fascinating* seer since we met him."

Arishen was pleasantly surprised. He had not realised that Miette found him so interesting. Although, thinking back to the night they had met, she had asked him more questions than anyone else.

"Are you going to be a mind mistress when you're older?" Arishen asked her. Kalydron laughed loudly and Master Reuben chuckled in amusement at the suggestion. Miette stared angrily at the three of them before storming away.

"What did I say?" Arishen watched in confusion as she disappeared into the classroom.

"Let's just say, it isn't necessarily your visions that has Miette infatuated with you." Kalydron smirked.

"I ... what?" Arishen stumbled over his words.

Kalydron shook his head as another group of lintep approached them.

"Arishen, I presume?"

Arishen's stomach lurched as he looked up. A lintep with round, soft features looked down at him. Her gaze was so intense, Arishen felt like an insect for her to study.

"Ah, Mistress Emeline." Master Reuben stood. "I trust you won't mind if Tommaso joins you for this session. He has been shadowing young Arishen here for a number of days now in the event that he has an important vision."

He nodded to Tommaso as the young lintep came up behind Mistress Emeline. Tommaso's friendly wave did little to ease Arishen's fear.

"That wasn't part of my plan for the morning," Mistress Emeline said slowly, turning towards Arishen. "However, I'm certain the students won't mind. Perhaps Tommaso will be able to show them a thing or two that he has learnt to do with the young seer."

Arishen cringed at the thought. He liked working with Tommaso, but did they always have to make him feel like a project for them to work with?

"It would be my pleasure." Tommaso beamed at her.

Emeline's long, black curls swirled around her slight frame as she opened the door to her room. Kalydron and Tommaso walked in, closely followed by two other lintep Arishen did not recognise. The bell tolled for morning lessons, but Arishen did not move.

"You'll be fine, Arishen," Master Reuben said. "I have faith in you and your abilities, but that means nothing unless you do too."

Arishen gave him a hesitant smile and rose to join Mistress Emeline's class. He closed the door behind himself and turned to face the small group. Mistress Emeline gestured encouragingly towards an empty chair next to Tommaso. Arishen sat down next to the only lintep in the room he trusted.

"Dezra, Kalydron, Sheridan, this is a very special prize I've awarded you for your research on seers and prophecies. We are extremely fortunate to have a human seer in Illaria. Such an opportunity has never arisen before.

"To begin with, you will each be allowed to ask a question of Arishen. Then if, and *only if*, he allows you to, you may see one of his visions for yourself.

"I must remind you that humans do not have the same abilities as lintep. He cannot shield his thoughts from you or project his visions into your mind, so you will respect his privacy and not pry any further than he is comfortable with. Is that understood?"

Arishen felt his stomach settle as Mistress Emeline introduced him. He had not expected this of the mistress who hadn't even thought to ask his permission before promising him as a prize to her students. The students nodded seriously.

"Good, now let's begin. Dezra, would you like to ask the first question?" Mistress Emeline took her seat on the other side of Tommaso.

Arishen studied Dezra. She was slightly older than himself. Her shiny brown hair cupped her chin making her slender neck stand out. She thought for a few moments before asking her question.

"When and how did you first realise that you were a seer?"

Arishen steeled himself for the start of the session. He closed his eyes, thinking back to his earliest memories. His dreams had always been there, but he hadn't always known what they were.

"I can't remember how young I was," he said. "I've always remembered my dreams, but I only realised what was happening when I was maybe seven or eight years old and heard about events in our Paradise that matched my dreams exactly. I tried to dismiss it at first, but it became more difficult the more it happened."

"May I?" Tommaso asked.

Arishen frowned and looked over at Tommaso curiously.

"You must understand that in Arishen's Paradise, magic was forbidden. Anyone who was suspected of having a hint of it was murdered. It was extraordinarily dangerous for him to have this amazing ability."

"Wow, how did you survive?" Dezra asked.

"Kalydron's turn," Mistress Emeline interrupted.

"You said you've always remembered your dreams, but do you only have visions in your sleep?"

Arishen tried not to grimace. "To begin with, yes, they were always in my sleep. I even fell asleep at some very inconvenient times just so the visions could come to me. It was only a few months ago that I began having waking visions."

"Sheridan, your turn." Mistress Emeline turned to a blond lintep. His eyes were as blue as Arishen's own. Arishen was shocked by the similarity in their appearances, it was almost like looking in a mirror or the feeling of a mostly-forgotten vision, but he had no time to stop and consider it as the session continued.

"What's the most important vision you've ever had?" Sheridan asked, without hesitation. Arishen was completely at a loss. He turned to Tommaso for help. The mind apprentice knew more about him than any other lintep, except perhaps Master Reuben himself.

"That's a rather difficult question, Sheridan. Many of Arishen's visions have saved lives. You need to narrow it down a bit."

Arishen reflected that there weren't any good questions these lintep could ask him. All his visions had been about bad things that were already happening or going to happen. There wasn't a single good or happy vision. Not really.

"Fine, then. Was your first waking vision an important one? Tell us about that."

Arishen closed his eyes for a moment and recalled the vision. It was not difficult. He could still feel the mounting terror as he remembered thinking they could not survive the attack, the sickening scent of burning flesh and hair, the fear afterwards that Rilla would die.

He gagged involuntarily, his heart beating erratically. Tommaso reached out a hand, but Arishen flinched away from it.

"Rilla and I were alone on the bank of the Bramble River. We were waiting for Eliséo to bring the others across when we were attacked by four men. We didn't know it at the time, but they had been hired by Lishe to find and kill Rilla. Well, they attacked us, and I knew we couldn't defend ourselves – not long enough for the others to reach us, anyway. That's when I had my first waking vision.

"Initially, I saw how I was going to be attacked seconds before it happened and so I could defend myself better. Any time I tried to focus on Rilla, all I saw was fire coming out of her fingers and burning the men."

"Did she do it?" Sheridan quickly asked.

"One question each," Arishen objected, looking over to their teacher.

"That's my question, then. Did she do it?" Mistress Emeline asked, clearly just as caught up in the story as her students.

Arishen sighed. "Yes, but please don't tell Rilla about this. She's a very private person. She won't be pleased to know we were talking about her."

"Rumours of that have been floating around the dining hall for days," Dezra said with a shrug. "At least now we know they're true."

That only made Arishen feel slightly better about telling them himself. He was not convinced that Rilla would look favourably on this turn of events.

"I have a question of my own, if I'm allowed," Arishen said. Mistress Emeline gestured for him to continue. "Do all seers have visions of bad things? I mean, does anyone ever have a vision of something nice happening?"

Mistress Emeline shook her head. "Even among the lintep, seers are rare. Perhaps Tommaso can answer."

Arishen looked over to his friend. Tommaso raised his eyebrows.

"I honestly don't know. I can tell you that I've only ever read prophecies of bad or unfortunate events, but that's not to say no seer has ever had a good event show itself to them. It could simply be that only the ones that deal with bad events need to be recorded or told to someone."

"What about the prophecy with Rilla?" Arishen asked before he could think better of it. "That's not actually about a bad event."

"That's true," admitted Tommaso, "but it was to help bring about the end of a bad circumstance. I'd say it falls into the same category."

"There's a prophecy with Rilla in it?" Kalydron asked in surprise.

Arishen closed his eyes in despair. The prophecy was well known outside of Illaria. Why didn't they know it here? Rilla was certainly not going to be impressed with him now.

"You've all had one question each. That's it now." Arishen crossed his arms, refusing to answer.

"Ah, yes, that's enough questions," Mistress Emeline answered hurriedly. "Arishen, have you thought about whether you might allow the students to see a vision for themselves? One of your old ones perhaps? One you think is not so important?"

Arishen wondered if it would be easier to show them old, short visions from the Paradise, rather than allow them to ask him more questions.

"If you don't mind, can Tommaso look at the visions first, just to..." He didn't know how to finish the question. He knew Tommaso would tell him if he was showing too much or not limiting his thoughts enough.

"Yes, of course," answered Mistress Emeline easily. "We shall proceed in whatever manner makes you most comfortable."

Arishen was again surprised by this teacher. He closed his eyes and thought back to his earlier visions. It was insignificant to anyone but himself, but all he could think of was the vision of Kalid fashioning wooden bolts for her door and window and sleeping with a chisel under her pillow. There were not many pleasant visions in his past, so this one would have to do.

He focused on the vision, brought it to the front of his mind, ignoring all other thoughts. When he opened his eyes again, Tommaso was ready for him.

With more care and respect than either King Lukys or Lord Aaron had used on him in the past, Tommaso touched Arishen's mind. Arishen felt the intrusion but could do nothing about it. To distract himself, he focused ever harder on the vision of Kalid. He saw it played over in excruciatingly slow detail before Tommaso left his mind.

"Thank you, Arishen," Tommaso said. "I think that is a perfect example. Mistress Emeline, would you like to have the first turn?"

She hesitated for only a moment. "I suppose there won't be many opportunities like this again. Thank you."

Once again, Arishen recalled the vision of Kalid. He was surprised to find that Mistress Emeline's touch was much subtler than even Master Reuben's. Had he not been specifically waiting for her to see his vision, he may not have noticed she was there at all. Dismissing the thought, and knowing that she must have heard it, Arishen focused on Kalid again until the older lintep left his mind.

"Remarkable!" she exclaimed. "And this is one of your *less* significant visions? It's amazingly detailed. Why didn't her face change at all?"

"Oh, that." Arishen cringed. "I never see faces. If I know the person, I can tell who it is, but I don't actually see any faces."

"How interesting!" Mistress Emeline cocked her head to the side as she studied him. "So, were you projecting her face specifically for me or does that happen with every reliving of the vision if you know the person?"

"I ... hadn't actually thought about that," he admitted. "I suppose when it's just me, I know who the person is, so it doesn't make a difference, but possibly because I'm thinking of that person you get to see their face."

"My turn?" Dezra asked, barely masking her excitement. Mistress Emeline nodded and Arishen quickly cleared his mind of everything but that vision. Again, he felt the lintep's touch, but this was much rougher than any other he had felt before. He tensed and instinctively grabbed Tommaso's arm.

"Gently, Dezra." Tommaso hopped into Arishen's mind to guide Dezra's movements. Arishen focused on the vision again, playing it in his mind much faster than it normally did. *Anything to get this girl out of my mind!*

"Sorry," mumbled Dezra, as she retreated. "I guess I need to practise my skills a little more."

Arishen didn't reply. He was still rigid from the shock of her rough intrusion. He felt his fear and anger subside too quickly and realised Tommaso was forcibly calming him.

Arishen sighed. *You can get out now. I'm as calm as you're going to get me.* After a deep, steadying breath, he finally met Dezra's eyes.

"I guess you're used to dealing with people who have walls around their mind, like Rilla and Plyke, but I don't have anything."

The young lintep hung her head in shame. Arishen felt horrible that she would have heard his thought about getting her out of his mind, but there wasn't anything else he could think to say to her. She would know he was lying if he said he didn't mind.

"Let's move along." Mistress Emeline broke the tension.

"I'm not so sure about this," Arishen said. "I don't have any control over what they do in my head. Master Reuben told me that unskilled lintep could damage my mind."

Mistress Emeline folded her hands in her lap. "I understand your fears, Arishen, but you must also understand that this is a rare opportunity for my students – even for myself. We will respect your privacy and my students will attempt to be as gentle as possible. Please do not punish them for lack of practise on humans."

Arishen shook his head, torn with indecision. He knew his position in Illaria was tenuous. The only reason he had been allowed to enter in the first place was because Rilla and Plyke had insisted they would rather die than leave him and Tika behind. Would they banish him for refusing Mistress Emeline's request?

"I suppose I have no choice." He rubbed his arms as a chill wind swept through the room.

"Thank you, Arishen." Mistress Emeline tried to catch his eye, but Arishen evaded it. "Kalydron, why don't you go next. Be gentle with Arishen. His mind has no defences. The lightest touch will allow you to see his vision."

Kalydron nodded as he stared at the pale and downcast Dezra. Arishen hoped the warning was enough to guide Kalydron's actions. He prepared himself again, focusing only on the vision of Kalid and waited.

Soon, there was another presence in his mind. Arishen tried to keep a grip on his vision but found it hard to concentrate. Random thoughts of Rilla kept clouding his mind. *Is Kalydron trying to find visions of Rilla?*

You can tell? Kalydron's surprised voice echoed in his mind. *Sorry. Please show me the vision you showed the others. I'll stop looking for Rilla.*

Arishen pursed his lips and tried to forget about Rilla, but the more he tried to forget about her, the more he thought of her. He tried desperately hard not to think of the vision where she shot flames from her fingers but realised too late that was now exactly what Kalydron was seeing.

"Out!" he yelled. "Get out now!"

Tommaso was instantly in Arishen's mind, creating a shield in front of the vision and gently ushering Kalydron out. Arishen felt them both leave his mind and hid his face in his hands. He couldn't help the tears that flowed.

"I'm sorry, Arishen," Kalydron reached out to comfort him. Instinctively, Arishen flinched from his touch. Kalydron dropped his hand. "I'm sorry."

"What just happened?" asked Mistress Emeline harshly. "Kalydron, what did you do?"

"I ... looked for Rilla," he admitted, sheepishly. "I didn't know it would be so easy."

"Kalydron, I expected better than that from you," Mistress Emeline chided him. "Arishen allowed this with the understanding that you would take a quick look and leave his mind not search through it to find what you want.

"You *know* he doesn't have a wall and can't hide anything from you. You had no right to do that to him. I'm afraid I must ask you to leave now."

Arishen wiped his eyes on his sleeve as Kalydron walked to the door. Why had the stupid lintep searched for Rilla? Why did so many things out of his control make his relationship worse with her?

"Don't tell Rilla, okay?" he called out to the retreating lintep. "She'll never forgive me if she knows what you saw."

"It wasn't your fault, Arishen," Kalydron pointed out. "I'm sure she won't be angry with you, but I won't tell her if you don't want me to."

"You don't know her like I do." Arishen shook his head. "She'll be furious with me, even more than if she finds out I told you about the vision before you looked for it."

Kalydron slumped his shoulders as he left the room. Arishen felt all eyes turn back on him. He knew what they were going to ask. There was one person left. Would he allow Sheridan to view the vision?

"Do you promise not to stray?" Arishen looked at him warily. "Don't think of anything. Just watch."

Sheridan nodded gratefully. Arishen wasn't certain he trusted this lintep but didn't think it could be much worse than what Kalydron had done. He tried to think of the vision with Kalid but couldn't concentrate. He kept thinking about Rilla and all the times his visions had affected her. Even the most recent one about Lord Aaron.

Without realising it, Arishen nodded his head slightly. In seconds, Sheridan was in his mind, seeing his vision of Lord Aaron and Anya walking in the tunnels of Goraburg as a Karlik lay in wait to kill them. He tried to think of Kalid, but all that happened was he merged the two together.

Lord Aaron was in Kalid's room with locked window and door.

The room shifted to a dark enclosure.

It shifted again.

Lord Aaron, Eliséo and a karlik were on a makeshift wagon. Anya and another two karliki – a male and a female – were dragging the wagon through the deep snow.

"I think we made the wrong decision," the female karlik grunted, as she pulled on a rope slung over her shoulder.

"We can't go back now," Anya replied through gritted teeth. "There isn't enough food there for the five of us to last until these two idiots recover."

"What was that?" the male karlik asked.

All three of them stopped, the wind howling around them, and listened.

"We must be near the Yoswen Stream now. That must be what you heard," Anya tried to reassure him. She took up her rope again and started forward. With a shout, she jumped back as four yoswen came charging at them through the snow.

"What was *that*?" Sheridan asked in surprise. "I thought you said you were going to show me a not very important vision. That looked quite important."

"Tommaso, I need Rilla." Arishen tried to calm himself. If Eliséo was asleep, he didn't know if Rilla would be able to help. He couldn't tell if this was happening now or was going to happen. Either way, it was bad.

"I've called her," Tommaso told him. "Now, please show me what you saw?"

Arishen forgot about the rest of the lintep and focused on Tommaso and the vision. He usually found it reassuring to have a more experienced lintep, like Tommaso or Master Reuben, in his mind. Training with them, he noticed they could focus on certain parts of the vision, slow down everything and take in all the details. This was *not* one of those times.

As the vision focused on the three people in the wagon, Arishen realised that the karlik was dead. He looked more closely at Lord Aaron and Eliséo. His heart skipped a beat. They weren't just asleep. The constant jolts from the wagon catching in the snow should have woken them. It was only when Eliséo's face turned to the side after a particularly nasty bump that Arishen saw the wound at the back of the elf's head. He certainly wasn't sleeping. He was unconscious, which meant Lord Aaron probably was too, otherwise the lintep would have healed the him.

"They're going to die!" he cried out in a panic, just before the door handle turned.

"Quiet!" Tommaso covered his mouth, but it was no use.

"Who's going to die?" Rilla asked as she ran over to him. "What did you see? Show me."

Arishen couldn't answer her. He just kept shaking his head.

"Tommaso can show you," Arishen mumbled. "Don't look in my mind."

He could see the fear on her face and knew he wouldn't be able to concentrate enough to show her properly, without tainting it with his own fears of what might happen next.

Rilla looked expectantly at Tommaso. She grew very still.

"Can you do anything?" Arishen asked, not quite knowing how to ask what he really needed to know. There were too many people still in the room. Too many people who didn't know about her secret bond.

"No, I can't. Not this time." Rilla shook her head, tears trickling down her face. "Has it already happened?"

"I don't know," he whispered.

Why do I always see things that make her world fall apart?

"Arishen, is there anything I can do to help?" Mistress Emeline gently touched his elbow. He looked at her without seeing. He was numb to everything.

"May I see the vision?" she persisted.

Arishen shrugged indifferently. The only person he didn't want in his mind right now was Rilla.

He barely felt it when Mistress Emeline brushed against his mind. There was no focus left in him. He couldn't hold onto the vision. It mildly surprised him how gently she sorted through his thoughts to find the source of his pain. The vision that proved Rilla's grandfather, Rilla's elf and Anya were all going to die at the mercy of yoswen.

His vision swirled until he was watching the movements from far above. The Yoswen Stream was just to the left of the party as they travelled north through the thick snow. A flicker of recognition caught his eye. The white ghost gum they'd entered Goraburg through, so many months ago now, was to the north-east. It would take them over a day to walk there through the snow – if they weren't killed or injured by the yoswen first.

"We know exactly where they are," Mistress Emeline announced. "Now we simply need to alert someone who can help us."

"But there isn't anyone," Rilla protested. "I can't..."

"Can't what?" Mistress Emeline asked curiously.

"Nothing. There's nothing we can do." Rilla tried to cover up her error. "Not now."

"What's going on?" Dezra asked. She was the only one who hadn't yet seen the vision. Arishen was too tired to show her. He could barely keep his eyes open.

Chapter Three – Slap

Rilla watched in surprise as Arishen fell asleep. He hadn't needed to do that with his visions for a while now. Seeing his vision brought her mixed feelings. Even though Elessa had reassured her Eliséo was still alive, it gave Rilla a sense of relief to see him. But with the knowledge that neither he nor Lord Aaron could protect themselves, a growing sense of terror was mounting. Her heart raced as she tried to smother her fear and come up with a plan.

What they needed was a way to communicate with Eliséo or, better yet, Anya. Even if Elessa told her how to communicate with birds, Rilla doubted Anya would be able to understand a message sent that way. Unless, perhaps, it was written. Rilla closed her eyes.

Elessa, is it possible? she asked as she showed the tree her idea.

Not for you, Elessa replied. *For that, you really do need to be an elf. Unless the bird was a fringa.*

There were no fringa in Illaria – of that, Rilla was quite certain. But what if they were to go into the Outworld?

"Horses," she said aloud, as she opened her eyes. "We need horses to get to the boundary of Illaria."

"How will that help?" asked the lintep teacher. Rilla did not recognise her. "We can't ride all the way to them."

"No, but we can call the fringa and maybe they can fly there," Rilla explained, hopefully.

"That's one idea," the teacher admitted, "but they are small birds and can't possibly reach the Lesa Mountains quickly enough. I think a better idea would be to get word to the crystal dragons. I don't know what's been going on, but there were two of them here a few weeks ago. Perhaps there is a way to get one of them to return."

Rilla stared at the teacher, a flutter of hope in her stomach. *Why didn't I think of that? When is Pyrid due to come back? They must have set a day.* Hurriedly, she sent out a few tendrils to find King Lukys. She found him in the audience chamber. If she disturbed him there, he would never forgive her. As she retreated from the room, she felt Aislen.

When is Pyrid due back? she asked the princess.

Not for another two days, Aislen replied, crushing Rilla's last hope.

Two days was too long. Rilla could feel Aislen's concern but was too distraught to explain any further. She pulled her tendrils back into her mind. She couldn't think anymore. Her mind was as frozen as her heart. As frozen as her elf and grandfather would soon be.

* * *

Aislen could feel Rilla's fear and despair with that one brief touch. Even as her young cousin retreated, Aislen could feel the girl bleeding out warmth into the air. It was subtle enough that anyone else might not notice immediately – other than Mistress Isis, perhaps.

Making as little fuss as possible, Aislen excused herself from the royal audience and followed the tendril back towards Rilla. If Isis were there, Rilla would not have been allowed to get to this stage, which meant she was in danger. As soon as she was out of the audience chamber, Aislen broke into a run. Without bothering to knock, she barged into the room where she could feel Rilla freezing to death.

A single glance told her that Mistress Emeline and Tommaso had not grasped the gravity of the situation. They were just as concerned about the collapsed seer as the motionless girl.

"Princess Aislen! What are you doing here?" Emeline cried out.

Ignoring the surprised teacher, Aislen quickly lit a roaring fire and fed as much heat into it as she dared. Slowly, and more calmly than she felt, she stood beside Rilla and placed a hand on her chest. She drew on the heat from the fireplace to feed into Rilla, but as quickly as the heat was replaced, Rilla let it out again.

"Mistress Emeline, I need you to calm her. I can't risk doing both things at once."

To her credit, the mistress didn't argue. Aislen felt Rilla's fear lessen, but the emptiness inside her cousin expanded, cold and relentlessly chilling. Shaking her head in frustration, Aislen continued to feed heat into the girl.

"What happened?" she asked no one in particular. "Why is she so upset?"

"Arishen had a vision," Tommaso answered. "May I project it to you?"

"No!" Aislen cried out before taking a moment to calm herself. "No. If you touch my mind, right now ... it's not a good idea. I need you to call Mistress Isis and Master Bastienne. Better call Kayte and Aurelius too."

Aislen heard Tommaso's whistle. It was a wise move. He did not have enough power to find them all. As she waited for the others to arrive, Aislen kept feeding heat into Rilla as fast as the girl was discarding it. There was only one thing she could think of to stop the cycle. But surrounding Rilla with her power, trapping her within, was not something Aislen wanted to try – especially not when Rilla trusted so few people as it was. She didn't want to become one of the many people who had betrayed her in her short life.

"Where are they?" she cried out in frustration.

"I don't know if they're in the castle," Tommaso told her. "They might not have heard my call."

"Dezra, Sheridan, run to every classroom. Get all the teachers you can even if they insist that they're busy. Get them now!" Mistress Emeline instructed her two remaining students.

The two students needed no encouragement. Aislen heard their footsteps racing away.

"What now?" Emeline asked. "Is there nothing else I can do to help?"

"I don't know what else to do," Aislen almost sobbed in frustration. "Calming her only made things worse. She's like an empty husk inside, drained of everything. What happened?"

"If you would only let me show you the vision," Tommaso insisted. Aislen tried to keep her temper with the apprentice.

"Tommaso, if you touch my mind right now, I cannot control what will happen. I may suck you into the same cycle Rilla has thrown herself into. I don't have the energy to keep both of you alive."

"I don't know who all the people were, but some of them, including Lord Aaron and an elf, are out in the Lesa Mountains, in the snow. They're either going to be attacked or have now already been attacked by yoswen," Emeline explained.

Aislen looked up sharply at the mistress. *Why is Aaron in the snow? It doesn't matter. At least he's alive. Eliséo really had saved him.*

"I don't understand why that would make Rilla react like this," she spoke her thoughts aloud. "Surely, the karliki can handle a yoswen?"

Thankfully Emeline did not question how she knew there were karliki involved, or why she seemed to know that both Eliséo and Aaron were not in a state to defend themselves.

"That may be the case, but there are four yoswen and only three karliki to fight them," Emeline pointed out softly.

Suddenly, it all made sense to Aislen. Of course, Rilla now feared that she would lose the one person who had never betrayed her, who had done everything in his power to keep her safe. The unfortunate thing was that there was nothing they could do about it.

Masters and mistresses flooded into the room. More than would be helpful, but Aislen wasn't in a state to argue. She was slipping into the same state as Rilla. Empathy may have been her strong point, but it was *not* the skill she needed right now. It was only making things worse. With her hand on Rilla's chest, she could feel her cousin's terror.

Too distracted to block it out, Aislen could not help but see Arishen's vision flicker through Rilla's mind. She narrowed in on Aaron lying pale and motionless in a makeshift wagon. If the boy's vision was true, Aaron would die. Aislen was not prepared to lose him. Not now. She had already almost lost him when he was attacked by a karlik. She couldn't do it again – not so soon.

"Aislen, control your feelings!" Bastienne shouted. The words sounded far away, but quite insistent.

Control your feelings. That's what she had always been told when she was younger. Her lack of control had been the reason the entire castle had drowned in her emotions many times in her youth. Instinctively, she practised the exercises she'd been taught long ago. As she calmed, she noticed that all the masters and mistresses were looking at her for direction.

"Rilla is distressed. Calming her didn't work. She is losing heat as fast as I can replace it. Does anyone have an idea how to help?"

"Why is she distressed?" asked Jorg asked. Aislen nodded to Tommaso who projected Arishen's vision to him. Jorg gasped audibly. "Good grief! What can be done?"

"That's not our main concern right now," Aislen told him sternly. "We need to help Rilla."

"But Lord Aaron ..."

Aislen interrupted him, "Can wait for now. There is nothing we can do for him. But I see you partially understand what has Rilla so distressed. Now, what can we do about it?"

"What was the vision?" Mistress Vika asked. Before Tommaso had the chance to show her as well, Mistress Emeline stopped him.

"It doesn't matter what the vision was," the younger mistress told them. "We don't need any more people distracted by it. All you need to know is that there is nothing we can do about it right now. We need to find a way to help Rilla. Princess Aislen cannot be expected to feed heat into the girl indefinitely."

"What happened when you calmed her down?" asked Bastienne.

"It made things worse. She is letting herself freeze and she doesn't care."

"Make her angry," he suggested. "It can't make things much worse, can it?"

"It might not make things worse, but how will it help?" asked Isis from beside him. "You may simply reverse the situation and have her draw in too much heat instead. I've seen her do that and don't want to have to fix *that* again."

"What's your suggestion, then?" Emeline asked Isis. "You know her better than most of us."

"I'm certain Princess Aislen has already thought of my suggestion, but it's not one I think either of us would be comfortable doing," Isis said quietly. Aislen looked up sadly. If they had both come up with the same solution and no one else could think of anything else, perhaps they had no choice.

"We could ask someone else to do it," Aislen suggested.

Isis shook her head. "Even if it isn't one of us, she would still never forgive us. Besides, that won't actually solve this. It will only keep you from having to replace the heat in her body. We'll still need to figure out a way to bring her back."

"If she's upset about my vision, maybe we can find a solution to that and make her understand it will be fine," Arishen suggested timidly from his prone position on the floor. Aislen looked over to find seer trying to prop himself up on an elbow. "Is there any way to reach the Lesa Mountains or the crystal dragons quickly?"

Silence greeted his question. Aislen looked around the room at all the masters and mistresses assembled. With some of the greatest minds in Illaria, it was ridiculous that they could not find a solution.

"What if we combine our powers?" Vika suggested. "Could we somehow reach them then?"

"No, combining them won't make them stretch further," Bastienne refuted.

"What's going on?" Kora asked as she entered the room with Plyke.

Isis quickly explained the situation to them. Aislen watched Kora closely. She was just as unusual as the rest of their family, but most people didn't realise. Perhaps she would have a reasonable suggestion.

* * *

Can we talk to Eliséo? Kora asked Isis directly. Even though Rilla had explained the bond between them to some of the lintep, it wasn't common knowledge and Kora meant to keep it that way.

It appears he's unconscious and she can't contact him, Isis replied. *But ...* She thought to herself for a moment. *Do you think it's possible for Aislen to talk with her tree? When Rilla first explained her bond to me, she told me anyone who has skin contact could potentially talk to her tree, her elf and anyone with skin contact to her elf.*

Anything is worth a try at this point, Kora shrugged. *Can you take over from Aislen so that she can concentrate on the tree? I'll explain when she is free from her task.*

Isis nodded slightly.

"Aislen, you're looking a bit tired. Why don't I take over for you?" Isis asked the princess, catching her eye and looking towards Kora.

"Thank you, Isis," Aislen replied, wiping her brow. "That would be most helpful.

You're certainly more skilled with heat and cold than I am. Perhaps you'll have more luck with her."

* * *

As soon as Aislen was free from Rilla, she turned to Kora. *What's your idea?*

Kora explained her theory. Aislen didn't immediately reply.

That could be dangerous, Aislen said eventually. *Rilla is quite powerful and even though empathy is not where her talents lie, she is still perfectly capable of sucking me into her state. In fact, I've already fallen into it once. If it hadn't been for Bastienne's reminder and my years of practise, I would have been just as lost as she is.*

You'd rather let her die? Kora asked bluntly. Aislen narrowed her eyes angrily.

"There are too many people here," Aislen suddenly announced. "If you think you can genuinely be of assistance, please stay. If not, return to your classes. Everyone in this room will be in danger from Rilla if things get out of control, so I want the minimum number of people here."

Many of the masters and mistresses looked suitably annoyed. In her raw state, Aislen could feel the annoyance rolling off them. They had just been dragged out of their classes by Emeline's orders and now that Aislen was free from Rilla, they were summarily dismissed. With low grumbles, most of them left.

Aislen looked around at those who remained. Emeline, Tommaso, Arishen, Plyke, Kora, Bastienne and, of course, Isis. *Where are Kayte and Reuben?* she wondered.

"Arishen, are you happy to work with Mistress Emeline rather than Master Reuben for the moment?" The young seer barely hesitated before nodding. Perhaps he had already realised that Mistress Emeline was more skilled with seers than his guardian. "Very well, then. The two of you work together with Tommaso to see if there is anything else you can tell us about the vision. Emeline, I know it's unconventional and more than a little dangerous, but if you can try to induce another vision, that may help us."

"In ... induce a vision?" Arishen stammered. "Is that even possible?"

"It is," Emeline replied quietly, "but I've only read of it before. As Princess Aislen mentioned, it's meant to be quite dangerous for the seer. I would suggest we focus on your current vision. We can try inducing a vision when you've trained up a bit."

"But I'd do anything for Rilla," Arishen replied instantly. "I owe her my life!"

"Rhanya bought your life," Plyke reminded him. "Rilla only kept us safe in the Outworld because of her promise to him."

Arishen shook his head, "You forget that she didn't tell anyone about my visions in the Paradise. She saved my life more times than I could ever repay her. What do you need me to do?"

"No, Arishen," said Emeline. "We'll see what more we can tell from your vision, but I refuse to help you induce another one."

Aislen hid her disappointment as Mistress Emeline stood her ground. She left the seer and his guides to their work, instead turning to the others. Plyke, Kora and Bastienne looked to her for direction. She knew both mother and son were well aware of Rilla's unusual bond, but Bastienne almost certainly wasn't.

"Master Bastienne, if you cannot think of a way to force Rilla to stop spilling out all of the heat within her, perhaps it would be best for you to leave us as well."

He cocked an eyebrow at her. "You still haven't tried my suggestion of making the girl angry."

"Bastienne, leave it alone," Isis looked up with fire in her eyes. "Making her angry will not help."

Bastienne held his hands up in defeat. "I know when I'm not wanted. I'll be in the library when you finish with her and want to explain exactly what happened here."

Aislen saw him make way for Mistress Kayte to enter as he walked out of the room. "Watch what you say in there," he told her, pointing back over his shoulder. "These people have no sense of humour. Apparently, I'm not to make her angry."

Aislen had no time for the old master. She motioned for Kayte to close the door behind her.

"What did she do this time?" Kayte asked, clearly annoyed.

"Kayte, have a little compassion," Isis growled through clenched teeth. "Not *everything* is her fault."

"It's *my* fault," Arishen called out from across the room. "If you need someone to blame, then blame me. If I hadn't reacted so badly to my own vision, maybe she wouldn't have either."

"Let's see it then," Kayte turned to him. Arishen paled as she moved towards him.

Aislen lay a hand on Kayte's arm.

"Not directly from Arishen," she cautioned. "I think Emeline can help us instead."

Arishen nodded gratefully. Aislen waited alongside Kayte for Emeline to show them the vision.

"So, she's scared that they're all going to die?" Kayte asked, in a softer tone. "I assume there's still no way to contact them?"

Emeline and Tommaso looked up in confusion. Aislen only shrugged.

"Then we need to calm her down," Kayte reasoned.

"I tried that," Emeline pointed out. "It made things worse."

Aislen did not miss the patronising way Kayte smiled at the mind mistress. "I do not believe she is calm. She may simply have gone numb, which can sometimes be confused as the same thing. If that's the case, it makes sense that she's worse off now."

"She was panicking," Emeline bristled. "I did what I needed to do to stop her from becoming completely hysterical."

Aislen stepped in to diffuse the situation. "No one is accusing you of anything, Mistress Emeline. Your efforts are greatly appreciated. I think we all need to keep ourselves calm now. The tasks we each must perform can easily spiral out of control if we aren't careful. Perhaps you could take Arishen to Reuben's rooms and continue your work there."

Emeline smoothed down her dress as she calmed herself. "Very well, Arishen, Tommaso, with me."

Aislen waited until they had closed the door behind them before turning to the healing mistress. "Really, Kayte? Sometimes, it would do for you to hold your tongue. Now, if you're so certain she made Rilla numb instead of calm, fix her yourself."

* * *

Kayte raised her chin defiantly and walked over to the motionless girl on the floor, being careful not to get in Isis' way. The night before, Kayte had been forced to show Rilla, Plyke and Shuut how to steal energy from another lintep. Rilla had almost killed her. Admittedly, the naive girl had no idea what she was doing, but that almost made things worse.

How did this girl always get herself into these situations? Kayte placed a hand over Rilla's forehead and closed her eyes.

The girl was devoid of all feeling – completely numb. Kayte shook her head in anger. She hated it when lintep dove into situations without thinking through the consequences of their actions. It so often led to someone else cleaning up their mess.

Counting down from ten, she calmed herself with deep breaths.

Rilla, I need you to concentrate.

There was no reply.

Rilla, come back to us.

Still no reply.

Rilla, wake up!

Nothing. No response at all. Kayte's anger bubbled over. She threw that anger into Rilla and slapped her across the face. Suddenly, there was fire in the girl's eyes.

"How dare you!" Rilla yelled, sitting up and pulling away from everyone.

"Well, looks like Bastienne was right after all," Kayte looked at Rilla smugly. "All I needed to do was make you angry."

"Kayte!" yelled Isis. "How could you be so reckless?"

Kayte crossed her arms and lifted her chin. "She's not bleeding out heat anymore, is she?"

Isis placed a hand on Rilla's arm and shook her head angrily.

"You didn't know it would work," Isis lowered her voice. "You could have pushed her the other way instead. *Then* what would you have done?"

"She's had plenty of practise calming me down," Rilla glared at the healing mistress. "You probably thought that would be the easier option, didn't you?"

Kayte shrugged nonchalantly.

* * *

Aislen held her head between her hands as she listened to the two mistresses argue. All the while her uncle was lying unconscious, somewhere in the Lesa Mountains, about to be attacked by a pack of yoswen.

"Enough!" she cried out, louder than she intended. When she looked up, all eyes were on her. "We do not have time for this bickering. I understand why Rilla panicked – I'm almost there myself. But it won't help anyone."

"There isn't anything we can do," Rilla pointed out. "Eliséo is unconscious. I can't reach him like that. You said Pyrid isn't due back here for two days, which will be too late."

"Arishen's vision doesn't show them dying," Isis pointed out hesitantly. "Perhaps they won't."

Aislen looked at the fear and doubt in Rilla's eyes and felt it all around her.

"Let's assume, for the moment, that they survive the attack. They won't be left unharmed and, almost certainly, won't be able to return to Goraburg without help. With Emeline's assistance, we've seen roughly where they are, so once Pyrid arrives, we can ask him to take a few of us there to help them."

"Assuming they're still alive when we get there." Rilla's voice trembled.

Aislen struggled to hold back her own tears. "We have to believe they will be. There's nothing else we can do for now."

"Mistress Kayte, will you give me some more healing lessons before Pyrid arrives?" Rilla asked the healing mistress.

"Oh, no. *You* won't be going," Kayte replied firmly. Before Rilla could protest, Kayte continued. "You are too close to this situation and if you injure yourself, or anyone else, no one will be able to help you. I will go."

"I'll go with you, then," Rilla insisted. "How could it hurt to teach me more before we leave?"

"Ah, Rilla, I think Kayte is trying to tell you that you won't be going at all." Aislen laid a hand on Rilla's shoulder. "Your power is too unstable. We cannot afford to have anything happen to you while our focus should be Aaron, Eliséo and the karliki."

* * *

"But ..." Rilla stood there helplessly, staring from one lintep to another. Everything was catching up with her. She had barely slept the night before. Her fear that Eliséo had died trying to save her grandfather had almost been too much to bear. She had tried to block it out all morning. But this ... it was all too much. Would she be forced to wait here while others went to save them? Would they really die now, after everything that had happened?

The tears finally started to flow. She collapsed to the floor in a sobbing heap. She barely heard the door open and close or felt the arm that wrapped itself around her, holding her close as she cried until there were no more tears to shed.

When she finally looked up, she was surprised to find Kora holding her and the room was empty. "Where did you come from?" she asked, sniffing quietly.

Kora smiled sadly. "You're not the only one who fades into the background when they're scared or upset. If people forget about you often enough, it just seems to happen more easily.

"When the others realised they couldn't do anything more for you, I reappeared so they could leave to organise who else would need to go with Pyrid."

"I wish they would take me with them," Rilla insisted. "I need to know that they're alive."

Kora looked at her strangely for a moment. "Can't you tell that from here? At least with Eliséo ..."

For a moment, Rilla focused on her link with Elessa, trying to feel anything of Eliséo. She let out a deep breath. "He's alive. For now."

"Let's just be happy with that and try not think about the 'later', just for now," Kora suggested. Rilla took another deep breath and smiled half-heartedly. "Good, now I need your help. I need to organise a more permanent solution for Abelin. You remember the lintep boy Plyke found at the broken Paradise? He can't stay in Illaria forever. I'd like for him to be the first student in my plan for a new school."

Chapter Four – Distractions

Cold wind bit at her face as Lishe pulled her cloak closer around her shoulders. The weather had turned from mild autumn to bitter winter in the space of just a few days. Bending her head into the wind, she rode her horse ever onward towards her hope – the only unbroken Paradise of which she knew the location.

She did not know how much time she had to solve this riddle before those meddling fools decided to destroy another one. Having no idea how they had destroyed that first one, all she could hope was that the humans from Deuterfoss would delay them. She had certainly left enough of a trail for them to find the broken Paradise and cause some trouble.

It's around here somewhere, she thought to herself as she looked along the small stream flowing through empty fields. She had followed the banwep along this very stream all those months ago.

"Along the stream, over to a small cluster of trees, barely worth a mention. Where *is* it?"

Lishe dismounted and led her horse as she walked through the long, damp grass. This weather had made everything damp, even when it wasn't raining. It must already be snowing in the Lesa mountains to be so cold down here.

As she walked, there was a slight resistance against her body. Irritated by the obstruction, she forged ahead, head still bent low against the fierce wind. Her horse pulled against the reins as she dragged her along.

"Come on, you dumb mule," she muttered, tugging firmly at the reins. "It's only wind."

Try as she might, she could not force her mare to come any further. She looked up angrily, but her jaw dropped before she could yell at the poor beast. The open fields had disappeared only to be replaced by a small country village. Thankfully, she was too far away for any of the humans to see her.

Turning around, she saw a blurred version of the fields. Quickly, she stepped back outside the Paradise boundary.

"So, you don't like the boundary, huh?" Lishe stroked the horse's neck thoughtfully. "Well, at least we found it."

She looked back towards the Paradise. It was quite amazing how invisible the boundary was from the Outworld. She had spent years trying to find them, but without the banwep's help, she may never have found one at all.

Time to try harvesting this power.

Lishe placed her hand on the barrier and smiled. Now that she knew it was there, she could feel powers intertwining beneath her fingers.

So much power!

If she ever managed to obtain all the power in these Paradises, no one would ever have power over her again. *She* would be the head mistress in Illaria and every lintep would fear and respect her. It gave her a heady feeling just thinking about it.

* * *

Kora tried to distract herself from her father's predicament. It was the only way she knew how to cope in these situations, of which she had been in too many. If she failed, all that awaited her was an overwhelming, crushing sensation that she would not survive.

Pushing the thought aside, she watched Abelin play with some of the younger students in the castle. Just like Tika, he immediately endeared himself to all around him. It helped that his Partner, Lorella, was such a sweet child. She was clearly in awe of all the magic surrounding her. Kora smiled at the way Abelin protectively watched over Lorella. Their Partnership would be a strong one indeed.

"So, what's your plan?" Rilla asked from beside her. "Where is Abelin staying at the moment?"

"Here, in the castle," Kora answered, pulling herself away from the young Partners. "I've put the two of them in one of the rooms specifically set aside for students. Father is paying for that, but it's a temporary solution."

Rilla arched an eyebrow. "Exactly how does Lord Aaron have so much money at his disposal? I never actually see him do any ... well, work, I suppose."

"Ah yes." Kora nodded. "Father never needs to work a day in his life. He and Uncle Kynon own a great deal of land in and around the city. Uncle Lukys owns the castle itself and much of the rest of the land. It is a rare lintep indeed, outside of the royal family, who owns their own property."

"So, that's why Lord Kynon can waste his days doing nothing." Rilla sounded quite unimpressed. She had every right to be. Kynon was well known for wasting his time. He never deigned to help Lukys or Aaron with running Illaria. In fact, it was only in recent days that Kora had seen him take an interest in politics.

When Kora returned from the broken Paradise, Kynon had taken her aside to ask about her lessons with Lishe and Nyssa. Apparently, her father had asked him to investigate the entire affair for him. Unfortunately, she had not been able to give him any new information. Her old masters and mistresses had told him all they could remember. Kora explained how they had experimented between lessons, but that only served to shine a light on Lishe's character – it did not show them what other skills she might have accidentally come across.

"Uncle Kynon isn't so bad." Kora shrugged. "At least he's doing his part to help solve the Lishe problem. What I need you for is to help me solve *this* problem."

She nodded towards the young lintep and his Partner. "Abelin can't stay here forever. I need to find a place for him and Lorella to live safely. Somewhere he can learn to use his powers without fear of humans and somewhere Lorella can live safe from lintep trying to use their powers on her the way all lintep in Illaria think it is their right to do."

"Didn't Master Bastienne say something about his town?" Rilla asked. "What was it called again?"

"Statera." Kora nodded. "Yes, he did say Abelin would be welcome there, but he's so young that I don't know if he could properly earn his keep. I don't really know how the town works."

"Well, why don't we find him and ask more about it?" Rilla suggested. "If you're going to start a string of schools, you may as well find out about the first town you plan to do it in."

Kora looked at Rilla thoughtfully. It was amazing how little anyone in their Paradise had noticed the girl. *Me included*, she admitted guiltily.

They found Bastienne in the library with Guiscard and Kynon, poring over a small book on the librarian's desk. The three old lintep did not look up as she and Rilla walked into the spacious room. A grated fireplace was lit, but it did little to warm the chill air down the long, dark aisles of bookshelves.

"May we interrupt?" Kora asked as they approached the men. As one, they jumped and looked over at them. "Master Bastienne, if we could have a moment of your time, we'd like to ask about Statera."

"Ah!" The old master's eyes lit up. "I'm always happy to talk about my home town. What would you like to know?"

Kora looked uncertainly towards Rilla.

"Where is it?" Rilla asked. "I mean, how far away is it?"

Kora suppressed a smile at the fact that Rilla already had a plan.

Bastienne nodded happily. "Kynon, I've got prettier company now. Don't wait for me. Guiscard, a map if you please."

Kora laughed at the look on her uncle's face as the old master linked arms with her and Rilla, leading them towards the chairs by the fireplace. Soon, they were settled with a map spread over Bastienne's lap. He pointed to a small dot, north-west of Illaria, towards the human town of Deuterfoss.

"This is where I grew up," he told them. "There were a few human settlements around Statera at the time. I can't say if they're still there. It's been a number of years now since I last returned."

"If I want to take Abelin and Lorella there, will you join us?" Kora asked hopefully.

Bastienne broke into a serene smile. "Nothing would make me happier. Do you plan to take them there soon?"

"Actually, that's the reason we came to see you," Kora told him. "I know you said they would be taken in by the people living there, but surely there must be a cost involved. I need to know that cost before we take them."

"The cost for the children would be negligible. You needn't worry about it," Bastienne reassured her. Kora wasn't convinced.

"Master Bastienne, I appreciate that two children might not cost much in the grand scheme of things, but I can't very well walk into a town I've never been to before and simply leave them there without providing for them. Besides, if I plan on creating a school of sorts for any other lintep children we find along the way, that can't be the solution for all of them."

"Why not?" asked Bastienne, rather obstinately. "It would be up to individual families if they want to take in the children. If they do, the children would be treated the same as any other family member.

"They would be taken care of and taught to use their skills until they are old enough to become an apprentice in whichever trade they choose. At that point, they will be earning their own keep and contributing to the society. So why can we not leave it at that?"

Kora wanted to protest, but each time she thought of something, he refuted it before the words were even out of her mouth. It couldn't possibly be that simple, could it?

"You're making a fairly big assumption that any of the families in Statera, and whatever other lintep community you know of, will be happy to take in a lintep child with a human Partner," Rilla pointed out. "What if things have changed since the last time you were there? What if they aren't as accommodating as you remember? I think Kora is right to be worried whether or not Abelin and his Partner will be accepted in your village."

"Things may have changed a little over the years," Bastienne conceded with a shrug. "But there is no chance that they have changed so much that an orphaned lintep *child* would not be welcome in my town." Bastienne waved aside their unspoken protests. "No, no. You listen to me now. I know you both had bad experiences in that Paradise of yours and, Rilla, I realise the human villages you visited on your way here were less than accommodating, but they were rather unique circumstances. A group of four apprentice-aged children with a banwep leading them – it isn't really an encouraging sight. Even in Statera, you may have met with a little opposition.

"However, every lintep settlement that I know of in the Outworld has always been very accommodating. We are an inclusive people. Have I not already told you that children are taught by the entire village rather than just their parents? If Abelin and Lorella are taken in, it won't be just by the one family – it will be by the entire town."

Kora shook her head, still unconvinced. "But we're not talking about just Abelin and Lorella. Who knows how many lintep children we'll find in the Paradises? It may be too much of a burden for any lintep settlement to take them all in."

"Very well." Bastienne braced his hands on his knees as he lifted himself from the chair. "If you are so very concerned about it, I will talk with my old friends in Statera and help you sort out the entire business. If you're so keen to spend all your money, perhaps they'll accept a new building or some food in exchange for taking in the children."

Kora shook her head but smiled at the old master. "Thank you, Bastienne." She tried to usher Rilla out of the room, but the girl walked towards Kynon and Guiscard before she had a chance.

"So, what made you jump when we came in?" she asked. "You wouldn't be trying to hide anything from us, would you?"

Kora walked over, suddenly very interested in what Rilla had noticed. The three old lintep looked guiltily at each other.

"Rilla, child, don't you have lessons to get to?" the librarian asked. "We wouldn't want to make you late."

"That's not one of your usual research tomes, Guiscard." Kora looked over curiously. "May I have a look?"

Guiscard moved to block her hand and obscured the small book of parchment into the folds of his robes, shaking his head. "Not this time, Kora."

Kora was about to protest when Kynon interjected. "It would be best for everyone, if the two of you were on your way now. Rilla, I believe you have an arrangement with Nicodemo to spar with him any time you have a free lesson. Why don't you head on down there?

"Kora, this school idea of yours sounds like it will take a lot of organising. Pér would certainly be quite happy to help you with that task. I suggest you take a little walk into the city to find him."

Kora caught Rilla's eye as her niece looked to her for guidance. She shrugged helplessly. "It looks like we both have prior engagements."

Kora glanced back over her shoulder as they walked out of the library, but Guiscard did not make a move to retrieve the book. She lifted her chin defiantly and closed the door behind her.

Chapter Five – Altercation

Leif drew his coat closer around his shoulders as he sat astride his mount. The twenty of them, including four of his own guard, had been riding for days to this supposed broken Paradise. Not for the first time, he wondered how anyone had convinced him that the rumours were worth following up.

They aren't. He shook his head. *I had to come along to stop these fools from starting a fight on my lands.*

"Chrislan, how much further?" he asked, irritably.

The burly blacksmith shrugged. "We should find it soon. We've already crossed the Pebble Stream. Hedgefall is two days' ride from here."

"What exactly are we looking for?" Talise inquired, strands of her long brown hair flying loose from her braid. "Hills, a forest, a cliff?"

Chrislan exchanged glances with the other men in their party.

"You don't know, do you?" she asked with an incredulous laugh. "We're travelling the Outworld, days from anywhere, looking for a broken Paradise, and you don't even have a landmark to look for."

"Well, now, let's be reasonable." Leif stepped in before another argument could break out. "There must be a forest nearby. No settlement, large or small, could survive this winter without fireplaces."

"There are clusters of trees all over the place." Talise gestured to the trees ahead of them. "Exactly which one should we head for?"

Leif ignored her sarcastic tone and scanned the horizon. There was a creek, winding its way down just a few hundred yards north of them. Every village also needed water.

"Let's follow that creek." He pointed in the distance. "Perhaps we'll find the broken Paradise along it."

The men grumbled agreement. Talise stared at him coldly. He avoided her glare. Why had he agreed to let her come along? He knew better than to have a lady along for this journey. With an inaudible sigh, he turned his horse towards the creek, leaving the others to follow as they would.

"Look, over there!" Karsyk cried out. "What's that?"

Leif followed the sight along his arm to a large clump of trees. "It's just a bunch of trees."

"No, it's not." Talise rode up beside him. "There's something behind them."

Leif looked again. Perhaps there was a smudge of colour behind the trees, but more likely, it was their imagination.

"We approach," he began, but before he could continue, Karsyk and Raleigh were already galloping towards the trees. "Fools! Follow me."

Leif fumed at the rash apprentices as the rest of the company trotted after them. Their idiocy could cost lives. He was not about to allow everyone else to pay for their brashness. His horse pulled roughly on the reins, but Leif held them tightly. If he lost control of this situation ... he didn't want to think about it.

Shouts of alarm sounded over the Paradise. Brynt grabbed a pickaxe and ran towards them. The five lintep guards who remained to protect them followed him closely.

By the time he reached the intruders, the fight had started. Brynt saw two of his farmers had fallen and a third barely managing to keep the horsed attackers at bay. He joined the fray, furious beyond reason. This was the third time his Paradise had been invaded and the second time they had come to blows.

Trying not to injure the horses, Brynt swung his pickaxe at the man closest to him. He struck the man across the shoulder and threw him to the ground. Brynt held the fallen man there, pickaxe against his chest as three of the lintep joined him. They unhorsed the other man and dragged him to his comrade.

Without touching him! How did they do that? Brynt stared wild-eyed at the lintep.

"Over there!" one of lintep shouted, nodding behind him.

Brynt turned to find a whole group of horsemen riding towards them.

"You bastards!" one of the fallen intruders yelled, clutching at his injured shoulder.

"Shut yer mouth!" retorted the only uninjured farmer. "Go, Brynt. We got these ones."

Brynt nodded at the lintep. Tiphaine stayed behind, Noémi and Rownyn flanked him as he prepared for the next wave of attack.

It never came.

The horsemen slowed their approach and stopped over twenty yards away. One of them, presumably the leader, dismounted and held his reins out to a woman before approaching on foot.

Brynt held his pickaxe at the ready. He could feel the lintep on either side of him tense at the man's approach, but they stood their ground.

"Get them, Leif!" came an angry voice from behind Brynt.

The blond man raised an eyebrow as he looked around Brynt to the man on the ground. He turned his attention back to Brynt with a shake of his head.

"I apologise for these two oafs," he said from a short distance away. "I am Leif, Duke of Deuterfoss. We heard about your broken Paradise and came to learn more about it.

"Unfortunately, some of my subjects are rather hot-headed. They've taken it into their heads that the lintep have invaded and destroyed your Paradise and that they need to save you. I assume that isn't exactly the whole truth, as you appear to have lintep at your beck and call."

"Duke Leif, is it?" Brynt asked, ignoring the comment about the lintep. "I've never heard of Deuterfoss. What business of yours is our broken Paradise?"

The duke stared at him dumbly. Brynt shifted his weight in agitation.

"Well, whatever your reason for coming here, I don't appreciate your men attacking my farmers."

The horsewoman approached slowly, stopping behind the duke. The blond man looked up at her and found his voice.

"We did not condone them galloping ahead of us. Karsyk is a well-known for his impetuous attitude. On my honour, we did not come to attack you," the duke told him.

Brynt finally lowered his weapon, though he noticed Noémi and Rownyn did not do likewise.

"My name is Brynt. I'm the ... Paradise leader." The title still did not sit right with him. How could he presume to lead his people? "If your boys hand over their weapons, our healers will patch them up."

"Lord Brynt, if you would allow me?" the lintep on his right spoke.

"Allow you to what, Rownyn?" Brynt asked, not comprehending him.

"I may not be the most skilled healer in Illaria, but I did learn under Mistress Kayte. I can easily heal those wounds, if they'll let me."

"Don't you touch me!" A petrified man screamed behind him. "You keep those lintep away from me!"

The Duke of Deuterfoss sighed loudly. "Please excuse Karsyk. It would appear he does not trust your lintep."

"They aren't *my* lintep." Brynt bristled at the comment. "If your boy is too stupid to let a gifted lintep heal him, he'll have to make do with whatever our Paradise healers can do for him.

"Noémi, take their weapons and bring that one to the healers. Rownyn, can you heal the other one here? And take a look at my lads too."

"Certainly, Lord Brynt," Rownyn replied.

Noémi and Tiphaine took weapons from all the Deuterfoss riders and escorted them into the Paradise. Only the woman and the duke stayed behind.

Rownyn took a quick look at the farmers, but they brushed aside his attempts to help them. Brynt saw they only sported bruises.

"I really do apologise if Karsyk and Raleigh startled you. That was never our intention," the duke said as he held out his hand. Brynt swallowed a sharp retort and shook the outstretched hand instead.

"No harm done. To my men, anyway," he replied with a huff, before turning his attention to the healer.

Rownyn was on his knees beside the other injured man, Raleigh as the duke had called him, a hand laid over his ribs. He remained motionless for long, agonising heartbeats. Finally, with a sigh, Rownyn sat back on his haunches.

"It is done," he said wearily.

Brynt looked at him closely. "At what cost to you, Rownyn?"

Rownyn waved away his concern. "I simply need to rest now. If you'll excuse me." He braced his hands against his knees to stand and headed back towards the Paradise.

Raleigh got to his feet and stared after the lintep. Brynt watched as he pressed his fingers against his ribs, then roughly pulled his shirt up to inspect further. "He ... my ... ribs were broken. At least two of them! He ..."

"He's not the monster you thought he was?" asked Brynt, sarcastically. "You'll be lucky if he ever says the same about you."

The boy had the good sense to look ashamed. Brynt shook his head and turned towards the Paradise.

"Come on, then. It's getting late and we'll need to find you a room for the night."

It took her two days. Two entire days to have any success. Not that Lishe called it much of a success to pull one tiny portion of power out of the Paradise boundary. She'd had less trouble taking more power from living lintep. Lishe breathed in the extra sliver from the Paradise, letting it settle inside her, as she placed her hand on the boundary and tried, once again, to take more.

At least it's a start, she thought as the new power was encased by the others. They all needed that at first – to be coddled by other powers, until they felt at home within her. If she concentrated, she could still tell each power apart from the other.

She had been harvesting power from other lintep for years now. It had been so easy to take power from the first lintep. Just like when she, Nyssa and Kora had experimented as students, she had covered him entirely with her power and tightened her grip on his, slowly pulling it out of him. It had been much easier than she had thought possible.

Lishe had found the man in a little town near Illaria. She had been surprised to realise it was a lintep settlement. Lishe had never heard of other lintep settlements when she was in Illaria. She remembered speaking to the old man for an entire afternoon. He had nostalgically told her of his much younger days when he'd had more power. He had boasted about being the only one left from a large group of them who had helped Princess Ophélie create her little Paradises.

Lishe had heard of Ophélie before. Everyone in Illaria knew of her. But this was the first she'd heard of the Paradises. The more she learnt about them, the more she wanted to find them, to somehow steal the power that had created them. Then she could return to Illaria to deal with her awful excuse for a father. Not to mention, she could become a powerful mistress. In fact, they could create a new position for her as Head Mistress. She smiled at the memory and the hope of becoming a mistress.

That first power had struggled for weeks to be free of her, but she had tamed it. After that, it had become second nature. She would feel empty without all this extra power inside her.

Chapter Six – Ophélie's journal

Guiscard waited until the girls had left before retrieving the book again. After reading the research Shuut and the twins had handed in, he and Aurelius had made discreet inquiries about where they had found that book.

He had cursed a hundred different ways when he'd found it. It was the same one Kora had shown him and Lukys all those years ago. He was certain of it even though he hadn't had a chance to look at it properly back then.

It looked like a journal of sorts. Ophélie had documented everything about the Paradises, but pages had been torn from the front. He couldn't remember what they were. Perhaps they had detailed exactly how the Paradises had been created. It made little difference now – they'd figured that part out with Bastienne's confirmation.

What Guiscard found most interesting about the journal was that it named the towns and villages where Ophélie had gathered her volunteers.

"And you say all of these are lintep settlements?" he asked Bastienne. The old master shrugged.

"I've heard of some of them, but only the ones nearest Statera. I wouldn't be surprised if she created Paradises near each of these groups of settlements."

"Do you have a detailed map of the Outworld?" Kynon asked.

"Not very recent, no," the librarian admitted. "Occasionally Eliséo will add to what I have, but it has been many years since it was updated. Wait here."

He walked purposefully to his own private desk, unlocked the drawer and sifted through a pile of parchment until he found what he was looking for.

"Here," he said as he laid the sheets out on the sunlit desk. "These are my most recent maps. Bastienne, can you point out where any of these settlements are?"

The old master leaned over the desk, tracing his finger from Illaria along Pebble Stream and landed on the far side.

"This is Statera." He tapped his finger over an empty place on the map. "Along here, you have Albercott, Garstiel and Bexent. Back when I was living there, we often traded supplies with those villages. Sometimes a young lintep could even move to find an apprenticeship which suited them more.

"I know Ophélie canvassed the area for lintep willing to help create her Paradises. We were among the first. She didn't yet know how many it would take to safely create them.

"She was young and idealistic, trying to follow in her sister's footsteps. Her idea of the Paradises was so idyllic, she managed to convince quite a few of my father's friends to join her. Not wanting to be left out, he joined them too." Bastienne shook his head. "He came back to us a broken man, with so little power it was barely worth mentioning. It was only then that I came to Illaria. Ophélie promised she would give me the best magical education possible."

"And do you think she did?" asked Kynon. "You seemed quite unimpressed with many of the older teachers when I spoke with you the other day."

"Well, she certainly assigned the best teachers currently in Illaria to me," Bastienne admitted, twisting his mouth to one side. "But it was on my regular visits back to Statera that I explored the opposite side of my power. *That* is still not being taught here, or so it would seem. It is something that should be rectified."

"And so it shall be," Guiscard assured him. "But today is not the day to make those changes. Do you know of any other settlements, lintep or otherwise, missing from this map?"

They spent the greater part of the afternoon plotting out the missing towns and villages on Guiscard's map. Bastienne revealed what he knew of them from his time in the Outworld – which were lintep, which were human, and which were a surprisingly peaceful mixture of both. Those were few and far between and, as Bastienne pointed out, could easily have changed over time.

"We need Kora's map," Guiscard muttered. "She told us that she found eleven Paradises. We need to see where they are and if it's at all possible that she missed some. This map may help us find them all."

"You shouldn't have sent her away so quickly," Bastienne admonished him. "I'll bring her back."

"She'll be with Pér in the city by now." Kynon got to his feet. "I'll show you the way."

* * *

Kora should have been annoyed at her veiled dismissal, but her thoughts kept drifting back to her father. She knew she had to keep herself busy and it certainly would be best to keep Rilla occupied. With an empty reassurance that things would work out, she sent Rilla on her way to Nicodemo for a lesson before wandering over the bridge towards the marketplace. It was early afternoon. Pér would still be at his stall. Perhaps he would not mind the company if she stayed with him awhile.

These days, she felt at a bit of a loss for what to do. She had her map, of course, but that only gave her so much of a role to play in the destruction of the Paradises. The only task she had, essentially given to her by Lukys, was the creation of schools for any lintep children they found once the Paradises had been destroyed.

"Lost in thought again, I see," the familiar voice called out to her as she passed by. Kora smiled and turned back towards Pér. "You would have passed me by completely, wouldn't you?"

"I would have come back, eventually," she told him, leaning in for a brief kiss.

"I forgive you," Pér whispered in her ear as she pulled away from him. "What brings you out into town, aside from me, of course?"

"Actually, I did come to find you," she admitted, her cheeks colouring at his smile. "I wanted to talk to you about the schools. I have a few ideas, but don't want to start planning anything without you."

Pér looked at her for a moment. She clenched her jaw tight.

"We can talk about schools if you like. But only after you tell me what's happened."

"No. There's nothing that can be done about it and telling you will only make you worry as well."

"Kora, I will worry whether you tell me or not. So out with it."

Kora looked around. There were a lot of people in the market square. If she told Pér what had happened and was overheard, it would likely cause widespread panic.

Father is in danger, in the Lesa Mountains. There is nothing we can do until the crystal dragons arrive to help us find him.

She expected Pér to cry out in alarm, to alert people somehow. He did not. His only reaction was to envelop her in an embrace just long enough for Kora to pull herself together.

"Stay with me a while," he told her. "I'll close the stall in a bit, and we can go back to my place. I've written down a few ideas about the schools for you to look at. Maybe we can go over them with Plyke later tonight?"

Kora knew he wasn't dismissing her father's predicament and appreciated that he was willing to help distract her. She could feel his hope at the question. He'd spent too little time with Plyke over the past few days. It was difficult with the two of them living in different parts of Illaria, Plyke with his lessons, Pér with his stall.

"Don't fuss over it, Kora," he told her. "We don't need to change anything right now. I'm happy with the time I spend with my son. You've raised a fine young man."

It was a wonder she felt so comfortable with Pér. He could read her fears as easily as she could read a book, yet she never felt the least bit intimidated or violated by it. Somehow, it was completely different to when lintep tried to actively read her thoughts or change her feelings by touching her skin.

"I'll stay with you." She pulled up a stool and sat behind him.

Later that afternoon, as Kora helped Pér pack away the wares, she saw Bastienne and Kynon walking through the markets. She raised an eyebrow as they approached.

"Are you looking for something in particular?" she asked them coldly.

"We're looking for you, Kora. Actually," Bastienne answered, unflinchingly, "we need your help". He looked Pér up and down. "Pér, I presume? He may join us if you so wish."

As Pér frowned, Kora realised he hadn't been introduced to the retired master yet.

"Pér, meet Master Bastienne. He was an advanced teacher when Nyssa and I were just girls. You wouldn't have been taught by him."

Kora and her father had quickly made Pér aware of the fact that Lukys would put him to good use if he ever found out how powerful the minstrel was. It had stopped him from showing his true power in lessons and prevented him from taking advanced classes.

"An honour to meet you, Master Bastienne." Pér extended a hand out to the old lintep. As they shook hands, Bastienne's eyes lit up.

"No, indeed, the honour is all mine."

Kora looked between the two of them suspiciously. Was there any way that Bastienne had managed to gauge Pér's true potential from a single touch? Would she and her loved ones ever be free from the way lintep presumed to meddle with them?

"Calm yourself," Pér whispered as he linked hands with her. Together, they joined her uncle and the master on the path back to the castle. "It's amazing how you survived in a Paradise so long without their lintep leader realising you were one too."

"Perhaps he did realise," Kora mused. "Perhaps that's the reason he never did anything to me. Especially if he knew he wasn't as powerful."

"There's a lot of 'perhaps' in those thoughts." Pér glanced sideways at her. "Do you really think he knew?"

She shrugged. "I don't know what to think anymore. He was clearly petrified of anyone realising he was a lintep. To disguise his race, he ostracised his own daughter from almost everyone."

"Almost?" Pér asked in astonishment. "There was someone willing to stand up to him?"

Kora smiled sadly. "An old healer, Rhanya. He had a soft spot for Rilla. The two of them could be found together almost every free moment they had. That was when you could see Rilla at all. I didn't realise until the day they left that she had been wrapping power around herself, making her virtually invisible, for most of her life. It was only then that I realised Erton must be a lintep." She shook her head angrily. "I must have done something, said something, to make him understand I knew. That was when his men tried to attack me. I fled in terror, so thankful that Plyke had already escaped."

She fought back tears. Pér disentangled his fingers from hers and draped his arm around her shoulders, pulling her close to him. He kissed her hair lightly.

"Plyke is safe. *You* are safe," he told her firmly, as though saying the words made it true. "He can't hurt you now and you *never* have to see him again. You never need to live in a Paradise again. *You* are the reason we can destroy those monstrosities."

Kora breathed in his scent, savouring the closeness. *How could I have abandoned you? Not once, but twice!* He held her closer, and she let the wave of calm and reassurance wash over her. He always knew exactly what she needed, and she loved him for that.

As they followed the older lintep into the castle, Kora clung closely to Pér. She should have felt safe, secure and confident in this environment, but the earlier dismissal paired with the sudden request to return rattled her.

When they entered the library, Guiscard was waiting for them. Pieces of parchment were scattered over his desk. Kora walked towards him curiously as he held out a small book to her. She presumed it was the one he'd hidden away from her and Rilla earlier that afternoon.

She took it and stared at it in disbelief. It was Ophélie's journal – the one she had torn the map out of before heading into the Outworld. She shook her head in annoyance. She should have taken the entire book with her, but that would have been too dangerous if it had slipped into the wrong hands.

"Where did you find this?" she asked emotionlessly. "I thought I hid it well enough that it would stay hidden."

"You?" asked Guiscard incredulously. "*You* hid it! Aurelius had to figure out what this book told us all by himself. If you hadn't hidden it, we'd have known more about the Paradises before you went out to destroy that first one."

Kora stared at him, her face a blank mask. "How did you find it?"

"If you must know, Shuut and the twins discovered it while researching the Outworld. I don't know how they came across it, but they left it in a much easier place for us to later discover."

"This book has important information. It's not for the casual reader. I think it should stay with me from now on." She held it close to her chest, immediately noticing Guiscard bristling with anger.

"*That book* will remain in this library." A light sparked in his eyes. He shook his head. "It was you, wasn't it? You're the one who tore something out of the front. What was it?"

Kora stood stiff-backed. "What did you need me for? You sent Uncle Kynon and Master Bastienne out to find me. Surely it wasn't simply to show me this book? What do you want?"

Bastienne stepped in. "There are a number of settlements listed in that book. We've plotted some of them on Guiscard's map and wondered if you passed any of the others in the Outworld. We have a theory that the Paradises are all located near them."

"Why do you think that?" Kora asked, as she leafed through the pages to find the list of settlements.

"Because I'm fairly certain the Paradise my father helped create is located near Statera. It only stands to reason that the same is true for most, if not all, of these settlements.

"I know Ophélie asked for help from more than one village at a time, so I would assume there is one Paradise per cluster of lintep villages. With your help, we were hoping to see if the settlements are near the Paradises you've found or if there may be more which escaped your detection."

Kora listened intently as the old master explained his theory. It was entirely possible that she had missed Paradises. After all, she only had an incomplete map to work with.

Reluctantly, she placed Ophélie's journal back on the desk and retrieved the map from her sash belt, placing it beside Guiscard's own maps, ignoring the old librarian's indignant gasp at the rough edge along the top.

She looked over the settlements Bastienne had plotted, compared them with the names in Ophélie's book and pointed out a few more that she'd passed by in her travels.

"How do you know they're all lintep settlements?" she asked. "I don't recall noticing that when I passed through them."

"I did," Pér replied quietly, at her side.

She frowned. "You?"

"You forget, Kora, I spent years trying to find you in the Outworld. I stayed in each town along the way, almost certainly longer than you did, trying to find any whisper of information to lead me to you. It wasn't difficult to tell that most of the people living in these places were lintep."

Kora refused to feel guilty about that, yet again. She looked away from Pér in time to see Bastienne's curious glance.

"The lintep in these settlements are usually quite guarded about their skills with outsiders. Many humans interact with them on a seasonal basis because they don't know they are dealing with lintep. They must have trusted you a great deal for them to have shown you their skills."

Pér shrugged. "I'm a friendly person. Besides, people tend to trust a minstrel more than any other lone traveller."

"Hmmm." Bastienne raised an eyebrow but said nothing more about it. "So back to the maps then. Did you find Paradises around these groups of settlements?"

Kora tried to ignore Bastienne's comments. Even though Pér's power had been exposed when she revealed he was Plyke's father, she still wanted to keep him out of Lukys' clutches. She didn't want everyone she loved to be forced to serve Illaria in whatever way suited their king.

She turned her attention to the maps before her and compared the two. "It does look like the Paradises I found are near these settlements. You can add Helsford, Hythebent and Baneforth around here. Burnkien, Dalreath and Bournebery are here, here and … here." She paused, racking her brain to remember her journey over sixteen years ago. "Danverness, Snowdrift, Hazelston and Rousting are here, on the other side of the Lesa Mountains.

"I mapped out all of the Paradises I passed through. I didn't find any near Gillenhop, Steyden, Warridean and Estilcrag. They're above the Crystal Falls. Is it possible they helped with one of the other Paradises?"

The three old lintep exchanged glances. Guiscard shook his head. "I don't think so. Those four are too far away from the other Paradises to have helped with any of those. How far did you travel around the Crystal Falls?"

Kora shrugged. "I didn't want to travel too close to the Drakos Mountains, so I stayed on the east side. It was difficult enough finding a way up the cliff to get to the lake. Perhaps Ophélie didn't actually recruit anyone from those settlements. You only know for certain that the lintep from Statera worked with the lintep from Albercott and Garstiel on this project. It's not necessarily true that the others worked together in groups or that Ophélie was successful in finding people to help create her Paradises everywhere she went."

"This does pose a difficult question, however." Bastienne tapped his fingers together in front of his face. "Even if we destroy each of the Paradises you found, how do we know we've destroyed them all? Is this how Rilla, the child from Paradise, is to fulfil the prophecy? Is she somehow the key to finding the rest of them and destroying them all in one fell swoop?"

"It always falls back to that poor girl," Kora said angrily. "Why must everything fall on her shoulders when we don't even know if she really is the prophecy child?"

"Kora, be reasonable." Kynon went to place his hand on her bare arm, but she flinched away. He shook his head as he pulled his hand back. "So, *that's* where Rilla got it from then. You taught her not to let anyone touch her."

"Rilla didn't learn anything from me," Kora retorted hotly. "Her father made sure that even *I* didn't attempt to speak with her. Whatever she learnt was on her own or from the Paradise healer. But I'm glad that is one thing she understood as soon as she arrived. That poor girl has been through so much – she doesn't need anyone manipulating her feelings."

"Whatever your own thoughts on the matter, Kora," Guiscard spoke softly, "Rilla *is* named in the prophecy. She must be involved somehow."

"Then explain to me how she has a crystal heart." Kora stood her ground. "And don't give me any nonsense about being raised among crystal dragons for the first few years of her life. She doesn't remember any of that, so they clearly didn't leave enough of an impression to give her even a metaphorical crystal heart."

Kynon shuffled his feet and avoided her gaze. She, Kynon and Guiscard were probably the only ones to know that a crystal heart was indeed involved, but it still didn't explain how that heart was meant to beat in Rilla, or anyone else.

"Let's leave that part for now." Kynon brushed the issue aside. "What about the 'song which will destroy that which was created'? If we're still assuming the prophecy child is a lintep, even if not Rilla, could we assume the song is the lintep whistle?"

"I've always found an actual song can be more powerful than the whistle, if one performs it correctly," Pér told them. "Just ask King Lukys why he refuses to allow me to play in the castle."

Kora shook her head at Pér. She saw the way Bastienne looked at him and didn't want him giving away all his secrets. Bastienne narrowed his eyes.

"I would love for you to give me a demonstration some time," Bastienne told the minstrel.

Kora's mind swirled with thoughts that she fought to keep hidden. *What would happen if someone with Pér's power used Anya's crystal heart to sing, the way that only he knows how? Could Pér teach them to do it?*

Chapter Seven – Nicodemo's dilemma

Rilla walked purposefully with her swords to the guardhouse. If she couldn't do anything else today, then she would take all her fears and frustration to the sparring ground. Perhaps Plyke and Shuut could join her after their lesson. As she neared the sparring ground, she saw a company of guards working with their weapons. They didn't give her a second glance as she sat to watch them.

Nicodemo caught her eye as he shouted out orders to his guards. He nodded to her but indicated that she should remain where she was. In anticipation of joining them, Rilla crossed her arms and began to study the movements. Before too long, she was standing, well away from the others, copying their routine. A few of the guards finally noticed her and began laughing.

"What's so funny?" Nicodemo asked sternly. "Have you never seen a child learning to fight before?"

"A child, yes. A Paradisian girl, no," one replied with a laugh. "She couldn't learn to fight if you spent all your time with her."

"An interesting prediction, Ramiro," Nicodemo said as he motioned Rilla over. She walked towards them with a cold calm settling inside her. "Perhaps you can show us how little skill she has."

Ramiro immediately stopped laughing and looked angrily at Rilla. "*Me*? Why should I?"

"Are you scared?" she asked him sweetly.

"Only that I'll hurt you, little girl," he answered with a shrug. "Go get a practice sword."

Rilla looked questioningly at Nicodemo. She much preferred using her own weapons, but when he shook his head at her, she placed her own swords on a small bench and went to find a wooden one instead.

She felt Ramiro's stare on her the entire time. She studiously ignored him and used the breathing technique Master Bastienne had given her. It helped to focus her thoughts on the wooden sword and the coming bout with Ramiro. By the time she'd settled herself across from him, she was completely calm and ready to spar.

"Right, in your places."

Rilla held her sword with both hands. It wasn't her preferred method of fighting, but that was what the rest of them were doing and she would certainly find herself at a disadvantage using one hand, even if this man wasn't more than twice her size.

"Attack and defend, go!"

Ramiro instantly attacked. She held up her sword to block his blow. Her shoulder exploded in pain as his sword jarred on hers. She stepped back out of his range and pulled her power out of her wall, wrapping it around her sword, making it one with her.

She took a steadying breath before allowing Ramiro to close the distance between them. He struck out again but, this time, she ducked under his sword and hit his legs with her own sword. He cried out in pain and cursed her angrily.

There would be no holding back now. The furious guard gave her no room to manoeuvre, no time to think. Everything was on instinct. She blocked where she needed to, using her power to absorb the shock, attacked where she could, making sure to make the few blows count.

"Halt!" Nicodemo called out. Rilla lowered her sword but kept a tight hold on it. She was in a battle fury and did not trust anyone, least of all the man who had just been trying to knock out her brains.

"So, Ramiro, you still think she's not worth training?"

Ramiro looked at him angrily. "You *knew*."

"I didn't the first time, but I still kept up my guard, which is more than you did. She should never have been able to strike you so early on. You underestimated her, gave her an opening and she took it. I daresay you'll both be sporting dark bruises by nightfall."

Rilla tried to hide her proud smirk as the guard glared at her angrily.

"Rilla, would you like to continue with the one sword?" She shook her head. "Go get another one, then. You can spar with Séverin. He'll be a better partner for you. Just mind you actually listen if he tries to give you pointers."

She cocked an eyebrow at him but nodded nonetheless as she went to retrieve another sword from the stash beside the guardhouse.

Séverin was waiting for her when she returned. His auburn hair glinted a fiery red in the sunlight. Rilla hadn't seen many lintep with red hair. She wondered if they were related in any way, but quickly banished the thought as he held his sword at the ready.

"Again," Nicodemo called out. "Take it in turns. Five attacks each and then you swap. Allow your partner to practise. You can parry, but if you are the defender, you are not to attack."

"You go first," Rilla told Séverin with a smile. "I need to size you up first."

He grinned and caught her off guard. Her side throbbed in pain.

"Don't let a pretty face like mine catch you off guard," he warned her.

Rilla stuck out her tongue at him as he struck out again. This time she caught his blade between her two and stopped the blow before it hit her. He nodded appreciatively at her skill, stepping back out of her range again. Rilla stood on guard, watching his every move, trying to sense when the next blow would come. Without thinking about it, her power swirled all around her, flowing out to where Séverin stood, taking in everything about him. Before he'd moved an inch, she swivelled out of the way, but held herself back from attacking him.

That was his third attack. Two more to go. Rilla focused on her power, on his stance, his sword. She was so attuned to his every move that his next two attacks fell well short of hitting their mark.

"How are you doing that?" he asked. "You seem to know where I'm going to move before I do."

Rilla shrugged. She was fairly certain this was another one of the ways she used her power differently to everyone else. King Lukys, or even Nicodemo, might not appreciate her divulging this information to all the guards.

It was her turn next. Rilla once more allowed her power to flow down her arms and around her swords, through the air surrounding her and over to Séverin. She had to think differently, now that she was attacking. But her power still afforded her an extra edge to the battle.

As she began each attack, she instantly felt how he was going to block or evade her blow and readjusted to counteract that. Four times out of five, she hit her mark. Séverin was breathing hard by the time they were done.

"Halt!" cried out Nicodemo. "Everyone take a quick breath before we start again. Séverin, Rilla, a word."

Rilla kept her distance from her sparring partner as they approached the head guard. She knew what was coming. Would it really matter if she told them what she was doing? Surely that would only make them better guards.

"You're doing something different to the last time I saw you," he stared at her closely. "You might have gotten the better of Ramiro quite easily, and to be honest, I almost expected you to. Séverin is another matter altogether. He's one of my best guards. Well-trained and perceptive.

"You not only managed to evade and block some of his blows but landed nearly all of yours on him. Even *I* find it difficult to do that. So exactly what were you doing to achieve that, young lady?"

Rilla weighed up her options. Isis had forced her to tell her entire class how she experimented with fire and they were only students. Disciplined guards should take the news more calmly and work to implement the changes if they agreed to do them.

"I used my power to help me," Rilla finally admitted. "I let it surround my swords and then sent it out to help me."

"Exactly how did sending it out help you?" Nicodemo asked.

Rilla saw Séverin smile.

"She let her power be her eyes. That's how she knew when I was going to attack just as I started and how she could evade my defences without a second thought."

Nicodemo stared at her in surprise. "How did you even know to do that?"

"Did *you* know?" she asked, equally surprised.

"Well, of course, but I never expected anyone as young and, pardon me but, inexperienced to have figured it out," he told her honestly.

"But, if you know how to do that, why haven't you taught your guards to do it?" she asked, confused. "I would have thought that would be one of the best ways to train them."

"You still haven't answered my question," Nicodemo evaded. "How did you know to do that? Who taught you?"

"No one taught me," Rilla replied, instantly becoming defensive. "It just happened one day, and I can make it happen any time now, barely without a thought."

"Well, that's a first." He cocked an eyebrow at her. "As for *your* question. I do teach my guards to do that, once I am satisfied that they can fight well enough without their power to save their lives. If you want a fair fight with Séverin, we can ask him to use his power or you can stop using yours. It's your choice."

Rilla stared, open mouthed, at his statement. It hadn't occurred to her that they might think she was cheating if she used her power. She simply knew that she was at a disadvantage age, height and power-wise. There was no way she would be able to defend herself against them without using her power.

"And I see by the look on your face that you've just understood exactly why I insist they learn to fight without power first. You should always assume your opponent might have as much skill with magic as you do, so if you can't beat them in a fair fight, you almost certainly won't with magic, unless you are somehow much more skilled than they are, making up for your lack of experience and skill with your actual weapon."

Rilla turned to Séverin, crestfallen. "I'm sorry," she told him quietly. "I didn't realise I was cheating. Would you spar with me again? I won't use my powers this time."

Séverin smiled casually. "But of course. Nicodemo is sometimes a harsh weapons master, but he has his reasons. I wouldn't ever want to be caught out in a fight to realise I wasn't skilled enough with my weapon alone to survive."

Rilla nodded and followed him back to the sparring ground. The other guards had gathered once again and Nicodemo called a start to the training.

"First group to my right. Second group to my left. First group, attack with purpose. Second group, allow them to attack and block if you see it coming. Only attack if they leave themselves wide open. Then swap."

Rilla was in the first group. She stood, swords at the ready, and watched Séverin. He calmly studied her every move.

Right, no magic, she thought as she attacked. Séverin managed to block her blow, but only just. Rilla smiled smugly, but immediately regretted it as Séverin took the opportunity to attack her. She blocked the blow, but he hit with enough force to plough through and make her hit herself with her own blades.

"I'm stronger than you," he told her. "No matter how well you block, I'm going to injure you sooner or later if you don't change your strategy."

Rilla grimaced and attacked again, spinning around to miss his wooden sword and struck him across his back instead. This time, she didn't take the time to revel in her victory. She was immediately on her guard, watching his every move. She anticipated when he would strike and moved so that he missed her completely. Unfortunately, she tripped over her own feet and fell flat on her face.

"And you're dead."

Rilla winced at the familiar mocking tone behind her. Shuut was lazily leaning back against the guardhouse, one foot against the wall, staring at Rilla with a look of disappointment. "I taught you better than that."

"You must be Shuut," Nicodemo said as he walked towards her. "You're more than welcome to join in. Rilla certainly attributes most of her current skill to you."

"Not sure I'm happy about that if *this* is how she's performing."

"Then perhaps you should show us how it's meant to be done," Ramiro smirked. "Grab a training sword and come on over."

Rilla dusted herself off as Shuut lazily pushed herself off the wall. Her sister strode over to the challenging lintep, looked him up and down with a raised eyebrow then strolled over to the wooden swords. She sifted through them, weighing a few in her hands before selecting one.

"Let's give these two some space," Nicodemo told the others. Rilla stood back with Séverin, fervently hoping that Shuut wouldn't permanently damage the cocky guard, even if he deserved it.

Ramiro had barely lifted his sword before Shuut attacked him. To anyone but those who knew her, it would have looked like she hadn't been prepared before he moved. Rilla thought that's what it must have looked like to all the guards. Rilla drew her breath in sharply, was momentarily distracted by Séverin who nudged her arm as he looked down at her, then she turned back to find Ramiro on his back.

"How did she do that?" he half whispered.

Rilla shrugged. "She's a trained banwep. How do you suppose she survived so long in the Outworld if she *couldn't* do that?"

Ramiro growled as he got to his feet. He lunged, but before the sword was fully extended, Shuut had already moved away and behind him, striking him across his back. He turned in a fit of rage only to take a blow to the stomach and another swipe across his legs, laying him flat on the ground once more.

Shuut stood over him, wooden sword at his throat. "I just killed you, twice." She looked over at Rilla and shrugged. "Guess my little sister isn't so bad after all. At least she managed to avoid getting hit, but Rilla, do me a favour and learn not to trip over your own feet."

Rilla shook her head and smiled. "One bout for old times' sake?"

Shuut nodded and walked well away from the prostrate lintep. Behind them, Rilla could hear Nicodemo reprimanding Ramiro for underestimating his opponent, yet again.

"It doesn't matter if she's smaller than you, not as powerful as you or even not a full lintep. As you can see, *anyone* is capable of flooring you if you let them. Ramiro, I want double training sessions from you for the rest of this week. If Shuut ever deigns to spar with you again, I expect you to be better prepared. That goes for all of you."

Rilla joined her sister in a free area of the sparring ground. She readied her swords and they sparred like they had in the Outworld so many times. It wasn't really any different now that they were in the relative safety of Illaria. Shuut still fought as though it were a fight to the death in the Outworld. What was the point of practising if you didn't take it seriously? It was just like the hunting game she'd had them play in the forest all those months ago. The boys had seen it as only a game, but Rilla had understood that Shuut was trying to teach them how to survive the only way she knew how.

Sweat was dripping down her back by the time Rilla begged for a halt. "I know you could keep going forever, but I'm already going to be half covered in bruises."

"Yes, you were a bit sloppy today," Shuut replied, looking at her closely. "Are you okay?"

"Of *course* not," Rilla answered between gritted teeth. She saw a flash of understanding in Shuut's eyes. Distractions could only help so much.

"Right, I guess we'll stop now."

"I'd like a turn, if you're still up for it."

Rilla turned to see Séverin, who had obviously been watching them. She looked over her shoulder at her sister, who didn't seem surprised by the guard's request. The other guards had started to pack their gear away, looking happy to be done for the day, though she noticed Nicodemo making a show of mending a leather tunic so that he could watch their bout.

"Why not?" Shuut replied offhandedly. "I need someone to cool down with."

Séverin flashed Shuut a grin as Rilla shook her head and walked over to Nicodemo. She put her wooden swords away, then settled down next to the weapons master to watch the show.

Shuut and Séverin circled around warily, neither lashing out at the other. Eventually, Shuut feinted and immediately backed away, watching to see how the lintep would react. He barely flinched, drawing her in closer once more. They danced around the sparring ground, neither willing to be the first to start their bout in earnest.

"Stop wasting time!" Nicodemo yelled out.

Séverin shook his head, but began pressing Shuut, forcing her to show her defences. Rilla held her breath as her sister leaped forward. It looked like Séverin's sword would hit her across the ribs, but somehow, it didn't. Shuut twisted, mid-leap, to land on his off-side. She struck him across the ribs while he was still lunging forward to attack the space she'd left empty.

He turned and backed away from her, a mischievous glint in his eye. Rilla knew he wouldn't make the same mistake again. She wondered if he'd done that purposely to force Shuut to show some of her moves. He had, after all, managed to best Rilla a few times and, though she wasn't a trained banwep, she was still better than at least some of the guards here.

So fast she almost missed it, Séverin darted in to attack Shuut, feinted to the right and landed to the left, forcing Shuut to change her direction too quickly. He struck her lightly on the shoulder and pulled away before she had a chance to retaliate.

Shuut showed no surprise, anger or fear. Rilla knew that for her sister, this was not just another bout, it was a fight to the death. She'd dealt him a savage blow, probably cracking some ribs and leaving a massive gash in his side. He'd given her a shallow wound in the shoulder. She was still winning, but if she didn't stop him soon, even light wounds would slow her down.

Rilla watched in fascination as they dealt blow after blow, as though they were trading pleasantries. Eventually, Shuut went to strike at his neck, stopping a finger's width short.

"You're dead," she panted before moving out of his range.

"I am," Séverin conceded, "but you're gravely injured and won't last out the day without a healer."

Shuut laughed. "Good thing my sister is one of the best healers I've ever met. Come on, Rilla, let's wash up before dinner."

"Will I see you again?" Séverin called out to Shuut as she placed her wooden sword with the rest of the gear and began walking away. Shuut looked casually over her shoulder and shrugged with a smile. Rilla thought she saw a light blush on her cheeks. She thought it hilarious that Shuut appeared to have won herself an admirer after thoroughly thrashing him.

Chapter Eight – Loreli's scouts

Loreli flew slowly over the Lesa Mountains. She had been unimpressed to learn that she would be sent to spy for the karliki, but the task had its benefits. It had allowed her to train a flight of young clear crystal dragons. She and Groldor had shared the training, flying in shifts with the younger ones.

Groldor taught them how to blend into the sky and make the most of their clear bodies. Loreli showed them how to search for things on the ground – a column of smoke from a campfire, a disturbance in water, leaves rustling too quickly or out of time with the wind. They were all giveaway signs that something was amiss below.

They'd been searching the Lesa Mountains for weeks without the slightest sign of the rebel karliki. She was beginning to wonder if the rebels even existed. Perhaps they only moved under the cover of night, which would make it more difficult to spot them. Loreli looked at the horizon. They wouldn't have long before the sun set.

"One more pass before we head home," she called out to her group of five trainees. "Snowcrest and Garnet, sweep up the river, as near the ground as you dare. Hoarfrost and Shard, over to the white ghost gum. If they're going to enter through the mountains, that would be the way. Luminosa come with me. We'll take another look at the north side of the entrance.

"If you see anything unusual, signal for everyone else to join you. When you finish your pass, head back to the Drakos Mountains."

Her trainees flew off to begin their last pass for the day. Loreli could see they were tired. For that matter, so was she. It had been a long day of nothing. She'd have a word with Celtan when she returned. This was no task for the crystal dragons. What could they do to stop the rebel karliki short of killing them?

"Over there," Luminosa called out. "Snowcrest is signalling. They must have found something."

Loreli turned to see where Luminosa was looking. Snowcrest belched a steady stream of fire. Garnet dove down to the ground.

"What is he doing?" Loreli growled as she flew towards them. "He's going to get himself killed."

As they neared the river, Loreli saw what had caused the commotion. A group of yoswen were darting towards an overturned wagon, swiping at it with their claws and then retreating.

Garnet hovered and roared. Loreli and Luminosa flew in as Snowcrest joined Garnet, blocking the yoswen's path to the cart. They roared at the ugly, stocky creatures, but the yoswen refused to retreat, instead clawing their way forward and swiping their thick paws with wickedly sharp claws at crystal snouts.

"Luminosa, turn over that cart, see if this fight is worth it."

"It's worth it," Luminosa told her gravely. Loreli craned her neck to see a gruesome sight. Two men unconscious – one with half his arm ripped off. Four karliki: two were dead, the other two clutched daggers and were staring, wild-eyed at them.

"Fire!" she roared. All of them belched out flames towards the yoswen, not giving the creatures the chance to retreat. Several yoswen managed to get close enough to strike at the dragons' eyes and snouts, distracting them from the others who were now approaching the cart.

"To me!" yelled a karlik from the broken cart. Loreli buffeted the yoswen with the force of her wings and lashed out at the four yoswen who were slashing at the sorely outnumbered karliki. The yoswen fell into the snow. Hoarfrost and Shard dived down, snatching at the yoswen with their razor-sharp crystal teeth. They shredded the creatures and tossed them into the river thundering past them.

"Again!" she roared at her trainees. "Luminosa, stay with me."

At her command, the other trainees took to the skies and dived down in waves, attacking from above with teeth and fire. Loreli and Luminosa kept a steady stream of fire aimed at the yoswen, to keep them well clear of the cart and the survivors it barely sheltered.

When the last yoswen was dead, the six dragons collapsed in a huddled mass on the narrow, snowy riverbank. Loreli huffed out a last curl of smoke and turned her snout towards the karliki and injured people.

"Who are you and what are you doing out here?"

"I am Anya Nikolaevna," the blonde karlik stood unsteadily. "This is Ermolai. That is ... was Rufina and Demyan. We were attempting to escort Lord Aaron and Ambassador Eliséo back to Goraburg. They were injured even before we were attacked."

"That elf causes nothing but trouble," Loreli growled. "I can't believe I'm going to save his life."

"He'll survive long enough without your help. Lord Aaron won't." Anya glared at her. She ripped the sleeve off her shirt and broadly tied it around the ragged, bloody stump of the unconscious lintep's elbow. "He needs skilled healers. We cannot help him now, even if we get to the lower caverns of Goraburg."

"The lintep, then?" Loreli growled.

Anya nodded.

"We can possibly close the wound, but that is all. How long did it take Pyrid and Celtan to fly you to Illaria?"

"Most of the day. "Anya shook her head, helplessly. "He won't last that long."

"Then what?" Loreli asked. "The crystal dragons can't heal him."

Anya looked at Ermolai, seemingly weighing up her options. With no little hesitation, she placed her hand in her pocket and held it tightly.

"I have ... a unique gift with me. Something the crystal dragons gave my family many years ago. Would that work?"

Loreli hissed. "*You* have that?"

"Have what?" Ermolai asked, looking from one to the other.

"Not now, Ermolai." Anya brushed him aside. "Would it work, dragon?"

"I don't know," Loreli admitted. "Celtan would be able to tell us. Snowcrest and Garnet, take the dead ones. Hoarfrost and Shard go ahead of us. Luminosa and I will take the others. Fly as fast as you can to the Drakos Mountains."

The crystal dragons moved to follow her orders immediately. Luminosa scooped up the unconscious elf and the other karlik. Loreli took charge of Lord

Aaron herself, after lifting Anya to her back.

Let my lucky stars be watching over me tonight. Don't let this fool of a lintep die on my watch!

Without waiting to see if the others were following, Loreli flew like the wind towards the Drakos Mountains.

* * *

Pyrid lay on his belly, basking in the sunlight. He was due to fly back to Illaria in another two days. Not that he minded the adventure, but the long trips were taking their toll on him. He was not as young as he used to be. Perhaps he should consider giving the task to one of the younger dragons.

But I don't want to miss out on the thrill of it all, he admitted to himself.

As he nodded sleepily, his gaze flickered across a shimmer in the sky. Those trainees of Loreli's needed more practise. He could see them flying towards the Drakos Mountains from miles away.

They're belching fire! What's happened?

He instantly belched out a reply column of fire, alerting all the crystal dragons in the crater that something was wrong. A few heartbeats later, the crater floor was covered with dragons of all colours and sizes. They left just enough room for the incoming trainees to land.

Stunned silence greeted the clear crystal scouts as they descended into the crater. Snowcrest and Garnet explained about the yoswen attack as Loreli approached, Lord Aaron in her front claws, Anya on her back.

"No!" cried out Pyrid. "What happened to him? Celtan, Lord Aaron is dying!"

Celtan pushed past the other dragons surrounding Pyrid, shouting at them to get out of his way. Loreli lay Lord Aaron down gently on the dusty ground while Anya, not waiting to be lifted from between her spikes, slipped and slid her way down to the lintep.

"Can your heart heal him?" she asked urgently. "Ermolai and Eliséo are right behind us. With the three of us ... although Eliséo is still unconscious."

Pyrid looked at Celtan uncertainly. "I've never heard of a crystal heart being used to heal. I wouldn't even know which words to try."

He saw the crestfallen look on Anya's face and wished he knew what to do. "Celtan, think of something – anything for them to say. We try that first, even just to stop the bleeding, then I fly him straight to Illaria."

"You won't get there in time," Celtan told him gently.

"Not if he's bleeding like that," Pyrid replied, gesturing to the blood-soaked cloth around Aaron's arm. "Surely we can stop the bleeding."

Celtan shook his head. "Not with the heart. There is another way, but it will leave terrible scarring."

Anya shook her fists at him. "I don't care what kind of scarring it will leave. If you know a way to stop the bleeding, you do it *now*!"

Pyrid struggled not to step away from the furious little karlik. He looked over at Celtan expectantly. The sapphire dragon visibly sagged.

"Anya, do you have a sword, any sort of blade?"

The karlik nodded and held out her still bloodied dagger.

"Place it on the ground. I don't want to burn you. I'm going to breathe fire onto it – as hot as I can. As soon as I stop, you need to take the blade and hold it against his wound.

"As I said, cauterising the wound will not be a clean way to work. It won't fix anything on the inside, but it will possibly stop him bleeding to death before you get to Illaria."

Anya placed the dagger on the ground and tore the other sleeve of her shirt off, ready to wrap it around the hilt when Celtan was done. She nodded to the sapphire dragon. The other crystal dragons moved back even as Luminosa descended with Ermolai and Eliséo.

Celtan leant down closer to the dagger, opened his snout a sliver and belched out fire as quickly as he could. The blade glowed bright orange, then white. He stopped and moved away, giving Anya room to pick up the blade, her sleeve wound around her hand. She knelt beside Lord Aaron and folded the shredded remains of his arm up against his elbow joint before forcing the flat of the blade against the skin. She turned the blade over once to make sure she covered the entire wound.

The karlik blanched and turned away from Lord Aaron to vomit. Pyrid turned back to see the angry and lumpy red flesh on the outside of the lintep's elbow and a charred mess in the centre. He stared at it helplessly.

"Pyrid, let's not waste any time. Grab Eliséo and let's go. Ermolai, go with one of these dragons to Goraburg and tell Lord Ilya what happened."

Pyrid was surprised at everyone, including himself, obeying the feisty little karlik. He placed Anya on his back, gently held Lord Aaron in one claw and Eliséo in the other. Before Celtan could order any younger or faster crystal dragon to complete the task, Pyrid took off and headed for Illaria.

Chapter Nine – Brynt's Paradise

Leif looked around the Paradise as Brynt led them towards the healers. It looked a self-sufficient little village, but there were many things about it which were completely foreign to him. None of the buildings had locks on windows or doors. Security was clearly not an issue here. The buildings were also spread quite far apart, not like the ramshackle buildings of his city that leaned on top of one another.

On the far side of the river, there were farming lands set out in neat plots, a windmill and other water related industries. This side of the river had more buildings, with the distinct feeling that they were isolated from one another.

Brynt led them through these buildings, reassuring some of the villagers that everything was fine, but otherwise, not speaking. What must it have been like for him to have his Paradise destroyed after feeling so secure within it?

Before long, they reached the healers' house but were refused entry.

"Your man is being well tended to," one of the healers told him. "Though if he would only agree to have a lintep work on him, he would be healed within moments."

Leif laughed mirthlessly. "You'd have more chance of convincing him to cut off his own hand than allow a lintep to touch him. Thank you for doing what you can with him. I'm sure he's grateful, no matter how much trouble he causes you."

"Now what?" Talise asked, once the healers had gone inside.

"I'll show you to the tavern." Brynt gestured for them to follow him. "I understand it isn't the same as Outworld taverns, but it's the only place large enough to house so many of you."

He led them to a large, empty building. A bar stood along a wall with twenty tables spread out before it and a stage to one side. There were no other rooms, no stairs leading to another level, not even a kitchen. Leif looked around curiously. It was a decent sized tavern, possibly capable of entertaining close to one hundred patrons.

"Where do your visitors generally stay?"

"Visitors," huffed Brynt. "We never *had* visitors. Then the Paradise boundary was broken, and we've been overrun ever since."

Leif chose his words carefully. "It seems as though the lintep didn't do any other damage than destroy the boundary. Can you tell me what happened?"

Brynt laughed. "We were invaded. Or so we thought. We saw a group of armed men approaching us and went to defend ourselves. A bunch of kids rode to stop us, but their soldiers didn't stop, so we attacked." He shook his head. "Such a pointless fight, what there was of it. They weren't attacking us. It's true, they came to destroy our Paradise boundary, with good reason from their side, but they never meant to hurt us.

"After the confusion was sorted, they left us some of their soldiers to help defend us against idiots like your boy back there, at least until we can defend ourselves. They're to send us out blacksmiths and glaziers to show us how to create locks for our doors and glass for our windows.

"They even helped us negotiate a trading partnership with Hedgefall. I'm loath to admit it, but those lintep aren't half bad. The karlik and the elf, I'm still not too sure about, and that sapphire crystal dragon of theirs, well, he just grows on you."

Leif gaped at the explanation then bristled as Talise closed his mouth with her fingertip.

"So, they ... it wasn't, there were others involved in this?"

Brynt laughed at him. "Aye, every race in the Outworld, including humans. They're determined to destroy every Paradise they can find."

"But, why?" asked Leif, still trying to gather his thoughts.

Brynt shrugged. "There's some lintep running around trying to steal as much power as she can. Apparently, these Paradises were all built with lintep power, so if she figures it out, she could become the most powerful being around. Problem is, she's already drunk on power and could lord it over everyone if she got it in her head to do that. So, they're trying to destroy all the Paradises before that can happen."

"How are they doing it?" Talise asked curiously.

"Don't know," Brynt replied. "They weren't very forthcoming about that."

"Will they leave soldiers at every Paradise they destroy?" Leif asked, ever the tactician. "Will they train your men to fight as well as secure your properties? Are they going to secure trading partnerships for all the Paradises?"

"Whoa now." Brynt held his hands up. "None of that concerns me. I'm happy enough with how they left us. What they do with the others is not my concern."

"It's *my* concern," Leif replied coldly. "How many of these Paradises are in my duchy?"

"Like I said, that's nothing we talked about. You'd have to meet with King Lukys himself to sort that out."

"I suppose I'll have to then," Leif muttered. "I'll speak to his soldiers before we depart. That still leaves us with your Paradise. It's within the bounds of my duchy."

"We ain't swearing loyalty to anyone," Brynt said in a low voice. "We've only just joined this Outworld and we'll be damned if any one of us is going to swear fealty to anyone."

Leif knew when to fight and when to let things slide. "Brynt, no one is asking you to swear fealty to them. However, the fact of the matter is that your Paradise happens to fall within my duchy. As such, you, and any of your people, are free to request help from Deuterfoss and we will do our best to aid you.

"If there comes a time when you decide you *want* to swear fealty, that is up to you, but I will never force the matter. As far as the rest of the Outworld is concerned, you are my responsibility and I will care for you accordingly should you ever need me to do so."

Brynt crossed his arms, but his expression softened. "Well, so long as we understand each other then. You can stay the night here. We'll talk more in the morning. You'll hear the bell for the evening meal. You're free to join us in the eating hall – just follow everyone else. " The flaxen haired man left them alone in the tavern.

Leif looked around at the sparse furnishings and spotted some bed rolls. "I guess we'll use these tonight."

Talise seemed less than pleased but remained tight lipped as the other men went to claim a spot for the night. Leif instead went to an open window and stared out at the Paradise beyond. A light footstep behind told him Talise would not be silent for long.

"I'm going for a short walk," he announced suddenly. "I'll meet you in the eating hall later."

He was only a few yards away from the tavern when he heard the door open and close again. He didn't slow his pace for Talise. Showing her too much favour, even out here, could be bad for her reputation. Then again, she'd never much cared what people said about her – as if there was anything they really could say.

"Are you going to talk with this King Lukys then?" she asked without preamble. "If he's going to destroy more of these Paradises in your duchy, that could prove troublesome for your warehouses."

Leif shook his head. "I don't think so. If this one is anything to go by, the Paradises appear to be self-sufficient. What really concerns me is whether or not these people can keep themselves safe." He turned to face her. "If those lintep hadn't been here, how many people do you think would have died today? And all over a misunderstanding! Imagine what would happen if some fools decide they're going to raid the Paradise."

Talise went pale. "What are you going to do about it? Like you said, they're your responsibility now."

"These people need to be trained to defend themselves or they'll have to build a defensive wall." He shook his head again. "Or both. I'll send for a squadron of soldiers to train and defend them, but that will only help this Paradise. I need to find out how many Paradises are in my duchy, how many are in neighbouring duchies, and make sure plans are made to ensure the safety of all of them."

He gazed at the lines of concern on her face. He hated to worry her, to burden her with his duties. It wasn't her responsibility. She always just seemed to be there when he needed to talk through a problem and often helped him find elusive solutions. He was coming to rely on her more than was acceptable, considering she was entirely unconnected with him. He brushed the thought aside. There was no time to consider his feelings for her now. Then again, when would there be time?

"Talise, go and rest. I'll see you in the eating hall later."

"Where are you going?" She rubbed her arms in the bitterly cold wind.

"Never mind." He didn't want her following him. "I'll see you later."

He expected her to argue with him. The expression on her face warned him that she would. But then she nodded and walked away. He stared in surprise at her retreating figure until she was back in the tavern before walking away. He needed answers and the only one who could give them to him was King Lukys. Perhaps the lintep soldiers knew the king's plans. If not, he hoped they could get at least send a message to their king.

Retracing his steps, Leif quickly found his way back to the healers' house. He knocked on the door and waited patiently, even though he knew there were no locks, nothing keeping him out.

His patience was rewarded by the appearance of a short, wizened old man, who looked him up and down suspiciously. "What do you want?"

"Good day to you, good sir," Leif responded, with a little bow. "I was wondering if any of the lintep are here. I have a few questions to ask them."

"Rownyn, there's someone here to see you!" The ill-tempered man didn't wait for the lintep before disappearing back inside. Leif tried to hide his surprise at the old man's manner.

Rownyn appeared at the door. "Ah, Duke Leif. What can I do for you?"

"I need information and I'm hoping you're the man to help me, Rownyn." He smiled broadly at the lintep, suddenly hoping all the rumours he'd heard of them reading minds and manipulating humans was nonsense.

Rownyn nodded. "That sounds about right. Follow me."

Leif was led down a dark hallway, past eight closed doors. Rownyn opened one of them, and ushered Leif inside. The duke was surprised, yet again, by the austere furnishings.

"Are all the rooms like this?" he asked.

"I'm certain that's not what you came here to ask," Rownyn replied, eyebrows raised. "But, yes, most of them are. These people live a very simple life."

"I think that makes my need more urgent." Leif shook his head. "Tell me, what do you know of King Lukys' plans? How many Paradises is he planning on destroying? Are they all located in my duchy or are some further away? Does he have enough men, soldiers like you, to protect and train them until they can do without?"

As he questioned the soldier, Leif was surprised at the sudden smile that appeared on the lintep's face. He couldn't fathom why.

"I think you are just the man King Lukys is looking for," Rownyn told him. "Would you permit me to escort you to Illaria tomorrow? If we leave at dawn, we should be there before midday."

Stunned, Leif stared speechlessly at Rownyn. *Illaria. I'm going to Illaria?*

Chapter Ten – Sudden Arrival

Edric was startled out of sleep by screams. Day was dawning, and his horses were bucking in their stalls and whinnying loudly.

"Secure the horses!" he yelled, pulling on his boots. His stablehands ran to do his bidding as he bolted past them towards the pasture. He had to find out what was causing the commotion before it was too late.

It did not take long for him to see what it was. A fire opal dragon was circling the pasture, angling lower and lower.

That damn creature is going to land on top of my horses!

A few stablehands had followed him out to the pasture. He immediately ordered them to round up the horses. Thankfully, the crystal dragon seemed to notice what he was doing and soared back up into the sky.

"Tika, run to King Lukys. Tell him what's happened. Make him come now!" Edric yelled at the awestruck human. Luckily, the boy did not second-guess him and immediately did as he was told.

* * *

Lukys woke to a persistent knocking. Angrily, he strode to his door and slammed it open against the wall.

"What's the meaning of this?" he roared, looking down at the terrified human boy.

"Pyrid is back. He's circling over the pasture. Master Edric is trying to get the horses out of his way. You need to come now!"

Aislen came running around the corner, already fully dressed. "Let's go!" She took Tika by the hand and dragged him towards the stairwell. "Father, get Kayte and follow us."

How does she do that? he wondered even through his irritation of being woken early. *She knew he was coming before he'd arrived. And what does she know to make me summon Kayte?*

Lukys hurriedly dressed and went to find Kayte. She was already dressing by the time he got there.

"Did Aislen warn you?" he asked as they practically flew down the stairs.

"She said you'd come to get me," Kayte puffed. They ran across the courtyard. "She didn't know exactly what about."

Together, they watched Pyrid land in the pasture, Edric yelling furiously at him. Suddenly, the stable master halted his ranting and stood petrified. Lukys glanced at Kayte and ran faster toward the massive fire opal dragon.

Anya climbed down his back as Aislen, already kneeling, rocked back and forth over something on the ground, head in hands, wailing in despair.

What's happening? Lukys panicked. He'd never seen his daughter like this before. He finally reached her and pulled her away to see what had caused her such grief.

"Aaron!" he cried, falling to his knees. "Oh, my stars! What happened?"

* * *

Kayte followed close behind Lukys. She stared impassively at the scene. Emotions could not help at a time like this.

"What has been done for him?"

"We were attacked by yoswen," Anya explained. "We defended as well as we could, but they got around us and tore off part of his arm. He was already unconscious before that…"

"We know about the other injury. Don't ask how. What have you done to his arm?" Kayte tried to focus the karlik.

"His arm." Anya nodded. "We stopped the bleeding. That's all we could do. Then we flew straight here."

Kayte nodded. "Edric, take Eliséo to the infirmary – they can help him there. Send two of the infirmary healers out to me. Lukys, you have a guest to take care of and a dragon to tend to. I suggest you ask your daughter to help you with your organising."

"I'm staying," he insisted, placing his arm around a weeping Aislen.

Kayte stared at him stonily. King he might be, but she did not need desperate relatives around while she worked on her patient. "Lukys, don't make me force you. Take Anya and Aislen and go."

"Come, King Lukys." Anya took him by the arm. "I was in a snowstorm for two days. I could use a cooked meal and a roaring fire to warm me."

Kayte nodded at her appreciatively. Slowly the king and princess got to their feet and followed the karlik and stable master. That left Tika.

"Tika, I know your first instinct will be to tell Plyke and Rilla about this. Don't. It will not help me to have them here right now. Do you understand?"

The small boy nodded, a tear rolling down his face.

"Pyrid, how much energy do you have to spare?" she asked, tentatively placing a hand on Aaron's elbow.

"Perhaps enough to help you until your other healers arrive," he rumbled. "The flight was … exhausting."

Kayte shook her head. "I'll try to spare your energy."

Kneeling beside Aaron, she heard his laboured breath. Forcing herself to take a few deep breaths, she focused on the problem at hand.

Fix the veins. Allow the blood to flow properly. The rest can wait.

She always needed a plan. With a hand on either shoulder, she compared the two, assessing the damage.

"Not a clean wound."

Painstakingly slowly, Kayte moved veins, allowing severed ones to connect back together to allow the blood to flow properly. She wasn't sure how long she worked before two of her most advanced students joined her.

"Mistress Kayte," Médard ventured as Vivek retched in the grass. Kayte rolled her eyes. Vivek was certainly skilled, but her stomach was not strong enough to be a healer.

"Médard, check his body. Search for any other wounds he might have," Kayte instructed him. "He was unconscious before he was attacked. Check the wound on his head and see if the two of you can fix it."

She spared no more thought for her students as she continued to work on Aaron's severed arm. Finally, the veins were all sealed or reconnected as she saw fit.

What next? She closed her eyes as she thought. *Fix the stump. Minimise scarring, hmph, if that's even possible!*

Kayte studied the red welts around Aaron's elbow. It was messy and brutal.

"This is a messy cauterisation. How was it done?" She turned to Pyrid, who had been watching her closely the entire time.

"Celtan heated Anya's dagger and the karlik pressed it against the wound." As Kayte shook her head, he continued. "We were too far from any healers. He was losing too much blood. If we hadn't done that, he would have died before we reached you."

"I thought the crystal dragons were all powerful," she glowered at him. "How did you not have the power to save his arm?"

The fire opal dragon growled at her. Flames rolled around in his translucent belly and flickered in his snout.

"According to the karliki, the yoswen ripped off part of his arm and started gnawing on it before their very eyes. There was nothing left of his arm to reattach."

Kayte struggled to swallow the bile which flooded her mouth. She stared back at the dragon, unable to speak. Shaking her head, she returned to Aaron.

"He must have taken a blow to the back of his head," Médard told her as she prepared to work on the lord once more. "It looks to be a few days old, but I can't understand the pattern of healing. It almost looks like he began healing himself normally, sped up suddenly and then purposely stopped. After that, it healed much slower. How is that even possible?"

Kayte's head swirled. If she hadn't already been kneeling, she would have fallen. It really had worked then. Eliséo helped Aaron heal himself. But then ...

"Tell me, did either of you see the elf before you came here?"

Vivek nodded. "His wound matches this one."

Kayte bit back tears. "I need you both to go back to the castle, go to my classroom – classes will have started by now. Gather my students. Vivek, bring half to the infirmary for the elf. Médard, bring the other half here. I was mistaken. *Both* of our patients will need more energy than the three of us can provide."

She stayed with Aaron while her students sprinted to the castle. His breathing was less ragged, but still more laboured than she would have liked. He would survive until her students arrived. Of that, she was certain.

* * *

Rilla sat uncomfortably outside Mistress Kayte's classroom along with the other advanced students. Marilisa stood to one side with her group of friends, whispering and sniggering behind their hands. Through her bond with Elessa, Rilla's enhanced senses allowed her to hear every word. Instead of letting their jibes get to her, she smiled sweetly at them. At least that silenced them for a time.

Where is Mistress Kayte? Rilla wondered, yet again. When the bell for morning lessons tolled, all the other teachers had swiftly appeared to take their students into the classrooms, but Mistress Kayte had not arrived. No one had come to tell them if the lesson was cancelled, so they all sat there, waiting.

"Maybe she's sick," one girl ventured.

Marilisa sneered at her. "Mistress Kayte has never missed a lesson due to illness before. What's the point of being a healing teacher, if you can't heal yourself?"

Rilla rolled her eyes at the superior way in which her cousin talked to the other students but remained silent. She did not need to draw any more attention to herself than she already did by being the youngest in their advanced class.

Marilisa was still lecturing the unfortunate student when two older lintep came running down the hall.

"You five, go with Vivek. You five, come with me. Now!"

Rilla jumped to follow the lintep who had issued the orders, along with another four students. She groaned to see Marilisa among them but had no time to say anything before the two older lintep split up and ran towards the stairwells on either side of the hall.

They ran across the courtyard, to the stables. It was only when they reached the pasture and she saw Pyrid that Rilla froze.

"No, no, no, no, no," she cried.

"Médard, what's she doing here?" Mistress Kayte turned to look at Rilla.

"She's one of the students from your class," Médard answered in confusion. "Did you want her to go with Vivek instead?"

"No!" Kayte's frantic reply shocked Rilla out of her stupor.

"Where did Vivek go? Is ... was it ... Eliséo?"

Rilla shut her eyes to hide how brightly her eyes were glowing. *Elessa, is he here? I don't know,* her tree replied. *He's still unconscious. I don't know anything.*

"Médard, take her away. She doesn't need to see this." Kayte's voice softened.

Rilla almost allowed herself to be led away until she heard Marilisa.

"Serves the old coot right. Every time his family goes to the Outworld, bad luck follows them like a shadow. He should have known something like this would happen to him if he ever stepped outside Illaria again!"

Rilla's blood boiled at the casual insult tossed at her grandfather.

"How dare you!" she roared. Marilisa took a step back. Rilla flew at her cousin and punched her with such force that the horrible brat landed flat on her back, blood streaming out of her nose and mouth.

"That's enough!" yelled Mistress Kayte. "Médard, take Rilla away *now*! Marilisa, go to the infirmary. I can't spare any of your classmates for you."

Marilisa looked like she might protest, but instead held her bloodied chin up high and stalked off to the infirmary. Médard waited until Marilisa had gone out of sight and Rilla's anger had subsided before he attempted to usher her away from her grandfather. Rilla shook her head.

"Mistress Kayte, please tell me. Was Eliséo with Lord Aaron? Will he ... is he going to live?"

The healing mistress halted her work and looked up at Rilla. "They were brought here by Pyrid. Anya came too, but she's fine. Eliséo, he's injured, but he'll live. Please, just let Médard take you away. I promise we'll tell you everything when we're done."

Tears rolled down Rilla's cheeks as relief and sadness flooded her. She nodded and wordlessly followed Médard.

* * *

Lukys tried to focus, tried think about anything but Aaron's arm. Eliséo was injured too, but his wounds were slightly less serious – Anya had assured him of that. She was there, the karlik, sitting across the table, eating a steaming bowl of stew.

"I suppose there's no better time to discuss the next Paradise," he ventured. "Do you need to return to Goraburg after ... this?"

Anya shook her head. "The rebels were all found and dealt with accordingly. Lord Ilya is as safe as he'll ever be. He has Kazimir to guide him and a council of fiercely loyal karliki behind him. I am not needed there."

Lukys nodded mutely. It took Aislen nudging him to bring him back to the moment.

"Very well, then our next step is to plan exactly how many people need to come this time and how we're going to get there. Has Kora, or any of the children for that matter, told us how long it will take to travel to their Paradise?"

Aislen closed her eyes beside him momentarily. "Kora is on her way."

Lukys thanked her and lapsed into silence once more.

"He'll be fine, Father." Aislen put an arm around his shoulder. "Kayte is the best healer in Illaria. She will do everything necessary to save him."

"She'll never be able to replace his arm." Lukys looked at her sadly. "He's had such pain in his life. I had hoped it was over. This..."

"If I may." Anya placed her spoon down. "Lord Aaron showed us what I imagine is only a fraction of his power in Goraburg. A man like that will easily be able to fight his way back to health. Afterwards, he will learn to manage. At least he is a lintep, with power able to replace his arm. Be thankful for that."

Lukys looked at her in surprise. It was true. If Aaron had trouble adjusting, his entire family would rally around him. This time, he would not be allowed to fall into self-pity and despair.

A gentle knock at the door preceded Kora. She walked in, not knowing what had happened, but Lukys knew there was no way to keep it from her.

Questions first, Aislen suggested. *Ask her questions, then tell her. She'll be no use to you otherwise.*

"Anya, I'm so glad to see you. Are you well? We were so worried after Arishen had a vision about the yoswen."

"Yes," Anya said shortly as she spooned into her stew again. Kora looked ready to keep asking questions. Lukys jumped in before she had the chance.

"What vision about yoswen?"

He saw the look that passed between Aislen and Kora.

"What vision?" his asked again, raising his voice.

Aislen looked at him guiltily. "Arishen had a vision about a yoswen attack, but we had no way of knowing what the outcome would be. I thought it best not to worry you, Father. Not without knowing for certain one way or the other."

It's the same thing we're doing to Kora now. Get the information you need from her and then tell her about her father.

Aislen's voice in his head did little to placate him. It was her touch on his arm that forced him to calm down.

"Kora, dear, we need some information about the Paradise you lived in." Lukys fought to keep the sadness from his voice. "How long do you think it would take to travel directly there, by horseback?"

She kept her eyes on Anya for a moment but answered, nonetheless. "Well provisioned, I would estimate at least two weeks by horseback. Is that really how you're planning on travelling there?"

"Without at least four or five crystal dragons to help us, we have little choice." Lukys shrugged. "They have been requested to search for the rebels in the Lesa Mountains and Pyrid has flown back and forth on a number of occasions already. I don't know how far we can push our luck with them."

"Their search for the rebels is over," Anya said flatly.

"Is Father back then?" Kora asked, a note of concern creeping into her voice.

Lukys hesitated. "Yes, he's back."

"Uncle Lukys, what aren't you telling me?" Kora's voice trembled. "Did the yoswen hurt Father?"

Lukys avoided her gaze.

"He's alive, but he was injured," Anya told her. "Mistress Kayte is tending to him."

Lukys looked up. "He lost part of his right arm."

Kora stared in disbelief. "His *arm*? No, it's not possible. It can't be."

Anya shook her head. "We were outnumbered and outmatched by the yoswen. Lord Aaron was already unconscious when we were attacked. Ermolai and I held them off as best we could until the dragons arrived, but ... there was nothing else we could do."

"What?" Kora's voice was so small. Lukys looked over at Aislen. She patted his arm and went over to her cousin.

"Kora, let me take you to Pér. We have a lot to organise and you shouldn't be alone right now. We'll let you know the moment your father is back in the castle."

Lukys watched helplessly as Kora allowed herself to be led out of the room. When Aislen shut the door, he simply sat in silence.

"You don't have time to fall into a pit of despair," Anya told him. "Your people will need you to be strong when they find out what has happened. Don't let them see you like ... that." She gestured up and down, her face scrunched up.

Lukys rubbed his hands over his face. He was too tired for this. "You're right, Anya. I know you're right. I simply cannot believe it. Aaron has always been my rock. Even when most of his family died, he was always there for me." He shook his head. "Enough now. Let's get to organising. My stables house twenty horses but I don't think we can take them all out for such a long journey. Edric would know more details, but some may be too old, too young or close to foaling."

"You make too much trouble for yourself," Anya chided him. "Swallow your pride and ask those crystal dragons for help. I'm certain more than a few of them would be happy to fly away from their mountain, especially the younger ones."

"It's an idea," Lukys agreed. "I'll speak with Pyrid later today, when he's had a chance to rest."

Anya looked out the window as a large shadow passed over them. "No need to wait," she said. "Looks like Celtan has arrived, with a few of those clear crystal trainees."

Lukys crossed to the window just in time to glimpse a small flight of dragons heading towards the pasture. Not caring if Anya followed him, he darted out to meet them.

Chapter Eleven – The Fabled Illaria

Leif sat astride his horse, an overgrown hedge blocking his way. He looked across at Rownyn. "How do we get in?"

The lintep scratched behind his neck, avoiding his gaze. "Well, that's the tricky part. *I* can get in, and I can bring you with me, but well, I don't really have the authority to do that."

Talise came up behind them. "Why did you bring us here if you can't get us in?"

Leif glared at her irritably, wishing he had the luxury of being as tactless as she sometimes was. "I'm sure Rownyn has a plan, don't you Rownyn?"

Earlier that day, he had left the rest of his men in the broken Paradise with orders to send a message for a squadron of soldiers, craftsmen and supplies to Deuterfoss. There had been no choice but for him to bring Talise with him. He would not have trusted most of his men with her. He hoped, not for the first time, that he would not regret it.

"Of course," Rownyn replied with false bravado. "We simply need to hope that Master Aurelius is on border patrol. He often is. Now, what I need you to do is touch the boundary, just there. Push into it like you mean to step through."

Leif dismounted and studied the boundary uncertainly. It looked like an ordinary hedge. How could that possibly stop him from crossing over into Illaria? With more confidence than he felt, the Duke of Deuterfoss stepped up to the boundary, put his hand against it and pushed with all his might.

"I can't get through!" he exclaimed. "How is that even possible?"

Rownyn shrugged. "These boundaries were created long before any of us were alive. We don't know how they were created or exactly how they work, but they've kept humans out for hundreds of years."

Talise crossed her arms, scowling. "If your people are so keen to keep us out, what makes you think we'll be allowed in at all?"

"As far as I know, there are at least three humans in Illaria at the moment," Rownyn explained. "Two of them came in with some lintep, after they'd fled their own Paradise. Funny thing, those lintep turned out to be Lord Aaron's grandchildren – some of the most powerful lintep in Illaria. Rumour has it that they refused to enter without their human friends. King Lukys had no choice but to allow them entry.

"Then, from that broken Paradise we just left, I heard they found a little lintep boy who has himself a human Partner. They both left in the care of Lady Kora. So, you see, there are already a few humans here. They *might* let you in."

Leif listened in enraptured curiosity. These lintep were a complete contradiction to all the stories he'd ever heard about them. He raked his fingers through his hair and motioned for Talise to dismount.

"We'll rest here until the guardians of the border arrive then."

They didn't have long to wait. A short while later, an old man pushed his way through the boundary, his grey hair catching in the twigs. Leif stood and instinctively moved slightly in front of Talise, who deftly swatted his arm. All he could think was that her father would never forgive him if something happened to her.

Pale blue eyes studied Leif as the old man took in the scene. "Rownyn, I thought you were stationed at the broken Paradise. What are you doing here?"

"Master Aurelius," Rownyn breathed a sigh of relief. "I was indeed at the broken Paradise, however, I thought it would be in King Lukys' interest to meet the Duke of Deuterfoss. It seems as though the broken Paradise lies within his duchy."

Master Aurelius nodded and turned to them. "In that case, I bid you welcome. What are your names?"

"I am Duke Leif, and this is Talise. Thank you for taking us to see your king." Leif shook hands with the old man. The strength within his grip belied his age.

"Don't thank me too soon," Aurelius cautioned him. "There may be a few humans in Illaria, but I can't pretend that everyone is happy about that. Stay close to me. No lintep would dare attack you while you're in the company of a master."

Leif swallowed hard. *What am I getting us into?*

"Holding hands now." Rownyn held out a hand to Leif. He gingerly took it and grabbed Talise's hand before he was half dragged through the boundary. It pressed in all around him, crushing his lungs, making it difficult to breathe. Suddenly, the pressure was gone.

He squeezed Talise's hand, to make sure she was still there, then looked around to see her pale face. She was quickly followed by Master Aurelius, who lost no time in leading their horses through the border.

"If one of you wouldn't mind letting me up behind you, we will reach the castle that much faster."

Leif shook his head. "Take Talise's horse. She can come up behind me. She's lighter than you."

"Many thanks, Duke Leif," replied Aurelius.

Leif trailed slightly behind the two lintep. They were deep in discussion about things he did not understand. Both looked up as shadows passed over them. Leif looked up to see crystal dragons – a whole flight of them – flying overhead.

"I fear something bad has happened. That's the second unannounced flight into Illaria today. We may need to hurry."

They galloped past tilled fields and farms, Talise's arms tight around his waist. Leif tried to concentrate despite that and took in as much as he could before they reached the cobbled streets of a city. Here, Master Aurelius slowed them to a walk.

"The streets are too crowded, and people will already be worried with all these dragons flying overhead. Stick together and follow us. There is another barrier before we reach the castle. I do not intend to leave you behind it."

Leif did not need a second warning. He kept his horse as close to Rownyn and Master Aurelius as he could. After they passed through the crowded marketplace, Aurelius stretched out his hand. Leif immediately took it and held Talise's arm tightly around his waist.

As they crossed over a cobbled bridge, he felt a similar pressure around him as that from the boundary, but not nearly so suffocating. Talise gasped and nudged his back. Leif looked ahead to see a brilliant sandstone castle before them. Carved figurines and stained-glass windows decorated the exterior. Even growing up in the fortress of Deuterfoss could not have prepared him for the sight. Deuterfoss was built for defence. Beauty had never factored into it. Black or grey stones all set together with little regard for anything but keeping out intruders.

Illaria was the complete opposite. Leif could see the defensive mechanisms – the island castle, the cobbled bridge reaching out only so far until the wooden drawbridge had to come down, the arrow-slit windows on the lower levels, giving way to larger windows higher up. But even with all of that, the beauty of the island castle was breathtaking.

Master Aurelius led them to stables on one side of the manicured gardens. The stablehands were struggling to keep the horses calm and safe within their stalls. Leif had no doubt that the crystal dragons had caused their distress.

"Settle there, Goldfire." A lintep man placed a hand on a palomino's nose. It calmed almost instantly. Leif wondered if there was some magic involved in that touch. Keeping his own horse back from the others, Leif watched as the man went from horse to horse, settling them in the same way. Some of the stablehands took their cue from him and followed suit.

In a short time, the stable was once more the quiet haven it normally would have been. Master Aurelius dismounted, motioning for Leif and Talise to do likewise. They stayed close to him as he and Rownyn walked up to the stable master.

"Master Edric, I hope you have room for three more horses in your stalls," the old lintep said with a smile. "I understand this is not the best time, but our need is urgent."

The stable master looked over the small company, his eyes lingering on Rownyn. "Weren't you one of the guards that went out that morning?"

Rownyn nodded. "I only left to bring these two to King Lukys."

"Ah, well, you won't find him in the castle. He went to see what that flight of dragons came for." He nodded behind him. "You'll find him in the pasture. Mind, he isn't in the finest mood, what with how Lord Aaron returned."

"Whatever do you mean?" asked Master Aurelius, fear creeping into his voice. The stable master didn't immediately reply. "Edric, what happened?"

"Best you go see for yourself. He's in the infirmary." Edric placed a hand on the old master's shoulder, a sad look in his eye.

Leif watched the entire thing in growing concern. Rownyn had been telling them all about the destruction of the first Paradise, especially the role of King Lukys and his family, which included this Lord Aaron. Clearly, he was a well-respected lintep. No wonder the king was out of humour if something had happened to him.

"Rownyn, escort our guests to the guardhouse and see to their needs. It may be that King Lukys is not disposed to meet them right now."

Leif went to protest, but a gentle hand on his arm held him back. Talise shook her head. This was one of the rare times he acknowledged her wisdom and kept his silence. Together, they followed Rownyn to the guardhouse with no indication of how long they would remain there.

Leif, Talise's arm tightly linked around his, followed Rownyn back across the manicured gardens to the guardhouse. It was not at all what he expected. His own soldiers lived in large barracks with four separate training grounds surrounding the keep itself.

The lintep guardhouse was barely worth the name. There was indeed a training ground, but it looked only large enough to accommodate twenty or thirty soldiers. There were only a handful of people training there. They were disciplined enough not to let a party of strangers distract them from their exercises.

One man, the oldest looking of the group, barked out orders for the next round of drills before walking towards them. Leif noticed the way Rownyn drew himself up to attention as the man approached.

"Rownyn, what are you doing here?"

Leif maintained his distance as Rownyn explained the circumstances that led to his return.

"I promised Master Aurelius to watch over them until King Lukys is available."

Nicodémo stared at them for a moment. "Right, take them to my sitting room. I'll be along shortly."

Rownyn nodded and ushered them through the training ground to the residences behind it. Leif audibly gasped at the sight. There were four smaller buildings leading up to one much larger one. That was the one Rownyn led them to.

Leif kept his silence as they were shown into a small but comfortable sitting room. Rownyn quickly set about putting a pot to boil over the fireplace and searched the cupboards for crockery.

"Rownyn, when we met, I thought you were a soldier," Leif said, one eyebrow raised.

"Well, soldier's probably not the right word for it." He scratched behind his head. "We're castle guards, really. You understand, it's not as though we have many enemies to fight since the boundary was placed around Illaria."

"Yet, the weapons in the training ground looked well worn."

"Oh, Nicodemo would never let us live it down if we didn't train every day, enemy or no enemy." He shrugged. "Good thing too. Means we were well prepared when Lishe attacked. Well, we would have been if it was any other lintep. She was a different story altogether – had half the guards, masters and mistresses looking for her all over the city, but not a trace of her could be found."

Rownyn was more talkative than Leif expected from a man in his position. He intended to find out as much as possible about these lintep before meeting their king.

"So why did this lintep attack?" he asked, a little too casually. "From where I'm standing, it seems like everyone in Illaria has a pretty good life."

Rownyn whispered conspiratorially, "I heard it was because she wants to stop some prophecy. She killed one of Lord Aaron's daughters and tried to kill his granddaughters too. That's why we need to destroy the Paradises as quickly as possible."

Leif tried to follow but was completely lost. He simply had too many questions. He tried to sort out the most important and settled on one.

"I fear we haven't heard of your prophecy in Deuterfoss. Would you enlighten us?" He took Talise by the arm and led her to a chair. They sat comfortably next to each other as though they were back in Deuterfoss, talking with an old friend. Leif smiled as Rownyn poured out two cups of tea and brought them over.

"Not really surprising you haven't heard it. Most of us hadn't heard it until recently, though apparently it came about not too long after the Paradises were first created.

When a crystal heart beats in the body of another
Their song will destroy that which was created
Every being will bow down to the child of Paradise
All will hail Rilla.

"And, you see, Lord Aaron's youngest granddaughter is called Rilla so now everyone thinks she's the prophecy child."

"So, that means she's going to destroy something?" Talise asked in confusion.

"Yes, you see, she lived with the crystal dragons for three years, so they say she has a crystal heart and will destroy the Paradises."

"That could mean almost anything," Talise muttered. Leif gave her a swift kick to the ankle.

"And exactly how old is this granddaughter of his?" Leif asked, covering Talise's badly judged comment.

"She's sixteen, but more powerful than almost every lintep in Illaria. She's already helped to destroy the first Paradise."

"Yes, I've been meaning to ask you about that. *How* did they destroy the Paradise?"

Rownyn shook his head. "No one knows but those who were involved or very close to the king. They keep it a closely guarded secret."

Leif nodded, sipping his tea. *And well they would if there is some crazed lintep running around trying to kill them.*

"There's good reason for that Rownyn." Nicodémo walked into the room. "It's so that affable men such as yourself don't go blathering about it to every person they meet."

Leif choked back a laugh as Rownyn's eyes bulged.

"The fault is mine. I should not have pried."

The older guard shook his head. "That may be true, but my guards should not have such loose tongues. Rownyn, join the others in the training ground. I want you to spar against every one of them. Perhaps then you'll be too tired to wag your tongue."

Leif cringed at the trouble he'd caused as Rownyn, red-faced, made to leave the room. Talise rose and swiftly blocked his path.

"Thank you, Rownyn," she said. "It was so kind of you to offer to bring us to Illaria. We will forever be in your debt."

Leif felt a twinge of jealousy as she stood on her toes to give the guard a swift kiss on the cheek. Rownyn blushed brightly, mumbled something incomprehensible and escaped the room. Leif sipped his tea to disguise his feelings though he was certain he saw a flicker of amusement cross Talise's face as she walked back to him.

"Well, now that Rownyn has told you more than he should, why don't you tell me about Deuterfoss. I confess, I've never ventured out of Illaria."

Leif found he instantly like Nicodémo. Had their positions been reversed, he would likely have reacted in exactly the same way.

Together with Talise, Leif described his duchy to the head of the guards until an older lintep appeared in the doorway. The thin circlet of gold atop his brow told Leif all he needed to know.

"King Lukys, I presume?" Leif immediately stood and inclined his head. Talise rose and curtsied by his side.

"Indeed. You must be the Duke of Deuterfoss," King Lukys said as he likewise inclined his head.

"Call me Leif. This is Talise, one of the ladies of my court."

"I'm sorry to have kept you waiting," Lukys said, exhaustion written all over his face. "We've had a rather trying day. I'm sure you understand how that can be. Rooms are being prepared for you as we speak. Please, join me in the council chambers. We can speak more comfortably there."

Leif and Talise thanked Nicodémo for his hospitality and followed King Lukys into the castle, up a twisted, winding staircase, to the council chambers. He pulled on a silver handle twice as he ushered them in.

"I apologise that there is no one else fit to meet with you today. We're all rather busy. Please, take a seat and tell me about yourselves."

Leif sat on one side of the long table, noting that the king sat across from them rather than on the ornamental chair that was obviously meant for him. He took that as a good sign.

"As you already know, I'm the Duke of Deuterfoss."

"Yes, you must forgive me, but I've only ever seen Deuterfoss on a map."

"I've only heard of Illaria in fables." Leif shrugged. "Deuterfoss, itself, is a fortress, positioned at the base of the Crystal Falls. The lands it controls stretches out along the southern side of the Bramble River, all the way to Bramblesk and out to the ocean, back again to the cliffs behind the city itself."

Lukys raised an eyebrow. "That *entire* expanse belongs to Deuterfoss, does it?"

"All except for Illaria, of course," Leif smiled at him. "In truth, it's only the villages and farms that we take care of. The lands themselves are not patrolled by my men."

"Mm hmm. Tell me, how did you come to be at the broken Paradise? I did not think any but the people of Hedgefall knew of the destruction."

Talise spoke up. "There are rumours floating all around Deuterfoss about it. Some say the lintep destroyed it for no good reason and should be stopped. Others claim there will be a full lintep invasion. But all sources agree on one fact – this Paradise was only the first."

Lukys sat back and tapped his fingers together in front of his lips. "Interesting. Very interesting. Do you have any idea how these rumours were started?"

Leif looked at Talise, eyebrows raised. "What did Karsyk and his friends say about that lady from Hedgefall?"

Her eyes glazed over as she thought back over that evening. "She was certainly from Hedgefall. Something about having cousins there, I think. They said she had long black hair."

Lukys sat up straighter. "Long black hair, you say. From Hedgefall?"

Talise nodded.

"I should have known," the king muttered under his breath. "Lishe!"

"They didn't say she was a lintep," Talise pointed out.

"No, but she was causing trouble, trying to incite you or your townsfolk to attack Illaria, correct?"

"Well, yes, actually."

"Lishe means to stop us from destroying the Paradises. She can't do it all by herself, so what better way than to find some humans to fight us? That's the second time she's tried.

"She almost succeeded the first time. Half the men from Hedgefall came to the broken Paradise, only a few days after the boundary had been destroyed. The only way they could have known about it so quickly was if Lishe was watching us and immediately went to find help."

"We heard that the broken Paradise has a trading agreement with Hedgefall," Leif pointed out sceptically.

Lukys' smile was tinged with sadness. "I attribute that partly to my cousin, Lord Aaron. He managed to calm everyone enough to avert bloodshed. The rest was up to the humans themselves."

Lord Aaron, the injured one, Leif thought. *The one Master Aurelius was so worried about.*

"Will he live?" Leif asked gently.

Lukys looked up at him with haunted eyes. "With one mutilated arm, but yes, he'll live." He shook his head. "On to other matters. Why was it you sought me out?"

"I wanted to know if you planned on destroying more of these Paradises, but it seems I already have an answer to that. I suppose the next thing is to ask if you know where they are located. How many are in my duchy? How many are in neighbouring duchies? Do you have enough soldiers to protect them all until they can protect themselves?"

"You've hit upon some of our most immediate concerns," Lukys told him as a maid came in to bring them light refreshments. "We know where many of the Paradises are, though we cannot be certain that we've located them all. From what you've told me, there are a number within your duchy – the rest fall outside it.

"As for my soldiers, well, you've seen my guardhouse. That's the extent of my soldiery. I'm sure you can understand, we don't really have a need for a standing army in Illaria. Most lintep would probably rely on their powers to defend themselves if they ever ventured into the Outworld but, to be perfectly honest, very few of them do so."

Leif nodded slowly. *Not enough men to patrol the Paradises. Probably not even for my duchy alone.*

"What are your plans then?" Leif asked.

Lukys poured out tea for the three of them, passing dainty cups to Leif and Talise. "I had planned to go to each of the larger cities to ask for more men, but if Lishe is getting to them first, I doubt I will have much luck. We have no choice but to destroy the Paradises, as quickly as we can. There is precious little time to concern ourselves with what happens to people afterwards."

"That's barbaric!" Talise cried out, almost spilling her tea. "How can you strip a people of their protection and then just leave them to their own devices? Why do you even need to destroy the Paradises? Why can't you leave them alone?"

"I see you don't know the extent of the situation," King Lukys sighed. "Lishe is a rogue lintep. She was a gifted, but disturbed student, who studied alongside my nephews and nieces. Because of her callous and vicious nature, her request to become a Mistress was denied, even though she passed every test of skill.

"She left Illaria and has been stealing power from lintep for at least the past fifteen years, that we know of, possibly longer. We understand that she intends to steal power from the Paradise boundaries. If that happens, there won't be enough lintep, crystal dragons or elves capable of stopping her. Who knows how far her ambitions fly? We must destroy the Paradises before she can take their power."

Talise went to complain, yet again, but Leif placed a gentle hand on her arm. She looked over in surprise, but thankfully remained silent.

"If this lintep is really as bad as you say, then I agree that something needs to be done, however, can't you stop her without destroying the Paradises?"

"That was indeed our initial thought, however, we've heard quite a bit about the Paradises and now understand that they are not necessarily the safe havens they were once thought to be. Many of them have become violent and dangerous places to live.

"Even if it weren't for that, if Lishe works out how to steal power from the Paradises, who knows how many other lintep might try to follow in her footsteps? Lintep who we wouldn't even know to look for until it was too late." He shook his head. "It's too great a risk to leave them untouched. I hadn't thought to be so involved in the process, but there you have it. Life has a way of twisting your path in ways you never imagined possible."

Leif listened to his explanation as he sipped at his tea. It did all make perfect sense, but the thought that all the people in those Paradises were to be left defenceless against any brigands in the Outworld left a cold pit in his stomach.

"I'll help you," he said firmly. "I've already requested a squadron of soldiers to travel to Brynt's Paradise along with craftsmen and supplies. I'll send a squadron to each of the Paradises in my duchy to await you, if you let me know when you expect to be at each one. I can write to the dukes and duchesses in neighbouring duchies to see if they'll spare any soldiers, but I can't promise that they'll agree to help."

The lintep king regarded him at some length. "Thank you, Duke Leif. That is ... more than I had dared hope for."

"It's least I can do to help in this situation. Besides, my soldiers grow restless. This will keep them occupied. They can help wherever needed in the Paradises and train whatever men and women they can. We can show them how to forge their own weapons and trade, or possibly provide, materials for them to make some."

"This all sounds well and good." Lukys tapped his fingers on the table. "However, the next Paradise we need to destroy is not within your duchy. It's the only one we are certain Lishe knows the location of."

"That does make it tricky," Leif admitted. "Do you have enough guards to leave at that one?"

Lukys nodded, playing with his teacup, not drinking. "Just barely, but we can stretch ourselves thin here. I doubt we will be attacked in the meantime. We might even be able to request the help of the elves. Silvaren is not too distant from that Paradise."

"I'll come with you." Leif banged his fist on the table. "I'll come and see for myself what happens when you destroy a Paradise, and exactly what sort of help they'll need. Then I'll send word back to Deuterfoss for my lords to organise everything we'll need for each Paradise."

"You mean, *we'll* come, don't you?" Talise said softly beside him. Leif glanced at the king who was looking studiously at his fingernails.

"Talise, this could be extremely dangerous," Leif cautioned her in a quiet voice. "What would your father say if I let anything happen to you?"

"I don't imagine it would be any worse than if you left me in Deuterfoss for your lords to fight over. He'll be inundated by offers for my hand with little choice but to accept one before my reputation is ruined."

She looked at him with big brown eyes that spoke volumes. The thought of his lords fawning over her without him around to put them on a leash, made him sick to his stomach. He shook his head, knowing she had just manipulated him, but not caring.

"Come then, but you write a letter to your father, explaining your own actions."

Talise's smile melted his heart. She really did have him wrapped around her little finger. What could he do but smile?

"It's settled then," Lukys rose, unsuccessfully trying to hide a smile. Leif could not help but return a wry smile of his own. "I'll show you to your rooms for the evening. The dining hall is on the ground level. You can find food there most times of day, however the evening meal is served when afternoon classes finish. You'll hear the bells tolling at that time."

Chapter Twelve – Broken

Rilla left her grandfather, torn by the idea that Eliséo might be just as badly injured. After all, he shared Lord Aaron's head wound. Perhaps the yoswen had gotten to Eliséo too.

Médard led her back to the castle, trying to take her somewhere safe, somewhere other than where Eliséo might be. She knew it was probably a good idea. She knew she should let him. But she couldn't.

"Where is Eliséo?" she choked out the words.

Médard turned to face her. "Mistress Kayte doesn't want you to go to him."

Rilla didn't object. She only stayed where she was and stared at him, tears rolling down her cheeks.

"He's going to be fine," Médard reassured her. "He wasn't as bad as Lord Aaron – as your grandfather."

"I just want to see him," Rilla whispered. "I *need* to see him. *Please!*"

Médard lay a hand on her shoulder. Rilla was too exhausted to react.

"Come with me then," he told her.

Rilla had never been in the castle infirmary. She knew it was there – Mistress Kayte had told her as much – but she'd never entered. Somehow, she knew any injuries forcing a lintep into the infirmary would need to be as bad as her grandfather's or like the farm boy Ratchin had helped back in Turon.

Her fears were confirmed as she walked in. She half listened as Médard explained that the austere beds lined the walls with one room in the centre of the infirmary containing all the supplies they might need. Most of the beds were empty, but the occupied ones proved her theory. Lintep with missing limbs; lintep with angry, red scars on their shoulders, faces, arms, legs – they were all here.

"Why are they still here?" Rilla quietly asked Médard.

He turned to where she was looking and replied equally as quietly. "Unless the injury is life threatening, as with Lord Aaron, we only heal as much as we need to until the lintep's own healing can take over. Otherwise, we'd end up injuring ourselves or become too exhausted to help other patients.

"Each day, we come back and heal them a little further. When their bodies have recovered enough, we send them home."

Rilla looked at each one as they passed, trying to determine how they could have come upon their injuries. She turned the corner and froze. The other half of her class was there with Vivek, crowding around a patient.

Elessa, do you see this? she asked as she took a step closer.

I see, her tree replied. *Courage Rilla. He's still alive.*

Rilla nodded and approached the bed. None of the students gave way. She was forced to go around them until she found an empty space.

Eliséo lay pale and sweaty on the bed. His head was turned towards her, blood smeared the pillow behind it. Long, swollen cuts marred his arms and legs. The students had clearly been working on him, but the sight of Eliséo, of *her* elf, so badly injured was too much for her to bear. Her knees buckled under her, but

Médard's strong arms were instantly around her side, holding her up.

"You're alive," she whispered as she reached out a hand to touch his cheek. His eyelids flickered at her touch. Rilla choked out a sob. "Oh, Eliséo, what went wrong?"

She instantly felt every wound, every gash, the gaping wound at the back of his head. She closed her eyes to further steady herself, tears struggling through the gap in her eyelids. Somehow, she forced her eyes open and looked over at Vivek.

"May I help?" she asked, voice trembling.

"I'm not certain that's a good idea," Vivek told her. "I don't know how skilled you are."

One of the other students, Marilisa's friend, looked over and sighed. "She's skilled enough, Vivek, and she has more power than all of us put together. Let her help."

Rilla nodded her thanks as Vivek waved aside some of the other students.

"You can start with that wound on his arm," she told Rilla sternly. "If I'm satisfied you know what you're doing, you can help me with his head."

Rilla instantly placed her hand over one of the smaller cuts on Eliséo's arm – no point in wasting her energy here. She spread the pain, little as it was, through her body and concentrated on the severed skin, knitting it neatly back together. It was such a small cut that it took only the tiniest fraction of her energy to heal it.

When she lifted her hand, the skin was smooth. Not even a hint of a scar was left. Vivek raised her eyebrows.

"Impressive," she said. "If you really have as much power as Eskil says, then I could use your help with his head."

Rilla smiled her thanks as Vivek moved aside. She walked over to join Vivek, trying to keep her breathing steady as she saw the bloody mess at the base of Eliséo's head. She placed a trembling hand over the wound, not caring that she would have his blood on her hands.

She listened to her power, felt everything that was amiss, but there was something else there – something familiar. Her eyes snapped open.

"Lord Aaron tried to heal him first!"

"Yes, that was my conclusion as well," Vivek agreed.

"But Lord Aaron has a matching wound," Médard pointed out.

"Is it possible this elf gave him energy to heal and opened up a wound on himself? It's messy, but not as bad as it could be. Lord Aaron must have tried to heal him a bit before they both passed out from the wound."

Rilla's head reeled. Vivek had just described exactly what Eliséo had tried to do with Aislen's help.

"Can I … do you mind if I use your head to see how it should all look?" Rilla asked. Seeing Vivek's hesitation, Rilla tried to reassure her. "I won't take any of your energy or open his wound in your head. I just want to make sure I get it right the first time. I promise."

She saw Vivek look past her to Médard, who nodded imperceptibly.

"Very well."

Rilla thanked her and placed her free hand on Vivek's head. She would have to be so careful now.

Concentrate, Rilla, Elessa told her. *One mistake and you could make a bigger mess than it is already.*

You're not helping, Elessa, Rilla chided her. *Don't distract me while I'm doing this.*

You remember I can lend you more strength, if you need it. Simply ask and I will provide.

Rilla nodded. To anyone else, it would simply look like she was steadying herself. To anyone else except Médard, who had been looking straight at her and must have seen her eyes glowing. She had no time to dwell on that now. Eliséo needed her.

She took a deep breath and set to work, comparing the wound on her elf's head to the lintep's pristine skin. She carefully pooled as much energy as she could safely spare to her fingertips and allowed it to spread in and around the wound.

Painstakingly slowly, she worked on the wound, reattaching severed veins, stitching back loose skin. There was so much that needed to be done. When she had healed as much of the inner wound as she thought necessary, Rilla focused on the outer layers of skin. There was a large chunk simply missing, not available to be stitched back together.

She considered the problem for a moment and took a chance, knowing she could stop as soon as she determined if it wasn't working. With the rest of the energy pooled around the wound, she focused it all on the skin. Without really understanding what she was doing, she changed that energy into her healing power, speeding up Eliséo's own regenerative ability. Slowly, skin began to grow over the wound until there was an impossibly thin and fragile covering.

Utterly exhausted, she withdrew her hand from both Eliséo and Vivek's heads and sank down to the floor. Gasps sounded above her as lintep leant over one another to see what she had done.

From a distance, she heard Shuut and Plyke call out her name, but she was too tired to even open her eyes.

Well done, my girl, Elessa's voice sounded in her mind as she succumbed to sleep.

* * *

Pér was working his market stall in the square when they arrived. Kora, moving inexorably slowly, with Aislen trying to lead her. He caught the princess' eye and immediately knew something was wrong. Before they were even half way to his stall, he'd already begun to shut it up for the day.

I'm having an awful lot of early closings these days, he thought. *I may need to start making other arrangements – playing in taverns at night perhaps.*

All thoughts disappeared as he felt the wave of hopelessness and despair coming off not just Kora, but Aislen as well.

"What happened?" he asked softly, as they approached, instinctively reaching out to hold Kora.

Back at your place, Pér, Aislen spoke directly to his mind. He only nodded and led them both away, one arm around Kora's waist, the other dragging his small cart of goods behind him.

He closed the door behind them and turned to face the two ladies. Kora was standing distractedly in the middle of the room. Aislen watched her closely, shaking her head.

"Aislen, what happened?" he asked, his stomach turning leaden.

"Pyrid returned with Anya, Eliséo and Aaron."

Pér swallowed the lump in his throat. "Were they ... alive?"

Aislen nodded. "Anya is fine. Eliséo was injured, but not as badly as Uncle Aaron. He ... will live. Pér, he lost his right forearm."

The world came crashing down around him. Lord Aaron was, without doubt, the most powerful lintep in Illaria, and the most skilled. Losing part of his arm, well, it was just unfathomable.

"How?" he heard himself asking through the roaring in his head.

"Anya tells us a karlik attacked while his attention was on the other rebels, so he was unconscious when yoswen ambushed what was left of their company. He was lucky to survive."

Pér looked over at Kora, who was still standing motionless, almost lifeless, in the middle of the room.

"Leave her with me." Pér rested a hand on Aislen's shoulder. "I'll sing her a song or two. That's always worked before. Even when she returned from the Outworld bringing her mother, brothers and baby sister home."

Aislen nodded with a sad smile. Pér noticed she didn't bother saying goodbye to Kora – there was no point. He closed the door behind the princess, then led Kora to a chair before the cold fireplace. He lit it to warm the ice-cold room, then filled a small pot with water and hung it over the flames.

He took his lute from the stand in the corner of the room and started tuning it while humming softly to himself. He sat on the floor in front of Kora and softly sang all the words that were in his heart, steadily looking her in the eye the entire time. Calm was not what she needed today – it was reassurance. Reassurance that everything would be well, but he could not give that to her. Instead, he would tell her what he knew everyone thought of her.

You've lost so much in your short life,
And let so many things go you never should have.
You bravely rise above it all.
You struggle through to be the best you can,
Yet life keeps knocking you down.
Don't forget how strong you are,
How strong you've always been.
So many of us count on you to be there for us.
You've always been the one we look towards when times are bad,
Don't fall now when we all believe in you.
We all believe in you because you are our Kora.

Somewhere during the song, Kora came back to him. She suddenly blinked and looked directly at him, really *saw* him. He continued playing, making certain she heard all of it. This was important.

Pér could feel her disbelief, her modest nature rising up. He simply sang on through it, trying to make her face the truth, that Aislen had chosen her to be the next heir for good reason. The people of Illaria would always trust and follow her exactly because of who she was. They would think nothing less of her for falling apart when she did – it made her fallible. Who could follow a leader without faults?

He continued strumming the lute, long after the song was finished. When he finally put it away, Kora held out a hand to him. He put the lute down, rose to his knees and kissed her on the forehead, her cheek, her lips. Kora returned his kisses as they fell into each other's arms.

* * *

Rilla woke to find Shuut sitting on a chair beside her bed. Her sister's face was a mask of anger and concern.

"That was stupid," Shuut said. "What you did with Eliséo, it was stupid. Rumours are circling the castle at this very moment. What were you thinking? What if you'd hurt yourself? What if you'd killed him?"

Rilla propped herself up on an elbow. "I couldn't have killed him," she replied levelly. "And I used only as much energy as I knew I had to spare."

"Oh, so that's why we saw you collapse straight after, right?" she asked sarcastically. "Master Aurelius told Plyke and I about Lord Aaron and Eliséo. I *knew* you were going to do something stupid."

Rilla waved her hand, irritably. "I was just tired, that's all. Anyway, it was worth it. Eliséo is out of danger now. I did just enough so that the others could focus on the finer details."

"Mm hmm, finer than, say, creating a new patch of skin where there wasn't any before?" Shuut drummed her fingers on her crossed arms. "You take too many risks, Rilla. You know you do, and you keep doing it anyway – no matter how many times you've been warned not to. I don't understand what comes over you."

Rilla looked at her sister, frustrated tears in her eyes. "What would you have had me do, Shuut? He's my elf. I'm bound to his tree. Elessa and I have both been in agony since he first fell unconscious. Do you have any idea the terror we felt? How could I have stood by to watch others, less powerful than I, try to heal him in little dribs and drabs when I knew I could do more myself?"

Shuut's expression softened as tears ran down Rilla's cheeks once more. She stood up and walked to the bed, sitting beside Rilla with her arm around her shoulders.

"I would probably have done the same thing," she admitted. "If it were you or Plyke, I would have died trying to save you."

Rilla clung to her sister as heaving sobs wracked her body. When Rilla had cried out all her tears, Shuut pulled the silver handle near their beds twice to send for food. Rilla watched as her sister fidgeted with the edge of her shirt.

"What is it?" she asked.

Shuut shrugged. "Lord Aaron's in the infirmary. They healed him enough to move him. I hear Eliséo has been waking for a few moments at a time. I can't guarantee either of them will be awake if we go there now, but I thought you might like to visit now that you've recovered."

Rilla smiled at the thought. At least they were both back in Illaria, safe as they could be for now.

"Let's go," she said as she rose from her bed.

"Uh, no, not yet. Not like *that*." Shuut pointed to Rilla's bloodied shirt. "I couldn't take it off you before putting you to bed. Go and have a bath. I've called for food. The maids can help us change the sheets, because you've bloodied those too."

Rilla looked down at her shirt. The light green material was stained with brownish red smudges. She turned over her hands to see that the one she had used to cover Eliséo's head was still caked with blood. She looked up at Shuut, who simply shrugged.

"Like I said, there wasn't much I could do with you lying unconscious on the infirmary floor. It was all Master Aurelius could do to make them let us take you back here. They insisted on keeping you there, to see if you had done any damage to yourself. We didn't know if they would find out about the bond if I let them examine you. I don't even know how much of a secret it still is with all the things you've been doing lately, but we did all we could..."

To protect me, Rilla thought. She nodded in appreciation then headed to the bath chamber. *Not that I'm doing such a great job of that myself these days.*

Chapter Thirteen – Best intentions

Lukys left his rooms early in the morning to discuss options with Celtan. The sapphire dragon had already agreed to escort them, along with the younger clear crystal dragons, to their next Paradise. However, given the circumstances, Lukys hadn't stayed long enough to work out the finer points with the dragon and time was running out.

Lishe had already travelled to two human towns, that he knew of, to incite anger and fear in the inhabitants. It had backfired with Deuterfoss but, from the sound of it, many of its people had nearly been swayed by her words. It was doubtful she had stayed in Deuterfoss very long. If she didn't pass by any other human towns on her way to the Paradise, she might very well beat them there.

As he strode out onto the pasture adjacent to the castle stables, Lukys gazed at the mass of dragons sprawled out before him, Pyrid and Celtan the only splash of colour. A few lazy eyes opened as he approached them, all but one closing again when they realised who it was.

"Well met, Lukys," Celtan greeted him. "How fares your cousin and the elf?"

Lukys grimaced. "They'll survive. I dare say, Aaron will surprise us all with some amazing skills we never knew were possible with our power and not feel the loss of his forearm very keenly at all."

"That sounds about right." Celtan rumbled out a laugh. "Now, I doubt you came out here so early in the morning to discuss those matters. What is it you want?"

"I need to sort out how many people can come to the next Paradise, with your assistance," Lukys told him. "How many of you will escort us? How many people can each of you carry?"

"All of my scouts in training are keen to assist you. These are the five who were with Loreli when ... the yoswen were stopped. I fear Pyrid will insist on going, though I would rather he rest."

At the mention of his name, the fire opal dragon opened an eye. "Celtan, at my time of life, all I ever do is rest. I've grown somewhat attached to some of these people. I want to help them and that's the end of it."

Celtan puffed out a curl of smoke. "Well, there you have it. It appears all of us will be accompanying you. The younger dragons can carry three people each, Pyrid and I can each carry four. Perhaps more over shorter distances, but let's not push it."

"That makes a maximum of twenty-three people." Lukys pulled his cloak around him in the sudden whipping wind. "I suppose I have some organising to do. With any luck, we might leave this afternoon and rest at the broken Paradise. It may be that Master Brynt may be able to give us some more information."

Celtan acknowledged him with a small nod, then closed his eyes once more. Lukys walked away from the sleeping dragons bracing himself for the long day ahead of him.

* * *

"Father, we've already discussed this." Aislen crossed her arms. "You will be staying behind this time. Please allow me to prepare myself for this task by organising it. How better to acquaint myself with what to expect than to make all the preparations?"

"I'm not so certain about that now," Lukys told her. "With everything that happened with Aaron and Eliséo, I don't think I could survive sending you into the Outworld."

"This isn't a debate, Father. You're still exhausted from the last trip," Aislen told him firmly. "If an accident is going to happen, nothing can prevent it. I will be surrounded by guards, talented masters and mistresses and crystal dragons. There can be no better protection for me."

Aislen watched her father carefully, trying to keep all her tendrils of power away from him. It would be unfair for her to influence him like that, though she knew she was well capable of doing it without him realising it. She could see the strain of the past few weeks catching up with him.

"Very well," Lukys sighed heavily. "You win. The dragons can carry twenty-three people between them. Choose wisely as all other help will be too far away."

Pleased as she was by his decision, Aislen was worried by his easy acceptance. Perhaps he was even more tired than she had realised.

When her father finally left, Aislen sent out tendrils to her most trusted friends, excepting Kora and Pér who were yet to resurface after the distress of the day before. It wasn't long before Guiscard, Braedan and Luisella appeared. Together, the four of them sat down to work.

"You said Kora is refusing to go to that Paradise," Guiscard reaffirmed.

Aislen nodded. "She wants nothing to do with the Paradise leader and, quite honestly, I can't blame her. In any case, it isn't necessary for her to come for this one. She has graciously agreed to make a copy of her map so that we can easily find it and the children will be coming with us to confirm the location."

"*All* of them?" asked Braedan. "That already makes five, with you included."

"Actually, it makes seven," Guiscard interjected. "Anya must go and there is no chance that Shuut will stay behind for this one. You may have many skilled lintep accompanying you, but she won't trust anyone else to guard her little sister against Erton."

"Alright, seven." Aislen brushed a curl out of her eyes, tucking it behind her ear. "We'll need at least one healer, probably two, which brings us to nine."

"Will you need Isis to help keep Rilla's powers in check?" Luisella asked gently. "You will likely be too busy to think of her and without Kora..."

"That only leaves Isis that she truly trusts. Isis too then." Aislen nodded. "Duke Leif of Deuterfoss and his companion, Talise, will be accompanying us on this trip to better see how his people can help with any subsequent Paradises."

"That's twelve," Braedan said. "You've room left for eleven guards, unless you can think of anyone else who should come."

"Personally, I would suggest Aurelius." Guiscard leaned forward on the chaise. "He is skilled in the all of the arts, more so than many other masters, and he has one more advantage – the children all trust him. They will listen to him. Aside from the guards, whom only Rilla and Shuut may claim any sort of acquaintance with, you only have Isis, Kayte, if she'll go, and yourself whom they know well enough to listen to. That may not be enough."

Aislen could see the logic in his argument. They were running out of time to decide. She sent out three tendrils and shortly after, Kayte, Isis and Aurelius were knocking on her door.

"Are the three of you willing to come to the next Paradise?"

"Do you really think it's necessary?" asked Kayte, eyebrows raised.

"Your skills may be more useful here than at the first broken Paradise," Aislen told her. "Erton is a hostile lintep by all accounts and has a number of loyal followers who may cause trouble when we arrive to destroy their Paradise."

"I can understand why you need Kayte," Isis said in her quiet way, "but what do you need me for? I doubt you'll need me to light a fire and, even if you did, there are many lintep more than capable of doing that."

Aislen exchanged looks with Braedan and Luisella before answering. "Rilla will need you, Isis. Kora refuses to return to this Paradise, and I will likely be tied up elsewhere. Rilla's powers are still increasing and very unstable. I have no choice but to allow her, and all those who lived there, to accompany us, but I don't want to risk their lives any more than necessary. I need you to keep an eye on them, Rilla especially. Make sure she doesn't take us all by surprise with some new erratic behaviour. It will be difficult for Rilla to face her father, knowing that he ordered the murder of the person she was closest to."

Isis nodded. "I had hoped not to miss too many more lessons for my students, but perhaps you are right. Rilla certainly needs someone watching out for her."

"And myself?" Aurelius asked. "Not that I mind coming along, you understand, but what role am I to play?"

Aislen took a deep breath. "I need you to fill in the gaps. I know you aren't as powerful as Aaron, but I think few are under the illusion that you are any less skilled."

"Your Highness flatters me." Aurelius bowed his head graciously. "I admit to being more skilled than many, but I think there is no lintep quite as skilled as Lord Aaron." He paused and looked at her with gentle eyes. "I doubt even the loss of his arm will detract from that."

Aislen offered him a faint smile, feeling her self-control wavering. Before her emotions engulfed her, Aislen closed off her feelings behind her wall. The last thing she wanted to do was accidentally influence the entire castle with her grief.

"It's settled then," she clapped her hands together softly. "Kayte, I'd like you to select another healer to come with us, whoever you think best suited to this task. Aurelius, if you think Jorg or any of the other masters or mistresses should accompany us, you can choose one of them. Isis, I'm going to put the children in your care. I'm certain you can deal with Rilla and keep the rest of them under control at the same time. Please let them know to prepare for the journey."

"When are you leaving?" Luisella asked.

"This afternoon. Ask everyone to meet on the pasture when the afternoon lessons are over," Aislen replied. "Luisella, could you do me a favour and ask Cook Palmyra to prepare enough food for twenty-three people? She'll probably complain at the short notice but apologise and explain that circumstances out of our control have forced us to move quicker than expected."

"Has anyone seen Kora today?" Braedan asked.

Aislen avoided his eyes. She knew all too well where Kora was. "I'll find her myself and bring her to the library. Can you wait there with Guiscard to make a copy of the map?"

Braedan nodded.

"Well then, we all have our tasks. Remember, the fewer people who know about this, the better. Clearly, we won't be able to prevent people from seeing us leave by dragonback, but they don't need to know where or why we're going."

Aislen smiled and greeted lintep amiably as she walked through the castle grounds and the market square. It was not uncommon for her to walk the streets to stay connected with her people, but it seemed of late that she'd barely had the time.

The crowd thinned out as she walked away from the market square, meandering through the streets towards Pér's house. She knocked solidly on the jacaranda painted door.

"Just a moment!" Footsteps sounded on the other side of the door. Pér opened it and stared at her. "Princess Aislen, what a surprise! Please, come in."

She followed him into the comfortably warm room. Kora was seated on the couch in front of the roaring fireplace, with a book opened on her lap. She glanced up at the intrusion, smiling slightly.

"Aislen, what brings you here?" she said as she closed the small book.

"You and that little book," Aislen replied. "Kora, we need to depart for the next Paradise, *your* Paradise, this afternoon..."

Before she could make her request, she felt the air around her heat up as the air directly around Kora froze. Aislen flinched. Perhaps Kora and Rilla were more alike than she had realised.

"I'm not asking you to return," Aislen quickly told her as Pér went to her cousin's side, took her hand and kissed it. "No one will ever make you face that man again. I only need a copy of your map. Braedan and Guiscard are waiting for you in the library."

"I'll come with you, my love," Pér said as the room returned to normal temperature. Kora gave a brittle smile but nodded.

"After that, perhaps we can visit your father. I understand he is much recovered since we saw him yesterday."

Tears sprung to Kora's eyes. She bit her lip and nodded.

"I'll bring her up to the castle," Pér whispered as he ushered Aislen towards the door. "She's not quite ready yet. I might play her a song or two to calm her down first."

Aislen nodded and walked out the door. She knew Pér's songs had unusual qualities. Much as he had tried to hide his skills from her father, Aislen had seen through what he was doing. Kora and Aaron thought they were fooling everyone by helping him, but she had always understood, always seen what was right there in front of her eyes.

She laughed to herself. *It's no wonder Plyke is so uniquely powerful. Everyone thinks Rilla is the amazing one because she is more flamboyant with her powers, but I think Plyke has a few secrets yet behind those colourful walls I've heard so much about.*

Chapter Fourteen – Trapped

Rilla walked beside Shuut down towards the infirmary. The air was cooler underground – much like the royal crypt. That thought sent a shiver down her spine. It was quieter than she expected it to be. When they reached Lord Aaron and Eliséo's beds, there was only a single healer sitting between the two of them.

Médard looked up as they approached. "They need their rest," he told them gently.

"We only wanted to see them," Rilla whispered as she walked up to her grandfather's bed. She didn't realise she was resting her hand on the sheets until Lord Aaron's hand slid over hers and weakly grasped her fingers.

"Thank you." His soft and tired voice found its way to her. Rilla tried to jerk her hand back in shock, but the weak grip of his fingers somehow held her firmly. "I heard Aislen's voice from so far away."

Rilla worriedly looked up at Médard.

"He's delirious," Médard told her. "He's been mumbling all morning about Aislen pulling him into consciousness long enough for him to use the elf's energy to heal himself. Load of nonsense if you ask me. Their hands must have touched at some point – that's all."

Rilla and Shuut exchanged knowing glances but said nothing. Carefully, Rilla disentangled her fingers from her grandfather's, bending down close to his face as she did so.

"You're welcome," she whispered in his ear. A small smile flickered on his face, gone before Médard noticed it.

"You realise the elf has a name," Shuut told Médard, to distract him from Rilla.

Médard shrugged. "I hear he's the ambassador or some such nonsense."

"It's not nonsense," Rilla said, more calmly than she felt. "His name is Eliséo and his position as Ambassador of the Elves has often been used to benefit the lintep. You should show him a little more respect."

Rilla felt Shuut's hand on her arm. Her sister wasn't skilled or powerful enough to change her emotions but, nonetheless, her cool touch had the desired effect. Rilla took a deep breath and counted to ten, like Master Bastienne had taught her.

"Might we have a moment alone with the patients?" she asked as calmly as she could.

Médard shook his head. "I'm under strict instructions from Mistress Kayte not to leave their side until Vivek comes to relieve me."

"Fine." Rilla tapped her teeth together. "We'll just stay for a little while before we're out of your way."

She sat on the edge of Eliséo's bed, discreetly placing a hand on his arm. From there, she could feel all his wounds. They were healing spectacularly well. Even the improvised new patch of skin she'd given him was doing well.

Perhaps I can just speed it up a little bit more, she thought to herself.

Don't you dare, Elessa immediately interfered. *You saw what happened last time you tried to heal him. You lost so much of your own energy that it took you an entire day to recover.*

Before she had a chance to retort, Médard was standing over her.

"Remove your hand from that elf." His voice was cold and steady. "I have strict instructions not to let you heal either of them any further."

Rilla bit her tongue and placed both hands in her lap.

"Please move away from the patients," he instructed her. "Mistress Kayte will be unimpressed if you push your limits again."

A rhythmic clicking on the floor announced the arrival of another lintep. Rilla looked up to see Mistress Kayte. The healing teacher raised an eyebrow at her.

"I see you've recovered from your reckless experiment," she said emotionlessly. "Did I not warn you that another move like that would land you in a beginner class?"

Rilla's temper flared. "They weren't healing him fast enough," she said pointing to the absent lintep students. "Vivek was focusing on the main wound herself while the others looked after the smaller cuts. She didn't have enough strength to do what I did."

"That will not change my mind. You will need to earn your way back to the advanced class. Master Vylor will be your healing teacher from now onwards." Mistress Kayte crossed her arms. "Did it ever occur to you that Eliséo did not *need* that amount of healing? Not so quickly, in any case."

Rilla glared at her in defiance but remained silent.

"Thank you, Médard. I need you to do me a favour," Mistress Kayte turned to her student. "Find Vivek to start her shift but come back with her."

Rilla sat angrily on Eliséo's bed as Médard walked away. She took comfort in Shuut as her sister placed a hand on her shoulder. Mistress Kayte did not turn back to them until Médard was out of sight. Rilla watched as the healing mistress made a sweep of the infirmary, making certain no other lintep were around them.

"Has Isis come to find you yet?" she asked them in a soft voice. Rilla shook her head, unreasonably irritated at her teacher's swift subject change.

"We came here as soon as we woke up," Shuut told her. "I thought Rilla might want to see the patients before morning lessons."

Mistress Kayte eyed them both, distrustfully. "Very well. In that case, I assume you don't know that we're off to the Outworld again this afternoon."

Rilla sucked in her breath. *Our Paradise! It's finally happening.*

"You said 'we,'" Shuut pointed out. "Does that mean *all* of us are going?"

"Wait, we can't go without Lord Aaron and Eliséo." Rilla looked at the two injured men.

A flicker of pity crossed Mistress Kayte's face. "I understand you've grown quite attached to them both, but we cannot wait for them to fully heal." She looked around again, then whispered. "Lishe has been causing trouble in the Outworld. We cannot afford to waste any more time."

Rilla felt the blood drain from her face. "Lishe?" she barely managed a whisper.

Mistress Kayte nodded. "Your Paradise is the only one she knows the location of, so we are in somewhat of a hurry to reach it before she can do any damage."

"Will I be your healing apprentice for this trip too?" Rilla asked, half-heartedly.

"No, Rilla. With this recent show of poor judgment and your connection to this Paradise, you are not up to the task. Médard will accompany us. He is quite the skilled young healer. You would do well to learn from his disciplined restraint."

Rilla should have been crushed by those words. Any other day, she would have been. But the fact that they were going to her Paradise, to destroy the tiny, evil world her father had controlled for so many years consumed her thoughts.

"Let's get to our morning lessons, Rilla." Shuut tugged her sleeve, pulling her out of her thoughts. "You don't need to miss any more than necessary."

"Everyone will be gathering in the pasture when lessons are done for the day," Kayte told them. "We will be stopping off at the broken Paradise overnight. Bring your warmest cloaks."

"Can we take Eliséo home?" Rilla asked, as Shuut tried to pull her away. "If he's out of immediate danger, I'm certain he would heal more quickly in the comfort of his own tree."

Mistress Kayte hesitated. "I'll speak with Aislen, but I make no promises. Now, off to class with you."

Rilla nodded, with a final glance towards Eliséo and Lord Aaron, then followed Shuut out of the infirmary.

* * *

Isis sent her tendrils out, feeling for Rilla, Shuut and Plyke. The girls were heading down to the infirmary, where she knew Kayte was headed as well. No need to tell them then.

"Where's Plyke?" she mumbled to herself as her tendrils left the infirmary to search the rest of the castle grounds. She smiled to herself as she found him. "I should have known."

Isis walked into the dining hall. Plyke was seated at his usual table with Tika, the twins and Dorian. The five of them had become fast friends almost from the moment they met.

"Good morning, boys," she greeted them as she approached. "Plyke, Tika, might I have a word with you?"

"Oh, don't mind us, Mistress Isis," Ulf said between mouthfuls. "We won't listen in."

Isis laughed lightly. "No, I'm certain you would *never* stoop to eavesdropping, however, I can't say the same for everyone in this hall."

Umi looked around conspiratorially. "You're right. We'll follow you out and make sure you're left alone."

"You'll do no such thing, Umi. I trust you almost less than I trust your brother."

Umi gave her an injured look, then laughed. "Well, I suppose we've earned that reputation. Go on, then, but return them to us before morning lessons. We barely get to see them anymore!"

"We'll see," Isis told her as she ushered the Partners out of the dining hall.

"Is something the matter, Mistress Isis?" Plyke asked in a whisper, once they had closed the door behind them.

"Not exactly." She drew both boys close to her. "We leave for your old Paradise this afternoon. Everyone will be meeting in the pasture behind the stables when your lessons end. Bring only what you need to."

The boys stared at her mutely.

"Did you hear what I said?" she asked them.

Tika looked at Plyke, but his Partner remained silent.

"Are the crystal dragons taking us?" Tika asked.

"Yes, so make sure you wear warm clothes. The last time you rode one, autumn had barely shown itself."

"Thank you, Mistress Isis." Tika smiled at her. "We'll make sure to prepare ourselves. Do you need us to tell Rilla and Shuut?"

"No, Mistress Kayte will tell them. I'm off to find Arishen now. Master Reuben or Timothée will need to bring him after he finishes his chores for the day."

She looked at the still silent Plyke. The boy was carefully keeping all his thoughts to himself.

"Plyke, it's important you attend your lessons today. We don't want to arouse any suspicion and I don't want you falling further behind in your studies. There will be fewer masters and mistresses this time and we may be away for a while longer than last time."

The young lintep nodded and turned to his Partner. "I'll see you later, Tika."

Isis and Tika watched Plyke head back up the stairs. Before the boy could leave for the stables, she touched his arm gently.

"Tika, is there anything you need to tell me?"

The human stared after his Partner for a moment before turning hazel eyes on her. "I know we all said we wanted to go back to our Paradise, to see it destroyed, but I don't think any of us were thinking further than that. It might ... bring back painful memories.

"I'm fairly certain you don't actually know everything that happened while we lived there. Not much of it was pleasant."

Isis frowned. Perhaps there was more to this task than Aislen realised.

"Tika, would you mind terribly if I ask you to accompany me to find Arishen?" she asked with a smile.

"Oh, Master Edric only allows me a quick break to eat with Plyke in the morning. I'm already running late for the rest of my chores."

"Very well, I'll escort you to the stables instead," she held out her arm. Tika took it with a wary smile.

"You want to know the worst things, don't you?" he asked her as they walked under the arched hallway to the manicured gardens beyond.

Perceptive little boy, Isis thought as she nodded.

"Princess Aislen has charged me with the care of the four of you," she told him. "It seems as though I don't know nearly enough as I need to about your Paradise."

Tika regarded her silently for a moment before bobbing his head a few times. "Well, you'll already know about Rhanya, our old healer, so I won't go into that. There are only a few other things I'd say are very important for you to know.

"Arishen has a Partner in our Paradise. Her name is Parthak. She threatened to betray him to Erton before we left. Their Partnership, well, it wasn't really all it should have been. She didn't know what he was before their ceremony and, being one of Erton's most loyal sheep, she couldn't possibly continue their Partnership when it would become dangerous for her as well.

"Then you have Erton. We all knew he was Rilla's father, even if he never allowed her to call him that. He's just plain mean. I don't think there is a single good deed I can place at his feet. He ordered the deaths of many people. His thugs, Belial and Torak, always did the deed.

"Plyke and Arishen had to hide who they were their entire lives. I don't think they're looking forward to going back. And Rilla, well, who would want to face a father like that again, especially now that she knows he kept so many truths from her?"

Isis absorbed his every word. He was telling her the truth, of that much she was certain. But something was nagging at her.

"Tika, you haven't told me about yourself. Is there a reason *you* don't want to return?"

He shrugged and shook his head.

"Somehow, I find that difficult to believe," she persisted.

"Erton already took everything away from me." He looked up at her with tears in his eyes. "There's nothing else he can do to me now."

"My goodness, Tika!" she gasped. "What did he do?"

The boy shook his head and turned away. They were nearing the stables now. There wouldn't be time for this later. Isis gently turned him to face her and looked worriedly at him.

"My mother," he whispered. "Erton had her killed when she admitted to me that I was her son. You know, in our Paradise, parents aren't allowed to let their children know who they are. We didn't know anyone had overheard, but they must have. Just a few days after that, Erton had her killed."

Isis' hand dropped from his shoulder, her mouth agape. "How did any of you survive such a place?"

Tika laughed sadly. "We didn't survive it. You'll see the scars if you look hard enough. I don't know what would have happened to us if Shuut hadn't stumbled into our Paradise.

"You might say it was the best thing that could have happened to us, but those first few weeks with her were almost as bad. We were still trapped – just in a different world with a whole new set of rules."

"Tika ... do you still feel trapped here?" Isis asked him gently.

"I think I could feel trapped anywhere if I didn't look at the bright side," he said carefully. "You could say I'm stuck in a lintep stronghold where any of the inhabitants could turn on me at a moment's notice simply because I'm human. I'd have nowhere to run to if that happened. I'm still a fairly unskilled person, so there is nowhere in the Outworld I'd be safe."

"You don't really think that would happen, do you?" she asked him, horrified by the thought.

"No, not really." He shook his head and smiled. "I don't feel trapped at all. I've always wanted to live in a world of magic. I get to live as close to Plyke as is reasonable. I'm learning the exact trade I always wanted to, surrounded by people who love me and my Partner. Honestly, Mistress Isis, the only way I could be happier is if I somehow got to use magic myself."

Isis smiled hesitantly at the boy before he ran off to the stables. Something about the way he'd said it had struck a chord with her. It almost seemed as though, without having ever had it himself, he missed magic as much as she would if she somehow lost her powers. The thought sent a cold shiver down her spine.

It was already mid-morning. Isis felt she had wasted time going back to her house first, to gather whatever belongings she thought might be useful on this trip, though in truth, there was little she could find to bring other than a change of clothes and her warmest cloak.

She knew Arishen would already be hard at work with Master Timothée. It surprised her to see Tommaso sitting in the corner of the workshop reading a book, until she remembered he had been assigned to the seer in case he should have any other important visions while Lord Aaron was away.

The morning that Arishen had had the vision of the yoswen was burned into Isis' memory. Rarely had she had to fight so hard for someone's life or fight with Bastienne and Kayte over it. One thing was certain – Rilla certainly kept things interesting for her.

Isis looked around for Master Timothée and found him instructing one of his journeymen on what looked like a particularly difficult procedure. She waited until he was finished to approach him. It amused her to see that Arishen barely lifted his head when she walked into the workshop. He clearly lived a very different life to his old Paradisian friends if he didn't recognise her.

"What can I do for you, Mistress Isis?" the master carpenter asked, wiping his hands on a rag hanging off his belt. "Don't tell me I've managed to convince you that you need a better cabinet for your clothes?"

Isis laughed. "No, Master Timothée. You won't convince me of that until the one I have falls to pieces."

"Ah well, then I'll see you in another few months," he said amiably. "What is it then?"

"I've come to ask you a favour." She leant in closer as some of the apprentice carpenters slowed their work to listen. "Might I ask that Arishen finishes his chores a little earlier today? I need Tommaso to bring him to the castle this afternoon, with a change of clothes and a warm cloak."

Master Timothée raised an eyebrow at her. "How long will he be gone this time?"

Isis shrugged. "I don't know. I doubt it will be less than a week."

"And I'm not to ask where he's going? Or where he went last time, for that matter?"

"I'm sorry, Timothée. It's safer this way." She looked over at the tall blond human. "I think the fewer people who know, the better."

"*You* may think that," he told her. "But there was a lot of speculation last time he disappeared for a few weeks. Some of the lads saw him riding out with a host of important lintep early that morning. It raised a number of questions as to why he should be so favourably singled out when he isn't even a lintep."

Isis was shocked. It hadn't occurred to her that Arishen's fellow apprentices might be envious of him.

"Trust me, Timothée, I'm certain Arishen would be safer here than where we're going. It isn't quite the honour your boys may think it is to be singled out like this."

"Oh, I believe you, Isis," he told her. "And I'm certain I wouldn't like to accompany you myself. But that won't appease the younger ones. Some of them are still angry that a human was chosen to be my apprentice when there is a long list of lintep still waiting for that chance. Your boy there isn't very popular around here."

Isis discreetly looked around the workshop. There were more than a few pairs of eyes on her, including some students she recognised from previous years. All of them glanced over to the seer with scowls on their faces and none of them were working near him.

Tika might not feel trapped, she thought, *but I'll wager Arishen does.*

"I'm sorry, Timothée, but there's little I can do to help that. If it will appease you, I can give the seer the choice to stay, but I doubt he'll take it."

"I'll take that chance," he told her. "Better than nothing."

Isis nodded and walked around the workshop, stopping at the workstations of those she knew, exchanging pleasantries and asking after their families. Had she not been so affected by Rilla's reaction to lintep changing her feelings through touch, Isis had no doubt she would have resorted to that as well.

As it was, her efforts made a little difference. It now drew less attention than it would otherwise have done when she stopped by Arishen's workstation.

"Please don't touch my mind," he said hurriedly as she approached him.

Isis frowned. "Are there lintep who do that to you?"

"Only a few times ... so far. But I don't like it." He shrugged, looking uncomfortable.

Trapped indeed, thought Isis.

"I haven't come here for your skills, Arishen," she told him softly. "I've come to ask if you wish to accompany us to your old Paradise. Master Timothée doesn't think it's a good idea, but the decision is yours and yours alone. All your companions will be coming. I'm certain they will miss you if you stay behind."

He looked at her, expressionlessly. She could only imagine what was going through his mind after what Tika had told her.

"You don't have to decide right now," she told him. "If you decide to come, Tommaso can bring you to the pasture this afternoon. Bring your warmest clothes."

"Wait." He reached out as she turned to leave. "I don't even know your name. Why do you care if I come or not?"

Isis smiled kindly. "I'm Isis, a mistress of fire and ice. I have the honour of teaching some of your friends. As for why I care, let me say, you might think it's just a moment in time, that you can set it aside and let it happen without you, but I can assure you, later in life, you'll regret it if you don't come.

"You might wish that you'd had the chance to tell Erton what you thought of him. You might wish to thank anyone who was ever kind to you, or helped you hide who you were. You might, and I realise you won't believe me now, you might even wish you'd had the chance to talk to your Partner again – to make her see what she missed out on when she betrayed you."

She left before he could answer. It was possibly a cruel note to leave on, but she knew those were the very things he would almost certainly regret not having had the chance to do if he refused to go back to the Paradise.

83

Chapter Fifteen – Adventure

Umi and Ulf impatiently waited until the door was closed before running towards it. They'd long ago learnt how to eavesdrop with an empty glass against a door. No one bothered trying to deter them. It would never have worked. They each held one against the large wooden door and pressed their ear firmly against it.

"This afternoon ... crystal dragons ... warm clothes ..."

They looked at each other excitedly. This was it! The moment they'd been waiting for. Adventure stared them in the face if they dared to look up. Before they could be caught out, they returned to their table and spoke in hushed voices.

"Where do you think they're going?" Umi asked.

"Who cares?" replied Ulf. "They're travelling by dragonback this afternoon. How many other chances do you think we'll ever have of doing that?"

"But how can we make sure they don't see us in a large pasture, with only crystal dragons to hide behind?"

Ulf grinned and waggled his eyebrows. "Have you been practising?"

Umi returned the grin, nodding. Her expression turned to one of concentration before she began to fade into the background. Ulf gave her an appraising nod before likewise fading.

"Not bad at all! Hopefully, they'll be too distracted by whatever it is they're going to do that they don't look for us."

Umi came back to full view. "So exciting! Just don't say anything in our lessons."

"Me?" Ulf asked in an injured voice. "You know *you're* the one who can't keep a secret!"

"Me?" Umi sputtered. "How dare you! Everyone knows *you* are the worst at keeping secrets!"

They were interrupted by a laugh. Dorian walked up to them, clutching at his stomach as his laughter rang through the dining hall.

"Before this gets out of hand, let me just tell you – you're both just as bad at keeping secrets as each other. Now, what's the secret you're trying to keep this time?"

The twins shook their heads. "We're not telling you!" they said in unison.

Dorian shrugged. "Suit yourselves. You're the ones who will be bursting by the end of the day."

The twins glared at him, then glanced sidelong at each other, quickly looking away.

"*I* won't tell," said Umi.

"Nor will I," replied Ulf defiantly.

"Right then, off to lessons." Dorian opened the doors to depart, the twins quickly flanking him.

"You want to know?" asked Umi quietly.

"No," Dorian answered firmly. "Your secrets always have a way of winding everyone up in trouble."

Ulf stifled a laugh. "You're going to miss out on the biggest trouble we've ever been in."

"And the biggest adventure," Umi said as she peered around Dorian to grin at Ulf.

As they walked up the crowded staircase, the twins pushed in closer to their friend. He shook his head.

"Just make sure you don't get yourselves in *too* much trouble," he cautioned them. "Don't forget how worried your mother was the last time one of your plots backfired. Twins with broken arms is not something I think she'd look forward to another time, especially now she knows how much of a pain you can be."

"*That* was a very specific exception." Umi lifted her chin defiantly. "We were dared."

"And you can't refuse a dare," Ulf chimed in.

"What if I dare you *not* to go through with this latest big adventure?" Dorian asked as they walked into their healing lesson.

"What big adventure?" Plyke asked curiously as he and Shuut suddenly joined them. The twins looked guiltily at him.

"Nothing!" they cried out in unison. Dorian laughed again as Plyke and Shuut watched the display in confusion.

"These two have a habit of thinking up mischievous plans, which almost always backfire. Sounds like they have another one up their sleeves."

"We do not!" Umi retorted hotly.

"We don't either!" Ulf cried out at the same time.

"Whatever you say." Dorian shrugged as Mistress Kayte entered the room.

"Settle down, class," she called out to them, her eyes lingering a little longer on the twins than the other students. "I have a special treat for you today. We're going to the infirmary, where you will get to see some injuries that my most advanced students helped me work on yesterday. This will give you an indication of how dangerous the Outworld can be and how lintep powers can be used to help in such situations. Follow me."

Umi and Ulf fought to get to the front of the class as Mistress Kayte led them out.

* * *

Aislen watched from the shadows as Kayte instructed her students on the different ways both Aaron and Eliséo had been healed, with multiple lintep working on them at the same time.

Plyke and Shuut hung back behind the other students but both listened intently. Umi and Ulf, as ever, jostled each other out of the way to get a better look. Braedan and Luisella certainly had their hands full with the twins, though she had never heard them complain about their children.

As the bell tolled for the end of morning lessons, the students hurried out of the infirmary. Even though Palmyra made certain to cook enough food for all of them, the best dishes rarely survived the first rush after the dining hall opened.

Once the infirmary quietened down, Aislen walked from the shadows towards her uncle. She laid a gentle hand on his arm. His eyelids flickered, but nothing more. Her heart ached at the sight of him.

"He's strong, Aislen." Kayte came to stand beside her. "He will survive this better than any other lintep could."

Aislen's lip twitched. She tore her eyes away from Aaron.

"Why did you call me, Kayte? I have many things to organise before we fly out."

"Rilla wants us to take Eliséo home. I know you've already decided who is coming, but I promised I would ask."

"Is he well enough?" Aislen glanced over at the elf.

Kayte shrugged. "I don't see that it would do him any harm. He was healed to the point where he should not need the lintep again. All he really needs now is time."

"It *would* mean leaving one of our guards behind." Aislen sat on Aaron's bed, looking thoughtfully at the elf. "However, Queen Liessa may be persuaded to replace that guard with another of her elves."

"I hear Master Ensil trains every elf himself. I doubt Nicodemo would begrudge his guards the opportunity to see an elf in action."

Aislen smiled at the thought. "I'll let him know we need fewer guards than we anticipated. Meet me here after your final class. We'll move him quietly. The fewer who know where we're going, the better."

* * *

"I don't like the idea." Lukys crossed his arms. "Once he recovers, Eliséo will be the only link to you. You expect me to simply accept your pronouncement that you're taking him home, when he isn't even conscious enough to make the decision himself?"

"Be careful, Father, that you don't start treating him as a prisoner rather than a most honoured guest. He has served both the lintep and the karliki very well and deserves to be taken back to his tree. We cannot deny him that right, especially as we pass so close to Silvaren that it will barely take us out of our way at all."

Lukys had the good sense to feel ashamed. His daughter was beginning to prove what kind of queen she would be when her time came. It pleased him, but he could not deny that it shone a light on all their differences, and he was none too proud of the fact that she was probably making better decisions than he was. Perhaps it was time to hand over more responsibility to her. When this mess with the Paradises was over, he would certainly do so.

He sighed and placed his hands on Aislen's shoulders. "You always think of others first. I've always admired that about you, Aislen. Just make sure you look after yourself on this journey. I would not want to lose you, even if it's because you risked your life to save another."

She looked up at him, eyes brimming with tears. "I love you too, Father."

* * *

"Are you sure about this?" Umi asked as they ran towards the pasture after their afternoon lesson. "What if we get caught?"

"Don't be such a worrywart," Ulf teased her. "Who cares if we get caught if we get to ride on crystal dragons? All we have to do is get there first, hide and then climb up before they leave."

"Why can't we climb up now and just wait there?" Umi asked as they faded into moving blurs.

"Because, the crystal dragons will feel us and tell the others. Better to do it at the same time as everyone else so they don't notice the extra movement."

* * *

Aislen kept her power wrapped around the four of them as Kayte and Médard carried Eliséo between them. According to Vivek, the elf had been in and out of consciousness all day, but never stayed awake for more than a few moments at a time. It would be good for him to recover in his own home. Aislen smiled. She'd never been to Silvaren before. It would be nice to see the fabled trees at least once in her life.

As they approached the dragons, Aislen pulled back her power, allowing the others to see them. She looked out over the gathered assembly. It was quite a different group to the last time. The most notable omissions were Lukys, Aaron, Pér and Kora. Her cousin had spent the morning with Guiscard, helping him to make a copy of her map. It was now safely tucked away in her own rucksack. Aislen tightened the straps a little more. Few people knew about it and she intended to keep it that way.

Kayte and Médard followed close behind her with Eliséo. Aislen planned to carry out the destruction of the Paradise boundary with a little more care than her father had, hopefully negating the need for healers, but she was glad to have them along, nonetheless.

Anya immediately went to Eliséo's side, assuming control of his bearers. They had clearly forged a strong friendship in these past few months. Aislen was happy to release his care to the karlik, though noticed Rilla watching enviously from a distance.

Her young cousin had been in Kayte's bad books too often of late. It was no wonder she stayed away from the elf. Her desire to heal him further could be potentially disastrous. Aislen wanted so much for Rilla to have a quiet few months to get used to her ever-increasing power and learn the skills that would keep her safe. It was unfair that she was so often placed in such difficult circumstances. Aislen marvelled at how much Rilla had endured in her short life.

Turning her attention aside, Aislen looked over at Leif and Talise. They were, as yet, complete strangers to everyone but Aurelius, who had only met them the previous morning. Aurelius had chosen Bastienne to accompany them. It was an interesting choice, but Aislen understood well enough how everyone had underestimated his skills.

She could see that the old lintep from Statera was careful to keep Isis in view. He had been quite impressed by her skills, and Aislen thought it was nice to see the fire and ice mistress receive as much attention from a skilled master as she deserved. On this trip, Isis would be well occupied keeping the former Paradisians, and possibly Shuut, out of trouble. Perhaps Bastienne would be able to help her.

Aside from those very few masters and mistresses, the remainder of the adults were castle guards, eight of them. Secretly, Aislen admitted to herself that she wished there were more of the teachers and fewer of the guards, but she understood the need for them.

"We will depart shortly. Tonight, our journey will take us to the broken Paradise. Pyrid knows the way, so he will lead. I will go with him. Aurelius, Leif and Talise, come with me.

"Kayte, Médard and Anya, take Eliséo on Celtan.

"Plyke, Tika, you can go together with Séverin. Isis, I want you with Rilla. Shuut and Arishen stay together.

"Bastienne, I leave you to take your pick of the guards to travel with you. Séverin, divide the remaining guards as you see fit."

Aislen climbed atop Pyrid, who had shifted around to face the others. She waited until everyone had settled themselves and were all holding tightly to the spikes in front of them.

"If anyone has any doubts about coming, voice them now," she called out. "We will not have time nor dragons to spare if you change your mind."

Silence hung in the air.

"Very well, then, let's be off."

One by one, the seven crystal dragons beat their massive wings and rose into the air. Pyrid circled over the pasture until all of them were airborne. He belched out a stream of fire in the direction he was heading, smoke and steam flowing over Aislen and her companions, and sped away into the distance.

Chapter Sixteen – Stowaways

Before the others arrived, they had decided which dragon they would go with so as not to trip over each other and be found out before they even left.

Umi scrambled up on Pyrid after the Outworlders – the ones Aislen called Leif and Talise. She made certain to sit far enough behind that they wouldn't notice her, but not so far that the crystal dragon himself would realise there was an extra person.

As the fire opal dragon beat his wings and took off, Umi held on for dear life. *Adventure has never been as dangerous as this before!* she thought as she closed her eyes against the ground falling away from her. *Please don't let me fall!*

It felt like half a day later when Pyrid started his descent. Umi stared, petrified, at the ground rushing up to meet her.

This is it! I'm going to die, and no one will even know where to find me!

She was jolted from her thoughts by Pyrid's firm landing. He was breathing hard as she scrambled down from his back, concentrating on keeping herself blurred.

"Are you sure you should be making this trip, Pyrid?" Aislen asked the fire dragon. Her hand looked tiny, resting on his snout.

"I thought you only named four people to ride on my back," he growled at her. Umi froze.

"I did," Aislen said as she looked around. "Here we are. Anya, Leif, Talise and myself. There's no one else here."

Umi's heart beat as fast as a hummingbird's as she tried desperately hard to keep her concentration. A dragon coming in to land behind her completely startled her.

"Umi!" Aislen shouted. "What do you think you're doing, young lady?"

"Um," Umi mumbled as she shuffled her feet in the grass.

"Where's Ulf?" the princess asked.

"He's not here," Umi lied. Aislen stared at her, one eyebrow raised. Umi slumped, unable to meet her eyes without giving in. "He's on the blue one."

"Oi!" Ulf shouted. He stalked over to Umi and poked her shoulder. "You little tattle tale! She would never have found me if you hadn't squealed!"

The princess came to stand over them. "I can assure you, neither of you would have escaped my attention for long. What were you thinking, stowing away like that? Never mind the danger you've placed not only yourselves, but everyone else in because of your foolish behaviour – think of your poor parents!

"I can just imagine how Luisella must already be fretting that she can't find you. Braedan is likely running all over the castle grounds looking for you. Did you even consider them in this scenario?"

Umi and Ulf shared a guilty look.

"We left a note," Umi admitted. "They won't find it until they search our chambers, but we *did* leave one."

By this time, all the dragons had landed. Umi realised they were the centre of attention, and the twenty-two other chosen companions were staring at them angrily.

"I should have known," Plyke muttered, shaking his head. "*This* is what you were talking about this morning."

Umi's anger flared. "We're not much younger than you. Why shouldn't we be allowed ... wherever it is you're going?"

Aislen laughed in disbelief. "You don't even know where we're going? How did you find out about this trip?"

"They eavesdropped," Mistress Isis guessed. Umi could have sworn she saw a smile flicker across the teacher's face. "When I took Tika and Plyke out of the dining hall to tell them, you two took it upon yourselves to listen at the door, didn't you?"

Refusing to look ashamed, and knowing her brother was doing the same, Umi nodded. Aislen looked at her and then back to Mistress Isis.

"I could take them back." Mistress Isis looked at the princess. Umi held her breath.

Aislen shook her head. "Not now, not tonight. I don't want to tire out the dragons. If there are any horses to spare in the ... village, we'll get someone to escort them back tomorrow morning. Otherwise, we have no choice but to bring them with us."

"Not on me!" Pyrid grumbled. "Loreli's scouts can take turns carrying them. I'm too old to be carrying so many people across the Outworld."

Celtan roared out a laugh. "It finally happened! It only took a little girl to do it, but Pyrid has finally admitted to being old."

Pyrid growled as the five clear crystal dragons joined in the laughter. Umi did not share their mirth. She had a feeling that, somehow, she was being made fun of and didn't quite like it.

"Master Bastienne, can I place the twins in your care?" Aislen turned to a crusty old lintep. Umi turned up her nose at the sight of him. "Do not trust them. They may look sweet and innocent, but these two have cooked up more mischief between them than all the other lintep living in the entire city."

The old master smiled deviously. "Children after my own heart. Fear not, Princess Aislen. They shall not escape my attention."

Umi looked at Ulf. All their plans for adventure had blown up in their faces. Admittedly, *not* for the first time. But this was meant to be their biggest adventure yet and they didn't know if they would get to go or even find out *where* they were meant to be going.

* * *

A large fire crackled and spat in the middle of their camp ground. The seven dragons had arranged themselves snout to tail in a massive circle, inner wings outstretched to keep the brunt of the wind away from the travellers.

Aislen rubbed her arms against the chill of the night. Winter had well and truly settled in now. It was a bad time to be destroying the Paradises. Each one would likely have enough food stored only for the people living there. The additional soldiers or guards to be posted at each one would stretch their supplies thin.

It was well into the evening by the time the children finally fell asleep. Aislen did not like to discuss sensitive matters with them in earshot, which was going to make this trip difficult.

The two Outworlders, Leif and Talise, were sitting side by side in comfortable silence, leaning against Pyrid's side. She knew they were not a couple, but the more she studied them, the less she understood why. It was clear they had feelings for each other. Perhaps humans saw things differently. Perhaps dukes were only allowed to marry for diplomatic reasons. Personally, she had never understood this obsession humans had for keeping their ruling class aloof from the masses. Illaria only worked as well as it did because she and her father worked hard to give the people what they needed or, when it was one and the same, what they wanted. It kept them safe, healthy and happy. There was no distinction of class in that matter.

"Duke Leif," she greeted him as she sat beside him. "Did you leave any of your men in the broken Paradise?"

The man nodded. "I asked Brock, my falconer, to send a message back to my lords explaining the situation to them, asking them to send out a squadron of soldiers. A few tradesmen and apprentices travelled with us there, so we left them to assist in our absence."

Talise laughed at the statement and was swiftly rewarded with an elbow to her ribs. Aislen, amused by their behaviour, struggled to keep a look of polite interest on her face.

"We left two men with their healers. The rest refused to leave again until we returned safely."

"Ah." Aislen nodded. "They knew you were coming to Illaria and didn't know if you would return from the mysterious lintep stronghold?"

"Something like that," Leif agreed, glaring at his lady. Aislen tried not to laugh.

"I don't suppose there's any chance you want to stay in this broken Paradise until we return from the next one?"

Talise covered a smile with her hand. "Those two children really messed up your plans, didn't they?"

Aislen shook her head. "The twins get themselves into trouble almost constantly. You'd think, with the amount of fighting that goes on between them, they'd never have time to think of anything else. But I'm constantly amazed by the new, and usually dangerous, schemes they cook up. This is, by far, the worst one. Their parents will never forgive me if I let anything happen to them."

"It's possible this journey will be exactly what they need," Talise pointed out. "It might knock some fear and caution into them. Sounds like the destruction of the first Paradise didn't exactly go as planned. If this one is anything like that, it might prove to them why they should have stayed back at the castle."

Aislen nodded slowly, a smile spreading on her face. "You've given me a fine idea, Lady Talise. If I can't find a way to send them home tomorrow, they're going to wish I had."

Leif looked between the two of them. "What did I just miss? The two of you have cooked up your own plan for those twins and I was sitting right here and missed it."

Aislen laughed as Talise patted his hand sympathetically. *Oh yes, I'm going to make Umi and Ulf rue the day they decided to stow away.*

Chapter Seventeen – Tika

Aislen shook the twins awake, a little more roughly than necessary, and Shuut just before dawn. The rest of the camp was asleep aside from Duke Leif and Séverin.

"What was that for?" Umi asked, looking around sleepily at the quiet camp.

"I'm going with Duke Leif to the village," she told them. "Make yourselves useful while we're gone. I expect everyone to be fed and ready to go by the time we return."

"What are you talking about?" Ulf asked, rubbing the sleep from his eyes. "Why is *she* smiling?"

Aislen looked over at Shuut, who had understood exactly what was happening. "Shuut will help you with whatever you need, but she's not going to do it for you. We won't be gone for long."

"Shall we, Princess Aislen?" The duke held his arm out for her. They walked away with Séverin following close behind, trying desperately hard not to laugh at the bickering that had already broken out between the twins. "I think I'm starting to understand what you and Talise were talking about last night. Remind me to never make an enemy of either one of you."

* * *

Leif led the lintep princess to the broken Paradise. It was clear from her reaction that she'd not been here before.

"Why didn't you come when they destroyed it?" he asked her.

Aislen looked around, taking in every detail. "Someone had to stay behind to run things in my father's absence."

"Well, what do you think of it?" He gestured to the sleepy village.

"It needs more security," Séverin answered before the princess had a chance. "We've now walked past at least half a dozen buildings, none of which have locks on their doors or any protection for their windows. They're either very trusting people, or stupid ones."

A voice from behind caused them all to turn. "Perhaps we were a *safe* people before our Paradise was destroyed. What need had we for protection against each other?"

"Ah, Lord Brynt." Leif nodded towards him. "It's good to find you well since we parted. Have my men given you any trouble?"

The stout human shook his head. "On the contrary, Chrislan has been hard at work, improving our forge to start the production of locks." He started pointedly at Séverin. "Apparently, we need more security now that the boundary is gone."

The lintep guard had the good grace to look ashamed. "I apologise, Lord Brynt. I did not mean to cause offence. I was merely trying to point out the work that we have to look forward to in the next Paradise."

"So, you're off to destroy another one then," Brynt huffed. "I wish you more luck than you had with this one. Who's this then?" he asked, looking at Aislen.

"Lord Brynt, allow me to present Princess Aislen of Illaria," Leif introduced them. "Princess Aislen, Lord Brynt is the leader of this broken Paradise. I'll leave you two to talk while I find Brock."

"He's taken up lodgings with the healers. You should find him there."

Leif nodded and left to find him.

* * *

Aislen suddenly found herself at a loss. This task of destroying the boundaries and keeping the inhabitants safe was a daunting one.

"Lord Brynt, I would appreciate a moment of your time." She held the man's gaze until it softened. "I understand things did not go too smoothly when my father came to destroy your Paradise boundary. If possible, I would like to learn from his mistakes."

"Well, that won't be too difficult," he grumbled. "Don't destroy the boundary and set a group of armed men at a run towards the Paradise."

Aislen almost choked. Brynt chuckled. "I see. They didn't exactly explain it to you that way, did they?"

"No. They most certainly did not," she said quietly. "I can assure you, it is not my plan to make it appear as though we are invading or attacking."

He gestured towards the Paradise. Aislen fell into step beside him, Séverin close behind.

"To be fair, I understand that wasn't exactly their plan either, but I saw the boundary disappear from view and raised the alarm at all the armed people I saw walking towards us. They only started running when a few of the younger ones took it upon themselves to try to calm the situation."

Aislen grimaced. "By any chance, would one of them have been a red-haired girl?"

Brynt raised an eyebrow. "Aye, it would. She and her friends had almost convinced us to stand down until we saw the others running fast behind them. From there ... well, I'm sure you've heard how things went."

"So, Rilla's way was working?" Aislen asked in surprise.

"I'd say the boy, the little one, had more of an effect on us. Strange, that. I never would have expected a mere child to avert a battle, but then again, it didn't quite work."

The little boy, Aislen wondered. She looked over at Séverin who only shrugged.

"Would you recognise this boy again if you saw him?"

The Paradise leader scratched behind his neck. "Maybe. He was here for a while. Him and that Partner of his."

Aislen smiled. "Tika."

"What was that name?" Brynt leaned in closer. Aislen repeated herself a little louder. "That's the one. I don't know what it was about him, but he managed to calm us down. He got us to listen."

"And then my father and his guards charged in, weapons drawn..."

Aislen walked on beside Brynt in silence. From what she'd understood, Tika had quite a way with animals as well. His bright and easy nature seemed to do wonders for everyone. Unlike Arishen, who did not appear to have made many friends among the lintep, Tika fitted in as though he were one of them.

"Have you given your village a name?" she asked Brynt as they neared a slightly denser cluster of buildings.

"Don't seem right to call ourselves anything," he replied with a shrug. "We never really saw ourselves as anything other than a Paradise. Now people are calling us the broken Paradise. Seems as good a description as any."

"True," Aislen said slowly. "It is an apt description, but there will soon be many more broken Paradises. Your village will need a name to distinguish it from all the others, if for no reason other than trading purposes. How will people know which broken Paradise to head towards if there is no name?"

"I s'pose you have a point there," he mumbled. "Maybe by the time you return from the next one, we might have a name for you."

Aislen smiled and nodded. "Tell me, Lord Brynt, do you think it would have made a difference to you and your people if my father had entered your Paradise and explained the situation before he had it destroyed?"

Brynt pursed his lips. "I honestly don't know. All I can think is if he had done that, we would have argued and possibly tried to detain him if he refused to change his mind. I think the only difference might have been an earlier chance for bloodshed, not that our men managed to injure the girl and the old man. I mean, there wouldn't have been any point fighting afterwards because at least we would have known that it wasn't an invasion."

"Yes, that's where my mind led me as well," Aislen sighed, trying not to dwell on the fact that she had left that "old man" behind with a missing arm.

"I think it's a mighty kind thing of you to try to find the safest way to destroy the Paradises," Brynt told her. "You're a sight better than your father on that score. Seems he didn't really think about that at all before he came charging in here."

Aislen cringed at both the compliment and the criticism but said nothing. She could feel Séverin bristle at Brynt's cutting opinion of his king, accurate though it may have been, but simultaneously glow with pride at the praise she'd been given. Sometimes, it was so difficult to keep her tendrils of power away from others. She couldn't help but hear their thoughts or sense their feelings, though she never used that to her advantage if she could help it. It simply didn't seem fair, no matter how much her father, and many other lintep, would argue that point to the contrary.

In that sense, Kora was more like her than almost any other lintep in Illaria. It confirmed, once again, that Kora was the natural and best choice for her heir. She would be good for the people of Illaria when it came to it. And with Pér by her side, the two of them could change things for the better. She would do her best to give them a good start in that, beginning with her dealings of the Paradises.

* * *

"I still can't believe she made us cook breakfast for everyone," Ulf fumed. He scooped up the last bite of his porridge as Shuut placed her empty bowl in front of him. He looked down at it, then scowled up at her. "What's that for?"

"I thought Aislen made it perfectly clear," she replied with a hint of amusement. "You cook and clean. Otherwise, you go back home."

"Some adventure this is turning out to be," Ulf grumbled as more bowls were placed in front of him. Umi gathered them up calmly.

"You wanted adventure? Well, looks like this is the price. We're lucky Aislen isn't sending us home right away."

"Suppose," Ulf mumbled as he joined Umi in cleaning the breakfast dishes.

They were just sitting down to rest when Aislen returned. Ulf scowled at her as she walked up to them. Umi was having too much fun enjoying her brother's foul temper to be in much of one herself. She was surprised they hadn't been sent straight home and was willing to do anything Aislen asked of her to keep it that way.

"There are not enough spare horses to escort you back to Illaria. I've sent Noémi, one of our guards from last time, with a message for your parents. They should receive it by nightfall," she told them without preamble. "They will likely still be in a state that you've put yourselves in so much danger. Master Bastienne will be your guardian while we are in the Outworld. Do not defy him. He may not be as powerful as Uncle Aaron, but I doubt he is less skilled. I have given him leave to make your lives a misery should you disobey him. Do I make myself understood?"

The twins nodded as one. The scowl left Ulf's face when he realised they really were to remain on this adventure.

"So ... where are we going anyway?" he asked Aislen. She raised an eyebrow.

"Best you don't know right now," she told them. "As I said, you've placed yourselves in a great deal of danger. The less you know, the less trouble you can get yourselves into."

A loud thud behind them startled the twins before they could protest again. Pyrid breathed hot smoke on their backs. Umi jumped and ducked behind Aislen. Ulf stood frozen in terror, trying to display a false bravado.

"Aislen, exactly where *are* we going?" the dragon asked in a low rumble. "Does anyone know the way?"

Umi and Ulf looked expectantly at their cousin. She *had* to tell the crystal dragons. After all, they were the ones flying.

"You two make sure everything is packed properly. I don't want anything left behind," Aislen told them as she led the fire opal dragon away from them.

* * *

Isis sat with her back against Celtan. From here, she could see everyone. It was certainly an eclectic group, even more so than the last time they'd gone to destroy a Paradise. Then, she hadn't been burdened with the task of keeping the children out of trouble. She looked over her charges. Plyke and Tika sat together, deep in discussion. Umi and Ulf joined them after a time, and it was almost like they were back in the dining hall of the castle. She marvelled at how quickly the four of them had become friends.

Rilla sat near enough to them but, somehow, she always seemed distant. It was only when they actively tried to engage her that she really joined her cousins. She seemed to prefer Shuut's quiet company.

Nyssa's eldest daughter had quickly helped the twins get the fire started so they could cook porridge for everyone, after which she'd pulled out her sword to do some drills. The old Paradisians had all joined her. Even some of the guards sparred with them.

That was the only time Arishen had joined in anything. Otherwise, he had sat on the outskirts of the clearing, watching everyone just as Isis herself did. Their eyes met, and he quickly looked away. Isis walked over and sat next to the seer.

"You're quite good with your daggers," Isis told him. "You certainly gave Tika a run for his money."

Arishen shrugged. "Tika is better with his bow. He only uses his daggers when Shuut forces him to. Most people can hold their own against him."

Isis sighed. He certainly had a negative outlook on things. "I hear you've been making friends in the castle. Miette seems to have taken quite a shine to you."

Arishen instantly blushed. "I ... she ... is a very nice person."

"You know, she's one of my brighter students," Isis continued, seeing the effect the mention of Miette had on him. "She is to be taught the very skill you prompted Rilla to use when the two of you were in danger. She was quite impressed that your vision saved the day."

"Oh, I wouldn't say that," Arishen brushed aside the comment. "It was all Rilla's doing."

"From what I hear, your visions have saved quite a number of people, more than once," Isis persisted. "Some might go so far as to call you a hero."

"Hah! No one would call me that! Especially not anyone where we're going."

Isis shrugged. "Some people are too blind to see the truly spectacular. It's their loss, really."

Arishen looked over at her, a strange look in his eyes. "Thanks Isis. It would have been ... nicer growing up in our Paradise if there had been more people like you."

"Surely there were a few people like me there," she said, even knowing how terrible it had been there.

"There were." Arishen nodded. "But from my visions, I know that some of them fled the Paradise or were attacked after we left. A fair few were ... taken care of before we left. Erton made sure of that."

A dark expression clouded his face again. Isis knew it was going to be difficult for him to go back to his Paradise. He would have to face Erton and his Partner after what they had both done to him.

"Arishen, you know your friends are always there for you, don't you?" she asked him gently. "You're the one keeping yourself apart from them when you don't need to. I'm sure they would appreciate your company before we leave. As bad as you feel about going back to the Paradise, it can't be a whole lot worse than they feel, don't you think?"

The blond boy looked over to where his old companions were happily talking with each other. He caught Tika's eye and, thankfully, the small and talkative boy motioned him over with big, unmistakeable waves. Arishen laughed and went to join them.

Isis breathed a sigh of relief. It was no wonder Kora had refused to join them. She was jostled out of her thoughts by Princess Aislen. "Isis, dear, I think we need to enlist the assistance of young Tika."

"Tika? Whatever for?" Isis asked in surprise.

Aislen looked sidelong at the twins. "Lord Brynt, the leader of the ... village, told me that it was that young boy who almost averted bloodshed. He gave me an idea for how we can go about this next time."

Isis nodded for her to continue.

"He is of the opinion that perhaps if they were warned beforehand, the potential for bloodshed might not have been quite as bad. It made me think, perhaps we can get Tika, and possibly the others, to go in and explain the situation before we do anything. What do you think?"

A cold chill shot through Isis. "Ah, Princess Aislen, that may be a good idea in most other ... villages, but it could prove to be quite dangerous in this instance."

"I could escort them in, to keep them safe," she suggested. "Perhaps with just a few of the guards."

"You haven't forgotten that Erton is Rilla's father, have you?" Isis whispered. "No matter how powerful Nyssa was, Rilla could not have become as powerful as she is without her father having some degree of power. He may have had to hide it the entire time he lived there, but that has probably only served to make him more imaginative with its use."

Aislen slumped down beside her. "So, not necessarily the best idea to give them warning then?"

Isis shrugged. "Some warning is probably a good idea, but we should be careful how we go about it. What if we ask the children if they know who the more sympathetic people are? We could try to warn them first and thus have more people to help us calm the rest."

"Calm the rest or control them?" Aislen asked grimly. "What if we find the ringleaders and neutralise them before we go in?"

Isis nodded. "I'd say that's a safer option. But would it be better to do that before we go in or after?"

Isis thought back on everything she'd heard about the Paradise. They knew nothing about the lay of the land. From Kora's reckoning, they were all set out the same way. Isis hadn't really had a chance to see the first broken Paradise, but she'd seen enough to notice a clump of trees in it.

"Rilla!" she called out to the girl, ignoring Aislen's startled look. She quickly joined them. "Tell me, if we destroy you know what, will it be instantly noticed?"

Rilla shook her head. "Only if there are people nearby and everyone generally stays away on pain of punishment."

"So, it's possible, if we come in from behind the trees, that we won't be noticed until we choose to be?"

The girl nodded. "You'd be on the far side of it. If we came in at a meal time with everyone else from that side of the stream, you might go mostly unnoticed until you reach the main group."

She was holding something back. Isis could tell.

"All suggestions are welcome, Rilla."

"It might be best if someone like Tika goes in first, maybe with Plyke. They might have some people welcoming them back and draw attention away from the rest of us."

Aislen laughed quietly. "It all comes back to Tika. That boy seems to be quite a wonder. Very well, Tika and Plyke go in first, but some of the more skilled lintep will accompany them, blending into the background. I refuse to send them in alone."

Rilla smiled. "Thank you. I think they'd appreciate that."

Isis shared a look with Aislen. "Yes, this will be a perfect opportunity for you to test your skills, Rilla. From what I've heard, you spent most of your time there blending into the background. You should be used to it."

The girl's eyed widened. "Well, that was when they wanted to ignore me."

"Don't worry, Rilla," Aislen reassured her. "They won't even know to look for you this time around."

Rilla nodded half-heartedly and rejoined her cousins. Isis hoped they were doing the right thing.

"Aislen, exactly who are you planning on sending in there? You can't send the twins or Anya."

"I've got plenty of time to decide on the way there," she replied, getting to her feet. "Let's go, everyone! We've a long day ahead of us. If we leave now, we might make it to our next destination by nightfall."

Chapter Eighteen – Silvaren

Eliséo woke and instantly regretted opening his eyes. The ground was rushing past him from a great distance. He closed his eyes again and worked his jaw open and closed a few times. His tongue felt thick and leaden.

"Where am I?"

There was no answer. He opened his eyes and tried to turn his head, but it was pressed firmly against a hard, blue surface. Fighting to keep his panic at bay, Eliséo reached out to his tree.

Elessa, where am I?

Well, you certainly took your time waking up, Elessa chided him. *We've been worried sick about you.*

I'm still worried about me. Where am I?

On your way home with Celtan. We'll be together by tonight. He could feel the smile in her voice. But there was something else. Hesitation.

Rilla, child, look who has finally woken.

You're awake! The force of her thoughts would have knocked Eliséo off Celtan if he wasn't tied down. *Are you okay?*

I ... don't know, he replied uncertainly. *I haven't had a chance to inspect my wounds, but my head doesn't hurt as much as it should.*

There was a guilty silence.

I guess I have you to thank for that then? He felt something pass between Rilla and Elessa.

Mistress Kayte is furious with me, Rilla replied.

Next time I see her, I'll be sure to praise your efforts, he told her, without reprimand. He was simply happy to be talking with Elessa and Rilla.

You haven't told him? Rilla asked Elessa.

There hasn't been time, his tree replied. *He only just woke up.*

Eliséo closed his eyes as Elessa shared Rilla's memories of the past few days with him. It was all he could do not to shed any tears at Aaron's terrible loss and at having this chance to be with Rilla when she faced Erton ripped away from him.

I will speak with Aislen. She will understand that I must come to this Paradise.

No. Elessa was firm. *You are not fit for this task. You need rest.*

Before he could argue, Eliséo could feel Elessa pushing him down into a deep sleep. He didn't have the strength to fight it.

I know what's best for you, she told him as he succumbed to her will.

* * *

Aislen saw the magnificent trees early in the afternoon. In truth, it was difficult to miss them. They were larger, by far, than any other tree she had ever seen. Each one had a black trunk and bare glossy black branches. She wished it was spring, then all the trees would be in full bloom. As it was, only a few scattered trees still had late autumn leaves.

Her excitement changed to trepidation as Pyrid started his descent. She had never spoken to an elf other than the ambassador before. Would they blame her for his injuries? Would they even be allowed entry to Silvaren? She should have asked her father these things. He had visited, many years ago, before she was born.

Aislen smiled. *The children have been here before, as well as Shuut and Anya. All will be well.*

Pyrid landed on a steep hill leading down to Silvaren. He had been here once before, with Anya and Eliséo. One by one, Celtan and the clear crystal dragons landed and immediately closed their eyes to sleep.

"Pyrid, are they unwell?" Aislen asked the fire opal dragon. He turned his snout to look at the small flight.

"No, they are only tired. The scouts are not used to such long distances and Celtan has barely been out of the Drakos Mountains at all these past twenty years. He is older than I am. The extra weight of those two children are not helping matters."

Aislen sighed and shook her head at Umi and Ulf's stupidity. "Will you cope if we request another elf join us in place of Eliséo?"

"We'll survive," he grumbled. "But from your map, I doubt we'll reach our destination tomorrow. We will need to rest before then."

Shuut walked up to them confidently. "You could stop in Turon. It's not so far from our destination and will mean that we are all well rested before we face ... that situation."

Aislen hid herself under Pyrid's wing and hurriedly pulled out her map. "What do you think Pyrid? Is it possible?" He looked under his wing, one large eye studying the map.

"Looks as good a place as any other."

Shuut grunted. "I know the Outworld better than most, old dragon. You should know that by now."

Pyrid refrained from answering her. In fact, for all her association with the crystal dragons, Aislen realised not a one of them had spoken to her the entire journey.

"Shuut, do you think the elves will welcome our entire party for the night?"

"I wouldn't count on it," the former banwep replied. "I've only ever visited by myself aside from the time I brought these four with me."

Shuut gestured to the former Paradisians, who quickly came to join the conversation.

"I can't wait to see Tameo again!" Tika bounced on the spot. "Do you think they're all still here?"

"Tika, Eliséo is the only elf who ever leaves. Of *course* they're still here." Shuut shook her head at the bright young boy. Aislen found she was smiling despite herself. Tika really was the key to so many things.

"Would the five of you like to accompany me?" she asked to a chorus of cheers. "It's settled then."

Aislen gathered the large company around her. "Anya, you may come if you wish. Mistress Kayte and Médard will help us with Eliséo but everyone else remains with the dragons, unless we send for you." She looked closely at the twins. "That includes the two of you. Master Bastienne is in charge of you. Slip away from him at your own peril."

"No fair!" shouted Ulf. "What do you expect us to do while you go and have fun with the elves?"

"Séverin, your swords could do with some polishing, couldn't they?" Bastienne called out to the nearest guard. Séverin smiled mischievously.

"Indeed, they could. Come here, you two. I'll keep you busy until the princess returns."

They walked down the hill with some trouble. Eliséo was an awkward burden to bear. Aislen turned to Kayte.

"Shouldn't he have woken up by now?"

Kayte nodded. "I thought he had for a moment, but the wind was so noisy I couldn't talk to him."

He did wake up earlier today, Rilla said quietly in Aislen's mind. *Elessa is ... making him sleep.*

Aislen looked at the girl curiously. There was something she was not telling them. *Can she wake him up again?*

Rilla closed her eyes for a moment. Eliséo began to stir. Once he realised where they were, he struggled against them and fell to his knees.

"No! Don't take me back there!"

The party stopped. Aislen looked at him in confusion.

"There are things happening in Silvaren that may prevent Eliséo from leaving again any time soon," Anya explained. "Did you bother to ask if he wanted to return?"

Aislen caught Kayte's eye.

"We ... no. We only thought to return him to his tree."

Anya grumbled to herself as she went to help the fallen elf. Without asking permission, Rilla went to his other side. She glared at Kayte, almost daring her to protest.

"I'm sorry, Eliséo," Aislen couldn't bring herself to look him in the eye. "We have no choice now. It will be too dangerous to take you with us. We thought the safest place for you would be with your tree."

"I'm sorry, Anya." Eliséo looked down at the karlik. "I had hoped to help you with all of them. I had hoped to see Ilya again before ..."

Aislen saw tears stream down Rilla's face. Clearly, the girl had not thought of these other consequences when she requested that they bring him home. Had she even known?

Shuut led the way down the hill and across into Silvaren over the narrow strip of land connecting the forested island to the mainland.

"Can we take him straight to Elessa?" Rilla asked, before they were surrounded by trees. Aislen looked over to Shuut and shrugged.

"You may as well," Shuut replied. "He isn't fit enough to present himself to the queen. I'll take Aislen and Anya to Silva. The rest of you may as well wait in Elessa."

Aislen forestalled the argument she could sense was about to happen. "That sounds like the most sensible idea. We most certainly will not be expected. The fewer of us who disturb Queen Liessa, the better."

They stayed together until Eliséo had been safely escorted into his tree. Aislen's fingertips accidentally brushed against Elessa's inner trunk as she made to leave.

You're the one who saved him. A vaguely familiar voice entered her mind and filled her vision with past events. *I thank you for that. I only hope you have not led him into further danger.*

I don't understand what danger there can be for him in his home, Aislen lingered, trying to understand the surreal situation.

The only warning I can give you is to be careful what you say to the queen. Do not tell

her you have ever spoken with me. Do not mention how you saved Lord Aaron's life
and endangered Eliséo's through Rilla's bond with me.

Aislen withdrew her fingers and clenched her fist. How was she going to explain
his wound without lying?

"Aislen," Rilla called out to her as she stepped onto the forest floor. Shuut and Anya
were already there, waiting for her. Aislen turned and caught the girl in her arms as
she hurtled down the steep walkway out of the tree. "Aislen, please don't say anything
about me. The queen, she ... well, she sees things differently to us. Please leave me out
of your conversation if you can."

"If any of you could stop being so cryptic with me, I might actually know how to
handle this meeting," Aislen replied through gritted teeth. "I will do what I can, but I
make no guarantees that, whatever this situation is, it won't get worse."

Aislen shook her head and followed Shuut further into Silvaren. Her excitement at
visiting the elves had withered like leaves in winter. Increasingly, she wanted nothing
more than to be away from this place and travelling towards the next Paradise. But
that would have to wait.

Shoving aside her trepidation, Aislen looked up at the magnificent conglomeration
of trees which were collectively known as Silva. Her breath caught in her throat. She
had heard so much about it. Such a dwelling should not be possible. The tree itself
was black, as all the other trees in Silvaren, but the glittering silver vines draped over
it signified that it was so much more than those.

Aislen found herself fighting the urge to touch this tree as she had accidentally
touched Elessa. She wanted to know everything about it, to share in its secrets, revel
in its joy and commiserate in its sadness. But to do all that, she knew she would be
forced to betray her dealings with Elessa and *that* she was not willing to do.

A tall and elegant elf with silvering hair descended the multitude of aboveground
roots to stand in front of them.

"I bid you welcome."

"Lady Eléna." Shuut bowed her head. "How did you know we were here?"

The former queen only smiled and looked at Aislen. "Anya, it is good to see you
again. Princess Aislen, I presume? Please follow me."

Aislen looked over at Shuut who only shrugged. With a brief glance towards Anya,
Aislen followed the retreating elf.

By the time they reached the throne room, Aislen had thought of and discarded
a dozen lies to explain how Eliséo had come by his wounds. If she spoke, there was
every danger that she would expose what had truly happened. Of the three of them,
only Anya was ignorant.

"Princess Aislen, what a rare and unexpected pleasure it is to meet you." Queen
Liessa was not what she had expected at all. She sat confidently on the throne, but
with a rigidity that spoke of discomfort. Her advisers stood along one wall, every one
of them avoiding the queen's gaze.

"Queen Liessa." Aislen inclined her head slightly. "It is a pleasure to meet you. I
trust I find you in good health."

"The pleasure is all mine. However, I do find it odd that you appear with no
warning, along with the karlik who took my ambassador away and seems not to

have returned him."

Aislen's mind raced. This was not the sort of reception she had anticipated. "We found that we were to pass close by Silvaren and decided to bring the ambassador home with all due haste. The reason he does not stand before you is that he is gravely injured."

Queen Liessa raised an eyebrow impassively, though Aislen noticed Lady Eléna visibly pale and reach behind her for support.

"He is recovering well. Our healers in Illaria gave him the greatest care possible and it seems as though all he needs now is rest. We thought he might heal faster in the comfort of his own tree."

She risked another look at Lady Eléna and saw her small smile and almost imperceptible nod. Queen Liessa looked down at Anya coldly.

"I did not lend you the services of my ambassador to have him so badly used. What happened?"

Aislen laid a calming hand on the karlik and took the edge off her anger.

"My lady, you knew he was to help us root out the rebels. That was never going to be a safe task. As it happened, Eliséo wasn't injured in action. It was only when he went to Lord Aaron's aid that he took on some of the lintep's injury himself."

"My queen?" Lady Eléna looked over at her daughter, who nodded disdainfully. "Did Lord Aaron also survive?"

Aislen wished she had a hand to hold. "Yes. He survived."

From the corner of her eye, she saw Anya look up at her but couldn't return the karlik's glance.

"Lord Aaron received a blow to the head, an injury which Eliséo now shares, while we were fighting the rebels. We were taking them back to Goraburg when yoswen attacked us. Lord Aaron lost part of an arm before the crystal dragons found us."

Stunned silence greeted her words. Aislen could feel the despair cascading from Lady Eléna, both for Aaron and Eliséo.

"Queen Liessa, if I may?" Shuut spoke too quickly to be silenced. "Eliséo has spent a great many years among the lintep. I am certain he knew what would happen to him as he went to Lord Aaron's aid."

The beautiful elf queen looked at her coldly. "So, he values his life less than that of a lintep?"

Lady Eléna gasped as Aislen used all her skill to calm herself. "My queen, Eliséo's respect for Lord Aaron is exceptional. I am certain he thought they would both survive if he shared the wound."

"You were always too lenient on the ambassador." Liessa looked at her mother scornfully. "He will be suitably punished for his reckless action."

Aislen stared in open wonder. How could the Queen of the Elves be so heartless? It was no wonder Eliséo wanted to stay away.

"We shall trespass on your good will no longer, Queen Liessa." Aislen took control of the situation. "We came to return the ambassador to his home. Now that we have done so, we must be on our way. Our mission requires the utmost haste."

She could see Queen Liessa debating whether to attempt to detain them, but eventually, she dismissed them. Lady Eléna moved quickly to escort them away.

Chapter Nineteen – Hidden dangers

"What did I miss?" Shuut asked as they left the tangled mess of roots below the massive expanse of Silva. "The last time I was here, she was so green she looked to you for every decision she made."

"Not here, Shadow," Eléna said quietly, then she continued in a louder voice. "It has been a while since your last visit. I will escort you back to Elessa for fear you may lose your way."

Eléna escorted them back to Elessa in silence. She lightly brushed her fingers along the trunk as she ascended to the main chamber. The former Paradisians rose when she entered the room. She smiled briefly at the sight of them. They had grown considerably since the last time they'd met though some of them looked the worse for wear. Rilla's red-rimmed eyes betrayed she had been crying. Eléna held up a hand to forestall their questions.

"I beg your good humour only a moment longer. I wish to see the ambassador."

Eléna glided up the winding walkway to her son's bedchamber, heart beating painfully fast. As she entered, two lintep who she did not know turned to meet her. The older one motioned the younger out of the chamber.

"Lady Eléna?"

Eléna inclined her head.

"My name is Kayte. I am one of the healing mistresses in Illaria."

Eléna barely trusted herself to speak as she saw her son so still on his bed of blankets.

"Princess Aislen told me he will live."

Kayte came over to her and placed a hand on her back. Slowly, Eléna closed the distance between herself and Eliséo.

"He is healing well. He willingly gave what he thought might be his life to save Lord Aaron. The whole of Illaria is in his debt."

Eléna smiled at the mistress. "I won't be long here. Please advise the others not to leave Elessa until I have descended."

Kayte raised an eyebrow at the dismissal but left the bedchamber without comment. As soon as she was gone, Eléna knelt beside her son and wept. Her tears quickly soaked the front of his shirt, but she did not care as his hand came to rest on her head.

"I could not let him die."

Eléna sat up and looked her son in the eye. "You would have broken my heart had *you* died."

"It would have made things in Silvaren less complicated."

Eléna shook her head. "Lately, I find myself questioning my own actions. I feel it may have indeed been foolish to abdicate in favour of my daughter. She has … changed much since that fateful day."

"Can you not reverse your decision?"

"Perhaps," she answered quietly. "Though it may result in the same situation as with Ilya and Vladimir, and I could not bear to put a child of mine to death."

"Liessa may not share the same feelings if she discovers the truth."

Eléna's eyes hardened. "*If* she discovers the truth, it will not be the queen who has the difficult decision to make." Eliséo did not answer, but only kissed her hand before succumbing to sleep. Eléna bit her lip and dried her eyes.

Once she was composed, Eléna descended into the main chamber. Tika, that dear, sweet boy, immediately ran into her arms. She smiled despite herself as she hugged him tightly then pulled back.

"I assume you are on your way to the next Paradise. Your haste must be great indeed, so I thank you dearly for bringing Eliséo back to us alive. I wish I could order another elf to go with you in his place, however, I no longer have that power. Of course, any elf may, of his or her own choice, decide to join you."

Shuut looked at her speculatively for a moment. "Princess Aislen, please excuse me. I find that I am missing the company of some dear friends. If we are to leave Silvaren tonight, I would wish to speak with them, if only for a few moments."

Aislen nodded with a small smile.

"You are welcome to stay here for the night, however, I would advise you to depart before dawn."

"Lady Eléna, we have no wish to trespass in Silvaren longer than her highness desires. As she did not bid us welcome herself, we shall return to the dragons tonight so that we may be on our way at first light."

Eléna nodded to the princess. "It would have been nice to have more time to get to know one another. I have heard people speak highly of you. Perhaps when things settle down, I might have the pleasure of visiting you in Illaria."

Aislen smiled, trying to hide a blush. "I look forward to that. Farewell for now." She ushered everyone down the walkway.

"Rilla, a moment if you please?" Eléna called out to the girl as she descended with the others. Rilla waved her companions ahead and walked back into Elessa's main chamber.

"I fear we may not have been very forthcoming in what we told you about the queen." Rilla looked up sharply at those words. Eléna laid a hand on her shoulder and squeezed gently. "Many things are changing in Silvaren. The queen may begin to make ... difficult requests of her ambassador. Requests which he may struggle with. Try to be forgiving of whatever decisions he might be forced to make."

Rilla tapped her teeth together. "I don't like the sound of that. Why does it feel like you're trying to warn me that a certain bond may need to be broken?"

Eléna shook her head. "That is but one possibility. An unlikely one, but a possibility, nonetheless. Have courage, Rilla. They both love you dearly and will do whatever they can not to hurt you. Go now. Your companions will be waiting for you."

She watched Rilla trail her fingers along Elessa's inner trunk as she slowly went down the walkway. Eléna saw the red smudged teardrops that remained in her wake. If she had not been watching, Eléna doubted she would have noticed them in passing they were so subtle. Her heart ached at the secretive care they all had to take. It was not what she had wished for her son any more than she had wished it for herself.

Shuut arrived back at the campsite with an elf at her side. He was clearly older than Lady Eléna, and his limbs looked so knotted and twisted that Aislen wondered that he could walk at all.

"Ensil has agreed to join us," Shuut told her. Aislen involuntarily coughed in surprise, wondering how this elf could possibly be of use to her. "He is the weapons master here in Silvaren. I'll wager he could teach your guards a thing or two if they're willing to listen to such a crusty old elf."

"Manners were never one of your strong points," Ensil muttered grumpily. "I might just change my mind if you don't speak more kindly to me."

"Ensil!" Rilla ran over to them. "Are you really joining us?"

The old elf huffed. "Someone needs to make sure you don't let those magnificent weapons go to waste. I hear you've been practising with the castle guards. How did that go?"

Aislen could tell Rilla was holding back a grin. "They only underestimate me once each, at the most."

"Master Ensil, we are greatly honoured that you wish to join us on this venture." Aislen nodded affably. "If you wish to spar with any of my guards, or your former students, you have my leave. Just don't damage them too much. We will need them at full strength if danger arises."

Ensil smiled mischievously. Aislen returned his smile, shaking her head.

"I want an early night for everyone. We have a long day ahead of us tomorrow."

Chapter Twenty – Measured breath

Aaron stirred and opened his eyes. He blinked and let his gaze wander until the room came into focus. He was no longer in the Lesa Mountains or Goraburg. This looked very much like the infirmary under the castle. He groaned as he tried to sit up.

"Aaron, you're awake!" Kynon cried out, startling him. "Rest yourself. Lukys is on his way."

As he looked at the beds beside him, a chill stole through Aaron's body. "Where is Eliséo?"

"They took him home."

"Alive?" Aaron closed his eyes against the answer. He could not bear the news.

"Of course, alive!" Kynon clasped his hand. "He sacrificed much for you, but not his life."

Aaron's breath ran out in a sigh of relief. If he had killed that elf ... The thought did not bear carrying through to a conclusion. Eliséo was alive. That was all that mattered. Almost.

"The rebels?"

"I do not know all the details. I was ... occupied with other matters. I know Anya arrived with you." Kynon smiled. "She's a feisty one, isn't she? Reminds me of you, in your younger years."

"Aaron! Thank the stars you're awake!" The king's voice echoed around the infirmary. Kynon laughed as the healers on duty shushed him. "Sorry, sorry," Lukys whispered as he quickly closed the distance between them.

"Lukys, good to see you too." Aaron smiled as he opened his eyes once more. "Maybe you can shed some light for me. What happened with the rebels?"

Lukys pulled up short and looked at him in surprise. "*That's* what you want to know about? The *rebels*?"

"That's the last thing I remember. We found their hideout. I detained the ones inside ... then my memory gives out."

"You ... don't remember anything else at all?" Lukys stared at him, eyebrows raised high.

Aaron shook his head and regretted it. He raised his arm to touch the wound, but only a tendril of power brushed against it. With measured breath, he looked down at his body.

"Not even what became of my arm," he said quietly.

Lukys' eyes filled with tears. "Oh Aaron! I'm sorry. There wasn't anything that could be done about it. Yoswen attacked your party while only Anya and two other karliki were alive to defend you. They did their best, and despite one of them dying to protect you, the yoswen couldn't be held back. One tore off your arm before a group of crystal dragons found you.

"Loreli and her scouts fought off the yoswen and carried you straight to the Drakos Mountains. The rest of your arm ... was eaten by a yoswen. There was never any hope of reattaching it."

"I see." Aaron swallowed hard. "Well, at least I escaped with my life, which is more than can be said of some of the karliki. How will I ever be able to repay them?"

"You saved their clan leader from the hands of his traitorous brother. Vladimir is dead. That is repayment enough."

They both knew it would be of little comfort to the families of those who were slain in the task. Ilya would have his hands full taking care of all the arrangements.

"What of Eliséo? Is Anya still here?" Aaron asked. "I'd like to thank her for ... everything."

Lukys shook his head. "Five clear crystal dragons and Celtan followed Pyrid here. The seven of them agreed to assist us. Anya has left for the next destination with twenty-two others. Aislen is leading them. They will take Eliséo home on their way through."

Aaron waved Lukys to silence with his left arm. "Leave me be now. I need to rest." Without waiting for an answer, he closed his eyes and turned away from his cousin. He thought he had dealt with all the pain in his life. He was not prepared to face the loss of his arm. Aaron almost laughed at the thought. *When would anyone be prepared to lose an arm?*

"Will you stay with him?" he heard Lukys ask Kynon before he dove down into oblivion.

* * *

Aislen took in every detail as they walked the streets of Turon. Shuut had convinced her it was the best place to rest before they reached the Paradise. It was far enough not to alert Lishe, should she already be near the Paradise, but close enough that the dragons would not have to fly more than half the next morning to reach it.

They had left the crystal dragons in a nearby fallow field. The land belonged to Cheyenne and Gavryle. The two had been rather vague on details, but they remembered Rilla had helped when Ratchin, a local lintep, had healed their son. It must have been a very grave wound indeed, for they volunteered to allow the crystal dragons to sleep there that evening.

"As long as they don't burn my crops," Cheyenne said with a nervous laugh.

"Pyrid is really the only one you need to worry about doing that," Celtan had grumbled.

Pyrid promised to only lightly scorch a small patch of land, off the field, to sleep on. Cheyenne had watched, frozen in place, as the fire opal dragon created himself a bed of ash.

Aislen smiled at the memory. The crystal dragons, Pyrid in particular, were growing on her. She was beginning to understand how Nyssa and Shuut had been manipulated by them. They could be quite charming, when they tried, and could disarm the most cautious of lintep.

"Where are we going?" Umi asked as they walked past openly curious townsfolk.

"Dell's Inn," Shuut replied tersely. "I have a ... friend there."

"You have to think about if they're your friend?" Ulf asked sceptically.

"We had a disagreement the last time we saw each other."

"Over me." Rilla nudged her sister playfully. "Surely you can find it in you to forgive her? After all, think of all the things that would never have happened if you had abandoned us here."

"Let's see." Shuut drummed her fingers on her cheek. "I wouldn't have been attacked by Lishe, hand two mind snares cast on me, found out that the crystal dragons had been manipulating me most of my life and, let's not forget, I would never have had to watch my mother be tortured."

Tika looked over at her cheerfully. "Look on the bright side, you would still be enslaved to the crystal dragons, you would never have had that rare and wonderful time with your mother, nor ever found Illaria and been taught to use your power. Oh yes, and you would never have discovered that you have a family, a *big* one, that loves you."

Shuut's scowl deepened, but Aislen could see the smile hiding behind it.

"We're here." The former banwep stopped suddenly. "Just try not to embarrass me. I have a reputation here."

"You *had* a reputation here as Laila out of necessity. You never need to be anyone but Shuut from now onwards," Rilla said quietly. Aislen saw Shuut give her an odd look.

Aislen raised an eyebrow as she walked past Shuut and into the dusty, but brightly lit inn. The others followed her closely. Loud music assaulted their ears as they shuffled out of the way of serving maids and patrons.

Shuut walked confidently to the bar. Aislen kept the others with her. This was beginning to look like a bad idea. How was a place so crowded going to have room for them all? She kept her silence as one of the barmen disappeared behind a swinging door. He was only gone a matter of moments before he reappeared with a rather large lady, who waddled her way around the bar.

The lady and Shuut stared each other down. Neither willing to be the first one to speak.

"Ratchin?" Aurelius strode forward as he called her name. The lady broke her stare to glance his way. Her eyes grew wide with recognition. She wiped her oily hands on her apron before heartily embracing Aurelius.

Aislen could not hear their conversation, but it was clear they were old friends. Ratchin completely ignored Shuut as she and the old master spoke. Eventually, she looked up at Aislen and made her way over to the large group.

"How many rooms do you require?"

Aislen hesitated. She had never stayed at an inn before.

"We have sleeping mats, so we don't require many beds. I think four or five rooms will be sufficient," Leif answered.

Ratchin looked at the gathered people and nodded tersely.

"I don't have time now but speak with Nadiya behind the bar and she will show you to your rooms. I'll come up when the kitchen closes."

Aislen thanked her and went to find Nadiya. The homely young lady fetched some keys from under the bar and motioned for Aislen to follow her. Aislen, in turn beckoned her companions to follow them as they headed to the stairs at the back of the room.

The music was still audible from the second level, but it was no longer so deafening that they had to shout to be heard. Nadiya handed four keys to Aislen and pointed out the rooms which they would occupy that night. There was a bath room at the end of the hall. They were to call if they needed hot water.

Aislen placed two gold coins in Nadiya's hand. The girl looked up at her wide-eyed. "Could you send up some hot food? We've had a long journey out in that bitter wind."

The girl swiftly flew down the stairs leaving Aislen to sort out the rooms. Aislen chewed on her lip. This was going to be difficult.

"Umi and Ulf, you're staying with me, Bastienne and Aurelius in here. They will remain with you whenever I cannot." The twins groaned in protest, but Aislen only nudged them into the room and nodded for the old masters to follow them.

"Mistress Kayte, Shuut, Rilla and Mistress Isis, you take one room. Plyke, Tika, Arishen and Ensil, you take another. Duke Leif and Lady Talise, you take the last room. Séverin, please assign the guards as you see fit."

As she assigned the rooms, Aislen could see protests forming on many lips, but none of them were voiced. Interestingly, Talise seemed more pleased about her room assignment than Leif. Aislen drew a long breath. It was going to be a long night.

* * *

Shuut unceremoniously dumped her rucksack and sleeping mat in her assigned room and stalked down the hall to the bath room. She noticed Rilla follow close behind but said nothing. It was a wonder Mistress Isis had let Rilla out of her sight.

"Make yourself useful and warm the water."

Rilla cocked an eyebrow but said nothing as she lit a fire in the hearth with her powers. Shuut ran enough water into each bath for them to soak their weary bodies. She waited until Rilla nodded before undressing and submerging herself in the warm water.

"You can't stay angry with her forever, you know."

"She lied to me."

"She saved my life."

"She manipulated me."

"She made you do the right thing." Rilla sighed. "Shuut, what will it take for you to believe that she did it because she loves you? She saved your life when your father abandoned you here. She never makes you pay for a room or your meals. She treats you more like a daughter than it seems Nyssa ever did."

Shuut stared Rilla down. This was *not* what she wanted to be thinking about. If she could have thought of any other place to stop for the night, she would not have suggested Turon. She was not ready to confront Ratchin over their argument. Especially not when it seemed the old lintep had been in the right.

Back in her room once more, Shuut's nerves were grinding on her. There were two beds in this room, but Aislen had assigned six of them, including the two guards. Four sleeping mats were spread out across the floor. Shuut paced back and forth. Too many eyes watched her every move. The banwep in her would not let her rest.

"I'm going out," she announced to no one in particular.

"Where?"

Shuut heard Kayte's question as she slammed the door shut behind her. She didn't bother answering. All she wanted was to be away from all of this – to be back on the streets that she knew so well, where she felt safe. At least, she *would* feel safe if she didn't have the distinct feeling that someone was following her.

She wound her way through market stalls, down through the narrower streets. Here, her sword would have limited use, but at least she couldn't be attacked by more than a couple of people at a time.

Listening carefully, she stopped and bent down, pretending to tighten the straps on her boots. The footsteps came to a halt. Shuut looked through the crook of her arm to inspect the alleyway. She couldn't see anyone.

As she straightened to walk again, the footsteps started behind her again. She could hear them closing the gap. Taking a deep breath, she timed her attack perfectly, pulling the sword from her back in a swift motion as she turned to face her hooded stalker.

Metal bit metal as the stalker blocked against her attack. She caught glimpses of his face as her blows forced him towards a wall. Recognition flickered in her mind. She brushed aside the distraction as the stalker pushed off the wall, forcing her back out into the middle of the alley. Her advantage lost, Shuut flicked the hood off the stalker's cloak back with the tip of her sword. His head jerked to the side along with the material. He stumbled and fell awkwardly to the ground, all the while keeping his sword at the ready.

"Séverin?" Shuut looked at him in confusion. She kept her distance from the guard. "What are you doing here?"

"Following you." He was unapologetic as he got to his feet. Shuut raised her sword as he stepped towards her. He stopped moving.

"Why?"

"Nicodemo put me in charge of his guards and Princess Aislen has made it abundantly clear that the royal family should be protected at all costs."

His words caught her off guard. "The ... royal family."

"Well, yes." Séverin looked at her a little less certainly. "You *are* Lord Aaron's eldest grandchild. You are part of the royal family."

Shuut mulled over the words in her mind. Would they one day call her Lady Shuut in Illaria as they had called her mother Lady Nyssa and called Plyke's mother Lady Kora?

"I don't need your protection." Shuut sheathed her sword. "I can look after myself."

Séverin shrugged and sheathed his own sword. "I know. But it would be remiss of me to allow any member of the royal family, no matter how competent with a sword, out of sight of my guards while we are in the Outworld."

"What makes you think I couldn't slip away from you if I wanted to?"

"Your years living as a banwep would help you in that, however, unless you are a lintep with enough skill and power to blend into the shadows, any of my guards should be able to find you."

Shuut scrutinised his words and felt a hole opening in front of her. "I have enough power."

"Yet, you choose not to use it." Séverin stepped closer, seeming to understand the effect his words had on her. "Why?"

"I ... can't."

"The masters and mistresses will teach you if you let them."

"I don't want to let them," she whispered. "It isn't mine to control."

"From what I've heard, your mother gave it to you of her own free will." He lifted her chin with the tip of a finger, forcing her to look him in the eye. "It was a gift. Something she hoped would protect you against Lishe. Why would you refuse to use it?"

Shuut bit back her tears. Tears! For crying out loud. When was the last time she had even cried?

"I don't want to become like *her*."

"Impossible." Séverin shook his head. "That would never happen."

"You don't know that. You barely know me at all."

"I know you well enough."

Her heart pounded in her ears as he leaned closer to her. She froze as his lips found hers. Surprised, she pulled back ever so slightly. He gently cupped his hands around her face and drew her in again. This time, she did not hesitate to return his kiss.

Chapter Twenty-One – Lady Shuut

The music stopped early that night. Perhaps the performers were tired. Perhaps they had felt the mood dampen just as Ratchin had. That princess was a powerful one – Ratchin could tell she was containing her feelings as much as possible, but it wasn't enough.

As the final patrons headed home, the kitchen fires were doused. Ratchin gave instructions for the following day before allowing the kitchen staff to depart. When they were all gone, she fetched her knitting from a corner of her room, took it to the taproom and waited at a corner table.

She had watched Shuut leave shortly after arriving. She had not yet returned. Ratchin was under no illusion that their previous encounter was the reason the young banwep was making herself scarce.

It pleased Ratchin more than she could say that Shuut had finally found Illaria. She wanted to hear everything that had happened since that fateful day, months ago, when she had forced her dear friend to take four helpless Paradisians into the Outworld with her once more.

"Ratchin?"

She looked up from her knitting to see Aurelius standing before her.

"Get to bed, old man," she told him with a wave of her needle. He did not listen to her, he never did. Instead, he sat across from her and leaned his head back against the wall with a sigh.

"You never came to visit."

Ratchin looked up sharply. "I never said I would. *I* sent messages and letters with most of the lintep I sent your way."

"But you never brought any of them yourself. I missed you. I missed your friendship more than any letter could fix."

Ratchin looked at him reproachfully. "You could have come to visit, any time you wanted to."

"I came *twice*." He waggled his finger at her. "It was your turn twice over."

"The villagers need me. I am content here. What I do is important." She laid her knitting down on the table in front of her and looked him in the eye.

Aurelius nodded sadly. "I know. I only wish we'd found a way to do these things together. To not miss out on our friendship for most of our years."

Ratchin smiled bitterly. "Don't fool yourself, Aurelius. We *could* have seen each other more. You could have left Illaria after you became a master as easily as I could have left Turon when we first met.

"But I am important here and you are important there. One or the other of us would have lost out had we left our home."

His mouth twitched. Slowly, he stretched out his weather-beaten hand across the table, his fingers lightly brushing hers. That gentle caress dissolved her bitter edge. As he moved to draw his hand away, she grasped it tightly.

Aurelius opened his mind, allowing Ratchin to see his memory of all the lintep she had ever sent his way. She hadn't realised there were so many. Even her own Shuut had found him.

"Lady Shuut?" Ratchin looked up sharply. "What do you mean *Lady*?"

Aurelius looked at her in surprise. "You didn't know? She is Lady Nyssa's daughter, as is that fiery young Rilla."

"Rilla? The prophecy child? I thought her name was Karinya." Ratchin laughed loudly. It was all too much. Shuut had tried to abandon her own sister! Aurelius smiled along with her but kept looking warily at the stairs.

"They're all asleep now," she told him when she finally caught her breath. "I can feel it."

"Then you must have forgotten how to count. Shuut left earlier this evening and has not yet returned."

"You're slipping if you didn't notice that handsome young guard follow her out." Ratchin winked. "I meant everyone upstairs is asleep now, as should you be. I don't know what is so important to bring you all here for a single night, and I don't want to know, but I assume you will need to be well rested for it."

"You're right. I need my rest for tomorrow." Aurelius cast his eyes down as he withdrew his hand and stood up. "You're always welcome in Illaria, Ratchin. I'm not the only one who would be glad to see you."

Ratchin remained seated. "You're always welcome in Turon."

"Will it always be like this, then?" he asked sadly.

"Perhaps ... perhaps I could visit once in a while when I don't think a lintep will make it on their own."

Aurelius creased his brow. "You don't have to wait for a lost lintep." He bent down and kissed her forehead fondly, then headed towards the stairs without another word.

* * *

Shuut walked into the dimly lit inn, Séverin close by her side. It felt strange, but nice, to have him there. To know that he wanted to be there – she found *that* the most difficult thing to reconcile in her mind. Most men she had met, aside from her family in Illaria, did not like her, did not want to be near her. They were either threatened by her skill with a sword or saw her as someone to swindle in the markets.

Séverin appreciated her sword skill and was not mistrustful of her defensive nature. However short the time they had known each other, he really did seem to understand her. She should have found that alarming, but she didn't.

A sound in the corner of the room drew her attention. Ratchin sat with her latest knitting project, huddled and shaking in the corner. The sight distressed Shuut more than she wanted to admit. She motioned Séverin up the stairs and counted the steps he took until she knew he had truly left them alone.

"What happened?" Shuut sat across the table from Ratchin. Her old friend lifted a tearstained face.

"It doesn't concern you." Ratchin wiped her eyes against the sleeve of her shirt and stared at her. "I won't say I'm sorry."

"No, I didn't expect you would."

"She would have died if you'd left her here. They all would have."

Shuut nodded. There was nothing else to be said about that. "Why didn't you ever try to take me to Illaria yourself? Was it because I am a half-blood?"

She watched as Ratchin's eyes teared up again. "No, child. I … If I had gone to Illaria, I doubt I would have left again. I couldn't do that to my town. They need me here."

"The distance is not so great." Shuut shook her head in confusion. "You could easily travel back and forth each year – even every few months if you wanted to."

"It was not the distance I feared. Some things are better left unsaid." Ratchin shook her head. "So, I hear you are *Lady* Shuut now."

Shuut immediately shook her head. "No, nothing of the sort. My mother was Lady Nyssa, that is all."

"Hmmm, yes and your little red-headed girl, she is your sister, Rilla."

"Half-sister, but yes."

"Are there any other details of your life which have changed since we last met?" Shuut crossed her arms. "Some things are best left unsaid."

Ratchin smiled sadly. "Yes, that is often the case. Perhaps one day we will be able to tell each other these things. Will you ever visit me again, do you suppose?"

"Yes. Perhaps. I don't know."

She watched Ratchin's face closely. There was true sadness, but she was not the only cause of it. Of that, Shuut was certain.

"I've missed you." Ratchin looked at the empty stairs. "I've missed so many things by staying here."

Shuut followed her gaze but could not follow her thoughts. "You don't have to stay here. You are free to go anywhere you want to."

"Shuut, have you ever seen me outside of Turon? Any further than the farms surrounding it?" Ratchin shook her head. "I belong here. I am needed here. My skills are not so great that they would be needed anywhere else. If I were to visit Illaria … I would lose too much."

"You might be surprised by how much you like it there," Shuut suggested.

Ratchin shook her head. "Enough. That's enough. I cannot! This conversation is not helping me."

Shuut could not follow Ratchin's thoughts. They were scattered and too quickly drawn behind her mental wall.

"You need your rest, and so do I. Perhaps we will meet again. I would very much like that but, if we don't, know that I always held your best interest at heart, even if you did not agree with me."

Shuut watched her leave, utterly confused by Ratchin's behaviour.

"I'm sorry I never said I love you," Shuut called out softly. Ratchin paused momentarily in the doorway before disappearing from her view.

Chapter Twenty-Two – Stolen gift

Lishe looked up at a ripple in the sky. She had been at the Paradise for over a week and had not had much success. There must have been close to one hundred different sets of power mingled together to create the boundary for this Paradise. One hundred, and she had only managed to take four tiny portions, barely enough to make a difference at all. The other powers stretched out thinly to close the gap left behind.

A second ripple caught her eye. She concentrated on it until it resolved into a shape – a crystal dragon. What was it doing all the way out here, so far away from the Drakos Mountains? She scanned the skies and realised it wasn't alone. She counted five of the clear ones before a sapphire and a fire opal one appeared.

No! Not already! she screamed inside her head. *I'm not done yet.*

She knew it must be a group of lintep come to destroy the next Paradise. Of course, they had chosen the one she knew the location of. Of course! How did they even know she would be here?

Wait, she thought, *they might not know I'm here.*

Lishe looked for a place to hide. There was barely anything out here. A clump of trees, but she couldn't reach them without going into the Paradise itself.

Nothing for it, then. She pushed her way into the Paradise and hid behind a large tree, where she could still peer out at the approaching dragons.

* * *

Ensil walked amongst his armed companions, offering advice wherever he deemed it necessary. He was pleased to see how much the Paradisian children had improved their skills since he had bestowed them with their weapons. It was clear to him that Shadow had influenced them to a great extent, but that was no tragedy, considering that he had influenced her to a great extent in her youth.

"I think that's enough for now," Princess Aislen called out from beside Pyrid. "I don't want my guards too tired to defend us should the need arise."

Ensil bowed his head and turned back to his trainees. With a few words, he thickened the air around all the weapons, so they could no longer move.

"Your princess commands you to cease and desist."

With a few more words, carefully muttered under his breath, he released all the weapons and removed the wards he had placed around them. Attempting to hide his smile at the astonished faces around him, Ensil turned and headed towards the lintep princess.

"How much longer until we enter?"

"The children will be noticed less when everyone heads back to eating hall at the end of the day's work."

Ensil huffed and went to sit by himself at the edge of the Paradise boundary. It surprised him not one bit to see Rilla walk hesitantly towards him. He indicated she should sit by his side.

"Out with it."

"I thought elves weren't so very powerful as that – except the one who wears the crown."

"Yes, I've heard that too." He nodded and smiled. "Funny thing though, there used to be a lot more us of with great power than there are now. It seems to have become less common as the years went by."

"That's ... odd." Rilla fumbled for words. "Can't the trees lend their power to an elf's own power?"

Ensil cocked an eyebrow at her. "To a certain extent, yes. However, if an elf is not so powerful to begin with, there is only so much more their tree can lend them."

The girl was silent for a long while. Ensil kept his peace, content to see where her mind led her.

"I don't believe you," she finally said. "I was not born with the same magic as you, but I can do some things now because of my bond with Elessa. I know she has lent me quite a bit of strength at various times. I think an elf's power is more tied to their tree than you say."

Ensil shrugged. "You are a unique case. A more conventional one to look at would be Eléna and Liessa. Both are bound to the same tree, yet one has plenty of power to call her own and the other has barely anything with that crown. How would you explain that with your theory?"

Rilla tapped her teeth together. "Well, perhaps elves are born with a certain amount of power themselves, but the trees should be able to amplify it more than it appears they do."

"Perhaps you are right," Ensil admitted. "There are many things we do not understand about the magnificent relationship we have with our trees."

They sat in silence after that. Ensil tried to hide the pain the conversation had caused him. There was much more to it than he had told Rilla. More that she had not figured out. It was not his place to tell her, nor could she solve the problem herself.

Eléna suspected the problem, but she'd had such a turbulent life that she had never explored the possibilities. He should have forced her to reveal Eliséo and make him her heir right from the beginning. There were so very many things he should have done. The only thing he could truly say he did not regret was fathering one of the most powerful elves who had ever lived. An elf who he dreamed could make a difference in the way Silvaren was run. There was nothing he could do about it now. Eliséo had made his choice a long time ago.

* * *

Rilla struggled to concentrate on anything. The sparring and her conversation with Ensil had distracted her. Now, with nothing else to do but wait for dusk, her mind kept drifting back to the Paradise.

She remembered every detail of that cursed place – the isolation hut, the healers' rooms, the children's hall. So many painful memories clamoured for her attention.

Focus Rilla. Elessa was in her mind – her tree standing steadfast in the swaying winds of her thoughts. *Don't think about the past. You have a new life now and you're going to help so many people in your Paradise to have that chance for themselves.*

She fell into her tree's embrace and wished she could stay there. Unfortunately, reality dragged her away. Tika, Plyke and Arishen came to sit with her, all looking as nervous as she felt.

"We'll be fine." She smiled half-heartedly. Her doubt was mirrored in their eyes. They all knew that no matter what happened, "fine" was not at all how it would be. Even if there was no bloodshed, Rilla would still have to face Erton, Arishen would still see Parthak, Tika and Plyke would have to defend their Partnership.

They sat in silence until Aislen walked over to them. "Are you ready?"

Rilla looked over and shrugged as Anya joined them. "Who's helping you this time?"

"I've given this some thought," the karlik replied seriously. "I think it's important that all of you have a part in this. It was *your* Paradise. You are the ones who made everyone realise why they needed to be destroyed."

Rilla didn't know whether to be shocked or pleased. It would certainly mean a lot to all of them. "Thank you, Anya. I ... thank you."

The karlik smiled sadly and patted her hand.

"I thought it only worked with three people," Tika pointed out, barely able to contain his excitement at having some involvement with magic. "Can we really all help?"

"I'm sure a few more won't stop it from working," Anya replied with a smile. "Now, Princess Aislen, have you decided how we're going to do this?"

Aislen nodded and called over the rest of their company. They quickly gathered around, including the stowaway twins who, Rilla knew, still hadn't understood what they were doing.

"*Most* of you know why we're here," Aislen said, staring pointedly at the twins. "We're going to do this differently to last time. Anya will help Rilla, Plyke, Tika and Arishen to destroy the boundary. Once again, we will not be showing you exactly how it is done, but these children have all been exposed to it before, so they are the exception. After that, Anya, I beg you to stay with the crystal dragons. I could not bear to face Lord Ilya should anything happen to you here.

"Umi and Ulf, you are sworn to absolute silence. We don't want to spread the word around Illaria. Things could get very difficult for your Uncle Lukys and I to manage if everyone knows before we're done. Do I have your word on it?" Aislen stared at the twins until they nodded in stupefied silence.

"Very well then. Aurelius, I realise I also entrusted the twins to you, but we may need your skills in the Paradise, therefore, I ask you to accompany us and Bastienne alone will stay behind. I trust you will be able to keep two children under control."

Rilla smiled as Bastienne grinned at the twins. "Oh, we're going to get along just fine. I'll be regaling them with tales of my youth. What could be more enjoyable for two youngsters?"

"Wonderful!" Aislen clapped her hands together as the twins groaned. "The rest of you, once the boundary is destroyed, will enter the Paradise in secret, with only the four former Paradisians, Duke Leif and Talise being visible. I assume everyone can manage that?"

Rilla wasn't surprised to discover that all the guards were skilled at blending into the background. It would, after all, be quite useful in their line of work.

"I can't," Shuut pointed out, "and I'm not staying behind."

"I will hide you," Ensil told her. "Stay by my side."

Aislen nodded and turned back to the children. "We won't be far behind you. Once we've located the Paradise leader, whom we know to be a powerful lintep, we will reveal ourselves. Be on your guard. This Paradise is hostile to all things magical, so our appearance will not be a welcome one. We need to neutralise the Paradise leader and his followers as swiftly as possible. Any questions?"

Rilla felt butterflies in her stomach as Aislen outlined her plan. It was sounding so much more dangerous now that they were here and about to do it. Plyke's hand found its way into hers. She clutched his fingers tightly.

"Let's go," Anya said as she walked towards the small forested area ahead of them.

This is it, Rilla thought to herself. *It's finally happening. We're destroying our Paradise and taking everything away from Erton, like he's been doing to everyone living here since he arrived.*

Somehow, it didn't make her as happy as she thought it would. It only made her nervous. Looking at the others, she could tell they felt the same.

They followed Anya to the boundary and repeated the words she told them as they all placed their fingertips on the crystal heart. As easily as the first Paradise, the boundary disappeared. The only difference this time was that silence greeted them. Rilla and Shuut had led them to where they knew they would be least noticed from the Paradise.

It was nearing evening. They would not have long before the bells tolled for the evening meal. Behind them, Aislen gave final instructions to Anya, Bastienne and the twins to stay away from the Paradise. There was already too much at stake here.

Rilla found herself walking through the trees, towards the isolation hut. She stopped short when she saw it. The crude hut was a ruin of charred wood and ashes.

"What happened here?" she whispered, taking a step back.

"Arishen?" Tika called out to the seer. Rilla turned slowly, in a daze to see Arishen heave the contents of his stomach onto the grass. "Arishen, what did you see?"

"You don't need to know," Shuut said, trying to bundle them along. Rilla pushed her arm away.

"Was ... was there someone in there?" she asked, hoping he wouldn't have the answer.

"What do you think?" he asked angrily, his voice rough from vomiting. "I won't make you see it, but just remember this is your father's doing!"

"Oh no, not that again!" Shuut hissed as she grabbed him by the shoulder. "We've already dealt with this. Rilla is no more to blame for this than you are. She couldn't stop it any more than you could. We're not here to lay blame on each other. We're here to stop that monster from doing anything like this again. Stop your bickering and lead the way."

Rilla listened to her sister as though from a distance, tears pricking her eyes. "Who was it?"

The seer shook his head.

"Please tell me," she begged.

"Rilla, you don't need to know." Shuut turned her away from the seer. "It won't change anything."

"I need to know what we're walking into, Shuut," Rilla replied, not caring that all the other lintep in their party had now gathered around them. "Who was it, Arishen?"

She saw him look over to Plyke and Tika. It was only when they nodded that he turned back to her.

"Remember that last night you drew everyone's attention away from me? You told some children a story about stars..."

"No, no, no, no, no!" Rilla fell to her knees. "How *could* he?"

"What's this all about, Arishen?" Aislen demanded.

"The star story was about inspiring people. Rilla told the story to some children to calm them down after I'd woken everyone in the dorm because of a bad vision," Arishen explained.

"It wasn't a story Erton would have approved of, but the children loved it. I remember their eyes lighting up as Rilla told them.

"My vision didn't show who told on them, but Erton found out they had been repeating it to each other and had two of them punished with the isolation hut. He never did that, put two people in. But he made an exception this time. Then he had Torak and Belial burn it down ... with the children inside."

Rilla had already pieced it together as Arishen spoke, but it didn't stop her from being sick when she heard it out loud. There were gasps and exclamations all around her, but she barely noticed it. All she could think was that this was her doing. Rhanya may have told her the story in secret, but she was the one who told the children. She should never have done it.

"Not now, Rilla." An arm draped around her shoulders, warmth flowing out of it. "You need to focus."

Rilla looked over at Isis, barely seeing her. It was then that she heard the bells tolling for evening meal. The sound brought her back to the moment. She would never let Erton harm another person. She had already taken his Paradise away from him – he just didn't know it yet.

"I'm going to make him pay," she said as she got to her feet.

* * *

Isis, watch her. Aislen quickly threw the thought to the fire mistress, hoping Rilla wouldn't hear it. This was going to be worse than she had anticipated. Rilla was powerful and, now, certainly emotional enough to do something rash. Aislen's only hope was that she and Isis could somehow prevent the worst from happening.

"It's time," she said aloud. "I need the four of you to lead the way. Pretend that you've returned with two new people for the Paradise."

"That story isn't going to work," Plyke pointed out. "Humans are only meant to be able to find one Paradise. As soon as they see us, they'll know we're either not human or the boundary is broken."

"True." Aislen breathed out. "Well, all we can hope is that they don't panic until we find and detain Erton. Let's go."

She let those still visible walk ahead ten paces before following them with her lintep guard. It played out exactly as they she had planned. They merged with all the other residents crossing over from the farm lands to the eating hall. She noticed a few flickers of recognition, but those people quickly averted their eyes. A handful of people let their gaze linger on Leif and Talise but even they did not say anything. It was clear none of them wanted to be singled out as troublemakers. Were they all loyal to Erton or afraid of him?

It was eerie how similar this Paradise looked to the first broken one. She knew she would be able to find her way around from just the quick tour Brynt had given her of his home. They managed to walk almost the entire way to the eating hall before the alarm was raised.

"What in the Outworld are *you* doing here?"

A burly man walked up to Rilla and poked her in the shoulder. Surprisingly, the girl didn't retaliate. She only stared up coldly at the man and spoke in an icy voice.

"Torak, why don't you run along and fetch Erton? Tell him Rilla is here to see him." The man looked uncertainly at another overly muscled man who walked up beside him. "Oh, and if either of you ever dare touch me again, I'll make you rue every day you placed me in that isolation hut."

Aislen was surprised to see a flicker of fear in their eyes. Torak ran into the eating hall, leaving the other man behind to watch them. By now, a small crowd had gathered around them. Whispers flew all around.

"What are they doing back here?"

"Never mind what. How did they get back in through the barrier?"

"Magic!"

"Magic!"

The chorus soon went around the small crowd. People flooded out of the eating hall as the cries became louder.

"What's the meaning of this?" a loud voice boomed from behind the crowd. It instantly parted to allow a lean, hollow-faced man through. He stopped short when he saw the children. "I believe you were banished to the Outworld. Leave this instant."

"You didn't exile us," Rilla replied calmly. "We left to get away from you."

"Then why ever would you come back?" he sneered.

Aislen shook her head, even knowing that Rilla couldn't see her. The girl took a candle from her pocket and held it out in front of her.

"Everyone still remembers that you are my father. Now they'll know what you are."

"Torak! Belial! Seize her!" Erton shrieked, pointing frantically at them. "Seize all of them! They return on pain of death."

Aislen felt her power merge with another's as she reached out to restrain the two bulky men. At least her guards were doing as they'd been told.

"Don't just stand there. Seize them!" Erton screamed as Rilla lit her candle, making the flame grow as high as her head for the briefest moment.

"Magic!" a Paradisian cried out. "She's a lintep!"

"And Erton is her father," Tika pointed out. "Which means your Paradise leader has been a lintep all along. He's been killing people, or driving them away, so no one would ever realise the truth and he could control you."

"Lies! All lies!" Erton sneered over the murmurs of the crowd.

Silence fell as a young girl walked past Erton. Aislen watched as the blood drained from Arishen's face.

"Even if he is a lintep, which I highly doubt, he never used his powers on us. He kept us safe from people like you." She pointed at Arishen. "This one was my Partner *before* I realised what he was. He sees things in his dreams – things that should be secret. He pries into your life without asking permission."

"That's not what happens," Arishen replied quietly. "I can't control what I see."

"Then you admit it's true," Erton said as he regained his composure. "You pry into people's lives. You see their secrets."

Aislen saw Rilla grip Arishen's fingers. The boy squeezed back and seemed to find his strength.

"I saw plenty of secrets," Arishen replied. "But I kept silent for fear of what you would do to me. I know all the people in your Paradise who would love to plot against you, those who have powers. But I also saw Torak and Belial killing some of them on your orders.

"I should never have kept silent about that, but now I have a chance to fix that mistake. Rilla, can you show them all my visions of the Paradise?"

That was it. Now it was getting too dangerous. Aislen revealed herself.

"Rilla is not skilled enough for that, but I am."

Amidst a chorus of gasps, shrieks and people fainting, Aislen signalled to her companions, all of whom became visible.

"I advise you not to try anything, Erton," Aislen told him. "My guards can and will detain you as easily as they are already doing to your own guards."

Erton was white with fury but remained still and silent. Aislen gently touched Arishen's mind. Though the boy was clearly afraid to let her in his mind, his anger fuelled his need. Master Reuben had trained him well. All the visions he wanted her to see were right there, waiting for her.

She took the visions and projected them to all gathered. Some of the Paradisians reacted with fear and anger at her touch, but most watched in shocked silence. The last vision was of a man being smothered in his sleep by Torak and Belial.

"Rhanya!" Rilla gave a strangled cry. The girl turned to another Paradisian. "Ursher, you told me sometimes it's just their time to die. How could you not have heard them coming?"

The man shook his head, sadly. "We had to keep silent. Do you really think we didn't know these 'accidents' were anything but that? We had no choice but to go along with it or be killed ourselves. You saw what happened to Rhanya when he helped *her*."

A finger was jabbed at Shuut. Aaron's eldest granddaughter glared at the man.

"I repaid my life debt to Rhanya by taking these children out of this Paradise. I could have easily left them behind to be executed, but I didn't. Each of you had a chance to step forward and try to stop it. As far as I can see, you're all to blame.

"You have this one chance to change your future. If you don't take it, *this* could be you."

Show them Arishen's vision of the isolation hut.

Aislen was surprised to hear Shuut's voice in her mind but lost no time in taking her suggestion.

"These children did nothing except retell a story told to them by Rilla, which had in turn been told to her by Rhanya. Erton has had innocent children killed."

It happened before any of her guards could react. Erton pulled a dagger from the folds of his clothes and threw himself at Rilla. The dagger bit deeply into skin, dark blood flowed out from the heart. Rilla screamed.

"Plyke!"

Aislen blinked in shock as she watched Kora's son fall to the grass. He had thrown himself in front of his cousin.

"Detain him and anyone else who struggles," Aislen commanded her guards but before they could do anything, Erton's feet and shins were surrounded by earth, rooting him to the ground. Ensil locked eyes with her for an instant and nodded.

"Kayte, see to Plyke."

The healing mistress was already on her knees beside the boy before Aislen had finished speaking. She ripped open his shirt, leaving the dagger untouched. Aislen looked on in horror as life seeped out of Plyke. How could this be happening?

"There's too much damage. I can't fix his heart. He needs a new heart and I don't have one to give him." Kayte looked up at Aislen with a bleak expression.

* * *

He needs a new heart. Rilla heard the words repeat themselves over and over in her mind as she struggled to breathe. Suddenly, it dawned on her. There was a heart, if she could take it.

Rilla knelt beside Kayte and closed her eyes. She stretched out her power in one long, thin tendril, seeking out the thing she knew would be Plyke's only hope. It was almost like that time back in Turon when she'd followed the fringa around Dell's Inn, except this time her mind didn't leave her body.

She carefully shot her power back through the Paradise, through the clump of trees, out to where the crystal dragons were waiting with Bastienne, the twins and Anya.

Anya, forgive me, Rilla thought as she let her tendril feel around for the crystal heart. She found it in the stonemason's pocket, wrapped her tendril around it and pulled. Anya was initially dragged along with it, but the crystal heart soon tore through her pocket and sped towards Rilla.

Within moments, the stone was in her hand. Knowing Mistress Kayte would stop her if she knew what she was about to do, Rilla leaned over Plyke, pretending to cry. She pulled out the dagger and sliced enough skin for her to see the wounded heart.

Kayte realised what she was doing a moment too late. Rilla had already pushed the crystal heart between Plyke's ribs down to his pierced heart. Her fingers, slick with blood, slipped as she tried to manoeuvre it towards the left side of the heart where it was damaged. To her surprise, the crystal and flesh began to meld together without her help.

"What are you doing?" Kayte asked in horror. "Rilla, you're going to kill him."

"He's already dying, and you said there was nothing you could do," Rilla told her through gritted teeth. "I can't just let him die."

"This isn't going to work! You don't know what you're doing."

"Then help me!" Rilla cried out in tears.

"Kayte, it's worth trying," Aislen said gently. "You and Médard should help her. There will be time enough for reprimands later."

Kayte shook her head angrily. "Rilla, Isis and Aurelius, I need a small portion of your energy. No, Rilla, don't argue with me. Your energy will suffice, and you can watch how we use it."

Rilla didn't waste any time pooling a decent, but not life-threatening, amount of her energy at her fingertip. She held it out for Kayte, as did Isis and Aurelius. They looked as drained as she felt, dark rings appearing under their eyes, as they slumped down on the grass.

Kayte took their balls of energy and placed them above Plyke's mutilated heart. Rilla put her hand on Plyke's arm so that she could see and feel everything that was happening.

Médard guided the balls of energy around the heart, allowing bits of them to rest around the wound. He then settled the rest of the energy in the crystal heart and passed that over to Kayte as he worked to collect the blood that was pooling in Plyke's lungs and redirect it back into his veins.

Rilla observed in wonder as Kayte took the energy in the crystal heart and spread it over every facet of the carved flower, changing it to once more resemble an actual heart. She worked slowly and carefully to bring Plyke's own power into the crystal heart. That was when it dawned on Rilla – the crystal heart was the power source keeping the dragons alive, but this one was so small, it couldn't work on its own. A portion of Plyke's power would always be needed to make it work. That, in turn, would amplify the power of the heart, making it keep Plyke's heart from failing. She had changed him forever. He would never be able to be separated from the crystal heart. What had she done?

Peace, little one, Elessa tried to soothe her. *You have saved his life. Nothing more, nothing less. He will not blame you for that.*

Rilla was doubtful. She pulled her hand away from Plyke's arm and drew her knees to her chest, rocking back and forth as she watched Kayte and Médard work for a long time on Plyke.

She felt a head settle on her shoulder as someone sat beside her. Tika had tears in his eyes as he leaned against her. She could feel his terror seeping out of him with that skin contact. Rilla put her arm around him and held him close as, together, they watched with bated breath.

"He'll survive," Kayte told them as she and Médard withdrew from Plyke. "That was a very rash decision you made, Rilla."

"But it saved Plyke's life?" Tika asked in a small voice. Kayte looked down at him in pity.

"Yes, it certainly did."

"Then I don't want you yelling at her," he replied firmly. "Plyke is her cousin. She may be the only other person out here who cares about him as much as I do. If I had lost my Partner when you could have saved him, but chose not to, I would *never* have forgiven you."

At that moment, Anya, with Bastienne and the twins close on her heels, came crashing through the crowd.

"What have you done with it?" she asked furiously. "Give me back my heart!"

Kayte raised an eyebrow at Tika. "You forget, there was more to this than Plyke's life."

Rilla looked between Tika and Anya, then down at Plyke.

"It's my fault Anya." She slowly got to her feet. "Plyke was injured. He needed a heart. I knew you had one..."

"It was not yours to take!" the karlik yelled before Rilla had a chance to explain. "That heart was a gift to my family from the crystal dragons to keep the karliki safe. You have *stolen* that gift without a hope of giving it back!"

"I'm sorry, Anya." Rilla knelt in front of the karlik, tears in her eyes. "I'm sorry! I know I can never repay you, but I couldn't just let Plyke die."

"Don't just apologise to *me*, Rilla," Anya replied hotly. "Who knows how the heart will work in the body of a lintep? It may be that it can never be used in the same way again."

Rilla lifted her head with hope. "It could be that its power is amplified because of his power."

"And what will you do if it isn't?" she asked bitterly. "Then you've stolen from the karliki and ruined the hopes of every remaining Paradise."

"No, she hasn't," Tika said in a small voice. "The prophecy said this would happen. *When a crystal heart beats in the body of another.*"

Rilla looked at Tika, stunned. How could the prophecy be about Plyke? It named *her*.

Chapter Twenty-Three – Thief

Lishe seethed with anger as the meddlers entered the broken Paradise. At least from this angle, she had gotten a glimpse of how they had done it. From what she had seen, it all came down to a stone belonging to the blonde karlik. Perhaps if she stole it, that would slow their progress.

Though, that won't matter at all if I can't find the rest of the Paradises, she thought to herself. *Surely, they have a map somewhere. I just need to find it.*

Her chance soon came. The karlik was suddenly dragged along the grass until something flew out of her pocket. She furiously ran after it with old Master Bastienne and two children following close in her wake.

A smile spread across Lishe's dirt-smeared face. She waited until they had crashed past her in the trees before wrapping more power around herself. No point letting the crystal dragons realise she was poking around where they would say she didn't belong.

As she approached the clear crystal ones, she saw they were all sleeping heavily. They must have flown all the way from Illaria to be so exhausted. She shrugged. That would make it easier to search the bags slung over their massive bodies.

Careful not to waking the sleeping beasts, Lishe methodically searched through all the bags on the clear crystal dragons. They were only full of spare clothes and food. The sapphire dragon's bag held a few pots in addition to more food. Lishe became frustrated. Surely, they would not come all this way without a map!

The fire opal dragon stirred and opened one lazy eye as she approached it. Lishe froze. Even with all her power wrapped around her, she was in no doubt that this looming hulk of crystal could burn her to cinders within seconds if it chose.

She waited, still as stone, until the dragon placed its head back on the grass and closed its eyes once more. Carefully and ever so slowly, she walked up to the bags slung over its side. She searched through them as gently as she could. The first was full of bandages and other medicinal supplies. The other had more sets of clothes. Just as Lishe was about to give up, her fingers closed around a small scroll.

Heart beating wildly, she pulled it out, tucked it in her pocket and fled to the safety of the trees. She sank down against the trunk of the biggest tree she could find and sat there, breathing hard, waiting to see if any of the crystal dragons had realised what she had done.

When she was certain they weren't coming after her, Lishe retrieved the scroll from her pocket and unrolled it. She couldn't believe her eyes. It was a map of part of the Outworld with circles around bits of ... nothing. Each circle was numbered from one to eleven. The first circle had a cross through it. The second circle – she peered at the map closely. This Paradise was exactly where the second circle was. She closed her eyes with a content sigh and leaned back against the tree. She'd found a map of the Paradises. Now all that was left to do was travel to the closest one and steal as much power as she could before they arrived. They were bound to realise, at some point, that the map had been stolen.

Then to steal that stone, she thought. *If I can steal that, I may be able to stop them completely.*

* * *

Eliséo shook violently, wrapped in his blankets. Elessa was not letting his thoughts through to Rilla but she was allowing him to see everything that was happening to her. He watched, helplessly, as her father pulled a dagger. Had he been there, he would not have stood as far back as Ensil. He would have been right by her side, sword drawn, protecting her.

He saw Plyke fall and cried out in shock. He laid his cheek on Elessa's smooth trunk, needing to feel something solid against his skin.

At some point, Eléna was by his side. She gathered him up into a tight embrace and held him, whispering soothing sounds, until he stopped shaking.

"We almost lost her." He looked up at his mother, helplessly.

"I know," she told him gently. "However, she is alive, and she saved Plyke's life. All will be well."

"How do you know that?" He pulled away from her in confusion.

"Ensil will not let Rilla out of his sight now. She will not be attacked again."

"No." Eliséo shook his head. "How did you know to come here? How did you know what happened?"

"What is the meaning of this?" Liessa yelled as she stormed up the walkway into Elessa. Eliséo noted angrily that she had not waited for permission to enter.

"What is the meaning of what?" he asked her calmly, hundreds of years of practise coming in to play.

"Your tree's unnatural bond with that lintep child has gone too far. Tell her to break it. Now."

A cold fury settled in Eliséo's mind as he ensured his thoughts were cut off from Rilla.

"Liessa, I don't know what has brought about this reaction, but I can assure you there is nothing *unnatural* in Elessa's bond with Rilla."

His sister glared at him through slitted eyes. "You will address me as *Queen* Liessa."

"*Queen* Liessa," he said curtly, though he kept his head held high. "My tree will not break her bond with the lintep child."

"I can make your life so miserable that your tree will do *anything* I say."

Eliséo kept his eyes firmly averted from his mother, though he was in desperate need of her advice. What had happened to make his sister react like this?

"I very much doubt that," he told her icily. "You have no power over us."

In a petulant fit of rage, Liessa stamped a foot on the floor. "I will strip you of your title of Ambassador of the Elves and never let you leave Silvaren."

"You could try, but you will never succeed in keeping me prisoner." His voice was deathly calm as he spoke to her.

"Then I will banish you to the Outworld and burn down your tree so that you may never see her again."

"Liessa!" Eléna held a hand out to her daughter. "Think what you are saying.

You cannot threaten to burn a tree."

Liessa stared coldly at her mother. "I will not be told what to do. You are no longer the queen, Mother."

Eliséo stood up, taking strength from Elessa to steady himself. Liessa turned back towards him.

"You have exactly one day to force your tree to end this abomination."

He looked at her with cold rage. There was a flicker of doubt in her eyes.

"Liessa, I think it high time we tell you a secret that has been kept from you for over seven hundred years. You are not the only one with a claim to the throne. I am your brother." He heard his mother draw in a sharp breath by his side but did not break his stare. "I control more power than you could ever imagine, even with your precious crown.

"I never wanted the throne, but rest assured that should you attempt to carry out your threat against my tree, I will defeat you. I will show everyone what kind of queen you are, and they will support me. It has always been the way of the elves to crown the most powerful among them.

"If you leave things as they are, promise never to lay a finger on Elessa, never insist she break her bond with Rilla, never threaten to isolate me from my tree or from the Outworld, then I will keep this secret. It is your decision, sister. Choose wisely."

Her expression did not change. Eliséo had expected some kind of reaction – anger, fear, disappointment – but there was nothing.

"You have exactly one day to make your decision," Liessa repeated herself. "I will expect to see you kneel to me before every elf in Silvaren tomorrow evening. You will apologise to them for the grief you caused them tonight and you will swear that your tree will break her bond with that girl. Otherwise, I *will* burn her down."

Before he could reply, she turned and left. Eliséo stared after her in silence. There was no way that he could ask Elessa to break her bond with Rilla, if it was even possible. He was left with no choice. In exactly one day, he would either be crowned as king or executed. His sister would allow no other alternative.

"You should not have incited her so!" Eléna hid her face in her hands. Eliséo had rarely seen his mother so emotional.

"I did nothing to her." He gestured to the empty walkway. "You both arrived, unannounced and uncalled for. You held me, and she threatened me. I do not understand what caused this."

"Elessa sent your grief out into Silvaren."

"She ... I don't understand."

"Perhaps she has never explained it to you before," Eléna said in a soft voice. "All of the trees are aware of the possibility, but few do it consciously. You've often asked how far away I can read thoughts. I think this is because you do not understand how I can always tell when you feel troubled.

"Elessa feels as you do all the way down to her roots. Silva's roots reach out to touch many of the trees of Silvaren and so your moods travel to me, even when you are not aware of it."

Understanding bloomed in Eliséo's mind.

"Then why has Liessa never felt it before?"

Eléna shook her head. "I have not taught my daughter many things which perhaps I should have. She does not listen to Silva the way she should – she never has.

"She only felt it this time because Elessa was overwhelmed by your fear. Your tree sent out your fear to every tree in Silvaren she touches and they, in turn, must have sent it out further. Liessa could not help but feel it."

Eliséo clenched his fists. "*This* is reason she wants Elessa to break her bond with Rilla? Because we feared for her life and now every elf in Silvaren knows it? Does she think other elves will race to ask a lintep or a human to bond with their tree?"

"No. Only I know the true cause of your fear. Elessa told me herself. Liessa only assumes it has to do with Rilla."

They stood together in silence for a long while.

"Do you ... have you yet decided what you will do?"

Eliséo glared angrily at his mother. "She has left me with no choice. I cannot and will not ask Elessa to break her bond with Rilla. She is too dear to both of us for that. I will tell our people the truth and they will decide."

Tears fell from Eléna's eyes. He knew she feared she would lose one of her children the next day.

Chapter Twenty-Four – Civil Strife

Aislen sat in the tavern, Séverin standing nearby, ever alert for trouble. Kayte and Médard were still with Plyke in the healers' house. Rilla and Tika had insisted on accompanying them, much to the chagrin of the Paradise healers. She shook her head at the absurdity of this place. They hoarded their knowledge to the point where even children were not to enter the different trade workshops. She knew Arishen had only followed them because he feared being left alone with the other Paradisians. She could feel a sad sort of hopelessness cascading out from him. That poor boy felt out of place no matter where he was. Aislen had asked Isis to watch over them, to make sure they didn't interfere with Kayte and weren't bothered by anyone else.

Duke Leif and Talise, with a few of the guards, had quickly set to work to find a way to isolate Erton. He was clearly the most dangerous person in the Paradise and none of them wanted to be constantly looking over their shoulders.

Bastienne and the twins were making friends among the children of the Paradise. Aislen had discreetly asked the old master to feel for any lintep, or half-blood among them. This would probably be the most dangerous time for their powers to be discovered, but also the most likely time for them to slip up and reveal themselves.

The rest of her guards were keeping a watchful eye on the Paradisians in case any trouble should break out during the night. Only Anya remained with her now.

"I'm sorry, Anya," she muttered, once again, head in hands. "We didn't know what she was doing until it was too late."

"Bah, that girl is too reckless." Anya thumped her hand angrily on the table. "She feels too deeply and can't bear to lose anyone close to her. I know her heart is in the right place, but she needs to slow down so she doesn't keep making a mess of things."

Aislen lifted her head. "She *did* save his life. That's something at least."

"I know," Anya relented. "In truth, I probably would have done the same thing if our positions had been reversed. What really concerns me now is what happens next? Can Plyke destroy a Paradise boundary by himself with the crystal heart within him? Or do we resort to asking the crystal dragons for another heart?"

"Well, Tika was right, the prophecy *does* say a crystal heart will beat in another's body, but that may not help us. I suppose I should go out and explain the situation to the crystal dragons," Aislen rose to her feet. "It will give them more time to discuss their options with one another. I also need to know how soon they will be fit to fly us back to Illaria. I can't justify keeping the twins in the Outworld any longer than necessary."

"Do you want me to come with you?" Anya asked wearily. Aislen shook her head.

"Séverin and I will bring back our packs so we can make ourselves comfortable. I assume most of our party will spend the night here. You're free to spend the night wherever you choose, though I'd feel better if you let one of the guards shadow you."

A few of the clear crystal dragons turned their snouts towards her as she entered the clearing. When they saw her, they lazily turned away and closed their eyes once more. They were truly exhausted. Thankfully, the next Paradise was closer to Illaria. They could ride there in a day with horses. That would be better than continually draining the crystal dragons of all their strength.

Pyrid and Celtan did not stir as she approached them. She laid a hand on the fire opal dragon's snout, stroking gently. A satisfied growl escaped him. He turned one golden eye on her.

"What happened?" he asked.

She explained everything to him, noticing as she did that the other dragons were listening closely, though their eyes were still closed.

"It won't work," Pyrid told her. "I don't think it will, anyway. The heart has enough magic to either beat or be used for other magic – not both. Your young Plyke may not need *all* the magic of the crystal heart to stay alive, but I doubt there will be enough to spare to destroy an entire Paradise."

"But the prophecy," Aislen began before Pyrid cut her off.

"It's a poem, Aislen. Not to be taken literally. The heart cannot work the way you suggest."

Aislen sighed. "We'll have to try it anyway. I think his own power will keep him alive in the moment it takes to see if the heart can still work in the way we need it to."

Pyrid looked over at Celtan, who pointedly kept his eyes shut. Aislen knew they would discuss the possibility of offering another heart once she was gone, but she did not hold much hope of that. Not when their first gift had effectively been taken from the true owners without their knowledge or permission.

"Tell me, Aislen, did you send anyone here after Rilla took the heart?" Pyrid asked her softly.

Eyebrows raised, she shook her head.

"You would do well to be on your guard. I do not think you are alone here. I felt someone here, though I couldn't see anyone."

"Lishe?" Aislen whispered. Pyrid only looked at her. Ice shot through her veins. Aislen searched her rucksack and found only clothes. Her precious scroll was gone! The memory of Kora's protectiveness, always keeping the map on her person intruded her thoughts. Aislen irritably pushed aside her overwhelming feeling of stupidity.

As twisted as Lishe was, she was still terribly clever. It would not take her long at all to realise she now held a map of the location of the Paradises and the order in which they were to be destroyed. Not allowing herself to panic, Aislen turned to her guard.

"Séverin, we'll take all the bags back with us. How soon will we be able to return to Illaria? The guards will need to stay behind to help the Paradisians."

"Ah, Princess Aislen," Séverin cut in as he gathered the bags. "I would be remiss in my duty if I allowed you, and the rest of the royal family, to travel without an escort."

Aislen sighed. "Very well, all but one of the guards will remain, leaving eighteen of us to return. I think Duke Leif and Talise may want to go to Deuterfoss to rally troops. In fact, we may need them to do so. We cannot spare many more guards for the other Paradises and speed is of the essence."

Pyrid joined the conversation at that point. "If we fly at a slower pace than we did to get here, we could leave tomorrow afternoon. Otherwise, we dragons will need rest for two full days. The scouts are good at what they do, but even Loreli does not make them fly such distances. As for Celtan and I, well, we're getting on in years. I dare say in our youth we could have flown these distances day after day."

"But what with Uncle Aaron utilising you more than expected, you're exhausted. Anyone can see that." Aislen nodded to herself. "Very well, if they agree, I may ask that Duke Leif and Talise are escorted to Deuterfoss with whoever is most recovered tomorrow afternoon. The rest of us will wait until you are fully rested. No doubt there will be things for us to take care of here."

"I'm ready, Princess Aislen." Séverin hefted the final bag off the dragons. Awkwardly, he slung some over his shoulders and others along his arms. Aislen almost laughed at the sight, but she was too weary. Instead, she sent out her power to lift as many of the bags as Séverin could not comfortably hold.

"Until tomorrow, then."

She turned and walked back with Séverin, her mind already racing. If only they had left Eliséo in Illaria, then she would have been able to ask Rilla to contact him – to alert her father to send out a group of lintep to the next Paradise to watch out for Lishe. Even riding horses to exhaustion, she would not be able to reach the next Paradise in less than ten days, but Lishe appeared to be capable of so much more than most lintep and could get there sooner.

Lishe also had the advantage of knowing the location of the next Paradise. Aislen would need to talk to Bastienne about it. The next Paradise was near his old home. Perhaps his father had taken him there once. She shook her head. Kora would be furious when she learned that the duplicate map had been stolen.

By the time they crossed the bridge to the main part of the Paradise, Aislen could hear shouting and the clash of weapons.

"Perfect," she said through gritted teeth. "We leave for a short time and the entire Paradise dives into chaos."

Séverin dropped their packs as they ran towards the commotion. Aislen couldn't blame him – there was nothing worth protecting. She dropped her own load next to his.

As they neared Erton's wooden dwelling, the noise grew louder. His followers were trying to free the three prisoners, while the rest of the Paradisians were trying to stop them. Aislen's guards easily held off Erton's so-called sheep, but there was little they could really do to stop them without causing injury.

The rest of the Paradisians were out for blood. Now that it had sunk in what their leader had really been doing to them, they would not be content until he was dead or gone. Aislen checked her mental wall and pulled her power away from them – she needed to keep a clear head.

She looked around at the mayhem. Carpenters armed with their tools, cooks armed with knives, others holding anything that would serve as a weapon, all of them swinging wildly at Erton's loyalists, who were themselves similarly armed.

The rebels hurled insults as much as weapons, striking at any who tried to stop them reaching Erton. His defenders – she wryly thought sheep did not aptly describe them now – fought on both fronts, against the rebels and the lintep guards. It wasn't a fair fight – their numbers were already dwindling as they fell, injured, to the ground.

Aislen searched for any way to stop the fighting. She looked at Séverin who gave her a hard stare. They both knew the only real way to stop this was to restrain all the humans with their powers. This was not the way it was supposed to happen!

Take their weapons! she sent the thought to every lintep within reach.

Powers overlapped as Aislen and the guards struggled to disarm the Paradisians. It barely made a difference. The weapons were dumped unceremoniously to the side of the building, but the Paradisians were now beating each other with tightly clenched fists.

"Stop!" A voice called out over the top of all of them. "Look at this! Look what he's doing to you when he's not even in control."

Aislen looked out over the angry mass to see Tika. Beside him, his Partner was hunched over, an arm wrapped protectively around his chest, with Rilla, Arishen, Kayte and Isis standing behind them. To her surprise, the fighting slowed to a halt. Some looked shamefaced and turned to face the small boy.

"I understand more than most what Erton has done to you. He killed my mother for no other reason than that she told me I was her son. My Partner now has a crystal heart because Erton tried to kill Rilla, his own daughter.

"You remember her? The poor girl whose name we couldn't even remember because we were too scared of Erton to use it? She spent half her life in the isolation hut because he was scared you would find out he is a lintep. But with all he did to us, you won't be any better than him if you try to harm him and his *sheep* now.

"And you," he said turning to Erton's followers. "How can you stand there and defend a man who has lied to you since he set foot in this Paradise? Parthak, he made you renounce your own Partner because Arishen was blessed with a precious gift – a gift you sneered at because it terrified you. Were you afraid he would see some horrible secret about you? All Arishen saw in this place was that your leader killed those who were helpless against him!

"In the Outworld, Arishen's gift saved our lives so many times. Plyke and Rilla's powers as lintep have blossomed into something I could only ever dream of possessing. Out there, wonders beyond your wildest dreams exist, but Erton has kept you too afraid of the Outworld to let you experience any of them.

"We've been guests in the elven forest of Silvaren, delved down into the karlik tunnels of Goraburg, visited the crystal dragons in the Drakos Mountains and now live in the lintep stronghold of Illaria. None of these things would have been possible had we not left this cursed Paradise to finally start living.

"Erton has been holding you back from all the wonders of the Outworld, but he can't hold you back anymore. The Paradise boundary is gone. Others will start to pass through this village on their travels. You are free to come and go as you please, but only if you break free of his hold."

Aislen listened in amazement as Tika's words had as calming an effect on the people as Aaron's powers usually did. The angry Paradisians backed down and a few of the loyalists looked down, ashamed of themselves. Of course, there were always going to be those who were too blind to see the truth, but there seemed to be fewer of them now.

Even the mention of the fact that their Paradise boundary was no longer there did not cause the outrage it should have. There were many problems they would need to solve, including dealing with the absurd situation that children didn't know who their own parents were, but Aislen was hopefully that could all wait until the next morning. She was too tired to deal with it now.

Tika, please ask them all to return to their homes. We can deal with this in the morning.

Aislen felt him instinctively flinch away from her mental voice before a smile spread over his face. This boy was so enraptured by magic, the mere touch of it was euphoric to him.

"Please, return to your homes. Parents, this is the last night you will ever have to spend away from your children. In the morning, you will be reunited with your family. We will find a way to fix all the problems Erton has created. Tomorrow."

The bulk of the Paradisians, including most of the loyalists turned away, some with smiles. She noticed a closeness between some which had been missing before – an arm around a waist, hands intertwined, shoulders softly jostled. The weight that had been lifted by Tika's words was palpable. Aislen found herself smiling despite the terrible evening.

The problem of the lingering loyalists remained. There were five of them. It was amazing that such a small number of people had controlled the rest of the Paradisians for so many years. Aislen could understand that they would not be happy to have their power stripped so suddenly and completely, but that did not change the fact that something had to be done with them.

"The five of you are free to return to your homes," she said as she walked towards the group, Séverin a pace behind her.

The young girl, Arishen's erstwhile Partner, stared at her with cold eyes. "You presume to tell us what we are free or not free to do in our own Paradise?"

"Parthak, just let it be," Arishen said, exasperatedly. "Erton is not the Paradise leader anymore. You don't need to act all high and mighty on his behalf anymore."

"I'm sure that would suit you, Arishen," she spat out his name. "You were never going to be anything more than a thorn in his side had you stayed. Too bad your visions couldn't save you from this."

She punched him. Or tried to. Her arm stopped mid-strike. Aislen looked carefully at the faces of all her lintep to see who had done it. Rilla hid it well, but a slight twitch at the corner of her mouth gave her away.

"His visions don't need to save him from the likes of *you*," Rilla sneered. "He has friends enough not to have to watch his own back in the middle of the night while Erton's sheep do his dirty work for him. You never deserved him as a Partner. He has found a peaceful and safe home in Illaria where half the lintep wish they were blessed with his gift rather than cursing him for having been born with it.

"Go back to your home now or join Erton and his minions in his prison. I don't care one way or the other but be aware that I *will not* let you hurt any of my friends. You've only seen a portion of my power. Don't force me to show you more."

Aislen was torn with indecision. Rilla was unpredictable at the best of times. She didn't want to imagine what else the girl was capable of if she felt any of her friends were truly being threatened.

"Let's go," Parthak told her group. "We'll deal with this lot in the morning."

Aislen watched as Erton's sheep walked away from their leader's house. She wasn't certain it was the best idea to allow them free rein, but they weren't here to become tyrants. And there was so much that needed to be sorted out before any of them went to sleep.

"Séverin, set a watch. I don't want any of them to step out of their residences tonight. We'll figure out what to do with them tomorrow. Duke Leif, Talise and Rilla, I need a word with you. The rest of you, try to get a good night's rest. There will be much to do on the morrow.

"Bastienne and the twins are in the children's hall with one of our guards. If any of you wish to join them, you are free to do so. In light of recent events, I suggest the rest of you lodge in the tavern tonight. I don't want us to be scattered too far from each other."

Chapter Twenty-Five – Rhanya's girl

"Rilla, you know this place the best." Aislen turned to her once the others had departed. "We need somewhere quiet to talk. Somewhere we won't be overheard."

Rilla shook her head and closed her eyes.

There is no safe place for us to talk. She opened her connection with Elessa and Eliséo. *Will it do any more harm to use the mist? If Erton had ears everywhere, so will his sheep.*

It is well past time when our bond could be kept secret, Eliséo replied woodenly. *Do what you must.*

Rilla flinched at the emptiness she felt within him.

Are you unwell? she asked in concern. Eliséo put up a wall between them.

Elessa, what's happening?

Nothing either of us can do anything about, the old tree replied sadly. *Do not worry yourself, Rilla. He will tell you when the time is right.*

Almost without thinking, Rilla led Aislen and the humans to the healers' house. She wondered if Rhanya's room had been used since his death. It was the only place she could think of where they would be undisturbed. Eliséo might not care who knew about their bond, but Rilla was still dubious about using her extra powers so openly.

She didn't bother knocking on the door. They had been coming and going half the evening. By now, the healers were used to people being in their house. She lay her hand on the door handle and hesitated. Shaking long distant memories from her mind, Rilla opened the door and ushered everyone in before her. She lit the lantern she knew would be on Rhanya's desk. Shadows flew eerily around the room, enough to show Rilla that no one had entered this room since she had taken Rhanya's healing pouch and filled it with everything she could fit in it. Her hand instantly went to her waist. She cringed, realising she'd stopped wearing the healer's pouch once she had reached Illaria and felt safe. It had been her constant reminder of him. Had she betrayed his memory by leaving it behind without even thinking about it?

Her hand strayed to her pocket. She breathed deeply, and her shoulders dropped as she felt Rhanya's note beneath her fingers. It was, undoubtedly, her most precious possession – more so than the tree pendant Queen Eléna had given her or the swords Master Ensil had bestowed upon her. Rhanya's note had given her the greatest gift of her life. That's where he had told her that *she* was the little star in his story. She had inspired him. Rilla still could not wrap her head around that thought. Rhanya had been everything to her. To think that she had inspired him was just unfathomable.

"Duke Leif," Aislen started, before Rilla cut her off.

"Wait!"

She closed her eyes for a moment. No need to show the humans her glowing eyes. She whispered the words for the mist bubble under her breath. In seconds, they were cocooned in a thick layer of air. Rilla opened her eyes again.

"We shouldn't be overheard in here," she told them.

Duke Leif stared at the mist around them, but Talise stared only at Rilla. She shifted uncomfortably under the woman's gaze.

"This isn't like the other lintep magic we've seen." The lady raised an eyebrow. Rilla looked over to Aislen.

"Yes, Rilla is one of our more ... special ... lintep. Her gifts are quite unique." Aislen gestured for them all to sit. Duke Leif and Talise sat upon the bed, Aislen sat at Rhanya's desk. Rilla looked around, the herb cabinet was behind her. She leaned against it and crossed her arms.

"I have bad news to report. My map has been stolen. It's only a copy, but that makes it no less dangerous in the hands of Lishe. I can't be certain she was the thief, but there are no other lintep in this Paradise who could have been near the dragons. Pyrid felt someone but could not see them."

Rilla's heart pounded in her ears. If Lishe was here, she was in danger. Why hadn't the rogue already attacked her?

Aislen continued, tearing Rilla from her thoughts. "Unfortunately, the map was not only marked with Paradise locations, but also the order we hoped to destroy them. It stands to reason that she will follow that order so as to steal as much power from the Paradises as she can before they are destroyed, presuming she has already found a way to do so. We could be terribly lucky and destroy them all before she has a chance to figure it out, but I don't think there is enough luck in all the Outworld for that."

"How far away is the next Paradise on your list?" Talise asked.

Aislen hesitated. "It's near Illaria. I would estimate it would take no less than ten days by horseback from here, and that's with fresh horses every day."

Duke Leif shook his head. "By all accounts, Lishe is a clever woman. I do not think she will ride for ten days to a Paradise that may already be destroyed by the time she arrives.

"Are there no Paradises closer to us? If I were her, I would head to one of those instead. It would throw you off my track – you wouldn't know where to find me next. It has the advantage that I would reach it before you're done destroying some of the others, which would give me more time to steal power from the boundary."

Rilla found herself nodding. Duke Leif had just described what she herself would do if she was in Lishe's position.

"She may have quite a bit more time than we'd like." Aislen looked at Rilla. "With the unexpected turn of events that took place here, we may have lost the ability to break the Paradises with such ease."

Rilla felt Talise's eyes on her again. She, in turn, studied the view from the window. It was getting late. The moon was already near the top of its arc. She tried desperately hard not to think about her father, the man who had tried to murder her in plain sight of everyone. How could a parent hate their child so very much?

"Then you'll have to find Lishe as quickly as possible." Duke Leif drew Rilla's attention away from her thoughts. "We'll need to return to Illaria, make another copy of the map and send out search parties for her while the rest of you figure out another way to destroy the Paradises. When the search parties locate her, they can send word back so you know where she is."

Aislen shook her head. "We cannot send messages over so great a distance."

Rilla cringed. She knew what was about to be asked of her. Her head was already shaking as Aislen turned to her.

"No, I won't do it."

"Rilla, please!"

"Don't make me ask. It isn't fair."

"You would rather allow Lishe to steal as much power as she likes from the Paradises until we destroy them all?"

Rilla scowled and tightened her arms across her chest.

"Rilla, child, give him the choice. He may surprise you. I think he may feel as suffocated as you do right about now."

Everyone jumped in surprised as Ensil suddenly appeared by her side. He must have been using his own mist to stay close to them earlier.

Not caring why Ensil was there, Rilla closed her eyes, trembling with fear and anger.

Eliséo?

He will not answer you tonight. Elessa was gentle but firm. *He ... cannot answer you tonight. The dragons will not have the strength to fly for at least another day. By that time, Eliséo may be able to discuss this matter with you.*

Rilla felt a cold chill run down her spine. Whatever was happening in Silvaren was her fault. *She* was the one who had suggested bringing him back to Elessa on their way to this Paradise. Had it not been for that, he would still be safe in Illaria.

Fighting back tears, Rilla shook her head. "He will not speak with me. Something is not right."

Ensil's eyes suddenly shone bright blue. He took an unsteady step back and fell awkwardly against the wall behind him, banging his head. Rilla instantly knelt by his side. Aislen and the humans quickly joined her.

"What happened?"

Ensil looked up at her with almost translucent blue eyes, tears streaming down his face. "My son has revealed himself."

"Your son?" Aislen asked in confusion.

"He what?" Rilla asked incredulously as she helped the ancient elf to his feet. "I don't understand. How do you know that?"

"There are many things you cannot begin to understand, young one. This is a dangerous time for Eliséo. If he still lives by the time we are ready to begin scouting, he will join us. If not, there are other ways." Ensil patted her on the shoulder, smiling sadly.

"Princess Aislen, let us make our plans. We will fly back to Illaria once the dragons are rested. There we will make more copies of the map. Duke Leif and Lady Talise shall take a copy with them to Deuterfoss and the other duchies sending out guards to all the Paradises.

"The other four clear crystal dragons will travel to Silvaren where, if things work out the way I hope, four elves will be waiting to join them. They will scout out the four Paradises closest to this one to see where your rogue lintep is hiding. When they have found her, they will send word so the rest of us know where to find her."

Aislen shook her head. "The dragons will not be rested enough for at least two days. Pyrid assures me that we can send one of the younger dragons, at a slower pace, tomorrow afternoon. Duke Leif, Lady Talise, your need is more urgent. I will send you with a guard and messages to Illaria. From there, you can fly to your duchies with new maps to gather soldiers."

Rilla listened without really hearing. *If he still lives.* The sentence hung in her mind. When Aislen tapped her on the shoulder, she dissipated the mist surrounding them. She did not notice Duke Leif and Lady Talise leave. She barely noticed when Aislen led her to Rhanya's bed and sat her down.

"Why did you have to say that?" Aislen asked Ensil roughly. "She's emotional enough just being in this Paradise. You did not need to make her worse."

"I could not lie to her." Rilla heard Ensil's reply, as though from a great distance. "Eliséo's life is in grave danger. All will be decided tomorrow night. Either he, or his sister, will die."

"No!" Rilla cried out. "He won't kill her. He couldn't ..."

Ensil turned to her slowly. "It may not be his choice, young one. Whenever there is more than one heir, the most powerful has as much claim as the eldest. Bloodshed may be inevitable on both sides. You must face the fact that Eliséo, himself, may be killed."

"What?" Rilla choked out. She turned to Aislen desperately. The princess looked as shocked as she was.

"What happens to Rilla if Eliséo dies?" Aislen asked the gnarled old elf. He shrugged. "Well, will she die as well?"

"I doubt it." Ensil looked at Rilla thoughtfully. "She is bound to the tree, not to Eliséo."

"Will Elessa survive his death?"

"It has been known to happen." Ensil scratched the stubble on his cheek. "Best not to dwell on these things. The more likely scenario is that Eliséo may be bound to Silva."

"How can he be bound to two trees at once?" Rilla gripped the bed beneath her so tightly her knuckles turned white. Ensil only shrugged again and walked out of the room.

Rilla reached out to Elessa but found her tree distant and distracted. Even worse was that Eliséo was completely unreachable.

"I can't lose them," she whispered.

∡ ∡ ⋈

Aislen would have slapped Ensil had Rilla not been watching. She'd been so worried about her cousin since the seer's vision of Eliséo and Aaron in the Lesa Mountains. Too many things were happening that the child had no control over. Aislen did not have to try too hard to empathise with her. The poor girl was forced to bottle up her feelings most of the time, like Aislen herself when she was younger. True, Rilla was getting a lot better at containing her feelings so she didn't overwhelm others, but there were still times when Aislen wished her cousin would ask for help.

"Aislen." Rilla looked up at her. "What do I do?"

Aislen checked her own walls, to make certain she hadn't leaked the thought out to Rilla. She looked at her young cousin with some hope. Perhaps she would finally learn to lean on others.

"You go to someone you trust and let them help you. Who do you trust Rilla? We'll find them together."

"I …" Rilla paused and looked around the room, tears filling her eyes. She shook her head. "Everyone I trust, they die or leave me behind."

Aislen risked the taboo of touching Rilla and held her in a tight embrace as the girl fell apart. She whispered soothing sounds as she stroked Rilla's fiery curls. Rilla trembled in her arms.

"Not everyone who loves you will leave you, Rilla." Aislen held her cousin tightly. "Your mother should never have been so selfish to leave you alone with Erton, but we cannot change that. All I can do is reassure you that your family, your *entire* family in Illaria will not leave you, no matter what happens."

Rilla sniffed and burrowed her face into Aislen's shoulder. "That's not true. Any of them could die, just as easily as Lord Aaron almost did. And even if what you say is true, what about Eliséo? Ensil said he might die tomorrow – that or he may become the king and be forced to bond with Silva. Either way, I'll lose him."

"You don't know that for certain. Even Ensil does not know what will happen. Just wait and see. I'm sure things will work out." Aislen tried to console her, though she barely believed her own words. She was surprised when Rilla flinched away from her.

"Things don't just 'work out'. Look at what happened today with Erton! He tried to kill me." Rilla shook her head. "He really, actually, tried to kill me – his own daughter – in front of everyone! How could he?"

"We don't get to choose our family, Rilla." Aislen was careful not to touch her again. "We only get to choose our friends and sometimes they just fall into our laps whether we want them to or not. You've had rotten luck with parents.

"There isn't anything I can do to change what your mother and father both did to you, but you have the power to not let it affect the rest of your life. You've already shown the masters and mistresses that you are not your mother's daughter when it comes to your lessons. You've shown everyone around you that you will fight to the death to save your companions, even to the point of stealing the crystal heart for your cousin when you thought you would lose him.

"Anyone who truly knows you will never compare you to your parents. They all know that you are far better than that. I've only seen glimpses from Arishen's visions and heard a little about Rhanya, but I'd wager he had more to do with forming your character than either of your parents. Cling to that thought, Rilla. Be the person Rhanya wanted you to be, not the person your parents tried to force you to become."

Rilla listened to her words in silence. Aislen felt all the hurt and anger within the girl ebb and fade away. Wiping the tears from her dirt-stained face, Rilla looked up at Aislen.

"The person Rhanya wanted me to be." Rilla smiled. "His little star."

Aislen saw her hand go to her pocket and clench something tightly.

"We need to banish Erton from this place." Rilla lifted her chin defiantly. "That or take him back to Illaria and let Lukys deal with him. If he stays here, his sheep will find a way to help him gain power again and it will still be a reflection of the Paradise we tried to destroy."

Aislen looked at her thoughtfully. "Banishing him probably isn't the best way. He will only wait until we leave and then return. We can take him back to Illaria."

Rilla nodded. "I think that would be best. We need to get him as far away from here as possible. What about his sheep?"

"I doubt any of them are lintep," Aislen pointed out. "They won't belong in Illaria and none of them, other than Torak and Belial it seems, have actually done anything terribly wrong."

"So ... they stay?" Rilla sounded crushed.

"Duke Leif may be able to negotiate for the duke of this duchy to take Torak and Belial away, but there isn't anything that can be done about the others. Don't lose hope, Rilla. These Paradisians are stronger than you give them credit for. They have survived in this harsh land for years."

Rilla nodded. "I suppose so."

Aislen got to her feet. "I think it's high time we return to the tavern. Tomorrow will be a busy day for everyone."

She opened the door and waited for Rilla. There was no way she was leaving her alone for even a moment.

Chapter Twenty-Six - Deuterfoss

Leif woke with Talise indecently close to him. He breathed in the scent of her hair and smiled. In such close quarters it might almost be seen as acceptable, but he thanked his lucky stars that none of his barons were there to see it. He watched her face as she slept, not able to continue hiding his feelings from himself. His resolve to keep her at arm's length was fading.

There really wasn't another lady in all of Deuterfoss to equal Talise. Her face had little beauty spots speckled here and there – things that the other ladies of his court tried to hide with their powders. Talise wore hers like badges of honour. That was just one of things he loved about her. She simply didn't care what anyone thought of her. It made her stronger, more self-assured. He laughed quietly as he reached out to move the hair out of her face. All the qualities he loved about her were qualities that most men tried to stamp out of their women.

She opened her eyes, smiled sleepily at him and closed them once more. He returned the smile without hesitation. He really should just ask her to be his wife, but he was afraid that for all her affection for him, she wouldn't like the life of a duchess.

You should just ask her. He heard a now familiar voice in his mind and looked over Talise's sleepy form to see Aislen seated at a table, looking at the two of them. She shook her head at him. *If you don't give her the option, how can she ever make the choice?*

He sat up, one hand still resting on Talise's arm. It felt like he was in a dream. Being spoken to by lintep in his mind, seeing their powers in full force, destroying Paradises – they were all things from old stories told around campfires. They weren't meant to be a part of his life. But now that they were ... he knew he would miss it when all of this was over.

Keeping Aislen's eye, he nodded towards a corner of the room. She stepped over several sleeping people to meet him there.

"When this is all over, do you ... will we..." he faltered.

Aislen frowned. "It would be difficult, but not impossible. There are a number of lintep in Illaria who would be happy to broaden their horizons. The only thing that stops them is fear."

"Of *us*?" Leif asked in disbelief. "What could you possibly have to fear from us? You're so powerful!"

A flicker of sorrow crossed Aislen's face. "There are very few lintep with as much power as you've seen displayed here. Most are not powerful enough to make any real difference to protect themselves if the need arose. Especially children whose power has not yet peaked. Many lintep have been killed by humans. It isn't something quickly forgotten."

Leif was shocked. He, of course, knew about the battles fought between lintep and humans, but it had never occurred to him that such magical beings could actually fear his kind.

"I ... would like to try. I think our world is a darker place because of the rift between us. Your people have already done so much to help my men. In the first broken Paradise, my men attacked even as I tried to hold them back. Instead of killing them, the lintep guards healed them – men who had attacked them! I hate to admit it, but I do not believe my men would have been so generous if they were the ones being attacked."

Aislen placed a light hand on his shoulder. "Most lintep have a gentle nature and, no matter where our true skills lie, we are all taught the art of healing. You may think it barbaric, but the way our children are taught these skills is to practise on each other, inflicting wounds and healing them. In this way, they come to learn the consequences of their actions and what it takes to make things better."

Leif listened in increasing wonder at this amazing race of people. "It *would* seem quite strange to our own healers, but I daresay if brawlers were made to heal each other, there would be fewer scuffles in our taverns." He laughed to himself. "What fun it would be trying to implement that in Deuterfoss!"

The lintep princess smiled at him. "I believe you are just the man to do that." She turned serious after a moment's thought. "Have you decided how to proceed when you return to Deuterfoss? Do you know how long it will take to fly to each of the other duchies and have soldiers sent out to the Paradises?"

"I have a standing army," he told her. "Only a fraction of them would be needed for each Paradise. A squadron of them have already been sent to Brynt's Paradise.

"It may be safest to send my soldiers out to all the Paradises within my duchy to await your arrival. Of course, the first troops will be sent to the next Paradise immediately. However, I don't know if I will be able to accompany them.

"I will likely be the one who travels to each other duchy to convince the dukes and duchess to send troops out to the Paradises." Leif looked over at Talise. "Though, I hope not to be absent from Deuterfoss for too long."

Aislen laughed at him. "You really ought to just…"

He cut her off before she could say another word. Talise had risen and was on her way over to them as they spoke. Even the way she moved bewitched him.

The lintep princess nudged him playfully. A crease furrowed Talise's brow for a moment before the lintep moved away from him. Leif tried to hide his smile.

Yes, I will ask her soon, he thought to himself.

Good. Aislen's voice sounded in his mind but he felt her retreat before he could rebuke her.

"When are we leaving?" Talise asked as she stepped over the last lintep between them.

"Not until this afternoon," Leif informed her. "We need the crystal dragon to be as rested as possible before we depart. It's a long flight back to Deuterfoss, especially by way of Illaria."

Talise nodded and turned to Aislen. "Is there anything we can help you with in the meantime?"

A smile found its way to the princess' face. "As a matter of fact, I think I have the perfect task for you if you don't mind working with one of my people."

Aislen stepped over towards Tika, the small-framed boy who had stopped the fighting the night before. Leif wondered why Aislen had called him one of her "people" when he was clearly as human as Leif and Talise.

"Tika." Aislen gently shook the boy awake. He was instantly alert, looking around frantically until he saw his Partner by his side. The boy took a deep breath and closed his eyes for a moment before standing up to follow the princess.

"Good morning," the boy mumbled as he rubbed the sleep from his eyes.

"Tika, I'm not certain if you've been properly introduced. This is Duke Leif of Deuterfoss and Talise, one of the ladies of his court."

Tika shook their hands, looking curiously at Aislen. Leif found himself as curious as the boy to know what the princess was thinking.

"I have a task for you, Tika. I think you would be well suited to it, but it's a rather large task and you'll need some help. Talise has offered her services and I daresay Duke Leif will do likewise.

"Last night, you said that it would be the last night parents and children would have to spend apart. It's a good point. I have no doubt that parents would have kept a close eye on their children, so matching them up should not be our greatest concern. What may prove difficult is reorganising the housing arrangements."

Tika stared open mouthed at Aislen. "You want me to do that?" he squeaked.

"Certainly not by yourself!" Aislen reminded him. "Lady Talise lives in a large city and I'm certain she would have faced some difficult tasks there. She will be more than capable of helping you organise this if you will allow her."

Talise, graceful as ever, easily slid into her new role. "Of course! I'd be more than happy to assist you, young Tika. To start with, we'll need paper and pens, or charcoal. Do you know where to find some?"

"The school room!" Tika replied happily. "I'll show you where it is."

He made to leave the tavern and then his eyes found their way to his Partner. Leif instantly understood his hesitation. "If you'll allow me the honour, I will watch over your Partner until he awakes and then escort him to you."

Tika nodded slowly, then walked with Talise out of the tavern.

"Well handled, Leif. Tika is very protective over Plyke, now more than ever."

Leif looked at Aislen intently. "I know Plyke is a lintep. That was made clear when we arrived, but Tika? He's as human as I am, yet you called him one of your people."

Aislen smiled. "Tika has wanted so much to be a part of magic his entire life. He gave up the chance to find a human Partner and took a lintep one instead. He works as a stableboy in the castle of Illaria and is more loved than half the lintep in the city. He belongs in Illaria, so I call him one of my people. He will be one of us until the day he dies."

Leif nodded quietly. This new world could work. It was already working. The only race he was still uncertain of was the elves, but with the care that had been taken of the ambassador back in Illaria it was clear to him that all the races could live together, quite amiably, if they only tried.

* * *

The morning passed in a flurry of activity. Talise co-ordinated everything with Tika. The boy was truly a wonder. Everyone trusted him so implicitly. He swiftly reunited parents with children and, in a few cases of orphans, found adults who were willing to care for them.

As Aislen had predicted, the bigger problem they faced was rehousing everyone but even that could not stand in their way. Now that old rules were being ignored, people were not bound to live in the building associated with their trade. If parents wanted to live together, they could. In the cases where they did not want to, the children were asked which parent they wanted to live with. It might not be a permanent solution, but at least it was a start.

By the time Leif came to find her, Talise was well and truly exhausted. He brought Tika's Partner over to them. Plyke's arm was around Leif's shoulders to help the boy walk – she could tell it was still a struggle. Plyke's face was pale and drawn tight with pain.

Paradisians drew back from them. Talise gritted her teeth until she realised it was not in fear, but in respect. She tapped Tika on the shoulder. The small boy turned and instantly ran to his Partner.

"Plyke! You're here. Are you feeling any better?"

Talise let the boys talk to one another for a few moments before intruding.

"Tika, it's time for me to go now," she told him quietly. "You've done a magnificent job. I look forward to hearing what other changes you implement while you're here."

The small boy reached up and hugged her. "Thanks for all your help!"

She hugged him back and tousled his hair. She couldn't keep the smile off her face.

"He's pretty amazing, isn't he?" she asked the duke as they walked towards the tavern to say their farewells.

"More than you can imagine." Leif smiled. "Plyke spoke of nothing but his Partner all morning. That boy has been working wonders his whole life from the sounds of it, most of it without even realising."

Chapter Twenty-Seven – Final day

Eliséo woke. Though he did not feel like it, he performed his morning ablutions and eventually sat in his chair – not quite ready to face the day. His steepled fingers rested lightly on his lips as he thought about everything he would lose today.

It would almost be better to lose my life than everything else. He allowed the thought to pass through to Elessa. Her pain flooded though him. It almost made him regret the thought.

You might still lose your life, Elessa warned him. *Do not think that because you are more powerful than your sister that she has no followers. You have lived away from Silvaren more years than you have lived in it. Many elves respect you, some have even tried to befriend you, but you are a stranger to most. They may not trust you enough to crown you their king.*

Eliséo could not argue with her. They both knew she spoke the truth. With a sudden sense of urgency, Eliséo pulled out parchment, ink and a quill. There were things he hadn't had a chance to say to his closest friends when in the Outworld. It hadn't crossed his mind that he might never see them again. Elessa did not disturb him as he wrote page after page of letters.

Eventually, he set down his quill and stoppered the ink. Next, he lit a candle within a glass lantern and selected a stick of wax. One at a time, he rolled up the letters, wrote the recipient's name on the outside, dripped wax across the loose page and pressed down with his seal.

Why have you written one to Rilla? Elessa asked gently. *She will never forgive you if you do not speak with her today. The poor girl is scared enough with everything else going on around her. You should not force her to miss you today.*

Eliséo nodded. *I will speak with her, but some things are better left unsaid until...*

He dropped to his knees and pressed his hands and cheek against Elessa's smooth bark. Waves of love cascaded over him. Without shame, he wept until there was nothing left inside him.

He pulled down all his walls. *Rilla?*

Eliséo? Rilla panicked. She immediately shut her eyes. From the little he had seen, she was walking through a room full of people. *Wait until I get away from everyone. They'll see my eyes!*

It matters not now. Liessa knows and, by this evening, so will every elf in Silvaren. His chest ached as he said the words. *No more secrets.*

Then you'll tell me what happened last night? Rilla asked, opening her eyes and finding a safe place to stand. *Ensil said you revealed yourself and you'll either die or become the king tonight.*

He could feel the tears coursing down her face. So much pain for such a young girl. *I'm sorry, Rilla – for everything.* He explained what happened the previous night with Liessa.

I don't want to think about what happens if you die. Eliséo felt her push down her fear. *I want to know what happens if you become the king. Will you have to break your bond with Elessa? With me? Will we both lose you no matter what happens?*

Eliséo tried to remain calm. *I don't think any elf knows the answer to that. In living memory, every royal elf has been bound to Silva since birth. We have never seen what happens when a royal elf binds themselves to another tree before taking the crown.*

I will do everything in my power not to lose you both. I ... do not think I could bear the pain.

Eliséo gave Rilla as much time as she needed. He sat with a cheek pressed to Elessa's inner trunk and suffused them both with love. When his lintep girl had taken as much comfort from him as she could, he released her gently back to her day and restored the walls around his mind.

* * *

Rilla breathed deeply as Eliséo withdrew from her mind. She could feel that his walls were intact but knew that Elessa would allow her to reach out to him if need be. She looked around the tavern with fresh eyes. Many people had dispersed, presumably to deal with the problems in the Paradise. The rest sat here in relative silence.

It did not escape Rilla's attention that Mistress Isis sat quietly in one corner, seemingly busying herself by mending a tear in her cloak. Rilla guessed the fire mistress had drawn the short straw and was being forced to watch her.

A soft rustle of cloth in a darkened corner of the tavern drew Rilla's eye. The blond mop of hair revealed it was Arishen, huddled with his face towards the wall, shaking. Rilla walked over to him and held out a hand.

"Let's go see how much of a mess Erton made while we were gone."

He looked up at her with a tear streaked face.

"I've already seen it," he told her woodenly.

Rilla tapped her teeth together. She was fairly certain he hadn't left early that morning and come back again. The only way he could have seen it was if he'd had more visions. She crouched down in front of him.

"Have you dreamt of Kalid?"

A smile flickered across Arishen's lips. He shook his head.

"The last thing I remember you dreaming of her, she was putting locks on her doors, sleeping with a chisel under her pillow and never sitting in the same spot in the eating hall. You never dreamt she died, did you? Why don't we see if we can find her?"

She held out her hand again and smiled when he took it. Together they stood and moved towards the door. Mistress Isis carefully put away her needle and thread. Rilla knew they would be shadowed. Surprisingly, it didn't bother her.

As they stepped into the sunlight, Rilla's stomach rumbled. She glanced apologetically at Arishen who shrugged.

"I don't think any of us ate last night. Not with everything that happened. Unless you did when you disappeared," he told her.

Rilla frowned. She didn't think anyone had noticed. "Let's go to the kitchen then. The morning meal will be over, but they're bound to have more food."

"You're joking, right?" He grabbed her shoulder and roughly turned her to face

147

him. "This Paradise won't have changed overnight. They won't give you any food."

Rilla sighed. "Arishen, look around you. Do you see people going off to their trade like any normal day? *I* see people heading towards that table where Tika and Lady Talise are seated. They're smiling. Parents are holding their children close and kissing the tops of their heads. This Paradise *has* changed overnight, and *we* made that happen.

"Now, I'm hungry and I know you are too. I'm not waiting until they decide to serve food again before I eat. You can come with me to the kitchen or you can join them over there."

Arishen looked over to Tika's table and the Paradisians milling around it. Rilla saw him frown.

"You don't know, do you?"

He shook his head.

"Do you want to go there first? Maybe we can find your family."

Arishen's expression darkened. "I don't want to find them. Let's just get some food and go."

Wary of the sudden change in his temper, Rilla stepped lightly away from him and towards the kitchen. Except for a few young kitchen hands washing the morning dishes, it was empty. They barely batted an eyelid when Rilla strode in with Arishen to get some food. She picked up an extra apple for Mistress Isis and tossed it to her teacher with a grin when they came back out.

"Now what?" Mistress Isis asked, taking a bite out of the pale green apple.

Rilla looked at Arishen. "Are you sure you don't want to find out who your parents are?"

He shook his head despondently. "Who would want to claim *me* as a child?"

"You could at least give them a chance," Rilla suggested. "What harm is there in trying. Besides, isn't it better to know than not know?"

"Erton might have killed them off."

Rilla struggled to understand him. Every other child in the Paradise had been desperate to figure out who their parents were. Now that he had the chance, Arishen seemed strangely reluctant to take it.

Mistress Isis moved closer. "Arishen, would you like me to ask Tika if your parents have come forward while you wait here with Rilla?"

Rilla felt the small spark of hope fly through Arishen before it was smothered. She hadn't realised her power was flowing so freely around her. Arishen flinched before she had time to withdraw her power. She didn't have time to apologise before he answered.

"No, thank you."

"If you won't let her ask, then I will."

Before Arishen could protest, Rilla was already on her way to Tika. She felt the attention shift from Tika to herself as she approached the gathered Paradisians. To her surprise, more than a few people were smiling at her. She tentatively returned their smiles.

A small child looked up at her parents, who nodded, before running over to Rilla. Rilla remembered her as one of the children who had listened to Rhanya's star story.

"Thank you for freeing us, Rilla. You're my little star."

Rilla choked back sudden tears. Other children, made braver by this first child, came running up to surround her. They all started thanking and hugging her.

"Thank you, little star."

"Thank you, Rilla."

Unable to avoid skin contact with them, their esteem for her coursed through her veins. Rilla couldn't stop those very feelings flooding out of her and over all the gathered Paradisians. Soon, many of the adults were thanking her. Rilla tried not to panic at their reaction to her own reaction. It was all getting too much for her. Suddenly, Arishen, Tika and Plyke were by her side, pushed through the crowd by Mistress Isis.

"It wasn't just me," she whispered. "It was all of us."

"You're right," Plyke told her as he held her hand tightly. "It was all of us. The four of us, from this very Paradise came back to save them all. We did it!"

Rilla didn't know if it was his new crystal heart or his own empathetic power, but suddenly the crowd was shouting out all their names, thanking them all. Her knees trembled, but Arishen took her other arm and held her steady.

Eventually, the cheering died down. Rilla spied Aislen at the edge of the crowd with an intense look on concentration on her face. It surprised Rilla that she wasn't angry with Aislen for taking the edge off their feelings. The people stood silently, looking at Rilla. She stared at them blankly. Were they waiting for her to say something? Plyke squeezed her hand and raised his eyebrows towards the people.

"I ... uh ... I'm glad we could help you win your freedom from Erton. Just, don't let anyone like him be in charge again. Choose someone kind, practical and clever next time. Someone like Rhanya or Kalid."

She hadn't meant to say it. It just slipped out. She was only thinking of the few decent people she remembered in the Paradise – people who helped others even though it might end up hurting them.

A small circle gathered around a lone figure. Kalid stared at Rilla, a horrified expression on her face as everyone's attention was turned towards her. Rilla shook her head, realising what she had just done. Arishen's grip tightened on her arm. Plyke and Tika started laughing and the Paradisians all relaxed as though they had been released from a spell.

Rilla took the opportunity to escape the crowd.

"Don't even think about it!" She heard Kalid's protest as she walked away with her friends, Arishen a little way in front of them.

Rilla helped Tika with Plyke, their arms linked with each other's around Plyke's back. Mistress Isis walked alongside them. They were quite a distance from the crowd when they caught up with Arishen. Rilla felt Tika's arm stiffen.

"What is it?" she asked as they came to a stop.

Tika looked up at Arishen in agony.

"I'm so sorry, Arishen. I found out who your parents are, but..."

"They're both already dead?" Arishen asked despondently. "I assumed they would be. Erton would have tried to figure out who they were as soon as Parthak told him the truth."

"Well, no, actually. I mean, yes, your mother died when you were born but your father is still alive. Um, but, well."

He looked between Arishen and the ground several times before Plyke nudged him. "Out with it, Tika. Who is he?"

Tika scratched behind his neck, trying to avoid Arishen's eyes. "Turns out Torak and Belial aren't just murderers ... A lot of the children in our Paradise are theirs. Torak is your father."

"Torak?" Arishen shook his head. "No. That's just not possible. Who in their right might would ever want *Torak*?"

Plyke placed a hand on Arishen's shoulder. "It doesn't sound like she was given the choice. How could she have fought against someone as strong as Torak? From the sounds of it, he was ... experienced with forcing himself on women. You have a number of half-brothers and sisters."

"What?" Arishen backed away from them, pale-faced and clutching his stomach. "I can't..." He turned and stumbled into a run.

Rilla froze in disbelief. How could this happen? How could people stand by and let Torak and Belial get away with it? With a growing sense of anger, she knew Erton must have protected them. Her heart ached as she realised Rhanya would have known about at least some of the rapes and not been able to do anything but heal the women. Yet another reason Erton would have been happy to have him murdered.

In a blind rage, she strode towards Erton's residence. He was still being held prisoner there. Two lintep guards were posted at the door. She ignored them as she reached for the door. One of them grabbed her wrist. Instinctively, she pooled the heat from her arm to that one point and burnt his fingers just enough to make him release his grip.

She opened the door and threw her power at Erton before he could react. His legs were rooted in place with earth that had torn through the wooden floorboards to bind him. Rilla's power engulfed Erton, magnifying his helplessness. He remained motionless, but the whites of his eyes betrayed his fear.

"How dare you?" she yelled at him. "How dare you come into a peaceful Paradise, control people with your power and let rapists and murderers thrive while innocent people suffered? How dare you not tell me what I was? Were you hoping that my power would peak, and I'd die before anyone discovered the truth about you? Is that why you tried to kill me yourself last night? Me? Your daughter! What's *wrong* with you? How can you be so horrible? You evil, evil man!"

Rilla felt she was not alone with him anymore. Powerful lintep were in the room with her. They did not try to touch her or force her to calm down. They were just there. Shaking with rage, Rilla let her power close in on Erton ever so slightly. She could feel his difficulty breathing, his lungs struggling to expand with the pressure she placed on them. It felt good, to have him in her power – to be able to end his life if she desired.

But that wasn't what she wanted. Not really. She wanted him to suffer a long and painful life, knowing that everything he held dear had been taken away from him forever.

"You will never have the chance to hurt anyone again. I will make certain of that. If I ever hear that you have even attempted to hurt someone again, I will kill you myself."

As abruptly as she'd entered the room, she withdrew her power and left. Behind her, she heard Aislen leaving instructions for the guards to find a lock for the door and then footsteps hurrying behind her. She felt a tendril of both Isis and Aislen's power hovering around her. Rilla let them follow her.

Without thinking, she followed what had been her usual escape route, across the middle bridge, past the farms and into the tiny forest. Once there, her legs gave out under her. She fell clumsily to the ground. Isis caught her before she hit her head on the tree roots covering the ground.

"I'm sorry," she whispered. "You told me not to do that to Lishe, but I did it to Erton instead."

"No, you didn't." Isis stroked her hair. Aislen sat in front of them. "You stopped yourself. You had him completely in your power. You could have crushed the life out of him – but you didn't and *that* makes all the difference."

Rilla looked up at Aislen from Isis' lap. She had so little energy left. "You need to detain Torak and Belial, now, before they do anything else. They are rapists and murderers. I don't want to give them the opportunity to hurt anyone else, not when we can stop them."

Aislen nodded sadly. "I will see to it. Erton's residence is turning into the Paradise prison. Isis will stay with you the rest of today. Rilla, just try to..."

"Stay away from everyone else?" she asked bitterly. "Don't worry. I don't think anything else can possibly affect me so much today."

She caught the worried glance that Aislen gave Isis before she left but was too distraught to care.

Chapter Twenty-Eight – Silva's choice

Eléna watched as the sun moved across the wall of her room. She had not closeted herself away like this since her parents were poisoned. Any time she allowed her thoughts to land on Eliséo or Liessa, her heart started racing, her breath came in short, shallow gasps, her vision began to close in, and she cried uncontrollably. She could not bear to lose one of her children today.

She had been so careful, for over seven hundred *years*, to keep her son a secret – to keep him alive. Now all that work was undone, and she bitterly regretted the lost moments she could have had with him had she only been open about their relationship. Making him her ambassador had given him as much freedom and access to herself as possible. But it was never enough.

A silver vine dangling nearby lengthened itself to caress her cheek.

Let me in, Silva begged her. *You keep so much of yourself locked away from me. I want to help, but you never let me.*

You can't help, Eléna sobbed. *Tonight, I lose one of my children.*

Eléna was wrapped up in her own despair but couldn't help but feel Silva's pang of bitterness.

Eliséo should have been mine, but all these years, you kept him from me. Tonight, I could lose a child I never had the chance to know. Did you think I didn't notice the change in you when he quickened in your womb? Did you think I never noticed how careful he was not to touch me with his bare skin, even once, in all his long years?

Frozen in disbelief, Eléna closed her eyes, but there was no escape. Silva flashed her every memory that every betrayed Eliséo's heritage. Eléna broke. She allowed Silva to see everything she had kept from her over the years, to keep her children safe.

They spent almost the entire day together, sharing memories with each other, blocking out Liessa from their thoughts.

I will do everything I can to keep our children safe tonight.

Eléna smiled sadly. *I wish that were possible.*

* * *

It was mid-afternoon. Eliséo had walked around Silvaren most of the day. He had made a concerted effort to speak with the few elves he had any sort of relationship with and to exchange banal pleasantries with those he didn't. Some of the older elves were still distant towards him. They treated him as an oddity – albeit a necessary one.

Trying to dismiss their indifference, Eliséo headed to his usual retreat – Ensil's grove. It was here he had spent years of his life training with his sword. Today was no different. As he performed his routine drills, a few of the younger elves gathered around. Eliséo recognised them as the guides assigned to the Paradisians when they visited Silvaren all those months ago – Gioshué, Raeslin, Tameo and Telon. He motioned for them to join in and, to his surprise, they did. Unlike himself, they hadn't brought their own weapons and so sifted through Ensil's stores to find ones to their liking.

Once they were ready, they began to mimic his movements. He kept the drills simple enough until he had gauged their skill. He smiled. They weren't half bad.

"That's enough drills for now." He lowered his sword and they did likewise. "Has Ensil shown you how to protect yourself in a practise bout?"

Raeslin tilted her head to one side. "Do you mean when he does something to the blades so they don't cut?"

Eliséo nodded.

"No, he thought we wouldn't have enough power for that, so he never bothered to show us," Raeslin answered. Eliséo detected a hint of bitterness in her voice.

Did Ensil never shown anyone else? Did he only show me because he knew who I was and would be powerful enough?

Elessa rebuked him, *Pointless questions. Focus on the young ones and see what they can do.*

"We'll never know if you don't try."

They immediately brightened at the idea. He showed them how to do it, no longer caring if it revealed how much power he had. In fact, it made him wonder why Ensil could do it so well if he wasn't a royal elf and did not possess the crown.

To their delight, the young elves had varying degrees of success in their attempts. All four managed to create some form of barrier around their weapon, though some managed thicker ones than others. In practical terms, all that meant was that the thinner barriers would leave deeper bruises, but none of them would cut.

"Why didn't Ensil teach us?" Tameo asked angrily after his initial delight.

Eliséo shrugged. There were many things he was beginning to question about what Ensil had and had not told elves. Many of their legends had been passed down by him. Eliséo wondered how many he had made up himself. Was it only the one about no elf having significant power without the crown? Even Eléna had not known about that before Ensil told them all those months ago.

"Is there anything else you can show us?" asked Raeslin. "We might not be as powerful as you, but we can try."

Eliséo hesitated. "I suppose so. As long as you don't get upset if it doesn't work."

Grins spread across four faces as they nodded eagerly. Their enthusiasm infected Eliséo and he couldn't help but laugh.

"First thing, do you know how to cleanse the water in your room? The one for your daily ablutions?"

They nodded.

Well, at least there are some things they are being taught.

"Have you tried doing other things with air, water or earth?"

"You didn't mention fire," Tameo pointed out unhelpfully.

"No, fire is the last skill you should learn to work with. It is the most dangerous, so I need to know you can master the other skills first. So, have you tried anything else?"

With sidelong glances at each other, presumably to make sure they weren't the only one, the four elves slowly shook their heads. Eliséo was shocked. These elves must be well over a hundred years old. Why hadn't they been given even the most basic training?

In defiance of every act of secrecy he had employed in his life, Eliséo spent the rest of the afternoon with the elf children, showing them skills with each element other than fire, and demonstrating the different applications.

By twilight, a crowd had grown around them, his four initial students calling out to any friends they saw in passing. Many of the young elves had joined in the lessons. Eliséo noticed older elves leaning against trees, trying not to look too interested as their children practised skills that they had presumably never attempted to master themselves.

"What are you doing?" The cold voice behind him was unmistakable. Eliséo finished instructing the children on the latest bit of magic before turning around.

"I should think it quite obvious," he answered unflinchingly. "I'm teaching the children some magic."

She did not bother voicing her objection. It was clear in her demeanour.

"It's time, Eliséo. Force your tree to break her unnatural bond and bow down to me before every elf in Silvaren."

"Are you going to tell them that you threatened to burn my tree if I don't?"

He heard gasps behind him but did not know if it was for his audacity in not bowing down or Liessa's threat.

"You have been a thorn in everyone's side for too long, Eliséo. I demand you obey me."

Eliséo slowly got to his feet, deliberately holding fast to his sword as he did so.

"No. I think it is time for the truth to be known."

He looked around at the gathered elves and noticed a good few were missing. He did something he had very rarely attempted – asked the wind to carry his voice further than it should, so that it would sound all throughout Silvaren.

"My name is Eliséo. I am the son of Eléna and Ensil. I have more power than my sister, Liessa, and just as much right to the throne. I do not desire the crown, but I will not allow my tree, nor her bond with a lintep, to be threatened by the queen."

Silence greeted his words. Complete and utter silence, until Eléna came running and stumbling over roots towards them.

"Wait!" she cried out, arms held out before her. "This cannot be done here. It must be done at the foot of Silva." She paused to catch her breath. "Any debate or challenge must be done at the foot of Silva."

Eliséo frowned at the interruption. He looked over at his sister. She appeared just as cold as usual. Without even a glance in Eléna's direction, she walked past their mother towards Silva. Eliséo motioned for the gathered elves to follow her.

"Mother, what are you doing?" he asked her quietly. "I had their support here. Why are you moving us?"

Eléna gripped his arm with a trembling hand. "Silva will keep you both safe. She promised me."

Eliséo did not have the heart to tell her that Liessa would not spare his life if she was chosen by the elves. Instead, he placed his hand over his mother's and walked her over to her tree. Elves made way for them as they approached. They joined Liessa, who was waiting at a small alcove in Silva's trunk. Every elf in Silvaren was present.

Eléna released Eliséo's arm and stood between her children, heart beating wildly. "For over seven hundred years, I have lied to you. I kept the identity of my son a secret to save his life. I did not wish there to be a fight for the crown. It cannot be helped now." She turned to face each of her children in turn. "I would ask both of you to consider your options. Whichever of you is chosen today, you do *not* need to kill your sibling. You can choose another path."

Liessa touched the crown on her head. "I have already been chosen. That cannot be undone. All that must be decided today is if Eliséo will force his tree to break her bond with the lintep child and bow down to me."

Silence.

"Will you really burn down his tree if he doesn't?" a small voice asked.

Eléna searched for the owner. One of the young elves. She was ashamed to admit she did not know the boy's name.

"I will," Liessa answered firmly. "This elf *claims* to be my brother, but he is not bound to the royal tree. He has no way to prove what he is. He was brought into Silvaren as a foundling. He chose a ridiculously old tree to bond with and that decision has finally come to haunt him. If he was really what he claimed, Silva would have seen him at some point over the past seven hundred years and claimed him as her own."

This was the moment Eléna had been waiting for, and dreading. She took Eliséo's bare hand and placed his palm on Silva's trunk. She caught the brief glimpse of terror in his eyes before they began to shine as bright as the stars.

Elves cleared the area as the dirt and mulch beneath their feet rippled. Roots shot out of the ground and moved aside, creating a wide trench between them. Eléna watched, mouth agape, as Elessa wove her way through the trench until she reached Silva. The majestic behemoth that was Silva reached out to Elessa with her silver vines and encapsulated the smaller tree, making her part of the family.

When Eléna finally managed to tear her eyes away from the magnificent sight, she was drawn back to her children. Liessa's thin circlet of leaves crumpled and fell around her face. She watched as her daughter gently gathered up the withered vines from her shoulders.

It almost made her miss Eliséo's coronation. Silva and Elessa worked together to weave him a crown – Silva's vine decorated with Elessa's glossy green leaves, neat silver and twisted red flowers. It was the most perfect combination of all that was her son.

She stepped up to kiss her bemused king and embrace her dethroned daughter. Liessa angrily pushed her away.

"You *knew* this would happen. You knew this was the only way he would be crowned king. Our people would *never* have chosen this themselves."

* * *

Eliséo took off the crown and studied it carefully, turning it over in his hands. He was trapped. Silva had made him the king of Silvaren.

No, he corrected himself, *Silva and Elessa have both done this to me.*

He heard his sister as though from an ocean away, complaining to their mother, like a spoilt child.

"I did not know," Eléna defended herself. "Silva told me she would keep my children safe if I brought them to her. That is all."

"She hasn't kept *me* safe," Liessa moaned.

"Yes, she has." Eliséo stepped over to them. "Silva knew I would not have you killed. I ... could never do that."

Liessa looked at him in shock. "But ... I threatened to burn your tree."

"That may be one of the reasons she chose me over you, but it will not make me kill you. I have seen enough bloodshed in my life. I will not add to it needlessly."

"What happens now?" Liessa asked, eyes firmly averted from his.

Eliséo shrugged and held out a hand to her. "I don't know, but we can do it together." He held his breath and waited. Liessa looked at his outstretched hand with tears in her eyes. Hesitantly, she placed her hand in his.

"Together?"

Eliséo sighed in relief. "If you're ready to ride a dragon, that is."

Chapter Twenty-Nine – Revenge

Arishen ran.

Torak. It was worse than he could have imagined. He couldn't deny that some part of him, no matter how small, had held a hope that Kalid was his mother. It didn't matter now that he would never know his mother – the thought barely registered compared with who his father was.

A murderer. A rapist.

Arishen ran until he reached the isolation hut. The charred remains made him sick – again. His father had done this. *His father* had burned two innocent children in a prison they had no hope of escaping.

It was late afternoon. Arishen had been thinking all day. Now, he had a plan. Happy as they were, reuniting with their loved ones, Arishen hoped everyone would be too distracted to notice him. Keeping a careful watch on his surroundings, he sneaked into the oil store on the farming side of the Paradise. There, he found numerous large vats of oil. He wasn't prepared for that. He had been hoping to find smaller containers that he could easily conceal and transport by himself.

Looking around, he noticed a ladle hanging from a rusty hook on the wall. He smiled to himself, another plan hatching in his mind. It took him only a short time to locate the building with stores of fleece. He had heard some of the farmers calling it grease wool once. They had complained about the long and arduous process of cleaning the wool to remove all the wool grease.

Beside the tall heap, there were reed baskets. He selected a few large fleeces and piled them into the basket. Testing the weight of it, he put all but two back again. These ones would have to do.

He carried the basket back to the oil store. With care not to spill any on himself, Arishen used the ladle to pour oil over the wool until it was saturated.

He looked outside. The sun was almost gone. It wouldn't be long now. Arishen spent the remaining moments of precious daylight finding a suitable rock he could use to create a spark. He waited a little longer, just until the stars began to shine. Everyone would be in the dining hall, eating their evening meal.

It was time.

He hefted his basket and walked awkwardly to his destination. The reed baskets had a layer of something inside them that did not allow the oil to seep through, but that did not stop the top layers of wool from bouncing into his chest and soaking his shirt as he walked, some of it dripping onto the grass. In the distance, he saw the silhouette of two lintep guards at the door. Hoping they hadn't yet seen him, he took care to walk the long way around, moving behind other buildings to get to one of the three unguarded walls.

Arishen spread the oil-soaked fleece out against the wooden walls, careful to be quiet so as not to arouse the guards' attention. He rubbed his hands against the grass, but the oil would not come off. Cursing under his breath, he wiped them on the back of his oil-soaked shirt. He could always find another one in the tailors' building.

Silently, he unsheathed one of his daggers and dragged the rock against the blade. Nothing happened. His heart beat faster. There was no time to waste. The house had to be in flames before the evening meal ended or all would be lost. Feverishly, he scraped the rock up and down his dagger, faster and faster.

Sparks flew.

The fleece ignited. Arishen fell back in shock as the flames whooshed around the base of the building, feeding off the oil. It happened so quickly he didn't have time to react. A spark flew across to his oil-soaked shirt and roared to life. Terrified, he ripped the shirt off and threw it at the building. Then he noticed his hands. They were alight and sizzling. Oddly, he couldn't feel any pain – not until the fire had burnt through all the oil. The pain set in and the smell of burnt flesh made him gag. He screamed as his skin bubbled and peeled off in sheets. Then the pain disappeared. From inside the burning building, Arishen heard shouts of anger and fear.

Fire shot out around the door and through the windows, turning the shouts into shrill screams.

Unable to stop the vision, he fell to the ground, gaging between hysterical sobs.

Three men were fixed in place by Ensil's handiwork, earth ripped through the wooden floor and packed tightly around their feet and calves. Torak and Belial twisted and writhed, trying to free themselves. Erton stood still, hands outstretched.

Fire from the outer walls flew in towards Erton, scorching Torak and Belial as it dragged past them. Erton splayed his fingers widely and the fire shot away from them again, now spreading over the entire inside of the building.

Each time he tried to manipulate the flames they only grew worse. Flames spat through the gaps in the wooden door, running across the grass towards the only remaining lintep guard.

Without warning, the fire on his hands went out. He stared at the charred skin in a mute stupor. A strong arm around his shoulders guided him away from the burning building. As he walked away, he heard other people calling out in alarm as the fire spat and popped loudly in random bursts. Arishen felt his legs grow uncomfortably warm. He looked behind him at the same time as his protector grabbed him roughly by the arm and ran.

Behind them, the fire crept along the grass, snaking towards them. Arishen realised the flames were following the path he had taken with the oil-soaked wool. Raised voices reached them as people streamed out of the dining hall. Arishen stared at the burning building and the streaks of fire running through the grass in horror. *He* had done this. He *had* been trying to burn Torak and Belial the same way they had burned mere children, but *this* was not what he had expected.

Lintep guards were holding the Paradisians at bay while using their powers to control the flames threatening to engulf the entire Paradise.

* * *

Aislen ran out of the dining hall at the first sound of alarm. Erton's residence was barely a few hundred feet away from the dining hall. By the time she emerged into the night, the flames had already crept half way towards her. She instantly threw up a wall of her power to stop the fire reaching them.

Create a shield around the fire! She threw the thought out to everyone, without a care that most of the people surrounding her were not lintep. As she felt other powers merge with hers, she guided and moulded them into a dome around the burning building and the grass surrounding it. Just before she closed the dome, there was a great explosion from within. Shards of wood tore holes in the dome. She struggled to regain control as the heat of the flames threatened to claw its way back through her power and into her skin. Sweat streamed down her face as she pushed the heat back inside it.

With the dome whole at last, she took a moment to breathe and think.

"Séverin, get the people back to the safety of their homes. Anya, keep Umi, Ulf and Tika safe, somewhere far away from here."

"Alais, get the people back to the safety of their homes," Séverin said behind her. Aislen spared him a glance and finally realised he was cradling a half-naked Arishen, whose hands were covered in blisters and charred skin. She swallowed the sudden bile in her mouth.

"Séverin, can you heal him?" she asked in a softer voice.

The guard shook his head. "I've taken away some of his pain, but this is more than I've ever had to deal with before. I think it can wait until the fire is out, but then Mistress Kayte may need to tend to him."

"Take him to the healers then," Aislen instructed. "They must be able to help him until Kayte is free."

She turned her attention back to the burning building. Arishen was the only one with burnt hands, and no shirt, which meant he had probably started the fire himself. It suddenly became so clear to her. The murderers and rapists were inside with Erton now. All the people who had caused so much grief to everyone in the Paradise. He had seen their handiwork with the isolation hut and must have decided to do the same thing to them. What was she to do with him now? She pushed the thought away for later.

It paled in comparison with the one staring her in the face. She knew there were three people inside that building, people she had no hope of saving. The fire was roaring, spitting and exploding out of control. As weaker lintep exhausted themselves and withdrew their power, the fire reacted to each sudden rush of oxygen and smoke caught alight through the gap in the dome. Aislen and the remaining lintep extended themselves further to close the gap over each explosion.

They were already so tired from the long journey to get here and the events since arriving in the Paradise. How long could they keep this up before they all collapsed from exhaustion?

A few heartbeats after the final explosions, the fire went out. Aislen looked up incredulously. Without her direction, a number of lintep withdrew their power. Flames instantly roared back into life. Exhausted, Aislen extended her power further to reform the broken dome. The flames extinguished again.

Keep the dome steady. The flames will keep returning until everything within has cooled down or there is nothing left to burn.

A sudden movement by her side caught Aislen's eye. Rilla, arms outstretched, stiffened. Her eyes glowed a bright green.

What is the girl doing talking to her elf at a time like this?

Ensil was suddenly by Rilla's side, holding her hand and kneeling by her side. His eyes glowed a deep blue. Rilla looked down at him. Aislen felt the girl's power wavering in the dome.

"Ensil, stop distracting her. I need her to concentrate!" Aislen called out to the elf.

"No, *I* need her to concentrate. Rilla, you can smother this fire yourself now. Use Silva's power."

"I ... can't."

"Leave her alone! If she doesn't concentrate, this fire will revive itself and destroy the entire Paradise," Aislen growled.

"Rilla, listen to me," Ensil commanded. Rilla's power remained part of the dome as she turned towards the elf. "With Silva's power, you can command the elements."

"I've never tried anything with fire – only air," Rilla called out over the cracking and spitting flames.

Aislen kept a close eye on the two of them as Ensil whispered in Rilla's ear. Her eyes widened. Rilla's mouth moved inaudibly. Aislen did not see a difference in the fire. What she heard was a whirlwind of dirt gathering to one side. The swirl grew steadily until it had become an impenetrable sheet of dirt over the dome.

"Aislen, if we open the dome at the top, and keep the sides up, I'll drop the dirt," Rilla told her.

Aislen reacted immediately by whistling out to all the lintep helping – she didn't have any spare power to talk to them with her mind. Slowly, she felt the shape of the dome changing. As soon as the dome opened, fire exploded up into the sky. The sheet of dirt instantly dropped down. The fire was suffocated, but a sudden sweeping wind threatened to blow it all away.

"Rain, Rilla. We need rain!" Aislen called out.

"Hold your horses," Ensil chided her.

He turned to Rilla and spoke in her ear once more. Clouds gathered until the stars could no longer be seen. They changed from fluffy white tufts into ominous dark grey behemoths. Within moments, the clouds unleashed sheets of torrential rain. It spread out well past the bounds of the dome, soaking everyone to the bone. Rilla kept the rain falling until the dirt turned to mud and the fire nothing more than a charred memory.

Aislen walked towards the ruined building, pulled her power aside and walked into the dome. Under the mud, the blacked wood was still warm to the touch, but there was not even an ember in sight.

Stand down. She sent the message out to all the lintep. Exhausted, she pulled back her own power. The rain continued falling, but it lessened in intensity. All Aislen wanted to do was sink to her knees, but knew if she did, she wouldn't get up again.

Taking a deep breath, she looked around at the masters, mistresses and guards who looked just as tired as she felt. She hadn't really thought they would need so many lintep here. It was worse than the Paradise her father had organised to destroy.

"Kayte, there is work for you in the healers' building. Take anyone you think you might need. Isis, take Rilla and Plyke back to the tavern. The others should already be there. I want our entire company there tonight. Séverin, set a watch on our building. I doubt the Paradisians will attack each other tonight."

Every lintep hastened to follow her orders. Soon, she was left alone in the rain, staring at the hidden ruins of a building containing three corpses. She barely noticed some humans approaching her.

"Are they dead then? All three of them?"

Aislen turned her weary head to see a huddled group of women. She nodded.

"There was no way to get them out without burning down the entire Paradise. Especially not when they were rooted to the ground."

One of them, short, dirty-faced and angry, stormed through the rain and spat on the building. "You'll never get your filthy hands on me again!"

Aislen stared as the woman burst into tears. The other women crowded around the short one, hugging each other and sharing their grieved relief. She left them in peace. However much people might appreciate his actions, Arishen still had to be dealt with. She could not ignore these murders.

Chapter Thirty – Ice crystals

Leif pulled his cloak closer and held on tightly to Talise, who sat behind Rownyn, the lintep guard who had offered to escort them to Illaria for a second time. The icy wind tore through to his bones. Snowcrest had insisted that she could fly at least part way through the night. Leif had tried to dissuade her, but nothing had worked. The crystal dragon knew the hurry they were in and was enthralled by the adventure. Her mission was to take them back to Illaria, so that Leif could deliver Aislen's messages and collect four copies of the map, then to escort them to Deuterfoss and the other duchies so that troops could be sent out to every known Paradise.

There was so much to do. The very thought of it all made him tired. He closed his eyes for a moment. When he opened them, he was drifting through the sky. He looked up and saw the stars refract through the body of a white-tipped clear crystal dragon. It flew past him and then the stars were clearer. Such a beautiful sky!

* * *

"Leif!" Talise screamed as she clutched empty air. She had felt his arms around her waist go slack only moments before he fell from Snowcrest. Beating her fists wildly against the crystal dragon's side made no impression on the massive beast.

Rownyn turned towards her – his face pale. Within seconds, Snowcrest shot down towards the falling duke. Much as she and Leif had protested the need for a guard, she was now grateful Aislen had insisted. Talise was certain Rownyn had spoken directly to Snowcrest's mind.

She held on tightly as Snowcrest sped through the chill night air. Tiny ice crystals formed on her tear encrusted eyelashes. She was so very cold. Her arms went slack as she closed her eyes. A strong unseen hand held her hands together around Rownyn's waist.

Talise woke to the crackling of a fire. The warmth of it soaked into her like a hot bath. She opened her eyes and blinked, trying to clear her vision. Dawn was breaking, but the colours flew across the sky in sharp, uneven lines.

"She's awake."

A hint of relief? She looked around and saw Rownyn watching her. He moved aside and there was Leif, alive and whole – not crushed against the rocks from his fall. Something sharp stuck into Talise's ribs as she tried to sit up. Irrationally irritated, she tried to push the shard of crystal away. It sliced the palm of her hand.

"Ouch!" She pressed the wound against her lips as she searched for a way to staunch the bleeding.

"If I may?" Rownyn knelt beside her and took her injured hand. He covered it with his own and closed his eyes. Talise froze as the skin on her hand began to tighten and itch.

She tried to pull away. "What are you doing?"

Rownyn held her hand firmly for a few moments longer and then released it. Talise snatched it away and carefully examined the wound. The sharp pain was nothing more than a memory. The flesh around the wound was an angry shade of pink, all tightly drawn together. She probed it experimentally – it only hurt if she pressed too hard.

"Thank you," she said as she sat up more carefully. Leif continued watching her silently. She raised an inquisitive eyebrow at him.

"You almost fell." He was so matter of fact.

Talise shrugged, though she felt anything but calm. "You *did* fall."

"Yes," he said quietly. "I did. If it hadn't been for you, I probably would have died."

Talise looked away, tears stinging her eyes. The fear she had felt when Leif fell from Snowcrest's back had all but paralysed her. Her mind had refused to consider life without Leif in it. It had been an automatic reaction to beat her fists against the crystal dragon.

She saw a shadow pass over the ground beside her but was still surprised when Leif gently placed his fingers under her chin and turned her face towards him.

"I don't want to spend the rest of my life wondering if you love me, or if you'd like the life of a courtier. I don't want anyone to find a reason for you to return to your father's farm or marry one of my barons."

Talise's heart pounded noisily. She gripped her hands tightly to stop them from shaking.

"Talise, will you marry me?" His voice was so soft and uncertain.

"Of course, I will," she whispered, tears falling freely down her cheeks. She marvelled at his sigh of relief. "How could you ever have doubted that I would?"

Not caring that they had an audience, Talise drew Leif in by his shirt, kissing him full on the lips. They stayed locked in each other's embrace until Rownyn coughed pointedly.

"Begging your pardon, but if you've both recovered sufficiently, I have convinced Snowcrest that we should travel mostly by sunlight and at a lower height, to save us all from further incidents with the winter winds."

Talise flashed Rownyn a thankful smile, then pulled Leif in for another kiss.

* * *

It took them almost the entire day to fly to the first broken Paradise. Snowcrest had been true to her word and not flown any higher than necessary the rest of the way. That hadn't stopped Leif from pulling his cloak tighter around his shoulders in a panic whenever the wind suddenly chilled. Otherwise, his arms had been tightly wrapped around Talise's waist the entire time. He knew she was as terrified as he was because when he shifted his weight or slackened his grip, even momentarily, she instantly grabbed at his hands and held them firmly.

He hopped off Snowcrest's back and turned around to look up at Talise. Leif could still not believe that she had agreed to be his wife. He held out a hand to help her down from Snowcrest's back, but she refused it and simply jumped into his arms instead.

"Decorum never meant anything to you, did it?" he laughed.

She brushed his concerns aside. "People put too much stock in what others think is good and proper. I'm certain that's part of the reason you took so long to ask me to marry you."

Leif blushed furiously. Rownyn unsubtly turned his laugh into a cough.

"Snowcrest has agreed to wait here until we return tomorrow morning," Rownyn said. "The villagers of this Paradise remain wary of the crystal dragons. We should try to find Lord Brynt before nightfall. I don't know how many weapons his men will have forged by now, but I don't intend to find out in a hostile way."

The three of them walked through the broken Paradise as unobtrusively as possible. Leif took note of the locks on doors and metal latches on windows. Security was certainly increasing, but it wasn't enough. They were almost at the centre of the village, but no one had confronted them, not even his own soldiers who should have arrived from Deuterfoss by now. Leif looked around in sudden confusion.

"Where is everyone?"

Talise and Rownyn stopped and looked around as well. The silence was eerie.

"I don't hear anything," Rownyn said. "Not even sounds from inside buildings."

Leif scratched behind his neck. "I don't like this. Something is wrong. Let's find Brynt as quickly as we can."

They picked up their pace and headed towards the centre of the Paradise. They passed the industry buildings, the healers, the tavern – all were silent. Finally, they heard a sound coming from the eating hall. Raised voices were clamouring to be heard over one another.

"Bryntville!"

"No, I tell you, Bryntly sounds the best!"

"Don't be daft. We have a brook running through it! Bryntbrook!"

As Leif hesitantly pushed opened the door, the crowd quietened enough for one man to be heard.

"Brynt is our leader and we all agree on one thing – this is *his* town. So why not call it Bryntown so everyone knows it?"

Leif noted his soldiers were stationed all around the room, carefully watching the changing moods of the crowd. He spied Brynt sitting over to one side, head in his hands. When people began cheering and hooting their agreement, the Paradise leader shook his head, stood up and walked away from them.

"Bryntown! Bryntown!"

A pained expression crossed Brynt's face with every cry of the name. Leif motioned him over and the Paradise leader seemed only too pleased to have an excuse to get escape. Two soldiers followed Brynt out and saluted when they saw Leif.

"I see things have been going well since we were last here," Leif said with as straight a face as he could manage. Brynt glared at him.

"Once that princess got the idea into their heads that we should name our home, nothing would please them but to name it after me." He shook his head. "The fools!"

Talise laughed loudly, even as Leif shot her a warning look. She dismissed his concern with the wave of her hand and looped her arm around his instead.

"At least it sets a nice precedent for the other Paradises. They can all name their homes after their leaders. It will save endless debates on so important a topic."

"Actually, I'm surprised to see the three of you alone. What happened at the next Paradise? Where is everyone else?"

Leif exchanged glances with Rownyn. "Perhaps we can discuss that in private?"

Brynt raised his eyebrows but did not question him further. "Follow me then."

Chapter Thirty-One – New magic

Eliséo sat upon his throne. He simply could not get used to it. This was the very position he had spent more than seven hundred years avoiding and now that he was here, he expected to feel lost. So why wasn't he?

You've had hundreds of years of experience in the political arena, Elessa reminded him, with Silva exuding her agreement. *You may have been avoiding this, but I think your mother was unknowingly preparing you for this eventuality your entire life.*

Had I been given the chance I would have instructed you myself on many of these matters. Silva's voice was strangely familiar and comforting. Eliséo found it difficult to describe, even to himself. It was almost like coming home to a family he'd always known was there but had never had the chance to meet.

"Your majesty." One of his advisors drew his attention away from the trees. "This matter is urgent. You need to make a decision today."

Every matter in the past few days had been deemed urgent. It seemed as though his sister had only taken the time to implement procedures and policies that suited her rather than those that were urgently required.

After a ridiculously long time listening to his advisors and making *important* decisions on *urgent* matters, Eliséo looked up to find the room had cleared out. He breathed a long sigh of relief and stepped out of the throne room before anyone else could vie for his attention.

Elessa, where's my sister? Eliséo felt Silva's pang of disappointment. More than seven hundred years of talking with Elessa made things difficult. Silva clearly wanted to be part of their lives and every time Eliséo asked a question of Elessa rather than Silva, he felt her sorrow and Elessa's embarrassment.

Secluded in her chamber, as always.

You need to reach out to her, Silva told him. *She has too much anger to talk to me. Ever since we crowned you, she has put up a wall between us and won't let me in.*

Eliséo grimaced. Much as he saw his sister as a spoilt brat, he knew her pain was real. She had accepted his offer to do things together and then withdrawn completely.

Silva, where is Eléna? Her shiver of pleasure was palpable. He smiled to himself and blocked away the thought that such small gestures were immeasurably beneficial to their budding bond.

Eliséo walked down to the lake below Silva. His mother was waiting there for him. She held out her arms. Eliséo fought back tears of joy as he embraced his mother. Every elf knew he was her son now – he would never have to hide that again.

"You know, you can talk to me through Silva just as you do with Rilla through Elessa," she advised him. "You could even talk to your sister through Silva, if you so wished."

Eliséo avoided that topic for the moment. Instead, he took his mother's hand and laid it gently on his arm. Together they walked through their forest, drinking in the jubilation of their elves. As soon as the younger elves saw him, they raised their eyebrows hopefully. He laughed and nodded.

In the days following his coronation, he had set aside time to teach magic to any elf who wished to try it. His mother sometimes joined them for these sessions. Initially, only the children had been brave enough to try. Soon enough, however, many of the older elves had begun to join in. Eliséo still could not understand why magic had purposely been suppressed for so long in Silvaren. There were so few of them who knew enough to teach the others that their progress was painfully slow.

"Will you join us today?" Eliséo asked his mother.

"Of course, but I'm not the only one you should be asking," Eléna pointed out. Eliséo knew what she was thinking, but he did not agree that Liessa was up to the task. "She cannot prove to you that she is capable of helping if you do not give her the chance."

Liessa? he tentatively called out to his sister. There was no response, but he could feel her listening. *Will you join us at Ensil's tree to teach our people magic?*

He felt her anger rise before she bellowed at him. *I have less power than most of them! Why would they want me to teach them?!*

Eliséo immediately pulled back and glanced at his mother in concern. "*That* is the reason I have not asked for her help. She is bitter and full of self-pity. I cannot involve her if she does not want to be involved."

Do you not realise this is where all her insecurities come from? Silva asked them both. *This is what drove her to become so strict and severe. She thought if she took away everyone's voice, they could not question her lack of power.*

Liessa, dear, Eléna soothed her daughter. *As you well know, it does not matter how much power you have. Our people do not know how to use their magic. They will not care that you have less power without your crown. They will only be grateful that you show your face and help them to learn. Please, do this for me.*

"Do you think she will come?" Eliséo asked.

"Perhaps." Eléna shrugged. "It is difficult for her. She is justifiably embarrassed by her dethronement. It may yet be too soon for her to swallow her pride."

Eliséo pondered the problem of his sister. He had promised her a dragon flight, but his recent conversations with Rilla told him the crystal dragons would not pass by Silvaren for at least another week. Maps still had to be copied and distributed before anything else could happen.

"Mother, how many trees understand how to talk with Silva?"

The question clearly took Eléna by surprise. "I ... don't know. It may be more a question of which have ever bothered to try."

Silva, how far do your roots reach? Can you communicate with any tree in Silvaren, or is there a limit? Eliséo felt his own excitement surge through his new tree.

It is but a moment's work to communicate with any of the trees who touch my roots. It should be possible to communicate with others, as long as there is a constant connection of roots between trees, much like when Rilla allows others to communicate with you by allowing them to hold her hand.

Thank you, Silva, you have been most helpful.

In his mind's eye, he saw hundreds of silver blossoms burst open amongst Silva's leaves in her happiness.

Using his latest favourite type of magic, Eliséo asked the wind to carry his voice throughout all Silvaren. "At your convenience, would every elf please meet me at Ensil's tree. There is a new sort of magic I wish you all to learn."

"What are you up to, Eliséo?" Eléna asked him curiously. Eliséo only smiled and continued to lead her towards Ensil's tree.

He waited until all, except one, of the elves had gathered. He hadn't really expected his sister to join them but could not help but feel disappointment at her absence. His people looked at him expectantly.

"This may seem an odd request, but I'd like all of you to ask your tree if they are touching Silva's roots with their own. If your tree confirms that they are indeed, please sit down."

Around half of the elves sat on the ground with bewildered looks on their faces. Eliséo looked around at the standing elves, trying to figure out the best way to proceed.

"For the rest of you, look at the seated elves and see if any of their trees stand nearby yours. If they do, go and stand next to them."

"What are you thinking?" Eléna mumbled under her breath.

Eliséo patted her hand and smiled mischievously.

"Patience, Mother," he whispered back to her. In a louder voice, he addressed those elves again. "Talk to your trees and ask them to touch roots with the tree of the seated person. Once you've done that, please sit down where you are."

There were still a score of elves standing at that point. "Can the rest of you find any elves who have trees nearby yours? If so, go and stand next to them, ask your tree to touch roots with the seated person's tree and then sit down."

Only a handful of elves were still standing by this point. "Do any of your trees neighbour other trees?" he asked them hopefully.

Each of the elves shook their heads. He recognised them. Their trees were on the far side of where Elessa had stood. They would have been able to connect to Silva through her, had she still been standing there.

"I have an idea. You five follow me. The rest of you stay here with Lady Eléna. We shouldn't be too long."

Eliséo led the elves to the place where Elessa had stood for most of their lives. This part of the forest was strewn with unbonded trees. He looked around for a moment, trying to decide how to make everything work.

"Can everyone see their tree from here?"

All the elves nodded. Eliséo pulled at his lip, pensively.

"Please stand next to your tree then, and we'll go from there."

He waited patiently until they were positioned by their trees. Next, Eliséo walked to each unbonded tree to see if they could feel Silva's roots, or feel any tree's roots which were already connected to Silva's. In a short time, all of the unbonded trees were connected to Silva's roots. Eliséo smiled. *This might just work!*

"Could the five of you please ask your trees to touch roots with these unbonded trees?"

When they all looked up at him, expectantly, he spoke to Silva.

Can you send a message to every elf in Silvaren, asking them to meet us here?

Eliséo closely watched the eyes of the five elves surrounding him. They glowed brightly, then all came over to join him with bewildered expressions on their faces.

"Did you just do what I think you did?" one of the elves, Amauri, asked him.

Eliséo smiled broadly. "That depends on what you think I did?"

Amauri's eyes glowed a golden hue. *Can I speak with you now?*

It worked! Eliséo was beside himself with excitement. All his plans for the Outworld hinged on this magic. A type of magic he never knew was possible.

Soon, almost every elf in Silvaren was gathered in the grove. Many of the younger ones had glowing eyes as they discovered they could now speak to each other through their trees. It hadn't taken them long to make the connection. The older elves looked rather uncertain.

"As some of you have already realised, we are now all connected through our trees. You should be able to talk with anyone you wish, but most importantly, you can talk with Silva and myself."

"Why is that the most important thing?" Raeslin asked.

Her mother's eyes glowed amber as she undoubtedly scolded her daughter for her impudence.

"All of you will recall meeting Rilla of the lintep and her companions a few months back. What you may not realise is that they are striving to complete a difficult task before a rogue lintep manages to steal power from an almost limitless source.

"I ask for three volunteers join me in going to the Outworld to search for this rogue. However, all three volunteers must be skilled with their weapons. The Outworld can be a dangerous place for the unwary."

Ripples of excitement flew around the elves – mostly the younger ones. Eliséo was surprised to see a flicker of annoyance cross Eléna's features.

What is it? he asked her through their bond.

You should be asking for four volunteers, she told him firmly. *You are the king now. You cannot go gallivanting around the Outworld. I hate to mention this so soon after your coronation, but you've seen how few of the elves have any great power. You are the last hope of our people to regenerate their powers. You cannot continue to risk your life to help others.*

Eliséo struggled to keep the shock from showing on his face. Every elf was considering whether they had what it took to go into the Outworld and help with this task. He could not afford to show them any sense of uncertainty on his behalf.

We will discuss that later, Mother. For now, I believe I must go gallivanting. More skills than communication may be required.

* * *

When she was a safe distance away from the Paradise, Lishe studied the map. She could not believe her luck. It really did indicate where all the Paradises were, and the order in which they expected Rilla to destroy them.

The thought made her hesitate. She'd watched the destruction of two Paradises so far and, though Rilla was involved with the destruction, it did not seem that she was essential for it. So why did the prophecy name her? Would she still be able to stop the prophecy if she killed Rilla? Lishe raised an eyebrow thoughtfully. It was worth a try if she ever managed to get near the little brat.

Brushing that thought aside, she focused on the map again. The closest Paradise was marked as P8. It was down the river from this Paradise, along the coast. It would be easy enough to reach, but it was far from any other Paradises. For her plan to work, she would need to travel around to as many Paradises as she could before they caught her, *if* they ever caught her.

"Upstream then." She traced her finger along the map, then looked in her rucksack. "I'll stop in Rockford on the way for supplies and cross over to the other side of the Bramble River."

It was a good plan. Rockford would provide the easiest route across the river. The city had spread so much that the humans had created a massive stone bridge across the river for ease of trade with Firechester. Lishe had no respect for humans, but even *she* had to admit that bridge was a wonderful piece of architecture.

It took her almost three days to ride to Rockford. She had travelled mostly at night in case the lintep sent out their dragons to find her. In the city, she blended in with practised ease. They would not be able to find her here, even if they had managed to track her the entire way, which she doubted they had. It was remarkably easy in large cities, such as this one, to find an inn with an empty stall for her horse.

She stayed in Rockford only one night. Time was of the essence. It was still taking her too long take each single portion of power from the Paradises. She needed all the time she could get before they destroyed them.

They seemed very efficient at doing so. Each time, it had been over in a matter of moments. Lishe fumed at the thought. If only she could figure out how they were doing it – how she could stop them. Then she would have all the time she wanted to take the power within the Paradises for her own.

With everything she had, she wondered if even Lord Aaron would rival her for power now. She was certain that she could best most of the other lintep in Illaria, but he was powerful and skilful beyond measure. There were things he had done which she still could not figure out how to do. If only *she* had been his daughter. She would not have wasted her gift as Nyssa had. She would have learnt everything she could from him and become the most revered mistress in all Illaria. People would have come from miles around to ask for their children to be tutored by *her*.

It was all she had ever wanted. But they had denied her that privilege, even after she passed all the tests they had set her with flying colours. Fury had eaten her up from the inside, and she had left Illaria soon afterwards. There was nothing left for her there. If they would not give her their prized blue tattoos, she would give herself black ones, in defiance of everything they stood for. She had memorised them all. Had paid a tattoo artist to ink her each time she thought she had mastered a particular skill.

Lishe fingered the tattoos as she rode out from Rockford, saddlebags laden with bread, fruits, cheese, anything she thought would last until she reached the next town. The tattoos were still a comfort to her. They grounded her, settled her thoughts, kept her calm. She *was* a mistress. One day, she would return to Illaria, display her power for all to see and then they would be forced to place her in charge of all the other masters and mistresses in their castle. She would be the most powerful and skilful mistress ever and no one – *no one* – would ever have power over her again.

Lishe looked up at the boundary of P5. In a single day, she had created a tear in the side, like a cloth that had been roughly cut and could not be stitched back together again. She felt a smile stretch across her face.

It was getting easier to take power from the boundary. The more she took, the more willing the rest were to come. They had been together for so long that they felt incomplete without each other. She could feel that. She could feel *everything*.

Her mind wandered as her power began the coaxing process for yet another piece to leave the boundary. She still could not believe Aislen's stupidity in leaving her map unguarded. True, she had left it with crystal dragons, but what were they to a lintep like Lishe? It had been child's play to steal the map from right under their noses. She wondered if they had noticed the theft at all.

Lishe laughed aloud, as another sliver of power was pulled into her body. She had lost count of all the powers she now held. All she knew was that if she linked all her bits of power together, she could reach out for miles around her, further even than the precious royal family. When she next returned to Illaria, she would force them to make her the Head Mistress – no one would be able to rival her power.

She watched the tear in the Paradise boundary as it slowly grew bigger. By the time those fools reached this Paradise, she would have enough power to stop them in their tracks. She toyed with the idea of stealing power from every lintep who dared defy her. It was a thrilling thought.

Chapter Thirty-Two – Trial

Princess Aislen.

Aislen awoke at the sound of Séverin's voice in her mind. She sat up, wishing for more sleep. It had been a long and difficult night containing Arishen's arson. Aislen picked her way carefully through the sleeping bodies on the tavern floor. Once outside, she found Séverin attempting to delay Kalid from entering.

"It's about time. We need to talk."

Aislen was taken aback by the human's abrupt manner. She nodded a dismissal to Séverin and drew Kalid a decent distance from the tavern.

"How can I help you?"

"Who said I needed help?" she asked, crossing her arms tightly across her chest.

Aislen forced a smile. "Forgive my assumption. What would you like to talk about?"

Kalid bit her nails and stared at Aislen as though judging how much to say. Aislen tried to contain her irritation of being woken up for a human who didn't appear to want her help so much as need it.

"I can't ignore what Arishen did."

Aislen raised her eyebrows. "Nor should you."

"It's just, I'm glad someone did it. But I wish it wasn't him."

Something clicked into place in Aislen's mind.

"I heard some women last night being grateful those men are now dead."

Kalid looked at her in sudden horror.

"No! No, no, no. Torak and Belial never got their filthy hands on me."

"Forgive me," Aislen replied with a shrug. "It seemed a common scenario."

"That's just the problem," Kalid told her. "It *was* a common scenario. And I'll bet every woman in this place felt safe last night for the first time in years. But there's enough of Erton's most loyal sheep making such a fuss that I can't let this go."

Aislen finally realised what the problem was.

"No, you can't let it go. You'll need to have trial for Arishen."

"A ... trial," Kalid sounded like she was testing out the word for the first time.

"Yes, you know, where people come forward to offer evidence for and against the perpetrator."

"I see."

"I assume you've been made the leader of your people now?" Kalid nodded. "Well then it will be up to you to hand out his punishment or set him free as you see fit."

Kalid shook her head. "No. I can't do that. I don't have any power over his life."

"Would you entrust that task to anyone else here?" Aislen asked gently. "I'm certain you already understand that's why your name came to Rilla's lips yesterday. She wouldn't trust anyone else here."

"Rilla? She's the one who got me into this mess," Kalid replied, almost angrily.

"Indeed. But if she hadn't, I think we both know Arishen's Partner would likely have taken power for herself and Arishen's life would now be forfeit. Would you prefer that?"

Kalid's shoulder's slumped. "No," she said in a quiet voice. "I'd better bring Arishen to the Assembly Hall. I don't suppose you'd like to come along and make sure someone doesn't kill him before we get there?"

"Just give me a moment to let one of my mistresses know what we're doing."

Aislen re-entered the tavern and spotted Kayte spread out in her own little corner of the room. The healing mistress was mumbling in her sleep. Aislen sent out a tendril of power to wake her. Kayte awoke with a short yelp. Thankfully, it did not appear to wake anyone else. Aislen motioned her over and waited for her outside. There was no use letting everyone know what was happening. It could only cause more trouble.

"Kalid has asked me to help her escort Arishen to the Assembly Hall. He will stand trial for his actions last night. Don't tell the others. I don't want to cause a riot at the hearing."

The tavern door creaked open and Tika stepped out.

"I'm coming too," he said in a firm voice.

Aislen looked at the boy with pity. He and Arishen were the only two humans living permanently in Illaria. That must have made him feel a stronger sense of camaraderie.

"I don't think that will be necessary," Aislen told him gently.

The fiery look in the boy's eyes surprised her.

"But I do, and this is *my* Paradise. I know it better than you do."

"How dare you speak to Princess Aislen in that tone." Kayte bristled.

"She's not *my* princess," Tika reminded her gently, but firmly.

Aislen weighed her options as they argued. Tika was right, but she didn't like it. What if he brought the others along? The trial would become about all of them instead of just Arishen. She noticed the sudden silence. Tika was looking at her oddly.

"You think I'm going to wake Rilla and Plyke for this, don't you?"

Startled, Aislen nodded.

"Well I won't. They both need to rest."

Kalid spoke up. "Actually, everyone here likes Tika. It mightn't be a bad idea to let him come."

"Very well," Aislen sighed. "Kalid, why don't you round up your people into the Assembly Hall. Tika and I will escort Arishen from the healers' house. Kayte, please stay with the others and *don't* tell Rilla and Plyke where we are if they wake before we return."

"I wouldn't dream of it," Kayte replied drily. Aislen shot her a look of annoyance but said nothing.

Aislen sat at the back of the Assembly Hall, with Tika by her side, curiously awaiting the outcome of the Paradise's first trial of sorts. Kalid stood upon a dais with Arishen sitting to one side. She had called on any Paradisians who wanted to have their say in the matter. At first, people were yelling over each other in an effort to be heard. When they would not listen to reason, Kalid had implemented the use of a "talking stick".

Anyone who wanted to speak was permitted only when holding the stick. It was passed from person to person as they ascended the dais. As his Partner, Parthak had been allowed to go first. She was livid.

"Arishen has defiled our Paradise with his repulsive actions. I should never have stayed silent about him when I knew what he was – that is my burden to bear. But I will not stay silent now.

"He is a seer. You all know this. He undoubtedly used those skills to see how, and when, the best time to attack would be and then he struck. Even I will admit that the lintep invaders had no chance to save Erton, Torak and Belial without destroying our entire Paradise, but that is exactly how Arishen planned it.

"We cannot allow him to go unpunished for viciously murdering three of our most loved and trusted Paradisians."

Aislen looked at Arishen. The boy was seated before the massed crowd. He did not face them, but hung his head low, as though ashamed of what he had done. Aislen knew that was not the case. A tendril of her power had found its way to him. He was seething with anger towards Parthak and looked away from her to avoid a nasty confrontation.

"Good riddance to them!" shouted one woman. Aislen recognised her as one of the women from the night before – the one who had spat on the building.

Parthak stared at the woman indignantly. "How dare you? Erton's life was worth more than yours ever will be!"

There was an uproar at her words. Aislen was surprised at the undercurrents of pain and anger in the hall. She withdrew most of her power within her walls, not wanting to take on the maelstrom of human emotions, but she still wanted to be able to sense the general mood.

Kalid held up her hands and called out for silence. Eventually, the angry voices subsided.

"Thank you, Parthak, for those heartfelt words." Kalid said sarcastically. She took the talking stick from her as she ushered the girl back into the angry crowd. "Ursher, you may speak now."

A middle-aged man walked up determinedly. There was so much anger in this room that Aislen had difficulty sorting out what each person was angry about. When she poked around further, she realised the anger was masking hatred and grief. Some people were even genuinely happy about Arishen's actions.

Ursher took the talking stick from Kalid and pointed at Arishen.

"This boy killed Erton and two of his most trusted men. None of us are here to dispute that – we all know he did it. The question we must ask ourselves is whether he deserves to be punished.

"In my years as a healer, I saw the brutalities Torak and Belial inflicted upon almost every person in this Paradise. The murders, ordered by Erton, were the least of it. As I'm sure you now know, Torak and Belial forced themselves upon many women. All these women could do was come to the healers to be treated afterwards. They could not tell anyone else or Erton would have ordered their death.

"These crimes are numerous beyond belief, and though Erton may only have ordered some of the atrocities committed, he was our leader. He should have been protecting us from people like that, not turning a blind eye to their depravities.

"From Arishen's own vision, you saw that Rhanya did not die of old age as we were forced to tell you. Torak and Belial smothered him with his own pillow. We heard them enter during the night. We heard the strangled cries as Rhanya struggled. But we could not raise a finger to help him, nor admit to the truth of what happened afterwards. Erton would have had us killed as well.

"Arishen may have done something despicable, but had I known he was doing it, I would have helped him, as I'm sure many of you would have."

Parthak and a handful of others strongly protested Ursher's speech, but their outrage was soon quieted by Kalid's upheld hands.

"Who would like to speak next?"

Aislen watched in annoyance as Parthak pushed forward one of her fellow protesters. Kalid reluctantly handed over the talking stick and stepped back.

"Lies! Everything Ursher has told you is a lie!" he yelled. "He accuses dead men of false crimes, knowing they cannot defend themselves against him. Will you stand there and let him?"

The room erupted into furiously shouted insults. There was nothing Kalid could do to calm them, nor did she appear inclined to. Aislen was about to use her power to suppress the most aggressive emotions when she saw Tika weave his way through the crowd. She was so distracted that she had not even noticed him leave her side.

Kalid handed him the talking stick as he approached her, a helpless look on her face. He turned to face the crowd and waited patiently until they finally noticed him standing up on the dais.

"Erton's sheep will never willingly admit what an evil man he was. By their association with him, they gained power themselves. I wonder if they are angrier with Arishen for committing this crime or for the irrevocable loss of their power?

"As I'm certain many of you can claim for yourselves, Erton irreparably scarred my life when I was only a little boy. He had my mother killed after she admitted I was her son. I don't know how many of you remember her, but my mother was a calm and gentle lady who worked with horses. All I have left of her is my love of horses and, hopefully, her gentle way. Erton stripped everything else away from me.

"I am not saying what Arishen did was right, but I can certainly understand what drove him to do it. Through his visions, he was forced to witness many of Erton, Torak and Belial's brutal crimes. He must have been driven to madness by these visions. Who can blame him for snapping like he did?"

His words had a calming effect on people. There was no outcry when he was done. Aislen was surprised to see a few people crying. Tika handed the talking stick back to Kalid and purposely avoided Arishen's stunned gaze as he returned to his spot beside her.

To Aislen, it seemed as though both sides had been discussed. All that was left now was for Kalid to pass judgment. The new Paradise leader was silent for a long while. She looked at Arishen with intense concentration. Aislen could feel the crowd start to tire. If Kalid did not speak soon, a few of the Paradisians would take matters into their own hands. It was precisely for this reason that Aislen had agreed to attend the trial. Though she was not certain that she had forgiven

Arishen's actions, she could understand what had driven him to it and did not want him to be dealt with too harshly.

Kalid made a sudden movement and clapped her hands loudly.

"I know most of us, myself included, feel safer now that our oppressors are gone. However, I am not blind to the fact that Arishen committed a heinous crime. His punishment may seem light to some of you, but considering it is this very thing which drove him to commit this crime, I think it will be punishment enough.

"Whoever wants to know the truth about their loved one's death or near accidents, they may ask Arishen. If any lintep are willing to assist, you may be shown the vision which will reveal it to you, as was done when Arishen first arrived back here."

Arishen visibly paled at the pronouncement. Already, there were people edging closer to him, clearly wanting to take advantage of his punishment. It was harsh, but Aislen could see the advantage in it for all those people who ever wondered if their loved one had really died of natural causes or not.

"That's barbaric," Tika gasped. "We have to help him!"

"Arishen must serve his punishment," Aislen replied, her shoulders sagging. "I can't do anything to help him."

Aislen walked away from the boy before he could object any further. She felt bad for Arishen – reliving those visions over and over would be tortuous for him – but Kalid was the leader here and Aislen had to respect her decision.

Chapter Thirty-Three – Rigid punishment

Isis watched Aislen enter the tavern. Something was amiss. Aislen was too distracted – too irritated. Before Isis had time to question her, she heard Tika's voice outside.

"Do you know where Isis is?"

"That's *Mistress* Isis to you." Kayte could be so stuffy and formal at times. Isis sighed and walked towards the door.

"Do you know where *Mistress* Isis is?" Tika asked in exasperation. Isis was surprised. He was usually the most placid of all of the children.

"No," Kayte replied shortly.

"I'm right here," Isis said, opening the door.

"Could we talk, somewhere a bit more private?"

Isis frowned but nodded. She led the boy away from the tavern. If their places were reversed, she wouldn't want Kayte listening in either.

"What's the matter, Tika?"

"It's Arishen," Tika replied quietly. "Kalid put him on trial this morning."

Isis listened in mounting horror as Tika explained what had happened.

"I … didn't know things would be so bad. I should never have convinced him to come back."

Tika looked up at her with pleading eyes. "You can help him now. Kalid said she would allow a lintep to help show his visions. You could do that, couldn't you? Then he wouldn't have to tell the same stories over, and over, again to different people."

"Isis, Princess Aislen just told me to let everyone know we're leaving this afternoon." Isis looked behind Tika to see Kayte standing there.

"Not without Arishen," Tika said firmly.

"He isn't one of us." Kayte shrugged. "He doesn't have to come."

"Kayte, we can't leave him behind," Isis told her. "What they're doing to him is brutal. Not only are they forcing him to relive visions but some of them are starting to blame him for not coming forward and saying anything when it was happening."

"They're what?" Rilla asked coldly. Isis hadn't noticed she was there. A small part of her cringed. Rilla had been so unstable lately – emotionally and with her power. Any little thing could set her off, let alone something as bad as this.

"Rilla, there's nothing you can do. Just leave it alone."

"No," Rilla answered softly. "I can't leave it alone."

"You can, and you *will* leave well enough alone," Kayte ordered Rilla. "If you attempt to intervene in the punishment Arishen has been given, I will stop you."

"You wouldn't." Rilla sounded unsure of herself. Isis watched the two of them in frustration.

"Rilla, I am asking you nicely, because I think you have enough respect for me to do what I ask. Please take Tika with you. Make sure Umi and Ulf are ready to leave as soon as the midday meal is over." Isis held her breath, hoping the girl would actually listen to someone for once in her life.

Rilla shook her head. "I'm sorry, Isis. I can't." She turned towards the Assembly Hall.

"Kayte, no!" Isis called out angrily as she felt Kayte's power fly past her towards Rilla. Within seconds, Rilla was standing rigidly. "You didn't have to do that. I was handling the situation."

"Yes, I could see how you were handling it," Kayte replied blandly. "The girl was readying herself to go into that Assembly Hall, fires blazing, to protect one of her own. We can't afford another disaster right now. We have bigger problems.

"You are free to deal with the Arishen matter any way you wish, as long as it does not cause further delays. By now, Lishe could be at another Paradise. With every passing day, she could learn how to steal more power. If we delay for every disaster this girl causes, Lishe will have more power than we can handle. We cannot afford to wait."

Kayte had already moved Rilla down to a beginner healing class. It was hardly a surprise that she would reprimand Rilla more harshly until she learned to control herself, but that did not help matters. The girl had been placed in Isis' care – *she* should have been free to deal with her as she saw fit. Encasing the girl with her power would *not* have been her first choice.

"I'm going to sort out this mess with Arishen," Isis turned on her heel.

"Make sure Aislen is happy to bring an arsonist back with us before you make any deals," Kayte called after her.

Isis stopped in her tracks. The thought that Aislen would not allow Arishen back to Illaria had not crossed her mind. She walked as quickly as she could, pulling Tika by the hand.

She found the princess in the tavern, making final preparations. Masters Graham and Bastienne were continuing lessons for Plyke and the twins.

"Aislen, I would like to give Arishen the chance to leave with us this afternoon. If I can arrange that with Kalid, are you happy for him to return with us to Illaria?"

Isis held her breath as she waited for an answer. Aislen carefully finished folding a spare shirt and placed it in her rucksack before turning to face Isis.

"It is a difficult question," Aislen said. "How should I explain his actions to my people upon our return?"

"They don't need to know," Isis told her.

Aislen shook her head. "The truth always has a way of getting out, Isis. The fact is that at some point in time, Arishen's actions will become known in Illaria. This Paradise is too far removed from anything they know. They will find it difficult to accept what he has done.

"If, as you have told me, he already feels trapped there, this will not make things easier for him. I'm not certain it's a good idea."

Isis shook her head. "But it's all my fault! *I'm* the one who convinced him to come here. He didn't even want to. If I hadn't convinced him, none of this could have ever happened. You can't punish him for that – not when he's already being punished in such a brutal way."

Isis was startled when Plyke spoke beside her. She hadn't noticed him.

"We're not leaving him here."

"Plyke, I know he's your friend, but his life could be in danger in Illaria after this," Aislen tried to reason with him.

Plyke only shook his head. "His life was already in danger in Illaria. Any lintep could turn on him for being a human. This incident might make them fear him more, but it won't put him in any more danger. If we leave him here, he *will* be in danger, from all Erton's sheep and especially Parthak. Just think for a moment what she would do to him the first time she finds him alone and vulnerable. I refuse to leave him here. If he stays, so do I."

"Me too!" Tika replied.

"Us too!" the twins chimed in.

Aislen pointed a finger at her young cousins. "You two have no say in the matter. I will be personally escorting you back to your parents the moment we land in Illaria.

"As for the two of you," she said, turning back to the Partners, "if you can convince Arishen to return with us, I will allow it. However, if any harm befalls him in Illaria because of this incident, I wash my hands clean of it. Is that understood?"

Isis let out a breath she hadn't realised she was holding, and the boys let out a whoop of joy. They took her by the arms, one on either side, and practically dragged her to the Assembly Hall.

Before she could formulate a plan, the boys had already burst into the Assembly Hall and were weaving their way through Paradisians to reach the front. When people noticed who it was, they began to give way, creating a pathway for them. Isis marvelled at the effect these two boys had on people, seemingly without noticing or trying.

"Kalid, we need a word with Arishen," Plyke said, as he signalled the new Paradise leader aside.

"He's in the middle of his punishment," Kalid told him bluntly.

"I can see that," Plyke replied coolly. "But from the look of him, he could use a short reprieve."

Isis looked over at Arishen. He was slumped in his chair, hopelessly staring up at the next Paradisian in line. As he spoke, pain rippled across his features. The woman muttered something under her breath. Isis couldn't make out the words, but it was enough to make Arishen cringe. There was no way for him to escape her fury.

When the lady had finished her turn, Kalid walked over to the dais and stopped the next person from approaching Arishen.

"I think it's time we give Arishen a chance to recompose himself." A general grumble started at the back of the hall and worked its way to the front. Kalid held up her hands. "Quit your whining. I didn't say his punishment's over, just give the boy a short break. He did help to free us from Erton's rule, after all."

Isis nodded to her appreciatively. Kalid barely spared her a glance. Together with Plyke and Tika, Isis walked purposefully up to the seer. He gazed up at them with haunted eyes.

"Never take revenge," he told them. "It isn't worth it."

"I may not have done what you did, but I know this Paradise is a better place for the loss of those three lives," Plyke said gently. He laid a hand on the seer. Isis noticed most of his hand was on Arishen's shirt, but a fingertip fell onto his neck.

Immediately, the seer began to recover. It was only a small change, but enough.

Firmly, she took Plyke's hand away. "I appreciate what you're trying to do, but we don't want him to appear too recovered or they will immediately begin again. Now, Arishen, you may not be aware, but we are leaving this afternoon. Do you intend to come with us?"

Arishen looked up at her in confusion. "They won't let me go until they think I've served out my punishment. I can't possibly tell them all they want to know so quickly."

"That's true," Isis conceded, "but if you're willing to let me try, we could speed up the process a bit."

"How?" Unsurprisingly, the seer was wary of her.

Isis had already formulated a plan. "Roughly how many visions of 'accidents' or deaths do you think you've had in this place?"

He shook his head. "I don't know. Hundreds."

Isis started. "Er … were all of them about deaths?"

"No. Maybe twenty were of deaths."

"And would you be willing to let me project them into everyone's minds like Aislen did? It might be quicker, and I daresay more effective, for them to see your visions. Then they'll know everything you know and will have no need to torment you any further. What do you say? Do you trust me enough?"

"I guess so."

It was the best answer Isis could hope for. Now to make sure she didn't hurt the poor boy. She was good at mind skills – they would never have let her become a mistress otherwise – but there were more than a few lintep she could think of better suited to this task than she was.

A second before she turned to the waiting Paradisians, Tika caught her wrist. She looked down at the boy, eyebrows raised.

"Thank you," he said softly. "For everything. I know you won't do anything to Arishen he doesn't want done. That's all we humans can hope for."

His comment cut her to the quick. Lintep would really need to change how they used their powers on humans when this whole mess of the Paradises was sorted out. Sooner with the ones they were in regular contact with.

She turned to the assembled humans.

"If you'll all give me your attention for a moment, I have a proposition to make." Isis waited until the murmurs around the room ceased and all eyes were on her. "Thank you. If you will permit me, I propose to show you all Arishen's visions from the first death or accident he can remember. It will save him having to tell the same stories repeatedly, and you will get to see exactly what he saw. Is this agreeable?"

Most people nodded, but about a score of them argued that they didn't want a lintep in their mind. Isis looked over to Kalid. The Paradise leader stepped forward.

"That's the best offer you're going to get. Take it or leave it. If you leave it, then you can leave this hall and never get an answer to your question. Go now."

To Isis' surprise, only a handful of people left the hall. With a nod, she turned to Arishen.

"Are you ready?"

"As I'll ever be," he replied. "Let's get it over and done with."

Isis sent out a tendril to Arishen's mind and allowed him to sort out his thoughts while she sent multiple tendrils out into the waiting crowd. She looked over at Tika and Plyke.

"No, not us," Plyke answered for the two of them. "We've seen enough. We don't need to see any more."

Once Arishen was ready, Isis began to feed the visions through to Paradisians. She couldn't help but feel their doubt as the visions began, but slowly, as she showed them details, which nothing but a vision could possibly give them, their doubt melted away into anger.

Fortunately, their anger was no longer directed at Arishen. The visions were such that the boy never would have had a chance to stop them, even if he hadn't been too scared to act. He saw them all as they were happening.

She purposely 'slipped' a few times and showed them Arishen's own fear when he woke screaming from a vision and waking the entire dormitory – Parthak's face close to his, threatening him.

By the time the bell tolled for the midday meal, Arishen had exhausted the store of all of his visions and the hall had cleared of almost everyone but a few stragglers, consoling each other in huddled groups.

Kalid pushed herself off the wall and walked over to them. Arishen looked at her defiantly.

"I don't have anything else to show you," he told her bluntly. Kalid tried to get some privacy, but Isis stayed as close to Arishen as Tika and Plyke.

"Why did you have a vision of me when I wasn't attacked?" she asked him. Isis looked inquisitively at Arishen. The boy shrugged.

"I don't choose what visions I have. I guess I was glad to have that one because at least I knew you were still alive. But I never had any more of you after that. The last vision I had of this Paradise, before we returned and I saw the isolation hut, was when Kora fled for her life."

"Oh." Kalid half smiled. "Well, I suppose other things took your attention away from us. Maybe now that you're back, you'll start having more visions of us again."

"Ah, actually, Kalid, we're leaving today," Plyke told her. "We were sort of hoping that Arishen would come with us."

Kalid seemed at a loss for words. "But ... you're going back to that lintep place."

Isis stepped in. "Yes, we are. Arishen is a very valued member of our town. He has been apprenticed to the best carpenter in all Illaria and his skills as a seer have saved numerous lives. It's his choice, of course, but he would be sorely missed if he remained here."

Isis pointedly ignored Tika's grin, as he exchanged looks with his Partner.

"Well, Arishen, what do you say? Your old life here in your Paradise, or your new life in Illaria?"

Arishen looked from Isis to Kalid, seemingly torn between two worlds. "Do I have to decide now?"

"Not right now, but soon," Isis answered, confused by his indecision. "We're leaving after the midday meal."

Kayte walked towards the tavern. She took her time, pulling Rilla along with her power. It wasn't a struggle. If Rilla had realised what Kayte was doing in time, it wouldn't have worked – Kayte knew she didn't have enough power to compete with the girl. She didn't bother speaking with Rilla. There was no point. The girl was clearly furious.

Let Aislen deal with her, Kayte decided. She didn't want to admit to herself that she was just a little afraid of how Rilla would retaliate if she released the girl when no one else was around. Rilla had a temper to match her flaming hair.

With no power left to sense who was inside the tavern, Kayte walked in virtually blind. A quick glance told her Aislen was not alone. Aurelius, Bastienne, the twins, Shuut and a few guards were with her.

"Aislen, a moment of your time." Kayte motioned the princess towards her. She didn't want to risk moving around, showing everyone what she had done. Aislen quickly placed her final few possessions in her rucksack and walked calmly over to them.

What have you done? Aislen threw the thought angrily towards Kayte. Kayte's eyes narrowed. Everyone always defended this brat of a girl. No one ever seemed to question her actions when anyone else would have been punished without a thought.

I've averted another of her disasters, Kayte retorted hotly. *She was about to go into the Assembly Hall and interfere with Arishen's punishment. I assumed you would rather I stop her* before *she delayed our journey.*

"Release her."

"I'm not hurting her, Aislen," Kayte protested. "I'm only stopping her from hurting others."

"Immediately." Aislen's tone brooked no argument.

Kayte hesitantly released Rilla, expecting the girl to explode. There was no reaction. Nothing. Kayte checked that all of her power was back within her body – that none of it had unintentionally stayed behind like a beginner student's, but it was all there. She glanced suspiciously at Rilla.

"Thank you, Kayte." Aislen's voice was oddly neutral. "You've done quite enough for today. Please make sure you're packed and ready to go."

* * *

Aislen forced herself to remain calm. True, Kayte probably hadn't had many alternatives, but what she had done was reprehensible. Especially on a child as volatile as Rilla, who barely trusted anyone as it was.

"Come, Rilla, let's have a little chat, you and I." Aislen went to put an arm around the girl's shoulder but noticed the tiny flinch at her movement. Instead, she gestured towards a corner table.

They sat together in silence for a while. Aislen tried to give the girl time to calm down. She knew the lack of retaliation was no indication of her mood.

"It appears you are often in Mistress Kayte's bad graces of late."

Perhaps it was not the best way to begin, but there weren't many better options.

"I'm not even meant to know that kind of magic is possible," Rilla replied with a quiet intensity. "What would she have done if I were any other student? Imagine if it was Umi or Ulf – she would never have dared!"

Rilla's voice rose along with her anger. Aislen shook her head, glancing over at the twins, who had instantly perked up at the heated conversation.

"True, she would most likely *not* have resorted to this," Aislen conceded with a nod. "But the trouble they get themselves into is of a slightly different nature to yours. They don't often put lives in danger – bones and property, yes, but lives, no."

"And she's put me in a beginner class again! Not even hers!"

Aislen had heard the rumour but had given it little credence. Kayte was certainly testing her boundaries.

"She has complete authority in her class, Rilla." Aislen spread her hands helplessly. "I cannot interfere."

"I suppose you can't interfere with Arishen's punishment either." Rilla crossed her arms. "You're just going to sit there and let them torture him and blame him until we go back to Illaria."

Aislen bit her lip. To tell or not to tell. "Have you considered that he may wish to stay in this broken Paradise? It was his home for years and his Partner lives here."

"She is no more his Partner than I am!" Rilla slammed her hands on the table and rose from her chair. "He *will* come back with us to Illaria. I can't keep my promise to Rhanya any other way."

"Rilla, sit down." Aislen readied herself for doing the unthinkable. "I forbid you to interfere. Isis has already gone with Tika and Plyke. They will deal with the situation as best as they can. If you go now, you will only make matters worse. Trust your friends to deal with this. Trust Isis."

She held her power all around herself, feeling the air for any change in temperature, any errant thought, but Rilla was keeping her power well contained behind her wall.

"Please get your things ready. You can join in with Aurelius and Bastienne's lesson if you have time."

Chapter Thirty-Four – Broken club

Arishen attempted to pick up a fork with his bandaged hand. After a while, he gave up. He was too distracted to eat anyway. How could he decide between a place he no longer belonged and a place where he often felt in danger?

"You're coming back with us, aren't you?" asked Tika. "You can't stay *here* after everything that's happened."

"It's different for you, Tika," Arishen replied bitterly. "Everyone loves you there. Your Partner lives within walking distance and your bond is stronger than ever. You've always wanted to be a part of magic, but you have no skills that they want to abuse."

"That's a little unfair, Arishen," Plyke replied. "There are plenty of people in Illaria who like you too. Miette will be heartbroken if you don't come back. Besides, did you ever think they don't want to abuse you? They are in awe of your skill and want to learn everything they can about it."

Arishen angrily pushed a pea into his mashed potatoes. "I know that! But every time they want to see a vision, half of them don't even bother to ask before jumping right into my mind. I don't have walls like you. I can't keep them out. They could do anything they wanted to me and I wouldn't be able to stop them. Did *you* ever think about *that*?"

A twinge of guilt rose in Arishen's chest. Plyke looked so hurt. "Look, I don't think all lintep are terrible, but they have a lot to learn about how to live with humans."

"We could be those people," Tika said quietly. "How else are they to learn if we aren't there to help them? Anyhow, your alternative would be to stay here, hope that Kalid will still take you on as an apprentice carpenter and that she's as good as Master Timothée. Then constantly be on your guard for Parthak and any of Erton's other followers who will *never* forgive you for what you did, even if the rest of the Paradise is overjoyed about it. Is that really any better?"

Arishen looked up at Tika. He was always so passionate about everything. Arishen had never been like that.

"She might come around."

"Parthak?!" Tika shook his head. "No. She never will. She will hate you forever, for what you are, the embarrassment you caused her and the danger you almost put her in. Why would you even want to wait for someone like *that* to change her mind when you have someone like Miette waiting for you back in Illaria?"

Arishen half smiled. *Miette!* True, she wasn't Rilla, but he could only pine so long after someone who ignored him so often. Miette would never ignore him. Miette would never be embarrassed by him. Miette might love him for everything he was.

A bench scraping against the floor brought him out of his musing. Tika and Plyke stood to go. "We're going to get ready now. You don't have long to decide."

Arishen nodded. His mind was made up. He would go with them. All that was left was to say a few farewells. He didn't want to leave things so badly with Parthak. Maybe if he apologised, she would forgive him. Maybe.

He left the eating hall and walked towards the school. Parthak was training to become a teacher, so it was as good a place as any to search for her. He pushed open the door, expecting to see students, but the room was empty.

At a loss of what to do, Arishen walked around the room and found himself at his old desk. He sat down and instinctively looked at the side of the desk where he had carved two names, years ago. He frowned. Both names had been scratched out entirely. There were other markings on the desk, he had not carved himself – dreams, magic, traitors.

Gritting his teeth, he stood up and made to leave the room. A shadow fell across the doorway.

"You can see how difficult things became for me when you left," Parthak said icily. "It wasn't enough that I had denounced you, I was still associated with a traitor to the Paradise. Enough children remembered you screaming in the night to realise your dreams must have meant something more than they'd first thought.

"Erton was rather forgiving, considering the circumstances. He gave me to Torak to *play* with."

Arishen cringed. "I'm sorry, Parthak. But you could have come with us. You could have left this world behind."

Parthak laughed bitterly. "Out there, I have no power, no standing. In here, I was well on my way to being respected. All I had to do was put up with Torak every now and then. Not so bad really." She shrugged. "I started to point out other women I thought he would *enjoy*. That made him grateful, less brutal."

As she told him, visions swam in his mind. Things she wasn't telling him, but he knew had happened. It was worse than reliving the other visions he had been forced to show people through Isis.

"You can come with us now," he offered. "I'm sure they would let you. After all, you're still my Partner."

Parthak spat at him. "I'm no more your Partner than Torak was my lover. All of this is your fault – everything I lost was because of *you*. I will make sure you never have a chance to regret it."

Arishen saw the vision a moment too late. The club smashed into him from behind. Pain exploded in his head. Everything went black.

* * *

"Where is he?" Tika searched for Arishen in the small group of people gathered in the tavern. "Let's go and find him."

"Maybe he decided not to come with us." Plyke laid a gentle hand on Tika's shoulder. "He knows we're leaving now. If he isn't here, then he must have decided not to come back."

"I don't believe that." Rilla crossed her arms. "Arishen would never decide to live here again. He was forced out by his Partner and when he returned, he killed three people and was tortured as punishment for that. What would ever possess him to stay here?"

Shuut sat on the ground, her head leaning on the bent knee in front of her. "He doesn't fit in back in Illaria. He doesn't really fit in anywhere. At least here he knows almost everyone and now they might leave him alone because they fear him."

Isis had been watching them closely. When she had returned with Tika and Plyke, Aislen had vehemently explained the need for her to closely watch all three of them, and Shuut, to make sure they didn't do anything rash.

The Partners were the least of her concern at the moment. Rilla and Shuut were a different matter.

"Well, I'm going out to find him," Rilla announced defiantly. "Who's coming?"

Isis sighed at the tone. She wound her way from the corner of the tavern to the four of them.

"We don't have time for this, Rilla," she firmly told the fiery girl. "Aislen has made it clear that we are leaving this afternoon no matter what. Arishen knows that. If he wants to come back with us, he'll find us. If not, we do not have time to traipse around the entire Paradise looking for him."

Rilla glared at her. "We're *not* leaving him here."

"We are. End of discussion, Rilla. It's time to go now. I have a duty to your family to return you safely back to them. Do not force my hand to something we will both regret." Isis looked at all four of them in turn. "Get your rucksacks, and let's go. Now."

* * *

Rilla angrily picked up her rucksack and strapped her weapons to her waist. Why couldn't they understand? Arishen would *never* choose to stay here.

Calm yourself, Rilla. Elessa's voice was instantly in her mind. *You will upset the balance of power within yourself and burn up. You cannot presume to know another person's mind. Perhaps there is more in this Paradise for the seer than you think. Perhaps there isn't. But that choice is not yours to make.*

No! I don't accept that. I'm going to find him. Now!

She closed herself off to Elessa and Eliséo. Arishen was one of *her* people. She had been protecting him most of her life in one way or another. For almost a year, she had actively protected him in the Outworld and then in Illaria. There was no way she was going to leave him behind in this broken image of a Paradise with people who did not appreciate him and would stoop to torturing him over something most of them were happy he had done in the first place.

Rilla picked her moment carefully and moved to one side of her erstwhile companions. She waited until Isis' attention was focused elsewhere and instantly whispered the words to bring up a solid mist around her. Within moments, it was done. She left the tavern to find Arishen.

* * *

Ensil was ill at ease in this Paradise. There were too many open spaces, too much opportunity for large groups of people to attack. He attempted to shrug off the feeling.

He focused on the five guards surrounding him. They had been more than pleased to have him along. His fame had apparently preceded him, and they had all been keen to make use of their time with him. Of course, he had lined all their weapons with compressed air, but other than that he showed them no mercy.

He grinned. The five guards stood ready to attack him with their swords. Ensil moved swiftly as the wind, using all his enhanced senses to full advantage. Every muscle they tensed told him exactly how and where they would strike next. He dodged in and out of their range while dealing them blows on the arms, chest, legs – anywhere they left undefended.

Soon, the guards were lathering up a nice sweat, their breath coming out in hard, short puffs. This was the moment Ensil shone! He used their deflated stamina against them and rained down blow after blow.

His sword stopped in mid-air. It would not budge, no matter how hard he pulled or pushed the hilt. Four of the five lintep guards attacked with full strength, forcing him to abandon his enchanted sword, and fight the guards with his bare hands and feet.

I'm getting too old for this, he thought to himself as he jumped and evaded yet another sword thrust. He mumbled a few words under his breath and the four attacking guards stopped mid-attack.

"You're cheating, Ensil," the fifth guard told him.

Ensil shrugged. "You started it. Now, I'd like my sword back, if you don't mind."

His sword floated over to him and landed gently at his feet. Ensil released the spell holding the other four guards in place and bent to pick up his sword.

Ensil, find Rilla!

The thought struck him so hard he stumbled and fell on his face.

"Steady on old man," called out one of the guards as he bent to help Ensil up. Ensil could see his blue eyes glowing in the reflection of the guard's sword.

What's happened? Ensil asked, surprised to be speaking directly with Eliséo.

I think she's doing something idiotic, Eliséo replied. *She's been forbidden from going to find Arishen, but I think she's gone anyway. She cut herself off from me and Elessa. I don't know what she's planning but you have to stop her.*

That girl is more trouble than she's worth, Ensil grumbled to his son. *Your tree could have chosen a better person to bond with if she wanted someone other than an elf.*

Not now, Ensil! Eliséo growled.

I'm going, I'm going, Ensil grumbled. *Let me know if she resurfaces.*

"You five, I need your help. Rilla has run off to find her friend. Likely she did this without anyone knowing and we need to leave soon. We need to search the Paradise for both.

"We work in pairs. You two take the other side of the stream. There aren't many hiding places there, so just run as fast as you can to search the area. The rest of us will search on this side of the river. Meet back at the tavern when you've finished your search. It would be good if we had a way to communicate with each other over the Paradise, but this is the best I can do for now."

"Princess Aislen could probably cover the entire expanse of the Paradise herself, maybe even Mistress Isis," one of the guards volunteered.

"Hmm." Ensil rubbed his stubbled cheek. "You come with me. We'll go talk to your princess while the others begin their search. Be careful. This girl is hot headed and powerful. If she thinks her friend is in danger, she won't care about repercussions in the effort to save him."

Four of the guards ran off to search for the missing children. Only Séverin remained with Ensil. With a shared look of annoyance, they set off for the tavern at a run.

There was a loud commotion as they approached the tavern. Tables were being overturned, windows and doors flung open.

"Looks like they've noticed she's missing then," Séverin puffed as they ran.

"That girl causes more trouble than anyone I've ever met before," Ensil retorted.

Séverin laughed. "You clearly haven't met her twin cousins then. They're worse than her but aren't as powerful yet."

"Oh, wonderful, so it runs in their family then. I suppose that means your princess will be difficult to deal with."

Séverin did not get a chance to answer before Aislen herself stormed out of the tavern, with Isis close on her heels. She stopped short when she saw them running towards her.

"Eliséo just told me she's made a run for it. She's gone to find Arishen and won't let anyone stop her, not even him."

"I can't sense her anywhere," Aislen growled. "I told her to leave it alone. *Isis* told her to leave it alone. That girl won't listen to anyone!"

"Sounds like she's got up a mist around her," Ensil surmised. "We won't be able to find her at all now until she wants to be found. Best bet is to find Arishen. Can you search for him?"

Aislen shook her head. "I don't know him well enough to get a fix on him."

"I might," Isis said. Her eyes went unfocused as she searched for the boy. She frowned. "I thought I had him for a moment there."

"Where?" Ensil asked.

"A large building, over near where the children sleep. But I can't sense him anymore."

"We'll start there. Let me know if you feel anything else," Séverin told her. "Let's go, Ensil. I have a bad feeling about this."

They ran towards the building Isis had indicated. It looked empty from the outside, until Ensil saw the shadows move. He signalled Séverin to silence. They stopped running, stepped lightly off the dirt pathway and hurriedly walked in a crouch the remaining distance to the building.

"Is he dead?" a girl asked in a cold, detached voice.

A few moments of silence fell before the muffled reply. "Not yet. I did hit him pretty hard though. It shouldn't be too long. Want me to hit him again?"

"No. He deserves to suffer through his death. Wait here and report back to me when it's over."

Ensil backed up against a side wall as the girl left the building. He sent Séverin to peek around when he thought it was safe. The lintep guard returned with a worried expression.

"It looked like the seer's Partner," he whispered. "I took a good look inside. I can only see two men there. They don't look very skilled, just big."

"Looks can be deceiving," Ensil replied roughly. "We go in together. They aren't lintep, so use all the skills you have. This doesn't need to be a fair fight. We leave one alive, barely. That's all."

Séverin nodded. Ensil enshrouded himself with mist – his power was not great enough to conceal both of them while they moved – and waited until Séverin had used his powers to blend into the background. It wasn't perfect, but in the darkened room, it would do.

They crept in quickly and quietly. As Séverin had noted, there were two men – one standing against a wall, foot up behind him, the other leering over Arishen's body, club at the ready for any movement. Ensil spared a brief glance at the boy lying motionless on the floor. If he was breathing, it was so shallow his chest was not rising visibly.

Ensil dropped his mist, sword at the ready, and lunged at the man standing over Arishen. The club came up automatically to block the blow.

Séverin took his cue and attacked the one leaning against the wall. The man gurgled blood as he slid to the floor. The sight clearly rattled the brute Ensil was fighting. He shouted out and brought his club down.

"No!" Rilla screamed and dove on top of Arishen. Distracted by her sudden appearance, Ensil's aim was off. Instead of slicing his chest, he slashed the arm holding the club. It wasn't enough. The club smashed down on Rilla's shoulder seconds before she put up a shield of mist. He heard her grunt as the heavy wood landed on her.

Séverin came up from behind the man and rammed the hilt of his sword into his head.

"I said leave one alive," Ensil growled.

Séverin shrugged. "He'll live. He'll just have a pounding headache when he wakes up. Can you get through to her?"

Ensil looked down where Rilla and Arishen lay, invisible on the ground. "That's enough of that, Rilla. You've caused enough trouble for one day. Drop your mist and open your bond."

The two children appeared – one unconscious, the other heaving sobs while clutching at her shoulder. Ensil shook his head in disgust.

I found your precious brat, he told Eliséo. *We might need to deny her the right to use Elessa's magic until she learns to use it responsibly.*

Just like you denied elves the right to even try their magic for hundreds of years? Eliséo asked bitterly. *Why don't you try protecting her the way you were meant to instead and leave me alone?*

Ensil drew in a quick breath. How many more of his actions over the past millennia would his new king find fault with?

"Séverin, can you ask Isis to call the others? We need to bring these three to the tavern and find the girl who orchestrated this mess."

The guard shook his head. "My power does not reach that far. I can run, though. I'll be there and back in a few moments. Can I leave you?"

Ensil waved him along. Séverin left at a run.

You could help her, Ensil's tree, Dystra, suggested.

No, replied Ensil gruffly. *That will only give Eliséo more cause to dislike me.*

You only have yourself to blame for that, Dystra reminded him. *If you will recall, I was against that decision in the first place.*

What would you have had me do instead? Ensil took his bait. He always did. *Too many elves were being corrupted by their power. I could not stand by to watch more of them fall.*

No, Dystra replied, *what you couldn't stand was the thought of Eléna falling.*

Ensil pushed back the memories Dystra was trying to force on him. He did not have time for this. Not when the dark-haired brute on the floor might awaken at any point, furious that his favourite club had been broken over the girl's shoulder.

Chapter Thirty-Five – Cinnamon scrolls

Aaron opened his eyes and cursed at the weak winter light streaming in through his window. Even in winter, when the days were shorter, they still started too early. He reached out with both hands to pull the curtains closed around his bed closed only to remember, with a pang of loss, that he only had one whole arm.

Swallowing the lump in his throat, he reached out with his power to pull closed the other side of the curtain. It wasn't difficult. Shaping his power to create the rest of his arm had been easy. The difficulty came in leaving it there permanently. It took a decent amount of his power to do that. What was left was still more than most lintep could dream of, but Aaron had always been used to so much more.

In the near darkness, he slumped back down into his pillows. He'd had a long life. There had been a few short years of happiness followed by decades of grief. No one could blame him for wanting to give up now. He was so tired. There was simply too much to care about. He didn't have the energy to care about any of it.

A knock at his door interrupted his sombre thoughts. He refused to get up to answer it.

"Father?" Kora's voice called out tentatively. "Are you decent?"

A small huff of amusement escaped him as he wondered how that could be her main concern. He shielded his eyes from the light as Kora drew back the curtains. She looked down at him with those pitying eyes. He was coming to loathe that look.

"Father, you can't stay in bed all day," she told him gently as she sat on his bed. "You know Uncle Lukys will find ways to keep you active and busy if you don't do it yourself."

"I don't *want* to keep busy," he grumbled. "I want to stay in bed as long as I like – all day if I want to. He has no right to drag me out every day to complete endless, useless, mundane tasks!"

Kora sighed. Aaron was coming to loathe that as well.

"Then get up before he comes to find you. We could take a walk around the gardens, or through the market. I'm certain people will be happy to see you." She hesitated a moment. "Pér would very much like to see you father. Perhaps we can visit him together?"

Aaron looked up at his only remaining child. She reminded him so much of his wife. Graesyn had been equally unsure of herself, not realising how much people loved her. Sometimes he wondered if Graesyn truly understood how much *he* had loved her – still loved her. She had been so sensitive. The tiniest things could affect her. Kora was just the same.

He relented. "I'll come." Patting her arm, he noted the smile and slight blush upon her cheeks.

"Shall I ring for breakfast?" she asked, as she rose from the bed.

"Why don't we pick up a pastry from one of the bakeries? I know you've always been fond of those cinnamon scrolls."

* * *

Kora walked arm in arm with her father. He probably did not need it, but she felt better knowing that she could support him if he fell. It surprised her when she realised that he was using his power where he would usually have done things with his hand, like steadying himself on the stone railing around the winding staircase.

They walked through the castle gardens, nodding heads and exchanging pleasantries with people. She could feel her father retreating behind a shell of indifference as people glanced at his missing arm and then pointedly avoided mentioning it. His pain washed through her with their skin contact. She carefully shifted her hand, ever so slightly, so that her fingers no longer brushed against his soft, weathered hand.

Kora breathed in the marketplace aromas as they walked across the drawbridge. The herbs and spices always reached her first. She smiled sadly as each brought back a vivid memory of playing with her brothers and sisters in their youth. When they reached her favourite baker, Aaron pulled them up short. Kora was amazed that her father still remembered these small details of her early life. They hadn't walked through the marketplace together in over twenty years.

The baker came out of his kitchen with a tray full of berry scrolls. He plonked the tray down on the bench and carefully moved the scrolls next to a selection of cinnamon ones.

"How can I help you?" he asked, gazing down at his pastries with a hint of pride. Before Kora had a chance to reply, the baker looked up and gasped.

"Lady Kora, Lord Aaron! What a pleasure to see you both again. Two cinnamon scrolls and a pumpkin seed loaf?"

Kora stared at the man in shock. That was exactly what the two of them used to order with Nyssa.

"What?" she asked incredulously.

"Oh, you're right!" The baker slapped his forehead. "Begging your pardon, milady. How could I not realise, what with Lady Nyssa not being here. Just one cinnamon scroll, then, and one pumpkin seed loaf."

He pulled out the order without confirming it with them and passed it over. Kora was in too much shock to pay the flour dusted man. Her father laughed, a rare and beautiful sound, and passed the man a few copper coins. Only, he didn't pass them with his hand. It seemed as if he was using a phantom hand made of his power.

The baker held out his hand for the proffered coins, then stared up at Lord Aaron with awe.

"Milord, you always were a wonder to the rest of us. I told my wife, I told her, that you wouldn't miss your arm. Not really. And here, I was right. I'll tell her, but she won't believe me. Who *would* believe me? They'll say that I made the entire thing up, that I didn't even see you today. That's what they'll say."

Kora loved the effect her father had on people. He never used his power to influence their opinion of him, they simply loved him for who he was and what he was capable of.

She took her cinnamon scroll and nibbled on it, savouring the taste. She had so missed cinnamon in the Paradise. Spices like that were a luxury. There was no extra space to grow them in the fields. Rhanya's garden alone had provided her with some small relief. At least he had grown some of the plants that she favoured as teas.

She had been wary of getting to know the healer. Even when she had first entered the Paradise, he already knew everyone there by name and all their usual ailments without the help of written records.

Knowing that the Paradisians were not tolerant towards magic, Kora had remained as unobtrusive in her use of it as possible. On occasion, when there had been epidemic illnesses, she had feigned the same symptoms to avoid notice.

"Such deep thoughts over a cinnamon scroll?"

Her father nudged her gently. Kora only shook her head. There were many parts of her life that her father did not know about and that she would likely never tell him. However, there was one part of her life that she was no longer happy to keep separate from the rest of her family.

"Pér's stall is just around the corner."

She quickened her pace in anticipation.

"Why doesn't he live in the castle?"

Kora stopped short.

"Pér? Live in the castle?"

"Unless he particularly wants to live in the town. He was never much of a merchant, as I recall, so I doubt he would noticeably miss that part of his life."

"But ... I..."

Her father patted her hand with his phantom hand.

"Kora, dear, I'd have to be blind not to realise that you spend more nights in his home than in your own room. Unless you feel more comfortable living out in the town, I suggest you bring him into the castle so that he can get used to it. One day, you will be queen and, if he wants to see you, he will be forced to live in the castle."

Kora only realised her jaw was open when her father gently closed it. Before she could reply, Pér came up from behind and kissed her cheek. Startled, she almost hit him, but he caught her elbow before it connected.

"Bad surprise?" he asked with a laugh.

"I don't think it was as bad as *my* surprise," her father told him. "I suggested you should move into the palace."

Kora felt his grip tighten on her elbow. She couldn't help but laugh.

"Father, we hadn't discussed anything of the sort."

"Well, it's high time you did. Plyke finally has a mother and a father who love him and each other. There's no reason the three of you shouldn't live together."

"I don't think King Lukys would welcome me into his castle," Pér objected with an embarrassed cough.

Kora looked between her father and her love.

"I think Uncle Lukys would make an exception if we asked him to. After all, it was only your songs he disliked, and he only objected to those because father and I convinced you to play songs specifically designed to make him mistrust you.

"But we don't have to decide right now. Your home is quite comfortable. I'm certain you don't just want to leave it behind."

Pér looked at her with eyes that made her heart ache. "I'd leave it in an instant if you asked me to."

Kora felt her chest tighten. "I ... I don't know. Your home has always felt so safe, so warm and inviting."

Pér caressed her cheek. "You only feel that there because I want you to. It would feel the same anywhere we live if we're together. If you want me to come to the castle for you, I will."

Kora was saved from making a decision by the flight of a white-tipped crystal dragon right over their heads. She could barely make out the shapes, but she counted three people on its back.

"They shouldn't be back already. Something must have happened."

Without waiting to see if the others were following, Kora ran towards the castle stables, her cinnamon scroll forgotten in her clenched fist.

* * *

Leif clung uneasily to Snowcrest as the crystal dragon flew in lazy circles over the top of Illaria. She had been instructed by Rownyn to wait until the field beside the castle had been cleared of horses before landing. Leif was very relieved that Rownyn was with them. Returning alone, under these circumstances, would raise more than a few questions.

His stomach lurched suddenly. He instinctively gripped Talise tightly about the waist as Snowcrest descended without warning. Since his fall two nights ago, Leif had a newfound fear of heights. Freezing air whooshed by him as they sped towards the ground. He closed his eyes against the ground rushing to meet them. *Don't crash! Don't fall!*

Snowcrest abruptly jerked up, beating her wings against the ground, and hovered for a moment before landing on the grass. Leif scrambled down, dignity forgotten in his moment of terror. He only belatedly remembered to offer Talise a hand, but she was already standing by his side, looking just as pale as he felt. Rownyn alone looked composed.

"What's happened? Where's Plyke? Where's my son?"

The words were screamed out hysterically as a lintep came running up to him from the stables. Leif did not recognise her. Still recovering from the flight, his mind could not keep up.

"He's recovering well," Leif answered before he could stop himself. "Wait, how did you know what happened to him?"

"Recovering?" The lady froze. "Recovering from what?!"

"Kora, slow down!"

A man with half an arm missing came jogging behind her, accompanied by a tall, muscular man. Leif assumed the one-armed man to be Lord Aaron – the one everyone had been so worried about when he and Talise had first come to Illaria.

"Lord Aaron!" Rownyn called out, a hint of relief in his voice. "You've healed."

Lord Aaron caught up to them as Kora, doubled over, asked again, "Recovering from what?"

"Lady Kora, do not be alarmed. Plyke is quite well now," Rownyn attempted to reassure her. "There was a little incident with the Paradise leader."

"I should never have let him go!" Kora cried. "What did Erton do to him?"

Leif placed a hand on Rownyn's shoulder. The guard stood down and allowed him through.

"Lady Kora, perhaps we might continue inside? There are a great many things we need to discuss."

"Leif, please," Talise said from behind him. "Look at her. She needs to know what happened to her son *now*, before she becomes sick with worry."

His fiancé stepped lightly around him and took Lady Kora by the hand.

"Your son intervened to protect Rilla. She owes him her life. None of us are entirely certain what happened next.

"The dagger that was meant for Rilla's heart struck Plyke instead. Then Rilla did something to fix Plyke's heart. I don't know what it was. She got into an awful lot of trouble over it and there was something said about not being able to destroy Paradises in the same way anymore.

"But she saved his life. It didn't take him long to recover at all. Mistress Kayte took care of him. He was quite well when we left – I promise you that. And Tika, that dear, sweet little boy, won't let anything else happen to him. You needn't worry."

Leif was amazed at the effect Talise's words had on the lintep. From the near-panicked state she was in to start with, Lady Kora was now breathing steadily and hugging Talise.

"Thank you," she whispered. "My son means everything to me."

"You're not the only one," Talise replied as she gently pulled back from the lintep's embrace. "From the looks of it, all his family and friends care for him enough that they will put themselves in danger to save him. Now, chin up and let's go inside so we can tell you everything that happened."

"Rownyn, is everyone else well?" Lord Aaron asked the guard.

Rownyn immediately stood to attention. "Yes, Lord Aaron. Princess Aislen and all the royal family were well when we left. Duke Leif has missives from your cousin. They should explain everything."

"Very well. You may report back to Nicodemo." Lord Aaron dismissed his guard with the wave of his good hand.

"Kora, dear, run along and let Lukys know we'll meet him in the council chambers. Pér, you're more than welcome to join us. Plyke is your son too, after all."

"Thank you, Lord Aaron." Pér inclined his head. "I'd appreciate that. I'll go with Kora now."

Leif watched the two younger lintep walk quickly hand in hand back towards the castle before his gaze returned to the old man before him.

"My good dragon, I do not recognise you, but if there is anything you desire after your long flight, you need only ask Master Edric, the stable master, and I'm certain he will provide it for you."

"So, you're Lord Aaron, then. Pyrid thinks the world of you. I'm Snowcrest."

Lord Aaron chuckled. "Well, I'm quite fond of Pyrid myself, Snowcrest. I'll send Master Edric out to see to your needs. Now, Duke Leif, my lady, please allow me to escort you into the castle." Lord Aaron gestured towards the stables.

Chapter Thirty-Six – Repercussions

Aislen felt anger and, if she was honest with herself, a good deal of uncertainty, bubbling inside of her. She had to fight so hard to keep it contained within – to keep her power tightly curled around her so that she wouldn't unduly influence anyone else. Doubtless, she wasn't the only one angry with Rilla, but she could not let her anger cloud the situation.

Once Kalid had taken charge of Parthak and her unconscious brute, Rilla and Arishen had been brought back to the tavern for Aislen to deal with. It was now clear that the seer would not be safe in the broken Paradise and would need to return to Illaria.

Aislen drummed her fingers on her crossed arms as she glared down at Rilla. Her shoulder injury was severe, but not life threatening. It was clear the girl was in a lot of pain and, quite frankly, Aislen was more than happy to leave her that way until she had learnt her lesson. Kayte and Médard were sitting in a corner of the tavern. They had already brought Arishen back to consciousness and were ready to work on Rilla as soon as needed.

"Explain yourself."

"I had to find him," Rilla sobbed through her pain. "I couldn't just leave him behind. Not when I knew Parthak would attack him."

"But you *didn't* know that," Aislen reminded her. "You only assumed it would. Since we arrived in this Paradise, the two of you, three including Plyke, have done nothing but act on instinct. I understand some of the time you were trying to help people, but you've caused endless amounts of trouble and seem to have no remorse for your actions.

"Exactly what do we need to do to get through to you? You are *not* invincible. You are *not* above the law. You are *not* to disobey your superiors. Do I make myself clear?"

"She saved my life," Arishen pointed out timidly. He sat awkwardly, clearly still in pain from the beating he'd taken. Kayte had only done the bare minimum necessary to save his life.

Aislen turned her angry gaze on him. These children were making her work so hard to keep her temper.

"Your life may not have needed saving if you hadn't set fire to a building, killing the three people inside it. Don't think any of us have forgotten about that."

Breathe. Count to ten and breathe. One, two, three, four, five, six, seven, eight, nine, ten. Breathe.

"We should have already left by now. Kayte, deal with Rilla. I don't think you need to remove her pain. Let her suffer the consequences of her actions. Once you're done, escort her outside the Paradise. Séverin, stay with them.

"The rest of you, get your things. We're leaving now. I've organised with Kalid to leave six guards behind to deal with the mess that is this Paradise until arrangements can be made for the Duke or Duchess of this duchy to take over. That means I need everyone on their best behaviour, including you two." She directed this last comment towards the twins. They, at least, had the good sense to look obedient. Perhaps this journey had done them more good than harm, showing how rash and stupid actions could have disastrous consequences.

* * *

It had been a long afternoon of flying. Shuut was exhausted. Going back to that Paradise had drained her more than she had expected. She had hoped they would wipe the smug look off Erton's face when he saw they were back and realised they had destroyed his Paradise. She hadn't expected him to attempt to murder his daughter, her *sister*, in full view of everyone.

She shook her head angrily. A year ago, she would never have been caught in a situation like this. In her life as a banwep, she had no attachments, no responsibilities to anyone but herself.

I also had no life.

It was a persistent thought. So persistent, she often wondered if someone was forcing her to think it, but her walls were too strong for that. Even without Nyssa's power, she had still managed to create walls to be proud of. The thought of Nyssa's power still nagged at her. Everyone expected her to be so happy to have that power, to want to use it because it would make her more powerful than most full lintep.

"Lady Shuut?" Séverin called out to her. The title still bothered her, but she knew he was using it to remind her she was part of the royal family and he would only have to follow her out into the town of Turon if she insisted on walking.

"Séverin, can't you just forget, for a moment, that I am who I am and just let me be?"

The guard shook his head. "Princess Aislen is even more protective now than she was when we first travelled to the Paradise. I am the only guard in our retinue. If you leave Dell's Inn, I will be forced to follow you, which will mean leaving the rest of the royal family unprotected. Much as I would love to spend time alone with you, *please* don't put me in that position."

Shuut was embarrassed to find herself blushing. She sighed and stepped back into the taproom and looked around. The children were upstairs with Aislen and Ensil. Kayte, Isis and Bastienne sat quietly at the bar, nursing ales. Aurelius sat in a corner booth with Ratchin, talking about old times. It had surprised Shuut to learn that they had formed a firm friendship in their youth. Ratchin had never spoken much about her past and Shuut had respected that privacy.

She swallowed her pride and walked over to her friend. At her approach, Aurelius made his excuses and went to join his fellow teachers at the bar. Ratchin made a show of wiping the table with a rag from her apron as Shuut sat down.

"I still miss you," she said softly.

"And I you," Ratchin replied gently. "But that is life."

"It doesn't have to be."

"Shuut, dear, I'm too old to go changing my life around. Can't you leave it at that?"

Shuut frowned. "No, I can't. The people of Turon will survive without you for a time. There is room on the dragons. Come back with us to Illaria."

At Ratchin's sharp intake of breath, she knew she had struck a chord. The large lintep woman glanced over at Aurelius and tightened her lips. Shuut put two and two together.

"Aurelius already asked you, didn't he?"

No answer.

"Exactly how well did you two know each other in your youth?" Shuut sat back comfortably, making sure that Ratchin knew she would not leave until she had an answer.

Ratchin looked up at Shuut, then over to Aurelius again. Her eyes lingered there for a long while.

"Not nearly so well as both of us would have liked."

"I'm here all night with nothing else to do. Do I really need to drag the story out of you?"

Ratchin sighed. "We first met a little while after I moved to Turon. I'd just met a lintep whose power was peaking and couldn't control it. I did my best to help him. I taught him enough for him to keep his powers, but I did not have the time to teach him everything he needed to know." She laughed at the memory.

"I didn't know it, but Aurelius had been watching our progress. He was amazed that someone like me, who had never been to Illaria and was not a trained mistress, could help peaking lintep so well. He offered to show us both the way to Illaria.

"Perhaps I should have gone with them, but I was just starting to build a name for myself. Many people in Turon had already sought me out for my healing abilities. It was nice to feel important. I knew if I went to Illaria, I would just be one of many, lost in the crowd. No one would notice me. I didn't want that."

Shuut listened attentively. She had never come close to guessing the truth of Ratchin's past. But she knew there was more her old friend was not telling her.

"That wasn't the only time you met Aurelius though, was it?"

Ratchin's eyes sparkled. "He left me with instructions on how to find Illaria and tried to wring out a promise that I would come and visit him. I thought about it, don't think I didn't, but there were so many people here who needed me.

"A few years later, he came back. By that point, he was just about to take the test to become a master. He was always so very talented. Two months he spent here, teaching me skills I had never seen before. Mind you, I taught him a thing or two about healing. We became quite good friends so when it was time for him to return to Illaria, he asked me to go with him ..."

"But you never went," Shuut finished her thought. "Why not? I don't believe your excuse of too many people needing your help. So, really, why not?"

Ratchin twisted her apron and avoided Shuut's eyes.

"I ... I was afraid."

"What in the Outworld could you possibly have been afraid of?"

Ratchin looked sharply at her. "I happen to like being well-known and needed. I like my room full of tokens from people I've helped. If I went to Illaria, I would have lost *all* of that. No one would have known me. I'd have had to work so hard to earn the respect that I already had here. And I was afraid that if I went to Illaria, Aurelius would be overwhelmed with his responsibilities and forget me."

Shuut shook her head.

"Shuut, dear, I can see your relationship with him is different. But if that young guard asked you to leave everything you knew to follow him to a place where he might easily forget all about you with all his other responsibilities, would you go?"

Shuut looked over at Séverin. She liked him. He was good with a sword, strong, safe, reliable. He seemed to like her as well, but she couldn't understand why.

"I suppose not," Shuut replied. "I don't think he likes me that much."

"There you go then." Ratchin folded her hands in her lap and sat back.

Shuut shook her head. "*This* is different. Aurelius came back for you when you didn't follow him. He asks every lintep you send him to tell him about you. He still remembers your friendship, quite fondly from the looks of it.

"Besides, even if not for him, you could come to Illaria for me, for all the other lintep you've sent there. You could come to Illaria for yourself! You wouldn't just be one of many. You're *Ratchin*. You could never be forgotten or cast aside by anyone."

Shuut got up from her seat.

"We're leaving tomorrow morning. I don't suppose we'll have any reason to come here again, at least not anytime soon. I'm not going to beg you to come, but I will miss you if you stay. And I'm not the only one."

Without waiting to see Ratchin's reaction, or give her time to reply, Shuut went upstairs to bed.

* * *

Looking up from the missives Aislen had written, Kora stared coldly at Duke Leif. "You lost my map."

"No." He shook his head emphatically. "We didn't *lose* your map. Aislen ..."

"*Princess* Aislen," Kora corrected him.

Leif visibly struggled to control his temper. "*Princess* Aislen thinks that Lishe stole it. Whatever the case, we need more copies of your original and we need to move faster now. I thought that was all explained in the notes."

Kora waved the letters in the air and looked at them dismissively. "These notes don't explain how Lishe got hold of the map in the first place. How do I know that any other copies we make won't be as easily misplaced by your fellow dukes and duchesses? That is, if they even agree to help?"

Leif shrugged. "As far as I understand it, none but another lintep could take power from the Paradise boundaries, so who else would *want* to steal them?

"As for whether or not the others will agree to help, we won't know until I visit them. Snowcrest has agreed to escort us to each duchy and I propose we leave as soon as possible. I don't know what Princess Aislen is planning, but I intend to make sure that we have soldiers at every known Paradise as soon as she needs them."

Pér put a hand on Kora's knee, under the table so the others couldn't see. It wasn't skin contact, but it had the desired effect. Kora took a deep breath.

"Very well, Snowcrest will not be rested enough to fly you to Deuterfoss until tomorrow morning at the earliest. In the meantime, I will have four copies of my map drawn up for you. If you need more copies, your own scribes can make them. Are we agreed?"

"Yes," Leif answered shortly. "Now for the other matter at hand. As soon as the other dragons are fully rested, the others will be returning. Unless plans have changed significantly since then, Princess Aislen plans on continuing the destruction in the agreed order, if possible.

"She will take one dragon herself and meet you at P2. The rest of the dragons will fly to Silvaren to pick up a group of elves. Apparently, they have found a new way to communicate with each other over distances, so they will spread out to the other known Paradises and search for Lishe. If any of them finds her, they will send word back to you ... well, that's the bit I'm unclear on."

Kora shared a look with her father and uncle. "I don't think you need to know anything more about that than you already do."

Lukys drummed his fingers on the table. "None of this really matters if what you say is true, Duke Leif. We cannot destroy the Paradises in the way we were. It will take us too long to understand how the prophecy works. All we can hope to do is find and stop Lishe."

"That won't be enough, Lukys, and you know it," her father pointed out. "If Lishe has figured out how, so could any lintep who set their mind to it. From what we now know, there could be hundreds, even thousands of lintep living in the Outworld who we don't know anything about. If they happen to stumble across even a single Paradise, they could steal more power than any lintep should have and become just as much a danger to everyone as Lishe now is.

"I think the time for secrecy is past. If the dragons won't give us another crystal heart, we will need to figure out another way to destroy these Paradises. The sooner we leave for P2, the more time we'll have to study the problem before the others arrive."

"We?" Lukys asked incredulously. "Aaron, I'm sorry, but you're not going anywhere."

Kora wanted to agree but instead found herself defending her father's rights. "Uncle Lukys, you may be the king, but we all know that father is more powerful and more skilled than you. If anyone has a chance of figuring this thing out, it would be him. You can't stop him from going into the Outworld just because you're afraid."

"I most certainly can!" roared Lukys before a wave of calm flooded the room. Kora looked at Pér with the hint of a smile. She could always recognise his power. He was only humming a few notes, but that was all it took for him to change the king's mood.

"Lukys, be reasonable," Aaron told him. "You can't leave Illaria while Aislen is away. I, however, can certainly go with a handful of people. I'm certain there are still some skilled lintep who would be happy to accompany me."

"You can count me in, Lord Aaron." Pér raised his hand. Kora looked at him, mildly surprised and shrugged.

"Me too. We can probably count on Guiscard as well."

Aaron slapped his hand down on the table.

"It's settled then! The four of us will journey ahead to P2 with a guard and try to solve this problem before the others arrive. Duke Leif will head out to all the human duchies with Rownyn and request soldiers be sent to all the Paradises. The elves will search for Lishe at all known Paradise locations."

Kora suppressed a laugh. Only that morning, her father had been in mourning for his arm. A short walk and an unexpected diversion later and he was organising the destruction of Paradises out from under his king's nose.

* * *

Aaron sat with Guiscard late that night. Extra scribes had been called in to create copies of Kora's map. They would have to work through the night to get them done by the time Duke Leif was ready to leave with his small retinue.

"Do you ever wonder what would happen if you could go back in time to change just one thing?" Aaron asked, tilting a glass around to make the honey mead swirl within it. Guiscard took a sip from his own glass.

"What would you change?" Guiscard asked.

"I suppose I was too young when my mother first went out to fight those pig-headed humans who started this whole mess. There was nothing I could do to change that. But there have been other things.

"If I hadn't taken my family to Silvaren, they might all still be alive now. If I had paid more attention to my girls when we returned, they might never have left."

He watched how the light from the fireplace created patterns in his glass. Such simple things could give him pleasure. With all the heartache in his life, Aaron had become quite good at finding pleasure in the little things. They were all he could ever rely on to be steady.

"Hmm, you would change a lot of things like that," Guiscard warned. "Out of all your grandchildren, the only one who still might exist is Plyke. Kora and Pér would always have found a way to be together. Rilla and Shuut would almost certainly *not* exist.

"Excuse me saying so, but had Nyssa not gone into the Outworld, she may never have found someone who could put up with her. She was talented, certainly, but she was smug about her powers and not well liked among many of her peers."

Aaron rested his chin in one hand and thought it over.

"I don't want my grandchildren to live in the same world I lived in. I don't want them to be afraid of humans and the Outworld. I want them to feel safe and secure wherever they choose to live."

Guiscard chuckled loudly. "Oh, Aaron, so do all parents and grandparents, but that will never happen. Even if we manage to destroy all the Paradises and reunite lintep with humans, there will always be small factions of each race who are not happy with the situation. I'll warrant even the elves and karliki would have similar problems if all four races were put together."

Aaron drained his honey mead, somewhat dispirited. "Does that mean you won't come with me to find a way to destroy those monstrosities?"

Guiscard waggled a finger at him. "Now, I didn't say that. I've been your friend for more years that either of us wish to remember. If you're going back out there with no idea of what to do, I'm coming with you. We both know I'm the brains between the two of us. You'll never be able to find a solution without me."

Aaron smiled to himself. In all Illaria, Guiscard was probably the only friend he had. Being the son of a princess had always made things difficult with the other children growing up. Their parents had clearly impressed upon them that they should respect royalty, which the children had interpreted to mean they should not speak with him.

It had been a lonely childhood. His only cousins were Lukys and Kynon, which only made things worse. Lukys was the crown prince and Kynon, well, Kynon was a spoilt brat. Even Aaron hadn't wanted to associate with him when they were children. But now...

"Do you think we should ask Kynon to come along?"

"Kynon? Really?" Guiscard blurted out. He paused, then added, "I suppose, he has changed in the past few months. It couldn't hurt to ask him."

"Tomorrow then," Aaron promised himself. "I'll ask him tomorrow. We can always delay for a while. The Paradise is not going anywhere."

Chapter Thirty-Seven – Trust

It was almost time for them to leave Turon. Aislen decided it was not worth detouring past Silvaren first. There was no point picking up any elves until they had a map and the lighter load might help the dragons fly faster to Illaria.

Aislen found the weapons master preparing his bag in his room. "Ensil, I think it's best you stay with us. With everything that has been happening with Rilla, we may need you to communicate with the elves. There may be times when she simply isn't capable of talking with Eliséo. You seem to talk with him in a different way. I ... confess I don't really understand it, but if you agree, it might be the best course of action."

She watched the elf mull over the idea and waited, slightly impatiently, for his answer.

"This is a difficult time in Silvaren, Princess Aislen. I must discuss these matters with my king."

"Your king?" Aislen asked in confusion. "What are you talking about? I thought Liessa was the queen."

"Ah, yes, we were quite distracted when it happened because of the fire." Ensil sat on the bed and motioned for Aislen to do likewise. "You may have wondered why I asked Rilla to use her elf powers rather than using them myself. It was in that moment that Silva chose Eliséo, over his sister, to be the ruler of the elves. Liessa is no longer the queen."

Aislen turned the thought over in her mind. From what she had understood, Liessa had only been queen for a very short amount of time. If Eliséo had been made king...

"Did Rilla somehow inherit even more power when that happened?"

Ensil shook his head. "It remains unclear. She has not properly been tested. I do not know what she is capable of, but I am certain she holds a great deal of power."

Aislen sighed. Yet another problem to deal with. She wondered if Rilla would be any easier to handle if she didn't have quite so much power.

* * *

Eliséo tried not to think about Ensil. His father had made a lot of changes in Silvaren that the elves didn't necessarily even know about. It felt like he was only just starting to scratch the surface. Ensil had made up the myth about the crown – that only the one who wore the crown had power.

Eléna had known that was not true but had never seemed to question it. She knew that he had power even without the crown. Why was it then, that so many other elves had so little power, even Liessa herself?

In the days following his coronation, he had come to realise that more elves than he had hoped possible had quite a decent amount of power. It would take time for them to learn how to use it all to a useful degree, but they were all so eager to learn. After hundreds of years, possibly over a thousand years, of not using their power, Silvaren was buzzing with the forces of nature.

You did this, Silva told him. *I've been waiting such a long time for my elves to be free.*

Why didn't you help my mother free their power? Or connect all the tree roots so that you could communicate with all elves? Eliséo could not understand it.

Your mother and I, we've had a somewhat mistrustful relationship, Silva admitted. Eliséo thought she sounded embarrassed by the admission. *It took her years to open up to me after her parents died. She has ever been wary of her people. We never did find out who murdered her parents or even why they were murdered.*

Eliséo thought back on his life with Eléna. She had done everything in her power to keep both of her children safe. He had assumed it was her motherly instinct. It had never occurred to him that there was some other motivation behind it.

Mother? he called out through Silva.

I'm coming, my son.

Eliséo smiled. It was strangely liberating to have her call him "my son". There would never be a need to hide who he was again. After over seven hundred years of secrecy, he still could not believe it.

Eléna walked through the glittering silver vines that marked the border between Silva and Elessa. Eliséo had chosen to keep to his quarters in his old tree, while still living with Silva. He did not want to make this change a negative one for any of them. Elessa was, and always would be, part of his life. Silva knew and accepted that. Eliséo was thankful that she was happy to let the two of them have their own quiet time for part of each day.

"How did your parents die?" he asked, as he held out his hand to her. Eléna drew in a sharp breath.

"I ... we don't really know," she faltered. "I was very young when it happened. I assumed they were poisoned, but it was so long ago now that I don't think we'll ever find out."

Eliséo could not accept that. "Why do you assume they were poisoned?"

"Eliséo, please, I've tried to put these things behind me." Eléna squeeze his hand. "I don't want to think about it now. What difference does it make anymore? They are dead and there is nothing that can be done about it."

"Mother, I'm about to go into the Outworld. I hope to take Liessa with me. That will mean leaving you alone." He took a deep breath, trying to steady his voice. "I would feel better knowing that whoever killed your parents has no reason to kill you. Do you even know *why* your parents were killed in the first place?"

She patted his hand. "I appreciate your concern, but I have looked after myself perfectly well without you here before. It won't make a difference that Liessa joins you."

"You don't know, do you?"

Eléna shook her head. "I assume there were elves who were unhappy with their policies. I never found the murderer, so I will never know for certain. In any case, I am not the ruler now – you are. If anyone is in danger, it will now be you."

She placed a hand on his cheek. He smiled and leaned in towards it.

"I've had years of training as the ambassador. Anyone who tries to kill me will have a difficult time of it – that has been proven time and again."

Eléna sat up straighter. "Enough of this. Have you decided which elves will accompany you? How many crystal dragons are we to expect?"

"Four. There should be four clear crystal dragons. I've been told they can carry three people each. One lintep will accompany each of them, so we can go in groups. Some of the younger elves have expressed a keen interest in visiting the Outworld."

"Do you really think that is wise?" Eléna asked sceptically.

Eliséo shrugged. "Possibly not. That is why I will only allow them to go if they are paired up with an older elf. Liessa and I will go. I will ask Ensil to come back with the dragons, so we only need another older elf."

"Who are the young elves? Or should I even bother asking?"

Eliséo grinned. "The four who were chosen as guides for the Paradisians when they visited Silvaren with Shadow. Gioshué, Telon, Tameo and Raeslin. All four have shown some promise with their power. I only foresee one problem with them."

"Which is?"

Eliséo hesitated. It was a problem he was avoiding. Ensil was not in his good graces. There were too many unexplained decisions the weapons master had made in the past that made no sense to Eliséo and actually may have been harming the elves.

"Raeslin is angrier than the others, but none of them are pleased that Ensil refused to teach them how to cover their weapons with compressed air when sparring each other. I haven't spoken to him about it, but it sounds like he didn't even let them try it before deciding they couldn't do it."

His mother frowned. Perhaps she had been unaware of that decision as well. Another time. These questions would be answered another time.

Silva? he opened his thoughts to Eléna and Liessa. *The crystal dragons will be here in a few days. Liessa and I will both be going into the Outworld along with four younger elves. We need one, possibly two volunteers from the older elves to join us. Whoever they are, they should be confident with their weapons and not opposed to dealing with humans and lintep, possibly even karliki.*

Can you ask the required trees to talk to their elves to see who might be interested?

Eléna smiled at him. "In all my years, I never considered such a thing. It never occurred to me that we could speak with other elves through Silva."

"Perhaps you trusted Ensil too much."

His mind tried to drag him down pathways he did not wish to go. There would be time enough later to contemplate everything.

* * *

The journey back to the first broken Paradise was uneventful. The plump, waddling lintep from Turon had joined them. That seemed to please a great many, but it mattered not at all to Ensil. He spent most of the flight lost in thought.

Ensil had tried to contact Eliséo, to talk with his son and king before they had left Turon, but he had been unsuccessful.

Your king is not inclined to speak with you, Dystra told him. *Eliséo is not as trusting as Eléna was. You may find this monarch more difficult to deal with.*

Ensil scowled. *Well then maybe you can talk to Silva instead. Princess Aislen wants me to remain with the lintep once the crystal dragons head to Silvaren. He has a few days to think about it, but the princess would like to know sooner rather than later.*

Eliséo must have realised that he had been withholding knowledge of their power from the younger elves. Had he also realised that the same knowledge had been withheld from the older elves as far back as Ensil was able to influence?

Not every elf goes bad, Dystra tried to reason with him.

He and Dystra rarely saw eye to eye. It was a wonder they had not severed their bond.

I heard that! Dystra said angrily. *You've always been afraid that no other tree would take you and you'd be left virtually powerless.*

Not all my power comes from you, Ensil reminded him. *I don't need you.*

You don't fool me, Ensil. For all your talk of not wanting elves to use their power for fear they'll go bad, you use it more than you think you should, and you'd be lost without it.

Ensil's scowl deepened. He ignored his bond with Dystra. His tree's thoughts had cut him too deeply.

* * *

Isis looked over her charges as they camped outside the bounds of Bryntown, as the broken Paradise was now called. Aislen and Séverin had found Brynt and were taking a tour to see how things were progressing.

"As I understand it, all five of you are now in beginner healing classes. Is that correct?" Isis asked.

Umi and Ulf nodded immediately, their eyes glistening mischievously. Isis resolved to keep a close eye on them. Shuut and Plyke barely looked up at her as they also nodded. Rilla, sitting a little apart from them, sent a smouldering look at Kayte and folded her arms across her chest.

"Very well. I think you could all do with a change of pace. You may not be aware, but Ratchin is known as one of the best healers in the Outworld. She has graciously agreed to give you a lesson in her specialty tonight. Mind her well. I do not want to arrive in Illaria tomorrow with five injured little royals."

Ratchin walked over to them and sat heavily on a log by the fire. She looked over them each in turn.

"Raise your hand if you have been physically injured, no matter how long ago."

All five of them raised their hands.

"Good. That will make things easier. What I want you to do is pick a partner whose past you don't know very well. I realise there are only five of you, but if you ask Arishen, he might agree to let you work with him."

Isis looked over at the seer. His eyes were wide and his face ashen.

"I volunteer myself in Arishen's place," she said.

Ratchin shrugged. "As you please. Now, what I want each of you to do, in turns, is see if you can decipher where and how your partner was injured from how their wounds have healed. It will not work as well if you already know their injuries, so you two, split up."

The twins groaned but went to find other partners. Umi sat next to Shuut and Ulf sat beside Plyke. That only left Rilla. Isis tried to hide her relief that the most volatile of the children had been paired with her. Rilla made no move to approach her, so Isis went and sat beside her instead.

"You should not need a great amount of power to do this so, Shuut, even you should be able to do it."

Isis glanced her way. She knew that Nyssa's oldest daughter and Ratchin knew each other quite well. Was it possible that Shuut had not told her what happened with Nyssa?

"You haven't told us how to do it," Shuut pointed out.

"There's a reason for that," Ratchin told her with a wink. "I want to see if you can figure it out yourselves. No cheating and don't tell the others if you figure it out first."

Isis raised her eyebrows and turned to face Rilla. "Do you want to go first?"

"I don't care." Rilla's voice held so much anger, Isis was almost scared to touch her, but she knew that skin contact would be necessary.

"I'll go first then."

She placed a hand on each of Rilla's wrists and sent her power in as the thinnest tendrils she could, searching for any abnormalities. It only took her a moment to realise it would take her all night to examine Rilla's body that way. Next, she asked Rilla to lie down and moulded her power to the shape of Rilla's body, gently laying it over her. Rilla instantly resisted the intrusion.

"I'm not going to hurt you, Rilla," Isis told her in a quiet voice. She did not want to draw any extra attention their way. "I just want to pass my power through your body to search for anything out of the ordinary."

She heard Rilla's teeth tapping together then saw her muscles relax. Isis took the opportunity to gently push her power through Rilla's body, making a note of everything it sensed.

"I can see you've had a broken nose, a puncture wound in your side, another in your left shoulder. I can still see the injury to your right shoulder from the other night. Nothing else. Have I missed anything?"

At the mention of each wound, Rilla's eyes twitched. Isis knew she had detected each of them correctly, though how she got them was a mystery.

"My turn, then," Rilla sat up and looked her in the eye. "I guess I should ask you to lie down as well."

Isis hesitantly lay on the grass. She trusted Rilla, mostly. She had never done anything to antagonise the girl, so there should be no reason to fear her. Yet fear her, she did. The difference between what she had done to Rilla and what Kayte had done, covering her entirely with her power, was quite small. It would only take a moment for Rilla to gain control of her while searching for old wounds.

"Thanks for the show of confidence," Rilla said bitterly, seconds before Isis felt the girl's power plunge through her.

She had expected it to feel like a gentle wind flowing through her. Instead, she lay rigid as a cold shock ran through her veins, froze her muscles and seized her bones.

Within seconds, it was over. The chill was gone, but Isis could not help but still feel cold. She drew her cloak tightly around herself and sat with her knees hunched up to her chest.

"Your left forearm is different to your right one. I guess something happened there – maybe you broke it when you were younger. I can't really tell anything else."

Isis flinched at the memory.

Ratchin came around to them. "Think harder, Rilla. How is it different? How might it have been broken?"

Rilla's face twisted into a scowl. Isis thought she was about to explode, but the fiery girl only took a deep breath.

"It was definitely broken at some point. The bones in the left arm don't look or feel as straight as the one in the right arm. It almost looks like tiny pieces are missing or were put back together by someone inexperienced. That's all I can tell."

Ratchin regarded them both closely. "Hmm. Isis, do you want to tell Rilla if she was correct?"

It was not a memory she wanted to relive. "I broke my arm when I was younger."

"Yes, we got that. Were the specifics correct?" Ratchin pinned her with a stare that Isis could not evade. She felt like a child badly attempting to keep the truth from her parent.

"More or less. I twisted my arm."

She set her jaw tightly as the memory flooded into her. One of the boys in the castle was not pleased to have a country bumpkin best him in his fire studies. He had pinned her arm behind her back and twisted it to breaking point.

Isis had been too afraid of the boy to seek assistance from a trained healer. They would have asked too many questions and she would have been forced to name him. She knew if she had done that, he would have made the rest of her life as a student a living hell.

Instead, she had done the best that she could, setting the bones herself over the course of a few days. She had feigned illness to absent herself from classes as she attempted to heal herself in her rooms.

Isis shook her head in an attempt to dislodge the memory. She noticed both Rilla and Ratchin's eyes on her as she evaded their questions.

"It's an interesting skill to learn, Ratchin, but does it really hold much purpose?" She did not want to sound insulting, but she needed something, anything, to get the attention off her.

The older lintep raised an eyebrow. "Let's ask your own healing mistress what she thinks of the skill then, why don't we?"

Isis motioned Kayte over to them and explained what they were doing. Kayte's eyes widened and a grin spread across her face.

"In all my years, I never thought to do that, or ask my students to do that. How did you come up with the idea, Ratchin?"

Ratchin reddened at the compliment and tossed her head towards Aurelius. "It was his comment, years ago, that made me think of it. I went to heal a farm girl, but it wasn't working, not as well as it should have. Aurelius suggested that there might be an underlying injury preventing my healing process.

"From there, it didn't take much effort to understand the girl's entire history from her previous wounds. I've done the same with almost every patient I've had."

"I don't remember you doing that with me when Arishen broke my nose," Rilla pointed out.

Ratchin warbled a laugh. "No, child, I didn't. Shuut was in a rush to leave Turon and you were so very defensive about everything that there was no chance you would let me do that to you. Besides, all I really did was patch it up a bit. I left the rest of the healing to your own powers."

Isis was curious despite herself. "Can you really tell exactly how a person was injured using this method? Even if a wound was completely healed by a lintep?"

"Aye. Every lintep leaves a marker of sorts, even if they are careful," Ratchin told them as her other students drew closer. "There is a difference in how bones look depending on if they were healed quickly or knitted themselves back together over time. If you only go skin deep, the muscles will have markers on them as well. It might be some scar tissue or a mismatch in size where the wound occurred.

"The skin itself may leave visible traces with scars, but even if those scars are healed with lintep powers, just underneath the muscles will tell you the story. When you've been doing it long enough, you come to understand how certain injuries occurred."

Isis held her breath as Ratchin gave her a pointed look.

"Some people wear their injuries as a badge of honour. Others tried to hide them away for fear it will tell people too much about them. Either way, it always helps to see if there are previous injuries where you're trying to heal, or it might just not work the way you expect it to."

"Can you reverse something that was done?" Plyke asked suddenly. "I mean, if you can see how it was done, could you reverse it?"

Isis felt Ratchin's power flow past her into Plyke. If she had felt more confident, she would have followed the older lintep to see what she saw. Ratchin studied Plyke for a long while, her face set in a frown of concentration. Eventually, she pulled back and sat up straighter.

"You're asking if I can pull that crystal heart out of you and fix your own one, are you?"

Plyke nodded. Ratchin scratched her cheek.

"I don't know. I can see there were three powers at work there. One was rough and powerful, the others were gentler, smoother and more focused, even if they lacked such raw power."

Isis glanced towards Rilla at that comment. The girl said nothing but hugged her chest tightly with both arms.

"I don't think I would be willing to try to reverse it. Not when it could kill you. I'm a healer. My first rule, my own rule, is to do no harm. I could not guarantee that you would survive a reversal, so I would rather not try."

Tika put an arm around Plyke's shoulder and led him away. Isis knew it must be difficult for the two of them. Their Partnership had always been interesting because Plyke was a lintep. Having the crystal heart made him even more different to Tika. Neither of them knew if their bond would survive when one of them died.

Isis saw Anya watching Rilla and could feel the pain flying off her in waves. She wondered if Rilla even realised what she had done to Anya.

Chapter Thirty-Eight – Jacaranda flowers

Plyke sat astride Shard, one of the clear crystal dragons, as they flew over the pasture and farmlands towards Illaria. It seemed odd to him that Illaria now felt more like home to him than anywhere else he had lived or travelled through.

When they arrived, it was almost as though they had never left in the first place. Master Edric immediately stole Tika away to the stables and Plyke was bundled off to his regular afternoon classes. He did not even get a chance to find his mother before he was swept back into castle life.

For Umi and Ulf, it was a different story. Princess Aislen had taken charge of them and marched them up, past the classrooms, to the levels designated for royalty. Much as he knew they would be in trouble, he envied them being allowed to see their parents before life settled back down to what passed for normal.

Together with Shuut, he walked into Mistress Isis' fire class. He was surprised at how easily their teacher settled back down into her lessons. Their fellow students tried to discover where they had been these past few days, but Plyke took his cue from Isis and remained silent or vague on the matter.

He did not want to tell anyone that he had been back to his old Paradise and destroyed it, that they had been attacked by the Paradise leader, that one of his friends had become an arsonist and murderer, that he himself now had a crystal heart in place of his real one. It was all too much.

"Plyke," Isis called his name softly as she touched his shoulder to get his attention. "I know Princess Aislen wanted you all back to your lessons straight away, but I think it may be best for you to take a little rest. Why don't you go find your mother?

"Shuut will you help him? I think we can spare you both from lessons this afternoon. I don't mind if you train with the remaining guards once Plyke is with his mother."

Plyke breathed a sigh of relief, thanked Isis and left the room with Shuut.

"Do you know where Kora would be at this time of day?" Shuut asked him. Plyke shrugged.

"I don't know what she normally does. She had barely returned before we left the first time."

"Let's search her room first then."

They walked up to Kora's room. Plyke remembered that it had been his room when he had first arrived in Illaria. It was strange to think that Lord Aaron had given him his mother's old room. He must have been so certain that she would never return.

A knock on her door confirmed that Kora was not in her chambers.

"Now what?" Plyke turned to Shuut. "I have no idea where to look for her."

"Can you try that thing everyone else in our family does?" Shuut asked him. "Send out your tendrils until you find her."

Plyke raised an eyebrow at her. "Why don't *you* do it?"

"Be reasonable, Plyke. I don't have enough power for that."

"You keep saying that to everyone, but we know it's not true." Plyke fixed her with a steady look. "Why don't you ever try to use Nyssa's power?"

"I don't want to talk about it." Shuut turned to walk away, but Plyke caught her by the wrist. "I said I don't want to talk about it."

"This isn't something you can avoid forever, Shuut," Plyke told her as gently as he could. "At some point, Nyssa's power will do something within you and you won't be prepared to deal with it because you've never even tried to use it."

"Her power was locked away pretty tightly by Lord Aaron. I don't think it's going to somehow just break free. Besides, it never seems to struggle. It isn't putting up a fight."

Plyke couldn't help but laugh. "I think that's a pretty clear sign that you're meant to be using this power. Nyssa gave it to you for a reason. Don't you want to find out what it is?"

"Enough!" Shuut wrenched her wrist free of him. "If you suddenly found yourself burdened with Kora's power, or Pér's power for that matter, you wouldn't be in such a rush to use it either!"

Plyke only needed to think about it for a moment before knowing exactly what he would do.

"You're wrong," he said quietly. "I would embrace their power. It would probably be more difficult for me because I didn't really learn to use my power properly from a young age like you, but I would do anything to bring me closer to my parents if they were dead. I can't understand why you don't feel the same way."

"Just leave it alone, Plyke." Shuut walked down the hall and disappeared behind her door.

Plyke looked angrily at her. He simply could not understand her decision. He tried to push it to the back of his mind, to clear his thoughts, but the castle dragged up too many memories. If his mother was here, he would have to search every room to find her and he simply did not have the energy to do that. Instead, he decided to take a walk through the marketplace instead. It was something he rarely had the luxury of time to do.

* * *

Unhappy about her disagreement with Plyke, Shuut grabbed her weapons. Sparring was always good for a distraction. They probably would not let her use them in the training ground, but if there was even a chance, she wanted to be prepared. The chambers were empty. Shuut idly wondered where Rilla was. Her sister did not have afternoon lessons today. As soon as her weapons were strapped to her, all other thoughts fled her mind.

When she reached the training ground, Shuut was surprised to see only a handful of guards. Nicodemo turned at her approach.

"Where is everyone?" she asked him.

He gestured to the guards in front of them. "This is everyone who hasn't been left behind at a Paradise."

Of the guards who were left behind, Shuut recognised a few including Ramiro, the arrogant one who had assumed that Rilla and Shuut would be useless with their weapons. Shuut smirked at the memory of the guard lying flat on his back.

Séverin was also there. He was paired up with an older doe-eyed lady. Shuut was impressed by the way she bore up against his attacks. She used her slender form and agility to her advantage, darting in and out of Séverin's range with fantastic speed. When they switched places and the lady attacked instead, Séverin had some trouble moving as quickly as she did. Instead, he used his blade-work to his advantage. His parries were amongst the fastest and well-timed that Shuut had ever seen.

Aside from these three and Nicodemo himself, there were only three other guards.

"You are welcome to join us, Lady Shuut."

Shuut cringed. "Nicodemo, can we agree that when I enter this training ground, my title does not enter with me?"

The head guard nodded with a smile. "I think that can be arranged. Now, if you don't mind, I'd like you to partner up with Ramiro – wooden weapons. Let's see if he's learnt his lesson since the last time the two of your sparred."

Shuut smiled mischievously. *This is going to be fun*, she thought as she looked at Ramiro. *I'm going to make this boy rue the day he insulted me.*

The guard sauntered over, passing his wooden training sword from one hand to the other. Shuut laid down her own weapons and picked up a few wooden swords until she found one which felt balanced in her grip. Likewise tossing the sword from one hand to the other, she squared up against the tanned, muscular guard.

She was ready for his attack when it came. Deftly, she flicked his sword to the side. She easily parried his advances. After sizing him up again, she began to extend some of the parries into attacks. Not as many hit their mark as she would have liked, but those that did get through hit his bronze skin hard enough to leave bruises.

Shuut could sense Ramiro growing angrier by the second. She was caught off guard by his next attack. It was very well timed. Ramiro parried back against her parry, hitting her sword with such force that her arm went numb and she involuntarily bent forward. Before she could switch hands, he had slammed the flat of the sword across her shoulders. Shuut collapsed to the ground and rolled out of the way a heartbeat before the next attack.

It was at that moment she realised that he was using his power. There was no way that he could have improved so dramatically in such a short time.

Nicodemo was distracted with his own opponent. No one was paying enough attention to realise what Ramiro was doing. Shuut knew if she called him out on it, she would only be seen as a weaker target because all of these lintep knew how to use their magic to give them an extra edge.

Tentatively, Shuut pulled out her power in long, thin tendrils and wrapped it around her sword, making it an extension of her arm. That was how she recalled Rilla explaining it to her once. Immediately, she noticed the difference. Her power could sense Ramiro's and allowed her to move seconds before her eyes tracked his movements.

It still wasn't enough. He clearly had more power than she did and had been using it this way for much longer than she had. Even with practice swords, Shuut knew he could still smash her bones or crack her skull if she wasn't careful.

Gritting her teeth, Shuut sought out Nyssa's power. She could feel it in there, struggling to get out and help her. This was *not* the way she wanted things to go. She had been perfectly happy leaving Nyssa's power locked behind a wall within her mind. She barely had time to reconsider her actions in the torrent of blows raining down on her from Ramiro. He had gotten into his stride and it was all she could do to stop every other blow from connecting.

Heedless of the repercussions, Shuut unlocked the wall. She had planned to pull out Nyssa's power slowly but didn't have a chance before it flooded out over her. In a panic, she tried to control it, while still defending herself against the frenzied guard attacking her. Clumsily, she tried to grab it with her own power, but it easily slid away from her. She stopped focusing on her fight and instead turned her attention to her mother's power as it flowed around her.

She noticed, with some surprise, that it wasn't rushing away from her. It was now pooled all around her, like a long flowing dress, covering every part of her body, extending out past her skin.

"Ow!"

The growled complaint came from someone in front of her. Shuut looked up to see Ramiro on his knees, sword held up against her. It was only then that she realised Nyssa's power had been working with her own instincts to attack Ramiro without her even paying attention.

"You're cheating!" he cried out angrily. Shuut smashed her sword down on top of his, disarming him.

"I was defending myself," she told him evenly. All eyes were on them now. Nicodemo and Séverin looked disappointed. The girl had a knowing look. Clearly, Ramiro had tried the same trick on her before.

"Shuut, did you use your power?" Nicodemo asked her, disappointment clear on his face.

Shuut glared at him. "I took my cue from Ramiro. When he started using his power, so did I. I will not allow him to have an unfair advantage over me in training so that he can falsely prove to you that he has improved."

Shock registered on Nicodemo's face.

"Ramiro, is this true?"

The cocky guard had lost none of his arrogance in the fight. He tilted his head up defiantly, not answering.

"I wouldn't be surprised if he did," the female guard said a little too casually. "He does it to me almost every time we spar."

Nicodemo stared at her incredulously. "Why didn't you ever say anything?"

The woman shrugged. "You never quite say it, but I always seem to have to work a little harder than everyone else to prove myself to you. If I pointed out every time he did it you would start to think me a nuisance."

"Well, I don't care if you think I'm a nuisance," Shuut told Nicodemo. "I will not be falsely accused of cheating when I was playing by the same rules as my opponent."

At her admission, Nicodemo lay down his weapon and dragged Ramiro from the training field. Shuut neither knew nor cared what his punishment would be for that little stunt. All she cared about right now was the power pooled all around her – power that was not hers but was not trying to escape from her.

She didn't know what to do with it. Every time she tried to interact with it with her own power, it slipped through her grasp.

"Shuut, are you feeling well?"

She looked uncomprehendingly at Séverin. His big brown eyes stared at her with worry. She did not answer him. He knelt beside her. She had not realised she was sitting on the ground until he did that.

"Maéva, find a mistress or a master – someone to help her."

"Why?" Shuut heard Maéva's query as though from a great distance. "She's old enough to know how to use her power."

"Just go." He did not yell at her, but his tone forced her to act. Shuut watched Maéva set off at a run and wondered why she was in such a rush.

* * *

The marketplace was bustling with activity. Plyke was overwhelmed by the noise, but mostly by the smells and colours. All the stalls had brightly coloured material awnings stretching out in front, creating shaded pathways for their customers. To Plyke, it seemed as though the stalls were organised into specific areas.

Fruit stalls were interspersed with vegetable stalls, which were, in turn, interspersed with hot food and drink stalls – baked breads and sweets, savoury pastries and pies, spiced teas and crushed fruit juices.

In another section, merchants sold bolts of cloth in a vast variety of colour, texture and weight. Plyke was amazed by the selection. Clothes in the Paradise had been handed down from one person to another, with little thought for anything other than practicality. The cloth had all been neutral, or hued with whatever they could find to use as dyes.

Other merchants had different wares for household such as clay pots and jars. All woodworked items were more trinkets than pieces of art. He had come to understand that true masterpieces were only found in the trade workshops such as the one that Arishen was apprenticed in.

As he passed one curious workshop, he stopped to have a closer look. It appeared to have musical instruments made of wood. Some were stringed, others had holes through long tubes. They reminded Plyke of the lute that Pér had played that night, so many weeks ago now, when Kora had first arrived back in Illaria.

"Plyke?" a woman cried out in confusion.

He looked up behind the stall and saw his mother.

"Kora!"

He ran straight into her outstretched arms, barely heeding the instruments in his way.

"Whoa, careful there, boy," Pér said as he gently moved some of the lutes out from under their embrace.

"Sorry Pér" laughed Plyke, as his mother squeezed him tightly. "I think Kora missed me just a little."

"A little? She worried after you every night. Especially when Leif and Talise returned early and told us what happened to you."

At the mention of his *incident*, Plyke went silent. It wasn't that he had wanted to keep it a secret, but he would rather they had found out from him, when he was ready to tell them. Not from someone else, when he wasn't even there to explain.

"Well, I'm back now and Erton is dead, so that won't be a problem anymore."

Kora visibly paled at that. "Dead? Did you, or Rilla ..."

"No ... not us." This was not at all how he wanted to tell them everything. He looked around at the marketplace. "Can we talk somewhere else?"

Kora shared a look with Pér. He nodded.

"I'll take you home, Pér will follow us once the day's trading is over."

Plyke nodded, thankful that his mother knew what he needed. Arm in arm, they walked through the marketplace. He had lost all sense of direction and did not notice until they had emerged from the throng of stalls that they were heading way from the castle.

Confused, he followed Kora down a maze of streets until they came to a two-storey stone house. The honey-coloured wooden door and shutters had been painted with masses of the small purple flowers Plyke had seen when he first arrived in Illaria. Plyke touched one of the flowers on the door. It had been painted with such exquisite detail, he thought it might even feel like the real thing.

"Jacarandas," Kora told him. "The flowers you're looking at so closely. They're called jacarandas. In spring, you'll see all the trees lining the streets start to bloom with these same flowers. Those leaves and flowers get into everything. If it wasn't such a glorious sight, Uncle Lukys would probably have done away with those trees years ago."

"Is this Pér's house?"

Kora nodded. She fumbled with a key, unlocked the door and pushed it open with both hands. Plyke peered inside. It looked quite cosy, warm, lived-in. He followed Kora through the door. There were a few items scattered around the room, a pair of small shoes, a favoured jacket – enough things for Plyke to understand.

"When you said 'home', you meant *your* home, didn't you?"

His chest hurt as Kora smiled and nodded. She filled a kettle with water and hung it over the fireplace before lighting the wood with flames from her fingers. With practised ease, she moved around the kitchen to retrieve two tea cups. She filled a small bowl with a selection of fruits.

Kora placed the items on a small table between the fireplace and the couch. She sat and patted a spot next to her. Plyke sat with a heavy heart. This was not at all how he had pictured the afternoon.

"Whatever's the matter, Plyke?" she asked him with an odd tone. "Did I upset you so much with talk of Erton?"

"No," Plyke huffed. "I just ... I didn't realise you'd moved out of the castle. I suppose I was just hoping I might get to live near you for a while, now that we can freely admit to being mother and son."

He looked away from his mother and, in a smooth and practised move, dislodged the lock of hair from behind his ear to cover his eye and hunched his shoulders.

He did not notice Kora's trembling fingers until they touched his cheek. He so wanted to lean in to her touch. Instead, he found himself turning away from her. It ripped his heart when her fingers curled back and pulled away from his face.

"I thought you would be pleased," Kora told him in a soft voice. "I thought, father suggested it, we assumed you might like it if we all lived together. Pér even made up a bed for you upstairs. I mean, we'll understand if you want to stay in the castle, we just hoped you might like to live in a house."

Plyke's head snapped up. "What?"

Kora moved away sharply from his jerky movement.

"You don't want to move away from me? You want me to live *here*?"

"Well, of course we want you to live here. Did you think Pér was happy, living so far from the two of us? Neither of us want to be parted from you, but I didn't think it fair to ask Pér to move into the castle. He's lived in Illaria longer than either of us. He was forced to build a life for himself here. I didn't want him to give that up just so we could live together."

Before Plyke could answer, the front door opened and Pér came in, dragging a small cart of goods behind him. Kora jumped up to close the door behind him.

"You always let too much of that winter air in when you come home," she remonstrated him with a smiling voice. Pér kissed Kora's cheek.

"And you always get so distracted, you never remember to take the kettle off the fire when it begins to boil."

She instantly ran over to the fireplace, put on two padded mittens and carefully took the kettle from the flames. Pér lifted the lid of the teapot for her before Kora had turned around. She smiled and rolled her eyes.

"I could have done that."

"I know." Pér shrugged. "But it always helps if you remember to do it *before* you take the kettle from the stove."

Plyke watched their evening routine with a sense of envy. This was *his* mother, living so comfortably with someone else. She had never been quite so comfortable around him. Neither of them seemed to notice he was there. He made to move off the couch until he realised Pér had sat beside him and placed an arm around his shoulder.

"Now, son, tell us all about that Paradise. Kora told me enough of it that I should understand if you explain what happened."

Plyke didn't get a chance to leave the house. He told them all the events, large and small, that had happened on the journey and in the Paradise. Kora moved around the kitchen and hearth room serving out the tea. Pér jumped up every now and then to help her prepare a meal for the evening.

The sun had already set by the time Plyke finished his tale. He had fallen into such a comfortable rhythm with his parents that he had not noticed the time.

"Tika!" he cried out suddenly. "Tika will be looking for me in the dining hall."

"Actually, Master Edric knows I'm living in the city," Kora told him. "He will have told Tika not to expect you."

"Oh." A heavy feeling settled in Plyke's stomach. "Of course."

Kora and Pér exchanged looks.

"We did consider asking Tika to live here, but we reasoned he would then be the only stablehand not living in the stables. I know he is well thought of, but I don't want to push things too far. There are others who might become jealous of his situation. Illaria is far from perfect itself and I wouldn't want anything to happen to Tika because of us."

"Yes, yes, you're right of course," Plyke said hurriedly. He knew she was right. It didn't stop him from feeling sick. This was the first evening meal they had not shared together since ... well, ever.

"It was bound to happen one day, Plyke." Kora put an arm around his shoulders. "Most Partners eventually find a mate and live separate lives. It doesn't weaken your bond to spend a little time apart."

Pér finished clearing away their dinner dishes and came over to them. "How about a song before we show you to your room?"

Plyke looked up at the mention of his room. He smiled at the fact that they had been so keen to have him in their lives that they had already found a place for him in their house.

Together, the three of them moved over to the fireplace, Pér picking up a small harp on his way. He plucked a few notes on it as Plyke and Kora sat on the couch. With just a few notes, Pér captivated Plyke's attention. His head swayed from side to side as he listened to the sweet melody.

"Could you teach me to do that?" Plyke asked when Pér had finished his second song. He felt a sudden rush of happiness as both Kora and Pér beamed at him. Plyke did not understand why that question had made them both so happy, but if that was all it took, living with them was going to be easier than he had imagined.

Chapter Thirty-Nine – Freely given

Aurelius hurried down the stairs, Ratchin close on his heels. The castle felt depleted with the absence of Aaron, Guiscard and Kora. He was one of the only masters free that afternoon. That explained why Maéva had come knocking on his door.

She had not been very forthcoming in her explanation of why they were needed. Something about Shuut and sparring with her power and collapsing. He sucked in deep breaths as he followed the guard down the twisting staircase and out to the training ground. He was getting too old to make such intense journeys.

Shuut was sitting on the ground, staring at nothing.

"What happened?" he asked Séverin once he had caught his breath. Ratchin was only a few steps behind him.

"Oh, my stars!" she cried out as she reached him. "That's not *her* power."

Aurelius sank to his knees. If this was not Shuut's power, it had to be her mother's. But they had been so careful to lock it away safely, unless Shuut wanted to try to access it.

"Séverin, did something happen to make Shuut want to use her power here?"

Séverin exchanged glances with Maéva.

"Ramiro pushed her," Maéva finally told them. "He isn't a very good guard. Nicodemo should have thrown him out years ago, but our skills aren't often needed. In any case, if he feels he is losing, usually against females, he starts using his power, knowing that most of us won't say anything because we don't want to appear weaker."

"So, Shuut used her power against him," Aurelius murmured to himself. "An odd reason to push herself into something like this."

Ratchin shooed the guards away. They moved to the other side of the training ground, though both continued to watch from their new vantage point.

"You don't seem surprised," Ratchin said.

It wasn't a question, but Aurelius knew what she was asking.

"Did Shuut tell you anything about her journey and arrival in Illaria?"

Ratchin shook her head.

"Ah. I suppose she would have told you sooner or later," Aurelius said as he sat back on his heels. "On their way to Illaria, they found Shuut and Rilla's mother, Nyssa. To cut a very long story short, Nyssa and Shuut were captured by a very powerful lintep. Nyssa voluntarily gave her power to Shuut to keep it out of Lishe's clutches.

"We helped Shuut to contain the power, thinking she would die if she couldn't learn to use it properly. She has refused to learn how to use Nyssa's power until now. But it seems as though Nyssa's power isn't trying to leave her."

Ratchin stared at him, her jaw hanging slack. When she finally recovered from the shock, all she could ask was, "How can anyone have two sets of power?"

"I'll explain that later," he told her gravely. "For now, we must tend to Shuut. Nyssa's power may not be trying to escape her, but the two of them are not working well together by the looks of it. Any ideas?"

"I've never experienced this before," Ratchin replied hopelessly.

Shuut, can you hear me? Aurelius attempted to speak straight to her mind. There was no reply.

He took a better look with his power. It was a mess in there. Shuut's power had been shoved aside as though it was worthless. Nyssa's power had taken up residence and refused to be put back behind a wall. He could see Shuut trying, but Nyssa's power kept falling out of her grasp.

"Ratchin, I'm going in there to repair whatever damage I can. If I do not resurface soon, find King Lukys or Master Jorg. Both helped with this the first time."

Not willing to leave anything to chance, he made her repeat the instructions back to him as though she were a student.

Satisfied that he had taken all reasonable precautions, Aurelius jumped in. Nyssa's power was greater than his, but it was rusty from ill-use. It did not realise it was being surrounded until it was too late. Unlike Shuut, who was trying to grab at sections of the power, Aurelius stretched his power into a thin sphere over the entire mass. He made his sphere smaller and smaller until the power was condensed into a tiny pouch of raw energy.

With a breath of relief, he held that power tightly off to one side as he searched for Shuut's wall.

What are you doing in my mind? The tone was indignant and dangerous.

Shuut! Aurelius cried out in relief. *I need to get Nyssa's power back into your mind, behind a wall.*

She was suspicious of him. He could feel her debating whether or not to trust him.

What if I don't want it anymore?

My dear girl, I don't think you have a choice. I don't know what would happen if I take Nyssa's power from you. Under normal circumstances, when this amount of power is lost, the lintep dies.

But it wasn't my power to begin with, Shuut argued.

True, but I don't know if that makes enough difference. Please, just show me where her power was kept in your mind.

Aurelius felt her hesitate. He closed his eyes and silently wished for her to see reason.

This way.

That was all he was waiting for. Aurelius dragged Nyssa's power through Shuut's mind to where it was previously contained. He pushed it inside, but before he could lock it up, the power began to flood out again. Aurelius managed to contain it again but could do little more.

* * *

Ratchin nervously twisted her fingers as she watched Aurelius. He had an intense look of concentration. At one point, he looked triumphant before falling into concentration once more. Beads of sweat began to form on his forehead. He closed his eyes and bent his head towards Shuut. After that, he did not move.

This was not at all how she had imagined her first day in Illaria. A girl who she treated more as a daughter than a friend collapsed on the ground with the man Ratchin should have called her dearest friend for life. She felt out of her depth here. This was not her area of expertise. She waved over the two guards who had stayed on the training ground.

"Can you find King Lukys or Master Jorg? I think Aurelius needs help and he said they are the ones who will know what to do."

They both ran off towards the castle. Ratchin was left alone.

"No," she said to herself eventually, "I will not stand by and do nothing."

She settled into a comfortable position, held each of their hands in her own and closed her eyes. She could feel what Aurelius had done. He was trying to contain it like a wild power, but Nyssa's power did not feel wild. Protective, yes, but not wild.

Shuut, listen to me, child, Ratchin reached out to the banwep's mind. There was the slightest flicker of recognition. That was all Ratchin needed. *Nyssa's power will not escape you. It had that chance and did not take it. Her power is trying to protect you but is leaving you powerless instead. You need to take back control of yourself.*

Her words must have made an impact. Shuut's glazed eyes snapped back into focus momentarily.

I can't, she whimpered. Ratchin was thrown off by her uncharacteristic weakness.

You can, and you will, she ordered Shuut firmly. *You have no choice. Nyssa's power does not need to be controlled or contained. It only needs to be put in its place. You're a trained banwep. You've never let anyone control your mind or your body. Don't start now.*

Her reprimand had the desired effect. Shuut began to struggle against the smothering protectiveness of Nyssa's power. Her own power was too small to cover Nyssa's power as Aurelius was doing. She would have to find another way. The two powers would need to co-exist in Shuut's body.

Ratchin kept her power within reach of Shuut. She was prepared to step in at a moment's notice. With a smidgeon of pride, Ratchin watched as the girl she had once trained to use her mind power proficiently now found a way to stop her mother's power from taking over her life.

Shuut convinced the greater power to pool closely around her body, but not flood her mind. With every passing moment, she took more of Nyssa's power from where Aurelius was containing it safely away from her.

Ratchin suddenly became aware of another power hovering around the three of them. Knowing that Shuut was now safe, Ratchin withdrew her power and opened her eyes. The two guards were standing nearby with an older man. His curly mop of dark hair oddly contrasting with his sharp eyes.

"Why was I called?" he asked sternly. "This is my one day free from lessons. I do not like being disturbed needlessly."

Ratchin crossed her arms. She was just about to give him a tongue lashing when Aurelius spoke up.

"Ah, that was my fault, Jorg. That *thing* we had to help Shuut with when she first arrived in Illaria needed to be dealt with again and I couldn't do it on my own."

Jorg did not look mollified. "It looks dealt with now."

"Yes, it seems as though Ratchin has quite a few more talents than she led me to believe."

Despite herself, Ratchin felt her cheeks flush hotly, but she refused to break her stare with Jorg. It almost looked like he was about to argue again but must have thought better of it.

"Well, as the situation appears to be well in hand, you will excuse me."

He did not wait for them to respond before turning on his heel and walking off again. Ratchin watched him go with little emotion. There was none to spare after what she had just gone through. She turned to find Aurelius staring up at her with a strange expression on his face – surprise and pride.

"Ratchin, my dear friend, how did you ever think you would get lost in the crowd here?"

Despite herself, Ratchin smiled at the compliment. Had she really wasted so many years of their friendship through baseless fear?

Chapter Forty – Three old men and a guard

Aaron dismounted from his mare. The copy of Kora's map said they were where they were meant to be, but he saw nothing. Not even a clump of trees. It was just a grassy field with a small creek running through it. Not at all a suitable place to spend these cold winters. He shivered in the chill air and drew his cloak closer around his shoulders.

"Let's spread out then and see if we can't find the boundary. Kora's map shows it to be here, a little to the east of Statera, Albercott, Garstiel and Bexent."

Guiscard, Kynon and one palace guard had come with him for the adventure. They had left against Lukys' wishes – he was always so tired and quick to anger these days. Aaron wondered if Lukys was feeling quite well. It would certainly explain his recent bout of bad moods. If his cousin had had his way, they would have dragged a handful of masters or mistresses as well as a few more guards with them.

Aaron grimaced at the memory of their argument. He had staunchly refused to leave Illaria so badly depleted. The guardhouse was already almost empty due to their expeditions to the previous two Paradises and teachers were complaining about having to accommodate extra students when Kayte, Isis and Aurelius disappeared for days or weeks at a time.

Edric had provided them with his finest horses. From Bastienne's description, they estimated it would take half a week to reach Statera and possibly another day to reach the Paradise. They had not counted on the fact that the bridge Bastienne had often used to take was in bad shape and could not carry the weight of one horse, let alone four. They'd had to travel along the stream until they came to a ferry crossing and had been forced to pay the ferryman twice the usual amount for him to agree to take the horses across.

"How did Kora ever find this Paradise?" he muttered to himself.

It was late in the afternoon by the time Guiscard's whistle could be heard along the wind. Aaron mounted Fleuris and rode over to meet him. Kynon and the guard were close on his heels.

"Now what?" Kynon asked as they stood and looked at the Paradise.

"Can we go in and spend the night indoors?" Guiscard asked. "I confess, I did not think of spending these cold nights outdoors when I agreed to your plan."

Aaron shook his head. "I don't think it would be a good idea to alert the Paradisians. They might not like the idea of us trying to destroy their Paradise. It would cause more trouble than it's worth just to spend the night under a roof. We'll set up camp here and start our work."

* * *

Shuut looked down at her hands. They rested, palms down, on a wooden table. On the outside, they looked no different. She reached out a hand to take the clay mug in front of her. It was hot – she knew it was from the steam curling up off the tea – but she could not feel that heat. She drew back her hand and looked at her palms. They were the same colour. One was not redder from the heat of the mug as she would have expected.

"It will take some getting used to, I'd imagine."

Ratchin was seated across the table from her. Shuut had not noticed.

"Don't let that power cloud your mind," Ratchin told her. "It does not own you. If you want to feel the heat of that mug, you feel it. Nyssa's power will protect you in every way it can, whether you want it to or not, unless you tell it otherwise."

Shuut looked at her hands again. "But I don't need *protecting* against a cup of tea."

Ratchin smiled knowingly. "Yes, dear. *We* both know that, but this power does not have a mind of its own. It acts on instinct. It senses heat and it shields you from that. It will likely work the same way with something cold, probably sharp items as well."

Shuut struggled to withdraw Nyssa's power from around her body. That was not going to work. Her own power was so little that it could easily fit behind her wall. How did Rilla fit *her* power in?

"Where is your power?" she asked. Ratchin raised her eyebrows.

"My power is safe behind my walls. It comes out when I need it to," Ratchin answered slowly.

"Isn't there too much power to fit there?"

Ratchin shook her head. "I've never thought about it that way. My power has always been a large part of me. It fits inside me."

"Inside you," Shuut mulled over the words. "So, not all in your head. Just inside you."

Concentrating so much it hurt her furrowed forehead, Shuut pulled Nyssa's power into her body, under her skin. It was like a body suit around her muscles and bones rather than over her skin.

She grinned at Ratchin. "It fits inside me."

* * *

Aislen quietly opened the door to the audience chamber. She knew how important these days were for her father and did not wish to disturb him before all his petitioners had been heard. It was oddly calming and reassuring to hear their complaints, no matter how petty or serious they were. *This* was what she was used to. It was what she had trained for her entire life. *Here* she knew what all the right answers were and could hand them out as easily as she could start a fire with her powers. She had not been prepared for the chaos of the Paradise. Many of the decisions she'd made there still did not sit well with her. She should have handled things better.

It took longer than she had anticipated for the audience chamber to empty, but she was happy to sit there until it did. Her father glanced over at her tiredly. He would have been told of her arrival the moment crystal dragons were spotted in the sky.

"I won't ask how it went. Duke Leif and his fiancé already told me."

Aislen smirked at the announcement. "So, he finally asked her. I wonder what pushed him over the edge?"

Her father looked at her oddly. Aislen waved the matter aside.

"There is quite a bit more to tell you since they left. Shall we have tea in your chambers?"

It was not a discussion she wished to have out in the open. Once they were safely secluded, she explained everything to him. He stared at her in silence for a long moment.

"I suppose I should congratulate you on the fact that it didn't get any further out of hand than this, but did you really think it the best idea to bring the seer back with you?"

"I didn't really have a choice," Aislen huffed, "unless I wanted half the royal family to remain in a hostile Paradise with a handful of guards. For now, his actions are unknown to everyone except those who were there and yourself.

"We have more pressing matters to deal with. Were you aware that Kayte moved Rilla down to Master Vylor's class? We will have to keep a close eye on her. I do not know how well Rilla will cope with classes that she thinks are beneath her."

"She won't have a choice," Lukys replied sternly. "With her grandfather off in the Outworld, *I* am responsible for her. If she has a problem with Kayte's decision, she will have to deal with me.

"With the loss of the crystal heart, I don't think she, or any of the others, will need to go out to the Paradises. At least not until we see if Aaron, Kynon and Guiscard have any luck destroying the boundaries without their help."

Aislen breathed in the sharp aroma of her mint tea and took a small sip.

"We still need to decide what to do with the crystal dragons. They have agreed to continue helping us. Through Ensil and Rilla, we have negotiated that the elves will assist us in looking for Lishe. It seems Eliséo has made changes since becoming king. The elves can all talk to each other over distances as easily as Rilla and Eliséo can."

Lukys scratched the stubble on his chin. Aislen absently noticed that it was at least two days' growth. It was unlike her father to neglect his grooming.

"Snowcrest is with Leif, that leaves us with six dragons."

"We can't let all of them go," Aislen pointed out. "We will need to keep a few with us so that we can fly out wherever Lishe is found."

"If Pyrid and Celtan remain, that leaves four crystal dragons. I haven't the faintest idea who we can ask to accompany them. I would suggest guards, but we have only a handful left. Nicodemo will flatly refuse to empty the guardhouse."

Aislen shrugged. "We can ask for volunteers out of those who have already been to a Paradise. At least they will know what to look for when searching for the boundaries."

Aislen scrawled down some names on a piece of paper and looked at them wearily. Most of them were children or teachers. Neither could afford to miss many more lessons.

"I can only see Bastienne, Kora and Pér who might not be terribly missed if they went."

Lukys shook his head. "Kora has moved into Pér's house. I doubt you will convince either of them to leave the other, especially if Lishe is involved."

"True, but perhaps we could send them together with Plyke and his new heart,"

Aislen suggested.

"Even if you could convince them, that still leaves us a lintep short."

"I could go out again," Aislen offered.

"No." Her father's tone was irrefutable. "Maybe it's time we let Kynon's family join in. What about Braedan and Daegan?"

Aislen raised her eyebrows. "Really, father?"

"Well, why not? Kynon himself has been quite helpful recently. He's even out there right now with Aaron and Guiscard trying to find a way to destroy the Paradises, since Rilla has ruined any chance we had of using the crystal heart."

"You don't know that, Father, it *may* still work with Plyke," Aislen tried to calm him, though she held as much hope for that as he did. "But I take your point. I'll ask Braedan and Daegan if they will go. Are we immediately sending Plyke to P2 now that he has returned?"

"I think so," Lukys decided. "He seems to have more control over his power than Rilla, but I don't like either of them missing out so many lessons while their power is still peaking. I wish had another choice. Perhaps when the dragons have rested, he can fly out with a guard."

Aislen kissed her father on the cheek. "I did miss you, you know."

He looked up at her in surprise, then smiled and caressed her face. "I only wish your mother were alive to see you. She would be so proud of you."

"Oh, really Father! After the mess I left in that Paradise, I highly doubt she would be proud of me."

"Don't sell yourself short, Aislen. You often do. If I had been there instead, it's likely the entire Paradise would have gone up in flames and, if any of us had survived, we would be covered in burns."

Aislen coughed in embarrassment. "I'll go find Braedan and Daegan now."

* * *

Lishe looked thoughtfully at the Paradise. She had managed to convince the remaining power there to merge together down at the bottom of the boundary, leaving a gap at the top. Her hope was that if the lintep came to destroy it, they would not notice any power had been taken. Better to have the element of surprise if she could keep it.

Time to move on. She did not like the idea of staying in one place for too long. That would only make her easier to find. *Not that it really matters when I have all this power.*

Her horse behaved well enough. The mare did not fight against the rope when she was tethered to a tree. The only problem was that the mare took time to get used to her scent every time she added more power to her growing collection. It was an annoyance, but not an intolerable one.

Once mounted, Lishe consulted her map for directions to the next Paradise. She clicked her tongue to make the mare move and was on her way with a smirk. Those meddling lintep would have a difficult time finding her.

* * *

Two days later, Aaron was growing increasingly frustrated by his futile attempts to destroy the Paradise. All any of them had managed to do was draw power away from the Paradise. The problem was that after they had done so, they could not release the power. It seemed as if the strands of power had become accustomed to their situation and were now afraid of being alone.

Aaron, Guiscard and Kynon had all managed to move power back and forth between the Paradise boundary and themselves but could not detach from the power unless it was connected with another. It was annoying.

"How are we to do this without the crystal heart?" Kynon asked angrily. "Why won't those blasted dragons just give us another one?"

Aaron and Guiscard exchanged exasperated looks. "We've been through this, Kynon. There was enough trouble with *one* crystal heart in the Outworld. If the crystal dragons hand another one out now, what is there to stop people asking for more? Can you imagine the trouble there would be if that happened?"

Kynon nodded to a spot behind them. "Well, what are you going to tell them then? That they've come for no reason? If we don't find a way to destroy these Paradises soon, all the troops Leif is organising to meet us will not be impressed at being stationed there indefinitely."

Aaron looked over his shoulder to the approaching troops. It appeared Leif did not take his duty as duke lightly. There were close to one hundred soldiers riding towards them, a banner whipping against its pole in the gusty wind. He noticed, with a wry smile, that the guard assigned to them drew closer, even though she could not possibly defend against such a large troop should they decide to attack.

The troops halted as a man with peppered black hair held up a fist. He alone dismounted and walked awkwardly towards them, the tailored sheets of metal covering his body clanging against each other at every step. Aaron watched him closely as he approached. The man was well armed and had the look of a warrior. He would not hesitate to attack if he felt threatened.

"Lord Aaron?" asked the man, his eyes wandering over the four of them.

"Yes," Aaron replied warily.

The man's eyes settled on him. For a moment, Aaron thought there would be trouble. He pooled his power around himself and could feel the others do the same.

"I am Commander Woodrow, reporting for duty."

"Ah," Aaron cleared his throat and held his power in check. "Commander Woodrow, allow me to introduce you to my cousin, Lord Kynon, our learned librarian, Guiscard, and our guard, Nedina.

"We have been here some few days already attempting to destroy the Paradise boundary. It is proving to be somewhat ... recalcitrant. If you would choose the best place for your troops to set up camp, we will stay out of your way."

There was a moment when Aaron thought Woodrow would protest, that they were ready for action and did not wish to set up camp, but the moment passed. Woodrow turned back to his troops and began issuing orders.

Aaron breathed a sigh of relief and gathered his fellow lintep around him.

"Tread carefully. Duke Leif must trust this man, but I have no doubt some of his men remember old stories told around the fireplace of lintep. We have not been thought of well in human towns."

Kynon huffed self-importantly while Nedina checked the sword in her scabbard, but Guiscard looked thoughtfully towards the humans. Aaron watched incredulously as the librarian walked purposefully towards Woodrow.

"Commander Woodrow, might I have a word with you once your troops are settled?"

The muscular human turned with an eyebrow raised at Guiscard. Eventually, he nodded and waved Guiscard away.

"What are you up to?" Aaron asked when he returned. "Did I not just tell you to tread carefully?"

"Oh hush, Aaron. I'm only going to ask if any of the humans would like to enter the Paradise with me."

Aaron sputtered. Guiscard only laughed at him.

"Why not let them see what the Paradise is like before we destroy it? I don't see it can do any harm."

Aaron shook his head and mumbled to himself as he walked back to the boundary border.

There must be a way to reverse what Ophélie did without the crystal heart.

"Kynon," he called out to his cousin. Both Kynon and Guiscard looked over to him. He waved them over. Nedina dutifully followed.

"Let's puzzle out the prophecy. Nothing else has worked so far.

When a crystal heart beats in the body of another,

Their song will destroy that which was created.

Every being will bow down to the child of Paradise,

All will hail Rilla."

Kynon gave him a withering look. "We all know the prophecy, Aaron. It's all about your granddaughter."

"But what if it's not?" asked Guiscard. "What if only the last part pertains to Rilla. After all, it only says 'All will hail Rilla'. That could be for anything. It doesn't need to be for destroying the Paradises. It doesn't even need to be *this* Rilla. It could just as easily refer to your mother, Princess Rilla, or any of her descendants."

"What does the crystal heart part mean?" Nedina asked hesitantly. Aaron could tell she still felt just a little odd travelling with three of the most important people in Illaria.

"Rilla lived with the crystal dragons for the first few years of her life. They say that was to give her a crystal heart, figuratively speaking," Kynon explained at length.

"What if it isn't meant to be taken figuratively, though?" Nedina asked. "I don't know much, but I think I puzzled out that they used an actual crystal heart to destroy the first two Paradises. All I keep thinking is that if we're trying to do it a different way, we don't have the crystal heart. What happened to it?"

Aaron regarded Nedina with newfound respect. None of them had taken that question any further and they all *knew* what had happened to it.

"In fact, the crystal heart does now beat in another body – not a crystal body."

"Is it in Rilla's body?" Nedina asked.

Aaron shook his head. "I don't suppose there's any harm in telling you now. It's my grandson, Plyke. The crystal heart beats in his body."

Guiscard smiled broadly. "So, Plyke needs to practise his lintep whistle and somehow free the powers with that. When is he coming?"

"I don't know. Unless they were greatly delayed, I suppose he should be along any day now."

* * *

Kora crossed her arms tightly. "No."

Lukys rubbed his temples tiredly. It felt like the hundredth time they'd had this argument. He wanted to send Plyke out to the Paradise where Aaron was waiting for them. They had already been waiting too long.

"Kora, I'm not asking your permission," Lukys told her. "Plyke will leave in the morning for P2. You may join him if you wish, but he *must* go. The four remaining clear crystal dragons and Celtan will head to Silvaren to fetch the elves.

"We cannot delay any longer. Lishe could be anywhere by now with your map. Every day, she could be growing stronger. We need to find her quickly. And we need Plyke to help figure out how to destroy the Paradises now that the heart resides in his body."

Lukys could see how close she was to stamping her foot.

"My son will not be treated as a possession. He isn't a tool for you to use however you like."

"Kora, dear, no one is treating him like a possession." Lukys' tone softened. "We have no choice now. The only crystal heart we can use is within him. The crystal dragons refuse to give us another. We only need to puzzle out how to use this one now. I'm truly sorry about what happened to Plyke, but can you really justify allowing Lishe to steal the power in every Paradise simply because you don't want to put your son in any danger? Think about every person, every child, who lives in a hostile Paradise."

It was cruel, and he knew it, but he had no choice. Plyke *must* be allowed to go to the next Paradise.

"You and Pér can join him if you like. Just let me know so that I can tell Nicodemo that we don't need another guard."

Kora's face was flushed. Her eyes were glistening with unshed tears. "We'll take him there ourselves."

Lukys heaved a sigh of relief. "Good. I'll let Nicodemo know so that he can arrange which guards are to go to the elves. We'll need Ensil to travel with you to Aaron."

"Not Rilla?"

Lukys coughed. "Uh, no, not Rilla. She has ... been having a few problems of late. Aislen and I think it best that she stay. In any case, the elves appear to have found a new way to communicate with each other over distances. If Ensil goes with you, you will be able to speak with us directly through Rilla."

"But what about the prophecy?" Kora asked, touching on the one point Lukys was unsure of himself. "It names Rilla. Don't you think she needs to be there too?"

Lukys scratched behind his neck. "About that. Aislen told me some of the things that happened in the Paradise. It's possible that when many of the Paradisians were calling out Rilla's name and praising her, that may have fulfilled part of the prophecy. It could mean that Rilla is no longer needed for the rest of the prophecy."

Kora looked at him pointedly. "You don't believe that though, do you?"

"I don't know what to believe," Lukys replied, throwing his hands up in the air. "But I think that girl has missed too many lessons. She will do well to be away from the Paradises for a while and have the chance to continue her studies uninterrupted."

Lukys bid Kora farewell and sent out a tendril to find his daughter. He found her in her chambers, with Daegan, Braedan and Luisella. Instead of calling them all to him, he left his chambers and walked down the hall to Aislen's chambers. He didn't have time to knock before the door opened for him. He shook his head and smiled at his daughter's way with her power.

"Well, Father, what did Kora say?"

"She and Pér will accompany Plyke to the Paradise. We can send Ensil with them and keep Rilla here. What have the four of you decided?"

Aislen looked at her cousins and waited for their nods before telling him anything.

"Braedan and Daegan have agreed to help. Luisella is keen to see a bit of the Outworld herself, if we can find someone to take charge of the twins in their absence."

Lukys laughed before he could stop himself. Aislen glared at him as Luisella went red to the tips of her ears.

"Ah, I'm sorry. That was uncalled for. I have it on good authority that Shuut and Master Bastienne kept the two of them quite well occupied during their travels."

Aislen nodded. "That's true. Even Ratchin and Isis managed to keep them in line for a while. Between the four of them, I'm sure they can manage."

"That's enough then. I'll go with the three of you to Silvaren. We'll pick up the elves and be on our way. The scribes have finished copying Kora's map, so we'll have one each."

"Father, are you sure you wouldn't rather I go in your place? I really don't mind."

"Aislen, I'm not changing my mind. You are my heir and you need to stay safe in these troubled times."

Aislen raised an eyebrow at him. "But you'll let *my* heir and her son go running off to a Paradise without a second thought."

Lukys stopped short at this statement. He had not been thinking of Kora as Aislen's heir. It gave him pause. Perhaps he should not have offered that she could go with Plyke. Well, the damage was done now.

"All the more reason for you to remain safe in Illaria. I'm putting the lives of our royal future in your hands. You'll have more than enough to keep you occupied with Shuut, Rilla, Marilisa and the twins."

Aislen groaned and rolled her eyes. Lukys suppressed a laugh.

"Right, off to bed everyone. We've got a long day ahead of us tomorrow. Aislen, would you be a dear and let cook Palmyra know how many lunches to prepare for the morning? I'll let Nicodémo know we don't need any guards for this run. I'm certain he'll be happy to hear it. I fear we've left his guardhouse quite depleted."

Lukys left Aislen's chambers as a round of farewells began. It was certainly going to be an interesting few weeks to follow.

Chapter Forty-One – Elves in the sky

Eliséo waited impatiently. Four crystal dragons were on their way to Silvaren and would arrive that afternoon. The other elves who were joining him had been selected. He was pleased that Liessa had agreed to come with them, especially in light of the fact that Princess Aislen had requested Ensil remain with the lintep for ease of communication.

It appeared as though Rilla was staying in Illaria. He thought it an odd decision but did not question it. Rilla seemed quite affronted and he did not care to upset his relationship with the lintep over this. Even more so than when he was the ambassador, he needed to keep a clear mind and a cool head in these situations. It would not do for the king of the elves to contradict the royal family of Illaria.

Liessa walked into his chamber and joined him at the window. Elessa had already been taller than many trees in Silvaren. Now that she was joined to Silva, she had shot up even further. The cosy chambers Eliséo had grown up with were now connected by much longer walkways than before and the chambers themselves seemed to have grown larger. He did not ask Elessa about it. He could feel that she was trying her hardest not to feel inadequate compared to Silva.

"They will not come any faster with you staring out the window," Liessa pointed out as they looked north, towards the mainland. "Are you ready?"

Eliséo nodded. "You?"

Liessa returned his nod.

"What about the others?"

"Gioshué, Raeslin, Telon and Tameo have been ready since you agreed they could come," Liessa laughed. The sound made him happy. Their relationship was still fragile, but her laughter was a good sign. "Kari and Farrow will be ready soon. They want to make sure they have everything they need for the Outworld. Kari is packing as much medicine as her rucksack can carry. Farrow is trying to placate mother. She still is not happy about our decision to leave."

Eliséo sighed. It had been difficult making Eléna understand the need for them to help the lintep. They had *discussed* the matter for a long time. Eventually, he had simply told her that it was something he felt he must do and that was the end of it.

"I suppose we had better call the children here. We need to work out who will travel with each of them. I quite like Raeslin. She has spirit." Eliséo smiled at the memory of her anger with Ensil. Before his mind could be clouded by thoughts of the weapons master, he called the children through Silva.

"I will take Telon," Liessa told him. "Kari has already expressed a wish to stay with Giosué. It seems the boy has shown a keen interest in healing, so she hopes to instruct him further while we're in the Outworld, should the opportunity arise."

"That leaves Tameo for Farrow," Eliséo said. "That should work fine. I am sure the two of them will get along."

He saw the expression on Liessa's face suddenly turn uncertain. Walking away from the window, he drew her to the cushions on the floor.

"You are worried." It was not a question. He knew she was.

Liessa took a deep breath. "What if we need to do magic, out there in the Outworld?"

"Then we do it," Eliséo replied simply.

"I do not think my power is strong enough to protect Telon, or myself for that matter."

Eliséo looked her straight in the eye. "I believe in you, Liessa. In the worst case, protect yourself with the mist bubble."

Liessa bit her lip.

"You have never tried it, have you?"

She shook her head. Eliséo told her the words and she spoke them aloud. A transparent mist rose around her. Eliséo reached out a hand and touched the mist. Instead of resting on a solid bubble of air, his hand passed right through it. Carefully, he took the crown from his head and placed it on Liessa's.

"Try again."

This time, when she created the mist bubble, he could not push through into it, though he could still see a shadow of her.

"It is no use," Liessa complained, taking the crown off her head. "This is *your* crown, not mine. I will not be able to keep us safe in the Outworld should it come down to it."

Eliséo was not listening to her. His mind was already lost in thought. Perhaps he could work out a way with Silva.

I know what you are thinking, Silva told him before he'd even asked her. *I do not think it will work.*

Have you ever tried it before? Eliséo asked. He felt her doubt. *Something small. Not a crown – maybe a necklace or an armband.*

While he was still deciding, a vine twisted around with leaves and flowers fell into his lap. He picked it up with a smile and handed it to Liessa, who took it gingerly.

"Put it on," he told her.

Liessa put her hand through the circlet and pushed it up past her elbow. It was too big. She opened her mouth, presumably to complain that it did not fit, but closed it again. The circlet had tightened around her arm, just enough not to slip off unless she pulled.

"Try the mist," Eliséo prompted her excitedly. Liessa looked at him dubiously but said the words to call forth the mist anyway. To his delight, a mist gathered around her. To Eliséo's eyes, she was still a shadow within it, but he could not push through to her no matter how hard he tried.

"It works!"

"It works?" Liessa asked incredulously. "Really?"

Eliséo could not stop smiling. He opened his mind to Silva and Liessa.

I want every elf coming into the Outworld to have something similar. Will it work best coming from their own tree or from you?

He felt Liessa's initial shock but was grateful when she did not object.

I cannot tell you that, Silva answered carefully. *I cannot recall this being done before. There is something familiar about it, but I have no actual memories.*

Then we experiment, Eliséo decided. *Please ask Giosué, Raeslin, Tameo and*

Telon's trees to create one for them and then send the children to us. Please do the same for Kari and Farrow when they are done packing.

Eliséo's head turned at the sound of footsteps approaching his common chamber. It could not possibly be the younger elves. They would not have had time to obtain a circlet from their trees yet.

"Eliséo, Liessa, what are you two doing?" Eléna asked as she walked swiftly into their view, her green and russet gown swirling around her ankles. "Silva seems quite agitated."

Eliséo exchanged a slightly guilty look with Liessa. His sister tried, unsuccessfully, to hide her arm circlet. Her movement only served to draw their mother's eye.

"What is that?" Eléna pointed to her arm.

Liessa deferred to Eliséo. He rolled his eyes at her.

"I want my elves to be as well protected as possible in the Outworld," he explained. "We are experimenting ways to increase the power of those who have little of their own."

Eléna paled. "Do you think that is a good idea?"

Eliséo was confused by her reticence. He knew he had her full support in teaching elves to use the magic they had so long been ill-educated in. How was this different?

"I believe it will keep them safe should they need it. I will teach them all to call up the mist bubble. That alone could save their lives."

He had Liessa demonstrate to their mother how well the circlet worked. Eléna was certainly impressed but remained doubtful as to whether it was a good idea. Before she could protest too loudly, a thumping of footsteps erratically ascended to them. The four elf children burst into the room, practically falling over each other in their eagerness to be the first to enter.

Eléna looked at them, eyebrows raised. She gestured towards them with a swish of her wrist. "Power in the hands of reckless children may not be as good an idea as you seem to think."

Eliséo did not want to dismiss her opinion, but knew he was running out of time before the dragons arrived. It would not be long now.

"If you would please place your circlet on your arm, as Liessa has done." The children did not hesitate, but quickly pushed their ring of vines up their arm and exclaimed in wonder as it tightened.

"I need each of you to try creating a mist bubble. I want to see if you have enough power."

Raeslin tilted her chin up. "You know we do not."

Eliséo suppressed a smile. "Just try."

Each of them did as he bid them. Tameo and Giosué's mist was powerful enough to keep them safe. Raeslin and Telon's were just a bit too weak for his liking.

Silva, can you add something of yours to each circlet?

He could feel her hesitation, but she did not object. Slowly, one leaf at a time was added to the circlet until Raeslin and Telon's mist was powerful enough to keep them safe.

"This is amazing!" Raeslin exclaimed. "Why did we not think to do this before?"

Realising her impertinence, Raeslin lowered her eyes. Eliséo did not think it wise to let her know he had been wondering the same thing himself. There were so many things he was finding out about their power now that he was free to use it. Unfortunately, many of those things angered him more than anything else. He pushed such thoughts from his mind, vowing to have a long talk with Ensil once this was all over.

* * *

The dragons arrived late that evening, far too late to depart immediately. Eliséo bid the lintep welcome and settled them into their chambers for the night. He had had little to do with Daegan, Braedan and Luisella in Illaria, but trusted King Lukys had a reason for choosing them for this task.

They had agreed to leave early the next morning. Eliséo invited them to spend the night in Silva, extending the same hospitality that was always extended to him in Illaria. He made certain that they neither lacked for food nor drink.

As the others stole away to their chambers, Eliséo noticed Lukys standing a little aside, attempting to get his attention. He walked over to the lintep king and gestured up to his own private chambers.

The two of them walked in silence. There was clearly something on Lukys' mind. Eliséo waited patiently until they were safely ensconced in his chamber, called forth a thick mist and settled down on a floor cushion. Lukys soon followed his lead, though took a few more moments to settle himself into a comfortable position. His years seemed to be catching up with him.

"King Eliséo," he began.

"Lukys." Eliséo held up a hand. "Have we not known each other long enough now to dispense with titles? At least when it is only the two of us."

Lukys gave him a tight, thin smile. "Eliséo, I do not want the elves to think we are using them simply as convenient messengers."

Eliséo started. "Indeed. I had not thought that. Thank you for putting my mind to rest."

Sweat beaded on Lukys' forehead. He wiped it away absently. It was not a warm night. Eliséo wondered if Lukys was ill.

"I would, however, be appreciative if you could let Rilla know that we have arrived safely so that my daughter does not fret."

"Rilla?" Eliséo asked slowly. "Not Ensil?"

Lukys shook his head. "Ensil agreed to travel to P2 so that we have an elf in every location. We thought it best that Rilla focus on her studies, in a safe environment, for the time being."

You have barely paid attention to the girl since Ensil saved her in the Paradise, Elessa chided him. *I could have told you everything if you had but given me time. You never have time for anyone other than Silva these days.*

Elessa, that is unfair, Eliséo disputed. *I warned both of you many things would change if I became the king. I have many responsibilities now.*

Elessa grew cold. *And you have magic to spread to the elves now. Nothing will get in your way of that. Have a care you do not do this for your own selfish reasons. You do not know what happened in the past.*

"Is anything the matter, Eliséo?" Lukys asked, drawing Eliséo from his tree.

Eliséo shook his head. "I was merely having a quiet word with my tree. She will ask Rilla to deliver your message."

Lukys looked at him for a long moment, then took a breath. "We should organise our groups for tomorrow's journey. We have Celtan, Hoarfrost, Shard and Luminosa. Pyrid insisted on going to P2 – apparently, he has grown quite fond of Aaron and now refuses to move from his side when he is in the Outworld. Garnet accompanied them so that everyone can return all at once when need be."

"I have a number of elves eager to join us on this trip. Along with myself and my sister, Kari and Farrow will accompany us. We each have a young elf ready to assist. I do not think I should fly with Celtan. He and I have had our differences in the past. I would not want that coming in to play."

Lukys cocked an eyebrow. "Very well. Perhaps your sister would like to fly with him. She might get along best with Braedan."

Eliséo smiled as he realised Lukys was trying very hard not to say what they were both thinking.

"It might be best if the two kings and the former queen fly separately," Eliséo suggested with an innocent face. "I could fly with Luisella. Kari, our healer, could fly with you on Celtan. Which leaves Farrow with Daegan. Does this sound amenable to you?"

Lukys attempted to hide his sigh of relief but failed miserably. Eliséo kept his face clear of any emotion, though on the inside he laughed fondly at the old lintep.

"We should get some rest, Lukys. I will ensure we have provisions to last at least a week. After that, each of us will need to make our own arrangements."

Lukys bid him farewell and left. Eliséo watched him go thoughtfully. It would not do to be interrupted for what he had to do next.

Careful with her, Elessa warned him, before he had even asked her to open his connection to Rilla. *She is angry and hurt. It would not do to make her feel worse.*

Eliséo drew in a deep breath. Sat on his bed and leaned back until his head rested against the inside of Elessa's trunk. He immediately saw all the memories he had purposely closed himself off from. They were distractions he could not have afforded at the time. He reflected that it might have seemed a cruel act, but that was not his intention.

Intentions don't matter when your action, or inaction, causes pain, Elessa told him firmly.

Shaking off her reprimands, Eliséo opened himself up to Rilla. He could see that she was by herself, in her common chamber. A book lay open in front of her, but she was not looking at it. She was staring out of the window into the windy night sky. Dark clouds obscured the moon, but the stars shone brightly.

Rilla.

Her attention immediately turned to him. She was open to him but remained cold and distant.

King Lukys has arrived with his companions. Please inform Princess Aislen.

There was no reply, though he knew she had heard him.

How are your studies progressing? he asked cautiously. He felt the sudden change within her as anger bubbled up to the surface.

My studies are wonderful. I had a beginner healing lesson today, followed by an intermediate practical lesson. My teachers are keeping a tight leash on me.

Beginner healing lesson? He had not meant to send that thought to her but was shocked into it.

Apparently, Mistress Kayte feels that I need to learn my place. She is refusing to teach me herself and will not allow me to progress any further until satisfied I can control my impulse to heal my friends.

Eliséo cleared his mind of all thoughts. The last thing he wanted to do was agree with Mistress Kayte in Rilla's own mind.

How are the boys? he turned the conversation to what he hoped was safer ground.

Plyke has gone off with Kora, Pér and Ensil to meet Lord Aaron at P2. I assume he's fine with such an escort.

Tika is happy in the stables and Arishen is still recovering from his wounds. I think it will still be some time before he can return to his apprenticeship. Master Reuben is taking him to the castle each day, so that he isn't left unprotected in the town.

Eliséo's head reeled. Elessa was right – he had been ignoring too much of what had happened in Rilla's life. There simply had not been time to live two lives.

Is there nothing the healers can do to speed Arishen's progress?

Rilla laughed bitterly. *They are disinclined to help him any further. His wounds are not life threatening and they believe he deserves to live through the natural healing process of his burns and beating as punishment for his crime.*

Eliséo was at a loss for words. How had everything changed so dramatically while he was not watching?

I trust you are well though? His words were certainly doing nothing to calm her.

Mistress Kayte began the healing process for my shoulder, but I too have been left to heal naturally as far as possible. Apparently, trying to save your friend's life and your cousin's life counts for nothing if you disobey others to do it.

There was little else Eliséo could think to say. Rilla was clearly not in the best of spirits and there was nothing he could do about it. He could see things from her viewpoint, but that did not mean that he agreed with her actions. Though Mistress Kayte's punishment was harsh, Eliséo could not think what else she could have done in that situation.

I fly into the Outworld tomorrow to search for Lishe, he told her. *Make sure you keep your link with Elessa open and don't stray too far from Aislen in case we need to you to communicate with her.*

In response, Rilla left herself open to him but turned her attention away so he could not speak with her. Eliséo could not blame her for being so angry with him. He wished he had more time for her.

Chapter Forty-Two – Broken heart

"This isn't working," Plyke pointed out, needlessly. They could all still see the Paradise boundary was there. No matter how many of them held his hand or placed a hand over his chest, the crystal heart would not work the way they needed it to. "It's broken."

"It isn't broken, dear," Kora tried to placate him. "Your heart is working just fine. It's doing exactly what a heart should be doing – keeping you alive."

Plyke tried to smile. He tried to not feel dejected, a failure, but it was no use. They knew now that the crystal heart would no longer work as it once did. His grandfather and the others had already spent days trying to destroy the Paradise boundary before he arrived with reinforcements. They had had no better luck that he.

"What are we going to do?" he asked sullenly. "Why can't we just ask Pyrid for another heart?"

Kora shook her head. "They already did. The crystal dragons are refusing to allow any more of their hearts out into the world. We have only seen the good they can do. I'm certain there is more to them than that. We aren't looking at the whole picture."

"So, what now?" he asked again. Kora shrugged with the shake of her head. Pér walked up to them and draped an arm around Kora. Even though Plyke was still a little jealous of their closeness, he marvelled at the effect Pér had on his mother. He felt waves of love flowing off Pér towards Kora. It made him wonder if everyone else could feel it too or if he only felt it because of his empathy powers.

Lord Aaron joined them. "No luck then?"

Plyke shook his head.

"Ensil!" Aaron called out to the elf weapons master. "Please let the others know that we cannot destroy this Paradise. All suggestions are welcome."

Ensil's almost transparent blue eyes shone brightly as he spoke with the other elves. From what Plyke had understood, Eliséo had done something when he became king and now all the elves could talk to each other whenever they wanted to. It was certainly an interesting notion. He idly wished there was some way he could talk to Tika over such great distances.

The thought of Tika made him sad. Plyke had agreed to come into the Outworld again without his Partner, but he wished there had been any excuse he could think of to ask Tika along.

The two of them barely got to spend any time together these days, especially since Plyke had moved into Pér's house to be closer to both of his parents. The three of them were still getting used to each other. It was nice to have them around and to help set up Pér's stall in the market place before his lessons started in the morning. He had only just started to get used to his new routine when he was uprooted and brought back to the Outworld.

"There is some suggestion of the lintep whistle," Ensil declared. "Apparently, more than a few people think this is the 'song' in the prophecy and wish for Plyke to try that."

Plyke looked despairingly at Ensil. He had only just started to learn how to use the lintep whistle. He could understand most things, but still had trouble doing it himself.

"Yes, we thought that might be the case," Aaron agreed. "Plyke, come along. I will teach you how to whistle the same thing as you say for the crystal heart to work."

* * *

Rilla sat in Master Reuben's advanced mind class with Taddeo, Odille and Zefiro, watching Arishen. He was sitting, huddled, in a corner of their classroom, terrified. It was no wonder – the last time he had been around lintep practising their mind skills had been with Mistress Emeline. He had not told her everything about it, but Rilla had understood well enough that he did not want another lintep in his mind, possibly ever again.

She was having trouble enough concentrating without worrying about him. Everything was going wrong lately, and she felt powerless to do anything about it.

Plyke had been taken to the next Paradise without anyone else. No one seemed to care that she was named in the prophecy anymore. Since she had stolen the crystal heart to save her cousin, she had been forgotten, tossed aside like a bothersome stone in a shoe. She did not want to be the prophecy child, but it was surprisingly painful to realise they no longer thought she was.

Even Mistress Isis was keeping her distance. Aside from the classes she taught, Rilla never saw her anymore. She felt alone and invisible, just like in her Paradise.

"Rilla?" Taddeo called out to her. She turned to look at him. "You did it again. You keep disappearing. Are you feeling ill?"

"No," she shook her head and gave him a weak smile. He was trying to engage with her. She should focus on him, but it was difficult with conversations going on in her mind through her link with Elessa.

Rilla noticed Taddeo's eyes widen. Her eyes must be bright green. He knew she was bound to an elf's tree. There was no secret about that any longer, but her glowing eyes were still a rare sight for them to see.

She listened to the conversation in the background. Anya had been right. The crystal heart no longer worked now that it was in Plyke's body. Yet another thing she had ruined. Her face flushed hotly with shame. At least no one in this class knew what she had done. She could hide, pretend that none of it had happened.

"Rilla, concentrate," Odille whispered harshly. Rilla cringed at the tone of her voice. She was ruining their lesson. She hurriedly told Elessa to block out everything she did not need to hear.

"Sorry." Rilla looked up and saw they weren't looking at her, but at the other students staring their way. She turned to those students. "Mind your own business!"

Master Reuben looked over at her shout. She didn't care. At least the other students had turned away from them. She turned her attention back to her group. Taddeo, Odille and Zefiro looked unimpressed. She knew she should not care what they thought of her, but it made her seethe inside.

She felt her blood begin to boil. In moments, Master Reuben was by her side, his hand on her shoulder, a finger touching the skin of her neck. It was cool to the touch. She realised how hot she was. She closed her eyes and counted long slow breaths to ten. The entire time, she worked hard to stop drawing heat out of the air towards herself. Instead, she radiated all the extra heat in her body in a wide circle around her.

"That will do, Rilla," Master Reuben told her as he lifted his hand from her shoulder. She looked up at him with gratitude. "Taddeo, start the exercise again. I think you will find Rilla is eager to focus on the task at hand now."

Focus. It was certainly what she needed. In an effort to not let her thoughts wander off again, she concentrated on her classmates.

"We've moved on from colours since you were last here," Taddeo told her. She knew it was a pointed comment about how many lessons she had missed, but Rilla refused to comment. "Now we are working on images. We've decided to work with flowers. So, think of a flower, create the image in your mind and pass it on to one of us. We will then pass it on to each other until it returns to you, so that you can see if it still looks the same."

Rilla nodded. She thought of the white finger orchid that she and Arishen had looked for in the Lesa Mountains. She pictured the four long, thin petals stretching out from the mouth of the orchid. Next, she pictured the main part of the flower, a petal standing up straight with a cup around it, enclosing the pollen inside it. Last, she pictured the delicate, thin, green stem, somehow capable of holding up such a beautiful bloom. Seeing the flower, she remembered how similar it smelled to freesias.

She held the image in her mind, then faced Taddeo. Not quite knowing how it should work, she covered the image with her power and floated it over to him. She felt his surprise when the flower reached him. Perhaps he had not seen such a flower before. There had been the rare few in the forest in her Paradise, but nothing compared to the great quantities she had seen in the Lesa Mountains.

In turn, Taddeo turned to Odille. She did not look so surprised. Neither did Zefiro when the image was passed to him. When Zefiro turned to her, Rilla prepared herself for his power to touch hers and purposely held herself in check. She did not want to overreact and accidentally hurt him.

The flower returned to her intact – more or less. The petals were more elongated than they should be and the cup at the top was fatter than she recalled, but it was still reminiscent of the white finger orchid.

"Whose turn is it now?" she asked, looking around at her classmates.

"How did you send me the smell?" Taddeo asked her. "I tried to send it to Odille, but I don't think I managed it."

"You didn't," Odille informed him bluntly.

"I ... don't know," Rilla replied hesitantly. "I just thought of the flower as a whole, scent included, and sent it to you."

"Send it to me, the same way you sent it to Taddeo," Odille instructed her. Rilla carefully formed the white finger orchid in her mind the same way as she did the first time. She recalled the scent and wrapped that around her flower before encasing it in her power once more. Carefully, she floated it across to Odille, just as she had with Taddeo.

"I think I know what happened!" Odille opened her eyes with a smile. "You didn't do it the same way we've been doing. We all thought of a picture of the flower and sent that. *You* thought of the actual flower."

"Well, yes," replied Rilla in confusion. "I thought that's what we had to do."

Taddeo, Odille and Zefiro laughed, but it wasn't cruelly. Rilla found herself smiling at their happiness.

"Let me try it!" Zefiro cried out excitedly. Rilla watched the look of concentration on his face. He looked over to her and pushed the flower at her. Rilla tried desperately hard not to crush his flower as it smashed into her wall.

"Oh, sorry," he mumbled.

Rilla shook her head. "No, it's okay. It just came at me faster than I thought it would."

Zefiro concentrated and tried it again. This time, the flower flew at her a bit slower. She caught it carefully in a pocket of her power. It was a small purple flower, that looked a bit like a pipe without the cup at the end. She scrunched up her nose at the intense honey scent that clung to it.

Carefully, without modifying it at all, she passed the flower along to Taddeo. From the looks on their faces, it appeared as though their new experiment was working.

"Nice jacaranda! Though, the smell is a bit too strong, Zefiro," Odille pointed out. "But I still got everything. My turn now."

They took turns the rest of the morning, passing flowers back and forth between each other. At one point, Master Reuben came to check on them and was impressed at the progress they had made. He brought their group to the front of the class so that they could each demonstrate this skill to the rest of their classmates. Instead of the jealousy that normally accompanied these revelations, the class buzzed with excitement.

When the bell went for the midday meal, students rushed from the room to reach the dining hall before all the best food disappeared.

"A moment please, Rilla," Master Reuben called out to her before she could leave the room. She turned back guiltily.

"I'm sorry, Master Reuben," she apologised, assuming he was upset with her over the way she performed the task. "I didn't know they were sending pictures to each other. I would have tried that instead if they'd told me."

He looked at her thoughtfully. For a moment, his eyes darted towards Arishen. Rilla almost followed his movement, but then he spoke.

"You don't need to apologise, Rilla. I was quite impressed that you did that and managed to teach your fellow classmates to do likewise. In fact, the reason I called you back was to ask if you don't mind taking Arishen with you to your next class. I have a beginner class in the afternoon, and they require more attention."

Rilla shifted her feet and purposely avoided Arishen's eyes. "I have my practical class with Master Aurelius' replacement this afternoon. There are a few students there who ... well, I don't know if Arishen will want to come with me."

"Isn't Kalydron in your practical class?" Arishen asked from beside her, his voice trembling slightly. Rilla nodded.

"Ah, I see." Master Reuben absently rubbed his chin. "Well, Arishen, you can't avoid him forever. He did express his regret for what he did to you. Mistress Emeline assures me he will not try that again."

Rilla looked over to Arishen. The injuries he sustained in the Paradise were still visible. His bandaged hands clenched and unclenched loosely.

"Come on then. Let's go before there's no food left."

She was careful not to touch his skin as she led him down and out to the dining hall.

* * *

Eliséo laid his hand on Elessa's inner trunk. It had been a much longer stay in Silvaren than he was used to. The two of them were still becoming acquainted with the additional bond with Silva and now it was time for him to leave.

Be careful, she warned him seriously.

I always am.

No. You are not, she retorted bluntly. *But you are the king now and the changes you have made in Silvaren will need you to carry on. Do not die out there or I will never forgive you.*

I love you too, Elessa.

He trailed his fingers along her bark as he walked away, stooping only to pick up his rucksack. As always when he travelled into the Outworld, he brought a spare change of clothes and his flute. His sword was strapped to his side in its sheath.

At the base of Silva, where the lake fed her roots, Eliséo met his new travelling party. They all looked over as he approached them, the four young elves fairly bouncing with excitement. He noted that his mother was there too.

"Have you decided to join us, mother?" he asked her jokingly.

She looked at him seriously. "It is bad enough that both of my children are leaving the forest on a fool's errand, do not joke about such things, Eliséo."

The lintep guests stiffened noticeably. Eliséo wiped the smile off his face.

"It is not a fool's errand, mother. Lishe is a dangerous lintep. If she is not stopped, she could wreak havoc in the Outworld. I am certain she intends to return to Illaria when she is finished collecting power. I cannot stand by and idly watch as she destroys their home."

He should have embraced her, he should have said a proper farewell, but he was upset with her choice of words. With a wave of his hand, he turned and walked away from her. He heard Liessa bid their mother a teary farewell, then her light footsteps as she caught up to him.

"She is only worried about us."

"She insulted King Lukys," Eliséo replied evenly. "Thankfully, he is grateful for our assistance and may not take her insult seriously."

They walked hurriedly through Silvaren, elves waving at them from the heights of their trees. Some of the younger elves followed them until they reached the thin strip of sand connecting the forest to the mainland. He sent them back to their duties before crossing over with his party.

On the side of the hill, Celtan lay sprawled across the grass with three clear crystal dragons. The sapphire dragon raised his head and huffed when he saw them. Eliséo took it as a good sign that at least he had not growled.

"Well met, Celtan," Eliséo greeted him.

"I still don't forgive you," Celtan rumbled. "But Pyrid is quite fond of you, so I've told Hoarfrost to not let you die."

Eliséo laid a hand on the old dragon's snout. "I am certain Pyrid will appreciate that."

"Let's not waste the daylight." Lukys came up behind them and handed out a map to each of the lintep. "We have a long way to fly today. I think it best that we all travel to P3 today. From there, we will have to go our separate ways to reach our Paradises.

"Kari and Giosué will come with me on Celtan to P8. Luisella, Eliséo and Raeslin will fly with Hoarfrost to P5. Braedan, Liessa and Telon will fly with Shard to P9. Lastly, Daegan, Farrow and Tameo will fly with Luminosa to P10."

Everyone shuffled into their groups and moved towards their dragons. Eliséo tested their communication before mounting Hoarfrost.

I expect everyone to keep in constant contact. You will check in with Silva every time you stop in your journeys. Any incident, no matter how small, is to be reported.

He heard their affirmative replies through their trees.

"On your dragons. Do not hesitate to protect yourselves and your lintep companions with your mist if need be. Fly well and be safe."

Eliséo mounted Hoarfrost after Luisella and Raeslin. The younger elves were all seated between the older riders, to ensure they did not fall off unnoticed. With a mighty beating of wings, the dragons took off one by one, flying out over Silvaren and the ocean to make a wide turn towards P3.

* * *

Rilla tried to ignore the fact that everyone in the dining hall was staring at them. She knew it was because of their extended absence and the state of the two of them when they had returned from the Outworld, but she still did not like it. In an attempt to ignore them, she led Arishen to the long tables laden with food. She took a plate and began to fill it.

The cooks always created many dishes for every meal. Rilla wondered how many people worked in the kitchens to provide such a feast three times a day. She moved along the table and breathed in the different aromas wafting from the vegetables. Peas were topped with slivers of mint leaf. Potatoes had been roasted with whole cloves of garlic and sprigs of rosemary. Pumpkins were spiced with cinnamon and sugar.

Forgetting the eyes of the crowd, Rilla heaped food onto her plate with her good arm, placing a thick slice of warm nutty bread on top to keep everything from falling off. She looked over at Arishen and saw he had not even taken a plate yet. He held his bandaged hands out in a pathetic gesture. Rilla cursed herself for not having thought about it earlier.

"Wait here," she said as she rushed her plate over to where the twins and Shuut were seated. She came back and made up a plate for Arishen, then took him over to her usual table. As soon as they were seated, Dorian, Miette and Kalydron came over to join them. Arishen and Kalydron exchanged awkward glances before looking away from each other.

"Oh, Arishen! What happened to your hands?" asked Miette in a horrified whisper. Arishen's face turned a deep shade of red as he attempted to pick up a fork. It dropped out of his bandaged fingers.

"Here, let me help you," Miette said as she picked up the fork. "I'm finished anyway."

Rilla tried not to smirk as Arishen turned an even deeper shade of red and stuttered his thanks to her. Miette waved it away with a "tish-tosh". Rilla elbowed Kalydron in the side when he began to laugh, earning them both a glare from Miette.

"We've missed you," Kalydron told Rilla as she diverted her attention away from Arishen. "Even the twins won't tell us where you've been and what happened when you were there. That's ... unlike them."

"Unlike them?" Dorian asked incredulously. "It's the complete opposite. I can't get anything out of them except they were punished with cooking and cleaning up after everyone."

Rilla looked over at Umi and Ulf. They avoided her gaze.

"Maybe they've finally learnt a lesson in discretion," Shuut said. "Something all of you could do with if you don't stop your questions. We went where we were needed and did what we had to do. We're back now, so if you don't mind, we'd like to concentrate on our studies. I have Master Reuben next with these three. What about you?"

"We're with Master Aurelius' replacement." Rilla nodded towards Kalydron. "I'm taking Arishen with me. Maybe we can walk him back into town when our lessons are over."

"Oh, I'll do that," Miette volunteered eagerly. "It's been an age since I walked through the town."

Rilla and Shuut raised an eyebrow at each other. They both knew Miette might not be able to keep Arishen safe by herself.

"Why don't we all go for a walk into town this afternoon?" Shuut suggested. "It might do us good to get out of the castle for a while."

"Good idea!" the twins cried out in unison.

"Aislen has been on our backs since we got back. Now that Mother and Father have gone, she's even more watchful over us than ever," Umi explained.

"Oh," Rilla said softly. "I just remembered. I'm not meant to leave the castle at the moment."

I need to stay near Aislen in case the elves need me to talk to her, she told Shuut with her mind. Shuut nodded almost imperceptibly.

"I'll take good care of them. You ... can go to the library instead."

Rilla nodded dispiritedly. The castle felt so empty. Almost all the adults were gone now, including Guiscard, which meant even the library felt cold and unwelcoming.

"I'll stay with you, Rilla," Kalydron said softly. "I can help you catch up on your lessons."

Rilla looked at him with a shy smile. She noticed Shuut's raised eyebrow but said nothing. The bell tolled for the start of afternoon lessons. Rilla quickly shovelled the rest of her food in her mouth before joining the others to rush to their classes.

Arishen walked close by Miette's side. She took hold of his arm and did not let go until they had to go their own separate ways. It made Rilla happy that Arishen had found at least one friend in Illaria. Miette's infatuation with the seer might not last, but she was certain their friendship would.

The door to Master Aurelius' room was open and students were already filing in. Rilla took Arishen in with her and quickly located an empty area of the room. She sat him down next to her.

Kalydron walked in soon after and immediately located her. He headed straight towards the empty seat on her other side. Rilla noticed Arishen tense beside her. It was going to be an interesting lesson.

An old master who Rilla did not recognise sat at the front of the class. She glanced over at Kalydron. He leaned in towards her.

"Many of the retired teachers have been called in lately to resume their duties while our usual teachers are off doing who knows what. This is Master Amyas. He's not bad, actually. A bit different to Master Aurelius, but no less skilled from the looks of it."

Master Amyas held up his hands for silence. The room eventually quietened down.

"Réne, would you please close the door?"

The arrogant boy rose out of his chair.

"No, with your power, not your hands."

Réne was seated at the front of the class, a mere few feet from the door. It took a few moments, but the heavy wooden door finally began to move from its place against the wall. Rilla watched in fascination. She wondered if he would still have been able to do that if he was seated further away.

"Not bad," Master Amyas conceded. "Now, move half way down the class and open it."

Réne's expression turned smug as he walked towards Rilla. She felt her dislike of him grow almost unbearable. All at once, Arishen's bandaged hand and Kalydron's smooth one were on her arms, one on either side. She wrenched away from both of them. Kalydron might not know any better than to touch her, but Arishen certainly did.

She looked up in time to see Réne's effort in opening the door. It was becoming a strain for him. Master Amyas ordered him to the back of the room to close it once again. Rilla watched the arrogant boy closely. He was trying, there was no doubt about that, but nothing was happening.

"My power does not extend that far, Master Amyas." He admitted defeat.

Master Amyas nodded affably. "Now, keep your power extended towards the door and stop when you can reach it well enough to interact with it."

Réne walked forward slowly, only a pace at a time, until he was almost back at the halfway point. The door moved painstakingly slowly and closed with a gentle click.

"And now you know your limit," Master Amyas told him before addressing the rest of the class. "Who else where knows their limit?"

A few hands were raised, but most of the class, including Rilla, remained motionless.

"In that case, I would like everyone to line up along the back wall. They still give out white pebbles when you start your training, do they not? Get one out."

Everyone did as they were told. Rilla hurriedly shoved Arishen in a corner of the room and stood beside him. She did not want Réne and his cronies getting anywhere near her friend. Kalydron shuffled and bumped past other students to join her. Arishen tensed again.

"He won't hurt you," Rilla whispered to him. The look Arishen shot her was confusing. She did not understand that look, but it certainly was not about Kalydron jumping into his mind.

Belatedly, Rilla realised she was the only one without a pebble in her hand.

"Rilla is afraid she won't live up to her royal heritage," Réne sneered. His sniggering friends were silenced by a glare from Master Amyas. Rilla blushed furiously as she dug out a pebble from her green velvet pouch. She held it tightly in her hand.

"All together now, move your pebble as far as you can across the room. Do *not* throw it with your power."

Rilla remembered the first time she had used the stones. Her mother had scolded her for losing one because she used too much power. Since then, she had practised, refining her touch, until she knew exactly how much was needed for a pebble.

She held her hand out in front of her, the pebble lying motionless in her palm. She pulled out a tendril of her power, no thicker than her finger. Carefully, she wrapped her power around the pebble, making sure it could not possibly fall. She ignored all the noise around her – the taunts and exclamations of her classmates, some of whom had already completed the task to their limits.

Slowly, Rilla lifted the pebble from her hand and carried it to the front of the room. She knew there was so much further she could go, but the wall stopped her.

A voice behind startled her. "Do you know your limit, lass?"

Rilla turned to see Master Amyas looking down at her. She shook her head.

"I know it's further than that," she said as she gestured to the pebble. He nodded, thoughtfully.

"Class, I understand you have not yet had any lessons in the courtyard, but I think it's about time you did. Follow me, please."

Rilla drew back her power, taking the pebble in her hand once more. She almost forgot about Arishen in her excitement.

"Come on," she called back to him. He hurriedly followed her. Together with Kalydron, they raced down the twisted stairwell into the courtyard.

"Test your limit again and sort yourself into groups of similar limits. I want you to pass more and more stones between each other and see if your limit decreases with the additional weight.

"If the extra pebbles make no difference, there are plenty of things in this courtyard that you can use instead. I warn you that I will tolerate no foolishness.

Whosoever of you tests me on that will be sitting on the side, missing out on their lesson."

Rilla stood on one side of the courtyard with the rest of her class. Once more, she readied herself to transport her pebble. Carefully, but trembling with anticipation, she floated the pebble across the courtyard. It quickly became apparent that she had pushed it further than the rest of her class.

When it bumped up against the wall on the other side, she looked over to Master Amyas. He curled a finger, beckoning her towards him. As discreetly as possible, she drew her pebble back and walked over to him. She only noticed his strategic position when she was standing next to him.

"Ask your blond friend there to walk out through the garden alongside your pebble. We'll work it out yet."

Rilla smiled and waved Arishen over to them. She explained the plan to him, but he did not look as excited as her.

"If your pebble goes past the wall, I won't be able to follow it," he told her.

"Oh." Rilla drew a deep breath. "Well, I doubt my power will go past there."

"Don't be too certain, lass," Master Amyas told her. "If you are being clever about it and using a thin tendril, your power may extend further than you imagine. If you think you can manage to keep your power in place, once you reach the far wall, follow it around to the stables. Your lad will be able to follow it there."

Rilla nodded excitedly. To her annoyance, Arishen was not nearly so pleased with the plan. Well, she was not particularly pleased to have to watch him all afternoon, so if she had to do that, this was the least he could do for her.

Blocking everything from her mind other than the stone, Rilla concentrated on her task. She extended her power as quickly as she thought Arishen could walk. It surprised her when she reached the far wall. Arishen was standing in front of the gate to the drawbridge, blocking the path of her stone. He pointed to his side and Rilla delayed until she had figured out how to move her power around like that without moving the initial portion's direction.

Eventually, she managed it. Slower than before, she continued to float her pebble until she had no power left inside her.

"That's it," she breath heavily. "That's as far as I can go."

Master Amyas did not move. "Kalydron, run and find the seer. Bring him back here." He turned to Rilla. "Do not retrieve your pebble until they have returned."

They waited for the boys to return. Rilla could feel her power stretched out to her limit. It was difficult to keep it there when every fibre in her body was calling out for her to retrieve it. Coloured dots began flashing before her eyes. She wavered on her feet. Her arms started shaking.

"Rilla, pull your power back," a voice told her firmly. She obeyed without question, after all, it was exactly what she wanted to do. The dots still flashed before her eyes, but now the sky turned dark. There must be a storm rolling in. She closed her eyes sleepily.

Chapter Forty-Three – Containment

They neared P3 late in the afternoon. With well-practised coordination, the four crystal dragons descended in a spiral. It had quickly become apparent that they would not reach the Paradise with enough light left to investigate and, as none of them wanted to be caught in the dark by Lishe, they had agreed to stop far enough away that she may not have noticed them.

As they had offered previous times, the dragons lay snout to tail and extended their inner wings over the party to create a makeshift shelter for their riders. It was a relief not to have to find enough firewood to keep them warm during the icy winter night.

Eliséo bade his elves practise their mist bubbles to ensure three people could fit within each one. He shook his head. It was too tight a squeeze for them.

"Kari and Giosué, hold hands and just one of you create a mist bubble."

He could see the bubble, faintly, but the gasps from the others ensured him they were hidden from everyone else's view.

"It was more spacious this way," Kari informed him once the mist had dissipated. "I do not believe that our mist bubbles are as strong as yours. Can we test if a lintep would be able to break through?"

Eliséo looked over at Lukys. He was certain to be the most powerful of them.

"What do you need me to do?" he asked.

"Kari and Giosué will create a mist around Luisella. Liessa and Telon will create a mist around Braedan. Farrow and Tameo will create one around Daegan. Try to speak with each of them through your powers," Eliséo instructed.

He nodded to his elves. They gathered around their chosen lintep and created their mist bubbles. Lukys stepped forward and concentrated.

"I can feel the bubble and, if I concentrate, I can almost see within them, but I cannot push my power through."

Eliséo used Silva to tell the elves to dissipate their mist. He waited until they all appeared again before creating his own mist, as wide as he could, around all of them. He staggered at the effect. It extended out past the crystal dragons. He had not experimented with his limits since being bound to Silva. Containing his emotions, he faced his elves.

"The last time I encountered Lishe's power, I was able to block it myself. I do not know how much more power she has stolen since then. From now on, any time you feel threatened or are within sight of a Paradise, use your mist. I will keep mine up until we go our separate ways."

Braedan made a strangled noise. Eliséo turned to him curiously.

"Won't that exhaust you?"

"That is doubtful," Eliséo replied calmly. "Elves do not need to sleep as often as other races. Our power works differently to yours. Once the mist is up, it does not take any effort to maintain it unless circumstances change."

Luisella laughed lightly at the look on her husband's face. She closed his gaping mouth and took his hand in hers, leading him away to settle in for the evening.

As his new lintep companions began to set up their sleeping mats for the night,

Eliséo watched them closely. He knew Lukys was skilful and quite powerful, but the others were relatively unknown to him. All he knew about them was that Braedan and Daegan were the twin sons of Kynon. Kynon himself was Princess Ophélie's son so, presumably, the entire family was powerful.

His attention turned back to Luisella. She had married into the family. He had no way to gauge her skills without asking.

"A copper for your thoughts?" Lukys asked as he sat beside Eliséo.

"My thoughts are worth more than a mere copper," Eliséo laughed. "I would rather know what *your* thoughts are. Presuming we find Lishe at one of these Paradises, what is your plan? Have your lintep been told how to deal with her?"

"We contain her. We contain all the power she has stolen until we find a way to strip it from her."

Eliséo stared at him. "Have you considered the possibility that she will be prepared for you? That you will not be able to contain her power and that she may steal yours or put a mind snare on you as she did with Shadow and Rilla?"

Lukys flinched.

"You did at least tell them it was a possibility, did you not?"

Eliséo tried to look Lukys in the eye, but the lintep kept avoiding him.

"Lukys, if you do not take the trouble to warn your family, I will be forced to tell my elves to kill Lishe on sight."

"No!" Lukys held out a hand. "You can't do that!"

"I will not put the lives of my elves, or anyone else, at risk. If Lishe cannot be detained and her power properly contained, I will order my elves to kill her. They have all been trained by Master Ensil and are more than competent with their weapons, despite their youthful appearance."

Lukys looked at him with flinty eyes. The conversation amongst the others had stopped. All eyes were on them.

"She isn't one of your subjects," Lukys answered carefully. "You have no right to decide what happens with her."

Eliséo regarded him coolly. "From the sound of it, she is not one of *your* subjects either, Lukys."

"Uncle, he makes a good point," Braedan interrupted. "We all completed our training a long time ago. I do not recall anyone teaching me how to 'contain' someone's power."

Lukys turned ashen. Eliséo had not realised that most lintep were not taught this skill. Nyssa had threatened to do it to Rilla and had forced Rilla to help her contain Plyke's power when it threatened to leave him.

"It is ... not a skill we widely teach," Lukys replied hoarsely. "I suppose I have little choice but to teach you now."

Eliséo listened as Lukys explained the concept to his lintep. Luisella's hand flew to her mouth, suppressing a cry. Braedan put an arm around her shoulders and drew her close to him.

"Let's hope we do not need to resort to that," Daegan said quietly. It was the first time Eliséo had heard him speak. His manner was much gentler than he had expected for such a refined and strict looking man.

Lukys appeared to have finished his lecture and seemed happy to leave things there. Eliséo gave him a moment longer to continue before pointing out the blindingly obvious flaw in their plan.

"The four of you will need to practise on each other, tonight. You will not have another chance, and this is as safe an environment as you will ever have for such an exercise."

He gestured to the mist bubble and dragons around them. Luisella began to shake her head, but was steadied by Braedan's hand covering her pale, slender fingers.

"You try it on me first, Lu," he told her with a forced smile. "I don't mind."

"I ... I can't," she whimpered. "What if something goes wrong?"

Lukys shook his head. "Nothing can go wrong unless you want it to. All you need to do is cover his body with your power and hold it steady. I know what you're concerned about, but none of us are like Lishe. We're trying to stop her, not become her."

Braedan squeezed Luisella's hand once more before letting go. Eliséo noticed his elves draw unobtrusively close so they could watch. This was the first time most of them would have seen lintep magic being used, though he doubted they would see anything with an exercise such as this.

Luisella sat crossed legged on the ground in front of Braedan. She drew a deep breath. Eliséo watched Braedan intently for any sign of what was happening. It happened so suddenly. The smile he had painted on his face to help his wife to have courage fell. The corners of his mouth began to twitch. The whites of his eyes grew larger. His chest began to heave up and down. Then, suddenly, he relaxed.

"I can't do it!" Luisella cried out as she buried her face in her hands. Braedan reached out a hand to her but stopped himself. Eliséo could see his internal struggle.

"You ... did well, Lu," he told her stiffly.

Eliséo felt a pit opening inside him. She had not done well at all. If Luisella was the one to face Lishe, she would almost certainly be stripped of her powers by the rogue lintep.

"Now do you see why we may have to resort to killing Lishe?" He turned to look at Lukys. The lintep king did not acknowledge his words.

"Try again, Luisella," Lukys said. "Try on me while Braedan and Daegan practise on each other."

Eliséo gave the lintep some space. He called his elves to the other side of their campsite and made them do weapon drills. When the time came, his elves would be prepared to do what they must, even if it meant Lukys would never forgive them.

* * *

Someone was patting her cheek, a little rougher than Rilla thought necessary. She swiped their hand away and opened her eyes. A blurry Master Amyas was learning over her.

"She's back," he called out. More faces appeared above her. Rilla tried to sit up, but a firm hand held her shoulder down. "No, lass, stay where you are. You've had quite the nasty turn."

Rilla focused on the faces again, trying to distinguish one from another. Some of her classmates were there – she could not remember their names.

"Where's Arishen?" she asked with a thick tongue. "Did Kalydron bring him back?"

"We're here, Rilla."

She tilted her head back to see the boys kneeling above her. They both looked pale. She frowned. Why were they so pale?

"Where did my pebble get to?" she asked, the words slurring past her lips. They looked at each other.

"We don't know," Kalydron answered after a long pause.

"Rilla, you need to rest now," Master Amyas told her. "Kalydron, help me take her to the infirmary."

"I don't need to go to the infirmary," Rilla said. Her tongue felt rough. She tried to sit up, but her limbs were too heavy.

"We can't carry you up to your chambers, Rilla. You'll have to stay in the infirmary until you can walk upstairs yourself."

She did not remember being taken to the infirmary, but there she was, lying on a hard, narrow bed. Kalydron sat on a stool between her bed and the one beside it. He looked over as she stirred. Rilla could barely remember anything of her afternoon after she pushed her pebble out to find her limit.

"What happened?" She noticed her tongue did not feel quite so heavy anymore, but it still felt strange to talk.

Kalydron scratched the base of his neck. "Master Amyas said you pushed yourself too far – that your power was stretched too thin."

Rilla closed her eyes to remember. "Yes, I made a thin tendril to stretch the pebble out as far as I could." Her eyes snapped open. "How far did it go?"

"We really don't know, Rilla," he answered as though he had already explained this to her. "I found Arishen standing at the front of the stables. Master Edric wouldn't let him pass. He said your pebble went through the stable. By the time I convinced Master Edric to let us pass, we saw your pebble whoosh past us towards the courtyard."

"Oh." Her voice sounded so small in the infirmary. "What am I doing here?"

Steady, but light, footfalls approached. Kalydron looked relieved.

"So, you're awake." Mistress Kayte sounded unimpressed. "Kalydron, you don't need to stay, unless you particularly want to."

"I'll stay," he replied quietly, but firmly.

"Suit yourself," Mistress Kayte shrugged. "Rilla, I'd have said this was yet another example of how you experiment without understanding the consequences, but it seems as though Master Amyas is partially to blame.

"Nevertheless, you should have known better. You must have been told before that if your power leaves you at any point it time, you will likely die. Now, you have proof of that. If Master Amyas had not realised what was happening in time, you would have stretched your power so far away from you that we would not have having this discussion right now."

Rilla frowned. "I only did what he told me to."

"Yes," Mistress Kayte sighed. "That's the only reason I'm not yelling at you."

Rilla pushed herself up onto her elbows, completely ignoring Kalydron's protests that she needed to rest.

"I should be the one yelling at *you*." Rilla felt the anger bubbling away inside her. It gave her fuel to burn. "You stifle me at every opportunity. Instead of teaching me, you reprimand me. Instead of helping me, you push me to the side. I should be out there with Plyke right now, but I'm *here* because of *you!*"

"Kalydron, get out of here, *now*! Find Isis. Find Aislen." There was a note of panic in her voice.

Rilla saw Kalydron leave, but she barely spared him a glance. "Eliséo is out there right now with King Lukys, trying to find Lishe. The lintep he brought with him have no idea how to contain her power. They've had less experience with it than I have, and yet *they* are the ones chosen to help.

"*I* was the one who doused the fire in the Paradise, but there was no thanks for that, there were only more reprimands when I tried to save Arishen's life afterwards.

"I saved Plyke's life. *I* did that. *You* were too afraid to try anything with him. You would have let him die, but *I saved him!*"

The anger boiling inside of her burst. She was surrounded by flames, but her skin was not burning. It was ice cold. The air she breathed in scorched her throat, but her power healed it as quickly as it burned.

* * *

Isis sensed the trouble before the warning call came. She was sorting through requests for training in extra skills in her classroom when a frantic whistle flew around the castle.

Isis, Aislen, the infirmary!

Papers dropped to the table and floor as she ran. No one was in danger in the infirmary, as far as she knew. There had been no major accidents recently. Besides, Kayte's management of the infirmary was exemplary.

Isis hitched up the long skirts she wore around the castle as she raced down the twisting staircase. She caught up with Aislen as she ran through the inner courtyard. Snow crunched under their feet and blurred Isis' vision as it began to fall in sheets.

Aislen opened the infirmary doors with her power moments before they reached it. Together, they ran headlong down the stairs into the infirmary. And stopped. It was hot in here – hotter than it had any right to be on a snowy evening.

Isis carefully turned a corner and saw flames burning in the middle of the room. Kayte stood in front of the flames, arms raised with hands facing the fire.

"What happened?" Aislen yelled over the roar of the flames. Kayte briefly turned her head towards them.

"Rilla's in there. It's her fire."

Isis heard their continued conversation in the background. She didn't care how it started or what Kayte thought might be happening inside. Isis knew this was her fault. She was meant to be keeping an eye on the girl, but since they returned, she had lapsed in her duties.

She sent out a tendril to investigate. Kayte's power acted as a shield on this side of the fire. Isis noticed, with some curiosity, that the flames spread no further on the other side of Rilla. Careful not to let any of the heat from the fire travel into her tendril, Isis probed past the flames. Rilla stood, arms outstretched towards the ground, fingers spread wide, her chin tilted defiantly upwards.

Gently, Isis touched Rilla with her tendril. The girl's skin was ice cold, but her body had not given out. Her heartbeat was steady, if a little slow. The fire was not coming out of her. It may have started that way, but now, it was feeding off the air itself, drawing all the heat out of it. Isis felt ice crystals start to form on her eyelashes. She absently wiped them away as her mind raced.

"Kayte, find warm blankets. We'll need them when this is over. Aislen I'm going in there with her. I'll cover the two of us with my power. Then I need you to cover my power with yours – suffocate the flames. Do it quickly."

Before they could object, Isis stripped off her bulky skirts, leaving only her undergarments and wrapped herself in layers of her power, head to foot. She took a steadying breath then walked into the flames, constantly telling herself not to let the heat past her power and into her body.

It only took a few steps to reach Rilla, but the roaring from the fire in those few steps made Isis' ears ring. Rilla did not acknowledge her – did not even look at her. It seemed as if she was in some sort of trance.

Isis put a gentle hand on the girl, but still got no response. Knowing she would have to wrap her power around them as snugly as she could, Isis unfurled part of her power. The heat was almost too much to bear. Instead of unfurling it completely, Isis loosened the layers of power around her and slipped it up and over Rilla's head, drawing the girl close to her.

"Now!" Isis screamed at the top of her voice. She hugged Rilla tightly, knowing it could be the death of her. The extended skin contact was sapping Isis of her body heat and feeding it into Rilla.

The flames still roared around them. Isis could not tell if Aislen was doing anything – if she had even heard the cry to start. She could feel her body going numb. The warm blankets she had sent Kayte to find would be useless if she and Rilla were already dead before the fire was doused.

This is my element, Isis told herself calmly. *Fire is what I know best. I will work with it now.*

Carefully, and ever so slowly, Isis allowed small amounts of heat from the flames to trickle through her power. She let the warmth flood through her body, careful not to allow too much. As soon as she warmed herself up, Rilla's body sucked that heat away from her.

This time, she allowed the heat to radiate through her body, straight into Rilla, warming the girl at the same time as warming herself. She focused all her attention on that single task. She did not notice Rilla's heartbeat steady into a normal rhythm. She did not notice the girl suddenly become stiff and try to break free. She kept all her attention on the warmth she brought to them. Until there was no more warmth left to draw on.

Isis looked up and saw the flames had disappeared. Rilla tried to back away from her. Isis let her go, but the girl did not move. She only stared around her wild-eyed.

"What have you done to me?" Rilla's heart was racing again. Isis could feel it through their close contact.

"I've saved you," Isis breathed out in relief. When Isis released her power from around Rilla, her legs gave way and she fell heavily to the floor. Rilla was over her in a moment, but Kayte pushed her roughly aside.

"Isis, are you okay?"

"Don't hurt her," Isis said, holding a hand out to Rilla. The girl hesitated for a moment before taking it. Kayte's eyes widened. Her cheeks flushed, but she let the girl past her.

Rilla's emotions hit her in a torrent. Fear, anger, sadness, rejection, hopelessness. It was too much for anyone to bear. There was no love there. No shining beacon to tell her everything would work out. She had nothing.

Isis sobbed and held Rilla closely.

"What's wrong with her?" Rilla asked. Isis heard it from a distance but did not have the strength to answer.

"You are," Kayte replied sternly.

The anger and sadness within Rilla deepened. Isis found herself shaking, not able to breathe.

"Kayte, leave those blankets with me," a gentle voice said. "You've done enough now. I'll come and find you later."

Warm blankets were draped over them and Isis found she could breathe again. She sucked in deep, long breaths, but did not let go of Rilla, even when Aislen's fingers tried to pry her loose.

"You can let her go now," Aislen said softly. "She's safe now."

"No, she isn't." Isis shook her head and looked up at Rilla. She had never noticed the fear in the girl's eyes before. Why was that?

Aislen sat down beside them and hesitated before wrapping her arms around them. Isis knew she would feel everything they were both feeling.

"Oh!"

It was what Isis had been waiting for – Aislen's realisation that Rilla was not okay. She did not feel loved. She had not felt loved since Rhanya had died. That wonderful healer who had taken her under his wing when she was scared and all alone in a Paradise where her mother had abandoned her, and her father ignored her. There was hot cocoa on a starry night. Whispered secrets. Shared stories. Trust, love and respect for one another. They had been united against a common enemy and had become stronger because they were there for each other.

It made Isis' heart ache. Her own parents had always been everything to her. She had missed them terribly when she had left their farm to live in the castle, but she always had their love. She had carried it around her heart as a shield against all the abuse she had been subjected to when the jealous rages hit her classmates.

Isis took that love, that shield and gave it to Rilla. She knew Aislen had felt it too. It meant more than she would ever be able to express that Aislen made that shield bigger by suffusing it with her own love.

Rilla began to tremble under their embrace, but it was no longer from fear or anger. Relief flooded out of her like a burst dam. She was still scared and angry, but those feelings did not overwhelm her.

Isis released Rilla from her embrace. She noted, with a wry smile, that Aislen held on just a moment longer, not wanting to let them go.

"I'm sorry, Rilla," Aislen said as she gently brushed the girl's cheek with her hand. "We should have been looking out for you. I forget you are the only child here without parents. Shuut has lived like that for so long that I ... suppose I assumed you would just go on like she does."

"I ..." Rilla choked on her words. "That's not your job."

"Oh, my dear, sweet girl!" Isis took Rilla's hand in her own. "Love is not a *job*. We both love you, as do many people in your life. You've just lived so long trying to protect others that you don't see their love.

"We should have realised you would feel alone now that most of your family is gone. I know even Shuut has been spending more time with Ratchin than with you lately. Perhaps I could come back to the castle for a while..."

Aislen held up her hand. "That won't be necessary. I will look after her. You have enough to do with requests for extra knowledge."

Rilla looked between them an expression of bemused incredulity fixed on her face.

"I could help," Rilla said quietly. "I'd *like* to help with the extra knowledge requests, if I'm allowed."

"I'm not sure..." Aislen began before Isis cut her off.

"It's not a bad idea, Aislen. We both know Rilla's power doesn't work the same as everyone else's in Illaria, as we have ample proof. If I'd trust any student to help me with this task, it would be her. She's probably the only one who will figure out how to do these things without any help."

Isis dared not send Aislen a message with her mind. With Rilla so close, it was possible the girl would intercept it unintentionally. Eventually, Aislen nodded and got to her feet.

"I'll alert the castle maids to make up a room for you. There are still a few empty teachers' rooms. Come along when you're ready. I'll have food sent to Rilla's room for the two of you."

Isis waited until Aislen had gone before she dared look at Rilla. She still had not let go of the girl's hand and was amazed that Rilla had not tried to pull away. It was a delicate spell she was under. Unadulterated love was a heady feeling for anyone, but even more so when it was so sparingly received.

* * *

Aislen headed towards Kayte's room once she had organised everything for Isis and Rilla. There was something she needed to do that she had put off for too long. It was not a pleasant task. Her father would probably object if he knew her plan, but he was not here, and she would not speak to him about this through Rilla. The poor girl had already been through so much. She rapped twice on Kayte's door and waited. The most skilled healing mistress Illaria had ever known opened the door and let her in.

Chapter Forty-Four – Wrong song

"There's no point staying here if we can't figure out how to destroy the barrier," Guiscard pointed out.

Aaron glared at him. "What do you expect us to do then? Leave Duke Leif's men here with a promise that we'll return one day with a solution. Then what? Let Lishe continue to steal power unobstructed because we gave up on figuring out the puzzle?"

The librarian pressed his hands against his knees as he stood up. "Face it, Aaron. We're out of ideas. Without another crystal heart, we cannot do this. You are only delaying the inevitable."

Aaron watched him walk away in annoyance. He knew Guiscard was right, but that didn't make it any easier to swallow the truth. They had tried what they could with the lintep whistle.

Over the past two days, he had taught Plyke various messages. Plyke had whistled them alone and in chorus with others. He had tried touching the barrier while they whistled and standing back from it. It did not seem to matter how many lintep joined in, the barrier did not seem to be affected at all.

"Grandfather?" Plyke said, walking over to him.

No matter how bad things looked, when any of his grandchildren called him that, Aaron felt better. It did not fix any of his problems, but it still made him smile.

"Yes, Plyke, what is it?"

"What if we have it wrong?" Plyke asked softly. "What if the song really is just a song? Not a lintep whistle at all."

"Songs have no power – not like the whistle."

Plyke frowned. "I don't think that's true. Pér's songs seem to have quite an effect on Kora. Doesn't his magic have something to do with that?"

Aaron looked at his grandson thoughtfully. Could they have had it wrong all along?

"I'll let you in on a little secret, Plyke. Pér is the only one we know of who can do that. I don't know if it's from lack of trying, or he simply has a unique gift, but I've never seen anyone else use their magic through song the way Pér does."

"You could say that about anyone," Plyke waved his hand dismissively. "Rilla and I both use our magic differently to others. I'm not certain what exactly Kora does, but I've seen enough people look at her in wonder to know that she uses her power differently to them.

"And look at *you*. How many other lintep do you think would be able to make their power replace their missing arm?!"

Aaron laughed despite himself. Yes, this boy had spirit. He might be softly spoken at times and often try to hide behind his Partner, but there was a sharp mind and a stubborn will there too.

"By all means Plyke, give it a try. Ask Pér to sing with his hand over your heart. There's no harm in trying."

Without needing to be told a second time, Plyke ran off to find his father. Aaron followed him at a more sedate pace. He motioned Guiscard and Kynon over to him and explained the boy's idea.

"It has merit," Guiscard agreed.

Kynon looked at them oddly. "I've never noticed this particular gift of Pér's. I'm certain Lukys would have exploited him if he could truly do as you say."

Aaron huffed. "That's exactly what we told Pér. Why do you think Lukys banned him from ever playing in the castle again? We orchestrated the entire thing so that he would play songs designed to make Lukys dislike him so that he had an excuse not to play in the castle anymore.

"Did you not listen to him in the market square that night soon after Kora returned? Did you not feel the effect his songs had on *all* the people gathered there?"

Kynon shook his head. "I didn't go out to listen. Why would I have wanted to hear the songs of a man who had been banned from playing in the castle?"

"Well, you'll have your chance to listen now," Aaron said as he patted his cousin on the back. "Hurry now, or Plyke will make him do it before we arrive."

The three of them quickened their pace, weaving their way through the tents surrounding the Paradise boundary. There was already a small crowd gathered by the time they arrived.

"I don't know if it will work, Plyke."

Aaron heard Pér's quiet protest as they approached.

"That's the whole point!" Plyke threw his hands up in the air. "None of us know if it will work, but we'll never know if we don't try."

"Do you need your instrument?" Guiscard asked him.

Pér shook his head. "It works better if I have my lute, but I can't play it with my hand on Plyke's heart."

"Fine, fine. Try just singing first. Let's see what happens."

Aaron chuckled quietly. He loved how Guiscard often took it upon himself to start organising and researching the best way to do everything. He drew the librarian back to give his family more room. Kora stood off to one side, a tender look of happiness on her face. It must be so nice for her to see her son and her love working so closely together.

Pér cleared his throat. The gathered crowed quietened to hear his voice. He tested out a few notes in a cadence, working his singing voice.

"*Be not afraid to fly alone. Fly free to the skies.*"

He sang it loud and clear. The song resonated about them, lifting the spirits of everyone in hearing distance, but it had no effect on the Paradise boundary. Pér slumped over.

"I told you..." he began.

"Tut, tut," Guiscard quietened him. "We have a number of experiments yet to try with the song. Kora be a dear and fetch Pér's lute. Next, he tries with his instrument, with Plyke making the skin contact for him."

Before he'd even finished, Kora produced the lute from behind her back with a wry smile. The librarian shook his head and waggled a finger at her.

"You, my dear, would make a fine librarian should the desire ever strike you."

Pér took the lute and strummed a few notes on it, humming to himself. He told Plyke to place his hand on his bare neck and stand behind him. Plyke did as he was told. Aaron held his breath in anticipation.

The song was sung again. It was certainly stronger. Was there a ripple in the Paradise boundary or had that just been his imagination?

"Much better!" Guiscard beamed. "I think you may have hit on a winning theory, young Plyke. We'll sort this out yet. Now Pér, I understand it is probably a difficult procedure but to start with, just teach Plyke your tune so he can join you in the song." Turning to Plyke, he repeated himself.

"Now, Plyke, you join in the song with your father. He'll teach you the tune he sings with it. If that doesn't work, he will explain exactly how he uses his power through it, then you try it together."

Plyke nodded dutifully and sat beside Pér to learn the tune. A little while later, they were ready to try it again. Aaron tried not to fidget. The anticipation of the song was working its way through his entire body. When they were finally ready, he stopped pacing.

Pér and Plyke sang together, their voices wavering as they tried to keep in tune with each other. Nothing happened. In fact, less than nothing – it was the worst attempt they had made yet.

"You're too agitated," Aaron told them. "I don't think it works when you're all worked up like that. You're both trying too hard."

Plyke looked at him in exasperation. "Of course, we're trying hard! We need to make this work."

Aaron shook his head, but before he could explain, Kora was at his side, a hand on his arm.

"What father is trying to say is that you can't force these things. I think you need to take a break. Pér will have to teach you exactly how he works his magic. It doesn't simply work because you need it to. It works because you *feel* it within you. Pér doesn't just start singing something as soon as he realises there is a problem. He takes his time, he thinks about it, he plays on his lute until he feels what he needs to do within him. It won't work otherwise."

Pér looked up at Kora with glistening eyes. Aaron could feel his wonder without even touching him. Kora knew him so very well, but he had never realised *how* well until that very moment.

"Off you go, away from all of us. Take our son and teach him everything you would have if I hadn't kept him from you for so many years."

Aaron could feel her guilt through their skin contact. There was nothing he could say to take that away from her.

Pér took both her hands in his and kissed them, and Aaron felt a guilty wave of relief. He saw the calming, reassuring effect Pér had on his daughter and envied him. Anyone else looking on would have seen that all it took was a kiss. Aaron was close enough to feel that there was more. Much more. Pér seemed to know exactly what Kora needed and, whether he knew it or not, his power worked with him to give her just that.

Aaron backed away from the two of them. This was their private moment. He did not need to be present for it. Guiscard and Kynon joined him in dispersing the onlookers. Commander Woodrow gave them a stern look.

"They need some peace and quiet. Come, show me your magnificent camp. Let me know if there is anything my fellow lintep and I can assist you with."

It was a good strategy. Without even using his powers, Aaron managed to turn the situation around. Woodrow was beaming proudly as he looked out over his soldiers. He mused that all you had to do was know what people cared about the most to make them understand that you appreciated them.

Chapter Forty-Five – Research

They decided it was best to leave the dragons far enough away from the Paradise that Lishe would not immediately spot them if she surveyed her surroundings. Tameo had argued the point of being left behind. He did not want to miss out on any of the fun. Eliséo was grateful that Farrow and Daegan had convinced him that the three of them had the most important job of all. If Lishe was there and the others couldn't handle her, they were to alert the dragons, who would sweep in to pick everyone up. Explained that way, Tameo had puffed up his chest proudly and stoically agreed to the position.

Eliséo instructed his elves to create a mist bubble around their group. They all held hands to make it large enough to walk comfortably. He knew he had more than enough power now to do it himself, but he needed them to practise the skill. It could make the difference between life and death for their assigned lintep.

Lukys had grudgingly given way and made Luisella, Braedan and Daegan practise with him until they were all exhausted the night before, but even that might not be enough.

"We still may need to resort to killing her," Eliséo told Lukys as they walked towards the Paradise. It would take a decent amount of time to get there. This region was quite flat and grassy. There had not been much cover for the dragons, so they had left the massive beasts in the longest grass they could find and hoped for the best.

"I will not entertain that thought unless we have no other options," Lukys replied stubbornly. "I do not believe anyone should go around killing people whenever the mood strikes them."

"Lukys, be reasonable. This is not simply because the mood strikes me. I have seen how far Lishe's power extends. I have seen the damage she can do, even from such a distance. My fears that your lintep will not be able to contain her with all her power is not unfounded. You will struggle, and my elves will be ready to end her life should you fail."

There was nothing more to be said. They had spoken at length about it and were each set on their own way. Eliséo hoped that whatever happened did not cause a permanent rift between the elves and the lintep.

The mid-morning sun did little to warm him. It barely managed to shine through the clouds. Eliséo was grateful that they were walking rather than flying. The air was so much colder up in the sky. He would need to remind the crystal dragons that people did not fare so well at heights in winter.

Studying Kora's map, he had realised that it was imprecise. Of the twelve of them, Eliséo was the only one who had traversed the Outworld before. He had no one else to confer with over the map.

You could try asking Kora, Elessa pointed out. *She's with Ensil at P2.*

Very well. Ask them and let me know if she remembers anything specific to help us find P3.

It took longer than he expected for Elessa to come back to him with a reply.

There is a crook in the river – one that almost makes a full circle. The Paradise boundary is just around it.

Eliséo told the others what they were looking for and they fanned out towards the river to find it in their groups. It took a moment for them to dissipate the large bubble around the nine of them and recreate three smaller ones. After that, Eliséo, Luisella and Raeslin headed straight ahead towards the river. Kari, Lukys and Giosué headed north. Liessa, Braedan and Telon headed south.

Raeslin walked with a bounce in front of Eliséo and Luisella, maintaining the mist by herself. Eliséo barely noticed as he kept his eye out for the crook in the river.

"She reminds me of my children," Luisella laughed quietly beside him. "They must be similar ages."

Her comment startled him. Eliséo assumed lintep were taught about elves just as elves were taught about all other races.

"I think you will find Raeslin is at least one hundred years older than your children, possibly more."

Luisella stopped dead in her tracks. Eliséo didn't hold back Raeslin quickly enough and the mist bubble barged into Luisella from behind, causing her to stumble. She fell, arms outstretched, into Eliséo's arms. He caught her just before she would have sprawled onto the ground.

"Oh, I am sorry, Luisella!" Raeslin raced back to them and attempted to help the lintep to her feet. "I did not see you had stopped. I was too excited about finding the Paradise."

Luisella stood shakily and dusted herself off. It had been a near disastrous accident so early in their campaign. Broken bones would not mend so quickly in the Outworld without the assistance of lintep healers.

"Are you really over a hundred years old?" Luisella asked the young elf. Raeslin nodded with a grin.

"I have almost reached my two hundredth year," Raeslin boasted. "Mother says my power will become stronger as I get older. Is that true, Eliséo? I mean, my king."

Her uncertainty on how to address him flustered Eliséo almost more than the question itself.

"I have not heard that before, but it is entirely possible," he admitted hesitantly. "Lintep power certainly appears to work that way, does it not Luisella?"

The dimple in Luisella's cheek deepened each time she spoke. "Well, for some more than others. It's true that every lintep's power peaks around their sixteenth year, and some have further peaks during that year though it is fairly uncommon."

Eliséo listened to what she wasn't saying. "Does it happen most for those who have great power to begin with, like Rilla?"

"It does seem to work that way. But we have no way of knowing beforehand who the powerful ones will be. All lintep have the same amount of power when they are younger."

"So, you will not know if Umi and Ulf will take their power from Braedan's family or yours?" Eliséo asked in surprise.

Luisella shook her head. "It doesn't work the same way every time. Some children only have as much as either one of their parents. Others will have the combined power of both. We have not managed to figure out how it happens, but it would be nice to know.

"Lintep power does not seem to be so strong now as it used to be, from what we can tell from old stories anyway. There are still some very powerful lintep, but they are now few and far between rather than common. I've been researching it in the library and trying to document it with people from Illaria, but I cannot seem to make any headway."

Eliséo listened in silence. He had seen a similar problem in Silvaren. Until recently, he had not realised how bad the situation was, but since trying to teach other elves how to use their magic, it had become painfully obvious that things were simply not as they should be.

It's here. Kari's voice interrupted his thoughts. *Head north from where we started. We'll wait for you.*

Eliséo put his questions aside for another time. There would be more than enough time to discuss these things with Luisella.

By the time they arrived, Lukys had had a chance to look around a bit. They merged their mist bubbles so they could converse more easily.

"The boundary is still intact," Lukys told them. "I can't see that it has been meddled with at all."

"How can you tell?" Eliséo asked him curiously. Lukys avoided his gaze uncomfortably.

"You can't really tell, can you?" asked Braedan with a smirk.

"Well, it seems to be the same as the first Paradise when we got there. I assume that means she hasn't been here."

"How does she steal power?" Luisella asked. "Does she take it all in one go?"

Lukys shrugged. "The Paradises were made up by a hundred lintep every time except the first. Each of those times, the lintep gave a portion of their power to the boundary and merged them together to create the Paradise. So, it's possible that Lishe will take one bit of power at a time, assuming she has worked out a way to do it."

Eliséo watched Luisella closely. Her expression had turned to one of intense concentration. When Lukys opened his mouth to talk again, Eliséo silenced him with a wave and gestured to Luisella. Her hazel eyes were unfocused, her dimple popping in and out as she pursed her lips. After a few moments of studying the Paradise, Luisella blinked and looked up at them.

"I don't think she can take all the power at once. It's difficult enough getting a grip on one part at a time. The effort in taking all of it at once wouldn't be worth it. Besides, even someone as disturbed as she is could not possibly think herself capable of handling so much more power in an instant."

Eliséo stared at her, open-mouthed. He wasn't the only one. Luisella raised her eyebrows.

"What? I told you I'm a researcher. This is what I do."

"So then, how do we find out if she has stolen any power from this Paradise?" Eliséo asked. Lukys and Braedan looked to Luisella.

"Let's take a walk around the boundary. Maybe if she takes enough power, there will be a gap somewhere. We might have to look closely to find it."

They walked around the Paradise. As Kora had described, it was quite a large portion of land, stretching over to the other side of the stream and encompassing the entire crook. The stream was not so large that they could not cross it, but in this weather, none of them wanted to get their boots wet.

Eliséo took Raeslin, Giosué and Telon aside before he attempted the next task.

"I have tried this before and know I can do it, but I do not want any of you to attempt this, or to ask Kari or Liessa to help you do it. I do not want you to explain to Tameo and Farrow what I am about to do. I will not have you endangering lives needlessly. Am I understood?"

Three excited faces bobbed up and down in agreement. It was reckless enough for him to do it, but he had done the same thing in the Lesa Mountains with Lord Aaron and a group of karliki over a much greater distance. This should not pose a problem for him.

"Everyone stand together and do not move until we have reached the other side of the stream."

He waited for them to huddle together before creating a mist raft beneath their feet. He asked the wind to move them gently across the stream. The sudden movement made some of them jerk out their hands to hold onto each other, but at least no one fell. In a few short moments, they were on the other side of the stream.

Eliséo dissipated the mist and continued walking around the boundary. He heard the excited whispers of the younger elves behind him and smiled at their enthusiasm for everything.

"How did you know you could do that?" Liessa asked as she drew close to him. Eliséo noticed Kari quicken her step to join them. There was no point in hiding the truth from them.

"I tried it when Lord Aaron joined me in Goraburg to help the karliki find their rebels."

"Had you ever tried anything like that before?"

Eliséo could tell Liessa was trying to keep the bitterness from her voice, but he could still detect a hint of it.

"I often experimented with my power when I was in the Outworld," he explained. "There was always less chance of someone out here realising what that amount of power in an elf actually meant. Elessa told me right from the beginning who I was and that I would need to hide my power from everyone in Silvaren. I think that is part of the reason she made me her ambassador – so I would have a legitimate reason to go into the Outworld and be free."

Liessa looked away from him, but he saw the pain in her face.

"I am sorry, Liessa. I cannot imagine what your life was like, growing up knowing that your power was not as great as Mother's, but know that for hundreds of years, I did not realise the full extent of the power I had either. Mother would place her crown on my head to convince me that was where the bulk of my power came from.

"Perhaps it was her way of trying to ensure that I would not be tempted to do great feats of magic anywhere but around her. I believed it for such a long time. It was only recently that I began to understand exactly how much power I have, even without the crown."

There was nothing more he could say. Their mother had lied to both of them. The fact that they knew it was because she loved them both did little to ease their pain.

I would have done things differently, had I been given the choice. Silva's voice in his head startled him. He instantly knew she was talking to Liessa at the same time. *Your mother had her reasons, but they were all based on fear. There has been too much fear in her life since her parents were taken from her. Secrecy rarely benefits anyone and often hurts more people than intended.*

* * *

Rilla sat in her room with Mistress Isis. Small stacks of paper were laid out on her table in organised rows. Together, they had been sorting through the requests for extra skills. They had split them up into easy and difficult skills as well as safe and dangerous ones. It had surprised Rilla that Mistress Isis did not mind her looking at the requests. Having read them all, she was not certain that she would have thought of many of them herself had she not been involved in this project.

The door creaked opened and Shuut sneaked in. Rilla immediately noticed the attempt at stealth.

"And where have *you* been?" she asked in a tone that she hoped sounded like an indignant mother. Shuut straightened and turned to face her with chin held high.

"I took Arishen out into town with the others."

Rilla raised her eyebrow. "That was ages ago. Surely you didn't have *that* much to say with Miette constantly flirting?"

Shuut turned bright red. Rilla would have laughed if her sister did not look so uncomfortable.

"What happened?" she asked, suddenly concerned. Mistress Isis made a big show of gathering all her papers.

"I might leave the two of you, now. If you need to find me, Princess Aislen has assigned me the room next to Aurelius on the next level down. Good night, ladies."

Rilla waved to the fire mistress as Shuut opened the door and let her out.

"What is it?"

Shuut rubbed a hand through her short hair and sat across from Rilla. "One of the guards likes me."

"I'd have to be blind not to know that," Rilla laughed. "Of course, Séverin likes you. You're probably the only one who can beat him so well without using their power."

"Well, what kind of banwep would I be if I couldn't do that?" Shuut blushed to the tip of her ears. "Anyway, after the last time I joined them in their sparring session ... I just thought he might see me differently."

Shuut had not explained everything to her, but Rilla had instantly sensed the difference that day. She had worked hard to not allow her power to float around, sensing all sorts of things that she was not meant to know, but it was difficult sharing chambers with someone. There were bound to be times that Rilla noticed things because of her power that Shuut might not want to talk about.

That had definitely been one of those times. Ratchin and Master Aurelius had brought her upstairs and stayed much longer than Rilla thought necessary. It had made her curious enough to let the hold on her power slip just a little. She was overwhelmed by the power emanating from her sister. They had shared a look, a single look, and that had been it. No explanation, no excuses. She had their mother's power and she was finally using it.

"If Séverin, or anyone, thinks worse of you now, they aren't worth knowing," Rilla told her bluntly. "I don't think it will make people like Ramiro think any better of you, but it might make them think twice before insulting you."

Shuut smiled shyly. It was an uncommon sign that she was not feeling confident. Rilla noticed it but was suddenly overcome by tiredness from her afternoon's excitement.

"I'm off to bed now. It's been a long day."

She got up and instantly sank back into her chair. She tried again with no luck.

"Guess I'm more tired than I thought I was."

"You can't get up, can you?" Shuut asked, a note of worry in her voice.

"Just help me over to the chaise," Rilla said. "I'll sleep there tonight."

"Rilla, what happened to you today? Why was Mistress Isis here?"

"I had a little trouble in my class is all. I overextended myself. I'm fine, really. I just need to sleep."

Rilla hoped that was true. After the incident in the infirmary, Mistress Isis had helped her more than she probably should have to get upstairs. Now that she was here and had been sitting down for such a long time, Rilla was starting to feel all her energy drain away.

"You look terrible," Shuut told her. Rilla tried to think of a retort but couldn't. She was too tired.

"I don't feel so well. Can you find Mistress Isis?"

Chapter Forty-Six – Thornborough

Thornborough was a solid fortress, just like Deuterfoss. From the air, they looked almost identical save for the fact that Thornborough had four tall walls rather than three. Each wall had a portcullis gate, though the northern one led straight into the river where the duke had erected a stone bridge allowing easy access for his people to the other side of the Bramble River.

Leif noted the new bridge with some interest. It was far superior to the old wooden bridge. Every spring when the river had flooded, the ferry had cracked, or the ropes snapped under the strain. It must have cost a great fortune, but if the city was prospering, then they would be able to afford it. There was little reason for Leif's people to travel to the other side of the river up near the Crystal Falls, so they had not even contemplated such a construction.

Snowcrest landed on the north side of the fortress. It seemed the quietest side for them to land, and they did not wish to attract more attention than necessary. A crystal dragon flying on the north side would not be so uncommon, considering how close Thornborough was to the Drakos Mountains.

"Shall I come with you?" Rownyn asked, once they were grounded.

"I think it's for the best," Leif told him. "I do not think anyone will notice you are a lintep just by you standing here, but I'd feel better if you came with us all the same. I can't imagine facing King Lukys if something happened to you."

"We also enjoy your company," Talise added with a swift kick to Leif's ankle. Rownyn laughed appreciatively as Leif bent to rub his wound.

"Snowcrest, we should be back tomorrow morning. Duke Ferris and I may not be on easy trading terms, but I see no reason he should need to detain us any longer than necessary."

"It's not far to the Drakos Mountains. I might fly back there for the evening and meet you back here," Snowcrest told them. "I don't know if Celtan sent back word about our adventures when we first agreed to come along."

"I wonder if you might convince them..." Rownyn barely had a chance to begin before Snowcrest cut him off.

"No!" Snowcrest growled lowly. "Celtan has already denied you another heart. I will not go behind his back to request another one."

Rownyn held up his hands placatingly. "We'll see you tomorrow then, with no extra hearts."

Leif clapped Rownyn on the shoulder as they headed towards the stone bridge. He was glad to have the lintep along. His sense of humour was a welcome breath of fresh air in these troubled times.

They wove their way through the wagons and people walking both ways across the bridge. Trade across the river had certainly increased since the last time Leif had visited Thornborough. He felt, rather than saw, Rownyn walking closer to them than usual. It was obvious he had not been around such large numbers of humans before.

"Relax, Rownyn," he muttered to the lintep under his breath. "You'll stick out like a sore thumb."

"Sorry. All of these powerless people at my fingertips, makes me want to assert my dominance over them," Rownyn joked nervously.

Talise laughed brightly, her fingers entwined with Leif's. He loved the fact that they could so openly show their affection now. They had not had much time for a detour, but Leif had insisted on dropping in on Talise's farmstead on their way to Thornborough.

Her father had been more than a little startled to have a crystal dragon land alongside his fields of corn, but he had all but forgotten about the cause of the fuss when Talise ran headlong into his arms. Leif loved the effect she had on people – not just those who were close in her life.

She had quickly, and quite simply, explained about their engagement. Leif had held his breath through her entire explanation. When her father walked up to him, Leif thought he might explode from lack of air. The old man looked at him sternly for long moments.

"Don't think this means you'll be getting a discount on your corn shipments," he'd said seriously.

"No sir!" Leif had almost saluted, falling back into his military ways.

"Well, alright then. Welcome to the family."

Leif's expression must have been incredulous as he remembered, with some chagrin, Talise and Rownyn laughing until they were red in the face.

"Leif?" Talise pulled him along. "Let's go."

Snapped back to the moment at hand, Leif squeezed Talise's hand and walked across the bridge.

It had been years since his last visit to Thornborough. Leif had not thought things could change so dramatically in that time. True, Duke Ferris had a different community to deal with, but the business of running a duchy was the same. The slums had overflowed from their confinement on the outskirts of the city. They now appeared to stretch over half the streets. The richer buildings, clearly belonging to nobles, were more opulent than he recalled.

"Is this what *all* cities are like?" Rownyn asked in a hushed voice.

"Only when their duke or duchess doesn't pay attention to *all* their subjects," Talise answered bitterly. "Some nobles think Leif is soft, that he lets the farmers and workers walk all over him. Others, like my father, realise that he simply treats everyone fairly and does not hand out favours to his nobles because they have money."

Leif was too aghast at the situation to mind how she spoke of his social peers. They were not leaders at all. They were exactly how Talise described them. Spoilt children at a party handing out favours to their friends.

"Can't something be done about it?" Rownyn looked at Leif, disgust written all over his face. Leif shook his head.

"Much like your king, Duke Ferris was not elected. His position was handed down through his bloodline. I would guess that, by now, all the nobles in his city are the same. The only way it will change is if there is an uprising from the poor, which would likely lead to more death than there currently is."

"Look at them, Leif." Talise pointed to beggars, too tired to even put up a hand.

"They don't have the strength to rise up against him."

Leif set his jaw and walked stiffly towards the fortress keep. He would need all his skills of diplomacy for this. Duke Ferris had never been one of his favourites, but the deplorable state of his city had put their relationship beyond all redemption.

Leif noticed everything on the way to the keep. The barefoot children, who scarcely had enough clothes to cover their bodies, without enough energy to play a simple ball game. The workers coming in from the fields at the end of a long day, dragging heavy carts behind them. Even those better off among the poor were bedraggled and depressed. They sold their wares in shabby stalls set up in the small market squares scattered throughout the city.

It felt like there was an invisible line from the poor to the rich. Once they had stepped over it, the streets were clear of household rubbish. There were no barefoot children, no beggars, no shabby stalls. The only poor people on this side of the line were the workers dragging their carts along behind them. Food and other goods still needed to be taken to the market squares in the rich inner circle and only the poor were fit to drag those carts.

Rownyn drew closer to Talise. This city must have felt so alien to him. In Illaria, it seemed as though almost everyone was treated the same. The masters and mistresses were well respected, as were most of the royal family, but they did not treat anyone else as their inferior. King Lukys and Princess Aislen often had public audiences – he had watched one of them himself. They listened patiently and without bias to their people. They handed out fair judgments and gave credence to all grievances.

In Illaria, you could *feel* the contentment on the streets. Leif had not seen a single beggar, nor a child without enough food or clothing. The air was calm and content.

Thornborough, true to its name, felt prickly. The atmosphere was tense. People felt like they were ready to start a fight at a moment's notice. They did not seem to be at all content. They mistrusted one another, and especially anyone they didn't know. It was different even to Deuterfoss, where many people did not know one another. But Leif and Talise had spent many an evening wondering the streets going to different taverns where they would not be recognised to see what the feel was in the city. They had always been welcomed. Perhaps not with open arms, but at least with a certain degree of respect for a fellow citizen of Deuterfoss.

Finally, they stood at the door of the fortress. There were guards posted at the entrance. This was a bad sign. Leif never posted visible guards at the entrance to his keep. He wanted people to feel welcome enough to enter should they have the need. The guards crossed their halberds across the gateway, blocking their path.

"State your business!"

Leif halted abruptly, drew his coat back and firmly placed his hands on his hip, close enough to his blade should he need it.

"I am Duke Leif of Deuterfoss. I have business to attend to with Duke Ferris."

The guard peered at him closely, then glanced at the other guard who shrugged. The first guard pulled a metal cone from the wall. A tube ran along it and disappeared into the wall. He pressed it around his mouth and appeared to be talking. Once he was done, he placed the cone to his ear instead and waited.

"Duke Ferris is currently engaged. You are to wait for him in the council hall. He will find you when he is ready."

The halberds were raised, and Leif stepped forward with Talise and Rownyn at his sides. It seemed that the first guard was about to protest when the second guard shook his head. Leif tensed, ready for a fight, until they were safely away from them.

Talise held his arm tightly. He put his hand over hers and drew her closer to him. For the first time in his life, he did not feel safe in another duchy. What had happened here?

"Do we really need his soldiers?" Talise whispered.

"There are no guards left in Illaria," Rownyn pointed out softly. "From Lady Kora's map, there are three Paradises in this duchy alone. We need enough soldiers to stop anything from happening..."

"Like in the last Paradise?" Leif asked through clenched teeth. "From the sounds of it, *that* was for a very particular reason that will not exist in any other Paradise. Even Bryntown was not so bad as that, and that was the first one. In any case, the soldiers I sent out to that village will be a great help to the people there – not only because of their swords. They will provide safe passage for skilled tradesmen to help build up the village into a safe place to live.

"So, yes, we need these soldiers. But I will not compromise the project if I think Duke Ferris will not agree. He could make things *difficult* if he took it into his head to do so."

Their hushed voices echoed off the stone hallways throughout the keep. Leif halted their conversation until he had found his way to the council hall. It was cold, empty and dark. Not even a single torch had been lit, let alone the fireplace.

They stood in the entrance, not wanting to enter such a forbidding room.

"I could, you know, if you wanted me to." Rownyn pointed towards the fireplace.

"Go ahead then," Leif told him. "We'll let you know if anyone is coming."

He turned back to the hallway with Talise, shivering by his side. They stared out at the hallway. It was poorly lit and just as cold as the rest of the fort appeared to be. The stone floors were missing their hallway runners. No tapestries or portraits hung on the walls. It looked like an old abandoned castle.

"It's done," Rownyn called out. "There is barely enough wood to keep it going, but it should last for a little while."

Leif ushered Talise in towards the fire. All three of them were freezing.

"Where are the windows?" Talise asked, facing the room while warming her back.

"The dukes of Thornborough have always been a suspicious lot. They did not want anyone able to spy on them during their council meetings, so there are no windows."

"Duke Leif!"

Leif turned around. The thin, metallic voice came from beside him, but seemed to fill the room.

"Duke Leif, pick up the cone."

The cone? They must mean the same contraption the guards had used at the gate. He looked around until he found it, nestled in the wall near the entrance.

"Yes?" he talked into it hesitantly.

"Duke Ferris will now see you in the royal audience chamber. We trust you remember the way."

Leif fought the urge to yell at the incorporeal voice. They had been treated with nothing but disrespect from the moment they had arrived. Had Duke Ferris arrived unannounced in Deuterfoss, Leif's guards would have escorted him in themselves and made sure that he wanted for nothing while he waited. Leif himself would have met him where he waited or sent one of his barons to find him.

He led Talise and Rownyn through the freezing fortress. Duke Ferris either did not care that most of his fortress was cold and dark or did not have the means to keep it heated during the cold winter months.

After several wrong turns, he found his way to the royal audience chamber. Torches lit the hallway leading up to it. There were guards standing to attention outside this door as well. Leif began to have a very bad feeling about this. The guards uncrossed their halberds and opened the door when he announced himself to them.

Leif wished Rownyn knew him as well as Aislen. She would have known to keep a tendril of her power in his mind so that he could talk to her if need be. This could become a dangerous situation very quickly.

"Duke Leif of Deuterfoss, well met."

The man who greeted him was not Duke Ferris. This man was a number of years his senior. Leif recognised him as one of Duke Ferris's elder barons.

"Baron Jayson, I see you are as well as the last time we met," Leif greeted him casually.

Baron Jayson coughed. "I am the acting Duke of Thornborough until the genealogists have worked their way through a mire of royal births to uncover who the next duke or duchess will be."

Leif's mind raced. Duke Ferris did not have any children – not for lack of trying – which would undoubtedly put the entire duchy into disarray should he die.

"What happened to Duke Ferris?" Leif asked stiffly. "He was in perfect health the last time he yelled at me."

"Ah, yes, well, there have been a number of problems with his heart since that time," Baron Jayson explained with many jerky hand gestures. "Each time, a tonic was found to revive his heart, until the last bout only a few weeks ago. I have taken over his duties until such time as a permanent replacement can be found."

"And will this permanent replacement see to the number of ill-fed, poorly clothed people within the city? Or will they be allowed to simply die alongside each other with no care from their leader?"

Leif knew he should have bitten his tongue and was mildly surprised that he hadn't received a swift kick to the ankles from Talise. His question was enough to make Baron Jayson pull at his tight collar.

"I presume you had some business other here than the state of Thornborough's citizens?"

Leif weighed his options. They needed soldiers and skilled tradesmen, but not from a duchy in the midst of an inheritance turmoil.

"How long do you think the genealogists will take to uncover the next rightful heir or heiress?" Leif asked in what he hoped was a leading manner.

"I do believe they will take some time," Baron Jayson replied. "Duke Ferris's family was already dwindling before he came into power. Since then, much of his close family has somehow taken ill or met with nasty, and often fatal, accidents."

"Are you in a position to order out soldiers and skilled tradesmen if they are required throughout the duchy?"

Baron Jayson eyed him suspiciously. "I am not certain I have such authority without a fight from the other barons and baronesses, but I believe we may come to another arrangement if we feel the need is great.

"Each of us commands our own standing army in our baronies. They are spread out fairly evenly throughout the duchy, so we could potentially come to an agreement with our own people. What are you suggesting?"

Leif looked over to Rownyn who shrugged and Talise who nodded.

"What do you know of the Paradises?"

Baron Jayson laughed. "They are mere legends. I don't know of anyone who has seen one. They are a fool's ideal of what the world should be like. I do not believe they exist."

Talise could not contain herself. Her laughter ran out through the chamber, bounding off the stone-cold walls. Baron Jayson's face froze.

"You don't mean to tell me they really exist, do you?"

"Hopefully, not for much longer, but yes, they exist."

"What is that supposed to mean? Why would they cease to exist? Why would you hope for that?"

Leif studied the man for a moment longer. "Baron Jayson, perhaps we could discuss this over a warm meal. We've been travelling through the winter winds for some time now."

Baron Jayson still looked startled – even after Leif had thoroughly explained everything over a hot vegetable broth. He kept glancing worriedly at Rownyn, though they had explained he could not actually manipulate Baron Jayson's mind the way old stories said they could.

"So, if I understand it correctly, you want soldiers and skilled tradesmen to travel to these Paradises, wait there until the boundaries are destroyed, then help the Paradisians to make their homes safe from the Outworld."

"Yes," Leif said, for the third time. "It won't take long to organise, and it will be a good exercise to keep your troops busy. Besides, if no heir can be found, your organisation of this matter could really show the people of Thornborough that you are the best person to lead them back to what they once were. To even out the difference between the rich and the poor – make sure your people get fed and clothed as they should."

Leif noticed, with a bit of satisfaction, that Baron Jayson had the decency to blush. He was clearly not blind to the situation in Thornborough, even if he had chosen to ignore it in the past.

They left the next morning, with promises that soldiers and skilled tradesmen would be sent out to the three Paradises in Thornborough. It might take some negotiating on Baron Jayson's behalf, but it would be done and within the timeframe that Leif had stipulated. He did not know when the lintep would arrive or which Paradise Lishe had reached, but he did not intend for any of the Paradises to be destroyed before there were people stationed there ready to help.

Chapter Forty-Seven – Protector

Plyke was exhausted. He had spent an entire day learning how to play Pér's lute. It was difficult enough learning a simple tune on the instrument, let alone use his powers through it.

He missed Tika's bright and easy nature, making him laugh and propping up his spirits any time they fell. Kora tried to do the same thing, tried to fill in the gap for him. He loved her for it, but she was not Tika and she could not help him any further.

"Are you ready to try again?" Pér asked hopefully. "I know we spent all day at it yesterday, but you're rested now, and the music will flow more easily."

Plyke tried to smile, but he could not muster fake enthusiasm for his father. Pér sat by his side.

"Plyke, I know I ask a lot of you. I know *everyone* is asking a lot of you. It isn't your fault that you have a crystal heart, but now that you do, we need you."

"I know," Plyke answered numbly. "I'm just so tired. We've been here for days and nothing is working. What was the point of all of this?"

Plyke did not understand the concern that flashed over Pér's eyes. He did not understand his father's urgency in taking him to Lord Aaron. He was too overwhelmed by these feelings that he had little energy left for anything else.

"Aaron, the troops need rousting. They are having an adverse effect on your grandson which is amplifying back over them and back again to him. If we do not do something soon, this will become a problem we cannot fix."

Plyke's grandfather looked at him. He stared up at him numbly. There was concern there, but Plyke could not understand why.

"I think your powers might be better suited to this than mine," Lord Aaron told Pér. "Why don't we organise a small concert for the troops? I'm certain they will appreciate it."

Plyke trotted mechanically behind Pér as his father walked around their camp, scouting out the best place for his music to travel. He caught glimpses of Lord Aaron talking with some of the more senior officers. Eventually, they began to shuffle off together towards the crystal dragons.

It was the fastest feat of organisation Plyke had ever seen, but he watched it all apathetically. He could not muster any enthusiasm. He sat where Pér placed him and barely noticed the people around him. There were some soldiers, some officers, all people he did not know. He had not made time to get to know any of them.

Tika would have. If his Partner had been here, he would have found out all about the soldiers' lives and been part of their daily routines. Even if it had not been his job, he still would have tended to the horses, earning him the respect of those who were in charge of them. Thinking of Tika made Plyke happy, but it made him miss his Partner something awful.

"Right!" Pér boomed out over the gathered soldiers, his voice bouncing off the crystal dragons who were curled up into a semi-circle. "It's time we have some fun here and have a concert. Who knows a good song?"

There were a few murmurs around him and finally someone shouted out a name. With a half-hearted protest, a soldier got up and walked over to Pér. Between the two of them, they got a tune started and all the soldiers joined in the raucous song. Plyke felt it enough to snap out of his haze and look around.

The soldiers were smiling, slapping each other on the back. Some had gotten up to dance, to the great amusement of the others. He found himself smiling, despite missing Tika.

Song after song followed with soldiers requesting and singing various barroom ditties. They stomped their feet and clapped their hands to beat out the time. Some had even brought along wooden flutes to play on during quiet nights. They quickly ran to get them and joined in the playing.

Pér stayed up there the entire time with his lute. Plyke knew he must be using his powers on the soldiers. He could see their mood lifting. He could *feel* their mood lifting. Suddenly, he understood what had happened. He pulled in his power, and wrapped it closely around him, far away from all the soldiers. It surprised him that he still felt as happy as he did before he took his power away from them.

"Welcome back, Plyke!" His grandfather patted him on the back. "It was a near thing there. Lucky you father is more in tune with you than I had realised."

Plyke looked up at him in wonder. "You knew he was doing this?"

"Well, of course I did. It was my suggestion, after all. Now you know his powers really do work through his music, perhaps you can try to understand it from the background, while no one is watching you, judging you, expecting you to learn it at a moment's notice."

Plyke hugged him. "Thanks, Grandfather."

Lord Aaron coughed uncomfortably and patted the top of his head. Plyke spent the rest of the afternoon, listening to the songs. It was a surprisingly educational experience. He could see how Pér was infusing feelings into his power and spreading it wide with his music. The daunting part about it was that Pér clearly had so many deep feelings in the first place, whether they were excitement, joy, sadness or love, that he could easily spread that out amongst his listeners.

Plyke knew he did not feel things so deeply. That was not to say he did not feel at all, but that he had been forced to become a calm, placid person while growing up in the Paradise. Of the two of them, Tika had always been the more emotional one. It made for a perfectly balanced Partnership.

Rilla certainly felt more deeply than either of them. Perhaps that was the reason she was named in the prophecy. They should be teaching her how to do it instead.

"Grandfather, why don't we teach Rilla?" Plyke smiled at the thrill his grandfather felt at that title.

"She does not have a crystal heart, Plyke. I do not know if she has a role in the prophecy any longer. Besides, I understand Rilla is having some difficulty with her powers at present. She ... should not be disturbed right now."

The way he said it made Plyke sit up and pay attention.

"What happened?"

"Oh, she's fine now, just fine," Lord Aaron replied, absently twisting his fingers. "Aislen and Isis are taking good care of her."

Plyke did not believe him for a moment. He ran off to find Ensil. With his tendrils of power stretched out, it did not take him long to locate the elf. They stretched out so much further than lintep were meant to be able to reach. Once, that would have scared him. Now, he took it in his stride. It had been passed on by Kora and Pér.

Ensil was working in a makeshift forge when Plyke found him. The hot embers were uncomfortably warm, even in the chill winter air.

"Can I speak to Rilla?" he asked.

The old, wrinkled elf looked up at the intrusion. "I don't know, can you?"

Plyke held his temper. His mother had sometimes played these word games with him. "*May* I speak to Rilla?"

"If you think it's necessary." Ensil shrugged. His eyes blazed bright blue for a moment. "No. She is not available right now."

"What are you talking about?" Plyke asked in annoyance. "How is she not available?"

"Young Rilla seems to be having trouble with her power. She's not in a fit state to talk to anyone, even through her bond."

Plyke left before the elf finished speaking. He ran back to his grandfather. Lord Aaron was the only one with the authority to send him back home. He needed to be with his cousin. She was all alone in Illaria. Shuut was clearly too preoccupied with Séverin and Ratchin to pay much attention to Rilla. Most of the rest of their family were away, aside from Marilisa, who didn't count, the twins and Aislen.

"I need to go back to Illaria!" he told him. "Rilla is having more than a little trouble with her power. She needs us. We have to go back."

"Plyke, we cannot go back just because Rilla needs us. We need to find a way to make this work here. If we cannot make it work, there won't be any point to Duke Leif sending out troops to every Paradise to await us. There will barely be any point to the crystal dragons flying elves and lintep all over the Outworld to find and stop Lishe. We *need* to find a way to make this work and you going back to Illaria to console Rilla will *not* help us to do that."

Plyke listened in horrified anger. His grandfather was being completely unreasonable. No matter what they had tried over the past few days, they could not break the boundary. Pér's song had made a little ripple, but it was not strong enough.

"I think we need Rilla. She's named in the prophecy for a reason. What if we can't get the crystal heart to work without her? What if we need her power too?"

"I daresay I have just as much power as she does. If your theory is correct, then it should work with me helping you."

Plyke was already shaking his head before his grandfather had finished speaking. He *knew* that was not the solution.

"Sorry, but you it won't work with you. You don't ... *feel* enough."

Lord Aaron looked at him oddly. "I don't feel enough?"

"Yes." Plyke shrugged. "That's the best way I can explain it. I don't feel enough either. That's why it works best for Pér. That's why I think Rilla will be able to help us. She is sensitive – she feels things very deeply."

Lord Aaron nodded. "She certainly does have a temper on her."

Plyke narrowed his eyes. "That's *not* what I meant. This is more than just about her temper. You don't understand her. You never have. Rilla is so much more than a ball of fury for you to control."

"Perhaps you're right. Perhaps I don't understand her, but I don't think we can just abandon this Paradise and fly back to Illaria."

There was no point in arguing further. He knew his grandfather would not listen. Instead, Plyke went to the one person he knew was always on his side, no matter what.

He found her, a little way away from the concert, away from the echoing semi-circle of the crystal dragons. Something clicked inside Plyke – away from Pér's power. Kora knew she could not help but be influenced by him. She looked up and smiled at his approach.

"Your father knows how to look after us both it seems." She almost sounded sad. Plyke did not reach out to her with his power. He still felt it was wrong to do that – it was what Kora had taught him.

"I don't need Pér to look after me now, I need *you*," Plyke said as he sat by her side. His mother draped an arm around his shoulder and pulled him close. He savoured the moment, breathed it in. His thoughts went back to Rilla. She had never had this from her parents. He was now certain that Rhanya was the only one who treated her like a parent, but only when no one could see.

"We need to go back to Illaria," Plyke told his mother. "Something is wrong with Rilla. Grandfather knows what it is and so does Ensil, but neither of them will tell me. It's something to do with her power, but it means she can't communicate with Ensil."

Kora looked at him closely. "What else is there?"

"Pardon?" he asked in confusion.

"You've figured something out and you need Rilla for it. What is it?"

Under the cover of Pér's concert, Plyke told his mother everything. The reasons he thought Rilla needed them. The reason he thought they needed her.

"They don't understand her, Kora, not like we do. We might not have had much to do with her in the Paradise, but since then, all the things she's done have made sense. She lives to protect us all. She's been doing it her whole life, even before Rhanya asked her to.

"I don't think anyone understands anything about her in Illaria. Mistress Isis gets close, but Mistress Kayte and so many of the others only see her temper or her quick actions. Well, I love her for those very things. Without them, we would all be dead. We wouldn't have even reached Illaria, let alone survived once we got there. She saved us all and now it's *our* turn to save *her*."

Kora's lips trembled as she drew him close. "If Father won't take you back, then *I* will. We can't take Pyrid. He'll only try to alert Father. Garnet is less loyal to him. There's only room for one other person. Do you think we need anyone else?"

Plyke shook his head. "The only other person we might need is Pér, but if we wait for him, Grandfather will find a way to stop us."

"Then we go now." Kora got to her feet and pulled her cloak closely around her. "With any luck, we won't freeze to death before we get home."

Chapter Forty-Eight – Blizzard

Eliséo sat upon Hoarfrost with Raeslin and Luisella in front of him. They were on their way to P5 when he felt something amiss. Elessa had shifted the barriers on her bond so that he could not access Rilla.

What is it? he asked her.

She should be fine, Elessa replied. *There appears to be a bit of trouble with her power and her emotions. They are wreaking havoc with each other.*

Can we do anything? Eliséo asked, cursing himself for ignoring her so much lately.

You do not have enough time for her, Elessa reprimanded. *I cannot do it alone or it will make things worse. She needs both of us or neither.*

Eliséo wished this was all over, that Lishe was stopped, the Paradises were all destroyed and all of them were safely back where they belonged.

You always waste time on useless thoughts, Elessa chided him. *You need to spend more time in the present, rather than in the past or the future.*

He blocked the rest of Elessa's thoughts out. He did not need her harsh reprimands to distract him. It irked him that he could not speak with Rilla. When he had left her in Illaria, all those months ago, he had promised that he would still be there for her through Elessa. It irked him that *she* had helped *him* more often than the other way around.

Eliseo? A voice called out to him, but it was not overly familiar. *Can you hear me?*

Yes, he actively thought, not knowing what was happening.

I think Lishe has been here.

He looked up at Luisella to see her glance back at him. He grinned. In all the years he had spent in Illaria, this was the first time he had spoken with a lintep like this.

How can you tell? he asked.

There is a gap in the boundary, over the top of the Paradise. I did not see one when we flew over P3.

Eliséo looked down. He had not realised there were already so close to P5. Against his own advice, they were flying right over it where Lishe would be able to see them if she looked up. The only advantage was that it was now late evening and the clear crystal dragons were even more difficult to see at dusk than during the day.

Can you tell if she is still there?

No. My power does not reach far enough to sense anyone down there and ... I don't want to risk losing my power to her if she is there.

Eliséo understood her reticence. If Lishe felt Luisella's power, she would likely not hesitate to pull it from the defenceless lintep.

Ask Hoarfrost to land. We need to be far enough away from the Paradise that Lishe won't see us, but near enough that we can, all four of us, walk there by the cover of night.

Hoarfrost flew in a wide circle around the Paradise until she found the perfect landing place, west of the Paradise. If Lishe looked towards them, the sun would blind her before she saw the crystal dragon. As soon as they landed, Eliséo created a thick mist bubble around them, crystal dragon and all.

"We travel to the Paradise now, under cover of darkness. Lishe should not be able to pierce through this mist, but I do not want to take any chances."

Eliséo watched the moon and stars as they travelled. Night was wearing on. Before long, dawn would break, and they would be more vulnerable if Lishe was still there. His mist bubble bumped into something solid, bouncing Raeslin back from her forward position.

"The Paradise must be here," Eliséo told them. "Raeslin, I'm going to dissipate my mist. I want you to create one around yourself and Hoarfrost. Do you think you can do that?"

Raeslin nodded. "I think so. What about you two?"

"Luisella is the only one who will be able to contain Lishe's power if we find her here. I will walk with her around the border of this Paradise. If Lishe is still here, we will find her. She is unlikely to waste any daylight lazing about when she must know that we will be looking for her. Our only advantage is that she cannot possibly know that the dragons agreed to help escort us around to find her. We shall walk quickly. If anything happens, Silva will let you know. Keep safe."

Raeslin hugged him. The sudden gesture shocked him. No elf, aside from his mother, had ever been this familiar with him. He held his arms out to the side, not knowing what to do.

"Please come back safely. You have already freed the elves so much in such a short time. Do not die and let it all fall back to how it was."

Raeslin stepped back from him with a grin. Eliséo did not know what to say. Instead, he dissipated his mist and waited there until Raeslin and Hoarfrost were safely hidden from view.

Hand on his hilt, Eliséo gestured for Luisella to start walking. She looked at him oddly before setting off. There was something about this lintep that he found unsettling, as much as he liked her bright and easy nature.

"I doubt I'll be able to find Lishe through your mist."

Eliséo nodded. He had assumed the same thing. He walked as quietly as he could beside Luisella. The tall grass in this field came up to their chests. At a moment's notice, they could duck and be hidden from view. It was an advantage as much as a disadvantage – Lishe could do the same thing.

"What do you think drove her to it?" Luisella asked after they had walked around the river side of the Paradise. "To start stealing power from other lintep, I mean."

Eliséo shrugged. "A lust for more power. Kora mentioned that she was not particularly powerful, but that her skill was unsurpassed in her classes. Perhaps she wanted more power to complement her skill."

Luisella shivered beside him. "I don't think I could ever have done that."

"Are you not content with your power?" Eliséo asked curiously.

"Barely content," she replied with a huff. "I have only just enough power to be useful. To be perfectly honest, if Lishe catches me off guard, I won't stand a chance."

Eliséo watched her expression closely. She was not bitter, but neither was she pleased. "Is that the reason you worry for your children? You do not wish for them to take after you with their power."

Luisella stumbled but caught herself before she fell. "I think Lord Kynon would have preferred a more powerful lintep for his son, though Braedan does not seem to care. He never has. Even Daegan has never taken offence to my lack of power compared with the royal family. Sometimes, I think he regrets his choice with Marilisa's mother.

"She's just like her, you know. Her mother was proud and cruel. She had more power than most lintep, other than the royal family. That was what gave her such ambition. Daegan never loved her, of *that* I am certain. Now, he spends much of his time trying to stamp out all traces of her mother from Marilisa."

Eliséo was shocked. He had never heard any lintep speak like this before. He had not thought there were any who would try to elevate themselves because of their power, not in any way other than to become a master or mistress.

"Was she a mistress then?"

Luisella laughed so loudly and suddenly that she covered her mouth with both hands, trying to stifle the sound.

"No. She did not wish to serve Illaria in any way other than providing powerful children."

"What happened to her?" Eliséo asked. He only knew the fate of Aaron's wife. Even Kynon's wife was still a mystery to him.

Luisella looked uncomfortable. "There was an accident in the castle one night. Daegan insists she was not involved, but only went to help. A fire started in the kitchen. Once it hit the cooking oil, it raged out of control. She died in the fire."

"You do not believe that story?" Eliséo was intrigued. This was the first he had heard of the fire.

Luisella shrugged as she trailed her fingers along the Paradise boundary.

"I was in the castle too. We were all asleep upstairs and didn't even know about the fire until it was already out of control. She was nowhere to be found. It was only after the fire was finally doused and they accounted for all missing people that we realised she must be the unclaimed set of bones in the centre of the fire."

"Do you think she started the fire somehow?"

"I don't know. There was no reason she should be in the kitchen at that time of night unless she was stealing food that she didn't want anyone to know about. Even doing that, I don't know how she could have accidentally started such a bad fire."

Eliséo thought about Kynon. He really did not know much about that side of the royal family. It was only recently that Kynon had finally started to take a larger role in the political life of Illaria. Eliséo had never had anything to do with Daegan and Braedan. They had never visited Silvaren and had kept to themselves whenever Eliséo had visited Illaria.

A snowflake landed on his nose. He stared at it with a smile before broadening his gaze to the rest of the sky. The clouds were a dark grey, closing in around them. Snow began to fall in sheets, blinding them to anything more than a few feet in front of them.

"Can lintep power control the elements?" he yelled through the roar of the snowstorm.

"No!"

The snowstorm quickly became a blizzard, blowing in from the Lesa Mountains. Eliséo created a mist bubble around them, giving them some relief. It was still freezing inside the bubble, but at least they would stay dry and not be buffeted around by the whipping snow-laden wind.

"What now?" Luisella brushed the snow off her coat.

"We cannot search for Lishe in this. If she was here, she would have sought shelter by now."

Luisella smiled. "Exactly. She doesn't have her very own elf and I doubt even *she* is insane enough to stay out in this blizzard to steal power. Let's scout around and find any good hiding places. If she isn't in one of them, then I think we're safe to assume she isn't still here."

Her plan was a good one. Good enough that he should have thought of it himself. He really did like this lintep. She was a clever one.

By that afternoon, the blizzard had eased off to a mild snowstorm. They had searched the entire area surrounding the Paradise for any makeshift or natural shelters. They could not find Lishe anywhere.

Eliséo checked in with his elves. Liessa, Telon and Braedan had reached P9. It had taken them longer to find theirs and so their search had only just begun before the snowstorm hit them. They had not devised the same plan as Luisella, so had spent much of the day huddled together, trying to keep warm.

Kari, Giosué and Lukys had only just arrived at P8. Daegan Farrow and Tameo had not reached P10 before the blizzard struck. They would arrive early the next morning if the snowstorm did not continue.

"What now?" asked Raeslin when they finally returned.

"Now, you let me take over this mist and the three of you get some rest. We will fly out tomorrow. If Luisella is correct about Lishe already stealing power from this Paradise, it is likely she will be at either P9, P10 or P6. They are the nearest ones. Rest now and we will discuss it in the morning."

Chapter Forty-Nine – Ask for help

Isis was already on her way up the stairwell when Shuut came racing down it. They collided quite heavily, and Isis's arm scraped against the wall as she reached out to catch the railing in an attempt to stop herself from falling down the height of the stairs.

"What happened?" she asked Shuut as she got to her feet and rubbed her grazed arm.

"I don't know. She looks terrible and she asked for you. Then she fell off her chair."

Isis wasted no more time. She ran up to Rilla's chambers and saw the girl lying where Shuut said she had fallen. As a precaution, she had kept a tendril of her power around Rilla when she had left. She knew something was wrong but could not put her finger on it.

Rilla was breathing shallowly, her pulse slower than it should be.

"Shuut, find Aislen."

"Why not Kayte?" Shuut asked instinctively.

Isis shook her head. "Kayte seems to make Rilla worse. Find Aislen and tell her to bring a healing teacher. I think this is beyond my skills."

Shuut ran off, leaving the door wide open in her wake. It did not matter. There were hardly any people left on this level of the castle. Isis knelt beside Rilla and sent a tendril in to her mind. The girl's power was not flowing all around her as Isis expected it would be. Instead, it was pulled tightly inside her wall. There was no way in or out that she could find, other than the locked trapdoor at the top of her tower.

Even in this situation, Isis could not help but marvel at Rilla. She knew that Plyke had only explained to her what he had done with his wall before she created her own. It was amazing that she had accomplished anything, let alone something so secure that a mistress had trouble finding a way in.

Rilla! she called out as loudly as she could inside the girl's mind. There was no response. Heavy footsteps brought her back to the room. Shuut had brought Aislen back with her.

"There are no other healing teachers in the castle this late at night," Aislen told her. "We either make do with Kayte or risk Rilla remaining like this for too long."

"What does that mean?" Shuut asked. "What happens if she stays like this for too long?"

Isis looked at Aislen's pale face. "She may die. Call Kayte, then. Just warn her ..."

"I already have," Aislen replied. "We had quite the discussion after this afternoon's episode."

"What exactly am I missing?" Shuut asked. Isis quickly filled her in on the events that had transpired in the infirmary that afternoon.

"And you trust Kayte to help her now?" Shuut yelled incredulously, just as Kayte herself walked through the door. Isis expected a quick and biting retort, but there was none. Instead, Kayte sat beside Isis and check Rilla's breathing and pulse.

"How long has she been like this?" she asked.

Isis looked to Shuut. "Not too long, I'd say."

"What started it?" Kayte continued her line of questioning.

"I don't know. We were just talking about the day we've had. She didn't really want to tell me. She said she was tired and wanted to go to bed, but she couldn't stand up. The next thing I knew, she was asking for Isis and fell to the floor."

"She couldn't get up? Did she try?"

"Yes!" Shuut yelled, throwing her hands in the air. "She tried to push herself up with her hands on the table, but her legs buckled under her."

Kayte shook her head. "She should not have walked all this way after that ordeal. She should have been kept in the infirmary under close observation."

Isis exchanged a worried look with Aislen. "We didn't know. We thought she might be more comfortable in her chamber."

"I'll need more energy than any of us has to spare. Who else is on this floor?"

"Only Marilisa and the twins," Aislen answered with a warning note in her voice.

"Bring them here now. I'll take a little from each of us and give it to Rilla. She lost too much energy today, first with Amyas, then in the infirmary. She might have been able to recover by herself if she hadn't walked all the way up here after that."

Isis refused to feel guilty. Aislen had told her what to do. Kayte had only been making things worse.

"I'll fetch the twins," Shuut offered.

Aislen sighed. "Mari will not be impressed, but I will bring her along."

Isis nodded gratefully and stayed where she was by Rilla's side.

"Why do you care for her so much?" Kayte asked when the others had left. "She's just a reckless little brat with a temper and no respect for anyone."

Isis shook her head. "You were inclined to believe that right from the beginning, just because of who her mother is. She's *not* her mother, Kayte. Rilla cares more deeply for her friends and family than her mother ever did.

"Every lesson she has in the castle, she spends trying to prove that she belongs. If you had bothered paying any attention to her skills rather than to what you call her lack of obedience, you might have seen that.

"Yes, she disobeys your orders and acts instinctively to save her friends and family, but have you ever stopped to consider why? It's not that she's irresponsibly compulsive. It's because she *needs* to protect them. They are the most precious things in her life and she's already had so many precious things ripped away without having a say that she can't stand to let it happen again. She would rather *die* than let anything happen to those she loves the most."

Isis was short of breath. She had rarely spoken so hotly to anyone, let alone Kayte. She was not sorry for having done so but bit her tongue when she saw Marilisa and the twins enter the room.

"I'm not helping *her*." Marilisa folded her arms and raised her chin, defiantly. "She got herself into this mess, she can get herself out of it without me."

"Mari, your father left you in my care, so you will do as I say," Aislen told her sternly. "You've hated Rilla since the day you met her because you finally have a rival your own age for power. Seems that you're the only one who cares about that. Now, put your selfish ways aside and help your cousin, or so help me I will do everything in my power to make sure you never have another thing that you want so long as you live."

Marilisa started at the words. Isis could see her jaw clench and unclench.

"What do you need?" she asked, through gritted teeth.

"Everyone in a circle around Rilla," Kayte instructed them. "I will take a little bit of energy from each of you – not so much that it should hurt you, but enough to revive Rilla."

Isis did not wait for Kayte to take energy from her. She pooled as much as she thought was safe into the palm of her hand and held it out in front of her. When Kayte turned to take it, she shook her head.

"Too much, Isis. That's why I called the others. I don't want this much from you."

Kayte took a little more than half of what Isis offered. Isis took the rest of the energy back within her. She felt depleted, but not as much as she had expected. Kayte had left her with more than enough to function normally.

Isis watched the others closely. Each of them looked tired, but not exhausted. She turned her attention to Rilla. The brave little girl was already breathing more easily. The colour had returned to her face.

"You three can return to bed," Kayte told the twins and Marilisa. "She should be fine now."

The twins looked at each other, crossed their arms defiantly and sat where they were. Isis admired their stubbornness. It certainly got them in a lot of trouble, but it also showed how much they cared for people. She was surprised when Marilisa did not immediately depart either. The oldest of the cousins looked troubled.

"What happened to her?" she asked, with a feigned air of indifference. Isis could see straight through it. She was terrified. "Is it because she doesn't know how to control her power?"

"No." Kayte shook her head. "Rilla doesn't work with her power the same way the rest of us do. She doesn't *control* it – not the way you're thinking."

"Then how did she end up like ... this?" Marilisa gestured to Rilla's prostate figure.

Isis raised an eyebrow at Aislen, then glanced over at Kayte. Her oldest friend always had trouble admitting when she was in the wrong.

"I believe there were a number of factors involved, but it had more to do with her emotions than her power."

"Her emotions?" Umi perked up.

"Like her temper," Marilisa explained to her younger cousin in a condescending tone.

"Actually, it was more fear than anything else," Kayte pointed out, studiously avoiding Isis' gaze.

"But she's safe here," said Ulf. "Her father is dead now. He can't hurt her anymore."

Marilisa sharply turned her head to her little cousin. He shrugged his shoulders at her. The brattish girl turned to the rest of them in turn, clearly trying to understand what she had missed.

"Not all fathers are like yours, Mari," Aislen finally told her. "You may think he is strict, but he is only trying to make sure you grow up to be a better person than your mother. Be thankful he loves you so much. Rilla was never so lucky as you."

"But I thought..." Marilisa looked down at Rilla.

"Erton didn't scare her," Shuut told them firmly. "It's her promise to Rhanya that scares her."

Isis shook her head. "These are not things we need to discuss right now. Rilla needs her rest."

"No." Marilisa held out her hand to stop Isis from rising. "I need to know what happened. I've never seen this with anyone before and if it has to do with her power and her emotions, then I want to know what it is."

"So that it doesn't happen to you?" Isis asked coldly. Marilisa blushed deeply but did not move.

"What promise can be so scary it results in *this*?"

"She promised to protect the boys," Shuut said, despite Isis' protests.

Marilisa frowned.

Shuut shook her head and laughed. "You can't understand why that scares her because you don't know anything about her. Aislen is right – all you see is a rival for your power who was allowed into Illaria with humans, breaking the only rule you've ever thought was important. You would have been perfectly happy to leave her and the boys out there to die.

"It's people like *you* that scare her. People who do not value her friends' lives. People who would just as happily let her friends die as help them. Now they are scattered, and she can't look after them all."

"How long does a promise last?"

Isis looked down to see Rilla clutch something tightly in her pocket before opening her eyes. She looked so defeated, lying on the floor, staring up at them. Isis helped her to sit up and retrieve the crumpled paper from her pocket.

To Isis' surprise, Rilla shakily handed the paper to Marilisa who read it aloud.

"My dear girl,

Do you remember the star story – big star and little star? Well, you, my dear, are the little star. I still remember the times you mouthed the words as I told you the story and always wondered whether you knew.

I feel certain they are coming for me tonight. Don't be sad for me. I've lived a long life. The past twelve years have been the best by far.

When I was born, this Paradise wasn't the place it is now. Were I in your position, I would be trying to leave as well. Remember, Rilla, if any of the other children follow you into the Outworld, you're stronger than all of them. Keep them safe.

Goodbye, my little star."

She handed the paper back to Rilla, who took it reverently and placed safely it back in her pocket.

"What does that mean?" she asked, sitting in front of Rilla. Isis was amazed by the change in her demeanour.

Rilla's voice was so faint. "It was a letter from my only friend in the Paradise. My father ordered his death that night. His dying wish was for me to keep the boys safe. So how long does a promise last?"

"Would they really have died without you?" Marilisa asked softly.

"At least five times over," Shuut replied. "Not counting when *you* tried to deny them entry to Illaria."

"I didn't know about this," Marilisa tried to defend herself, but the fight had gone out of her. "I didn't know."

Isis stared at her in surprise. This was not the Marilisa she knew – the haughty, self-important brat was gone. In her place was the person Daegan had been trying to mould for years.

"I'll help you," Marilisa said suddenly. "Tell me how and I will help."

"I ... don't think it works that way," Rilla protested.

Isis rested a hand on the girl's shoulder. "It *could* work that way. If you are willing to share the load."

Chapter Fifty – Calm the wind

Plyke snuck through the silent camp with Kora. He was fairly sure there were no soldiers left – they were all at the impromptu concert Pér was conducting. They had almost reached the dragons when he heard a sound behind them.

"Sneaking away again, Kora?" Guiscard asked, from the shadows.

Kora froze beside Plyke.

"Guiscard, I..."

Plyke instinctively stepped in front of his mother. "Actually, she's helping *me* sneak away."

Guiscard studied him carefully. "Would this have anything to do with the argument you had with your grandfather earlier tonight?"

Plyke did not answer. It was clear to him that Guiscard knew enough to either help them or hinder them, but he did not know the librarian well enough to judge which way he would lean. The old lintep chewed on a long piece of grass, until he came to a decision.

"Let's be off then. No point waiting until the concert is over and everyone wonders where we are."

"Sorry?" Plyke asked incredulously.

"You'll never get Pyrid's help without me. I'm the only one who knows your grandfather well enough to fool him. Let's go."

Plyke glanced at Kora. She winked and took his arm. Not having much choice, he walked with her towards the dragons. Guiscard waited for them to catch up before approaching the massive beasts.

"Are you sure you want to ask Pyrid?" he asked. "Wouldn't it be easier to convince Garnet?"

"We'll be flying with Garnet, yes, but he won't go anywhere without Pyrid's approval."

Guiscard cleared his throat noisily. The dragons did not stir. He tried again and again until Plyke could not help laughing.

"What is it, old man?" Pyrid asked as he lazily opened an eyelid. "We were trying to sleep, if you hadn't noticed."

"Pyrid, you've been sleeping almost since the moment you arrived," Guiscard chided him. "Poor Garnet must be out of his mind with boredom. I've seen him fly circles at night when he thinks you're truly asleep."

Garnet snorted nearby, his ruse of being asleep well and truly thwarted. Pyrid blew out a thin stream of fire.

"These young ones have too much energy to spare," Pyrid replied testily.

"As do these ones," Guiscard said, gesturing to Plyke and Kora. "That's why Aaron wants me to take them back to Illaria on Garnet until we can sort out how to fix this mess young Rilla put us in."

Plyke made to protest, but Kora held him back.

"The boy needs to continue his lessons and his mother refuses to be separated from him again. So, Garnet, what do you say? Are you up for a night flight where you *don't* have to hide?"

Garnet was already stretching out his wings before Guiscard had finished speaking.

Plyke marvelled at the way the librarian had smoothly lied to the dragons. He had made it seem like Aaron was trying to get rid of a nuisance rather than Plyke sneaking off.

"Why didn't Aaron come himself?" Pyrid asked.

"He needed to stay with Pér," Guiscard answered easily. "The troops were getting a bit downhearted what with being stationed in a place where there is nothing for them to do. They've organised a concert to raise the morale a bit."

Pyrid huffed. Plyke thought they were done for. He had given up hope when Garnet beat his wings.

"Enough talk. I'm ready. Come on up and let's be off. If we leave now, we should be there before dawn and I won't need to circle the pasture until the horses are cleared away."

"You be careful with these ones. Aaron will cut my heart out himself if I let you take them instead of myself and something happens to them."

Plyke grinned. He could not believe their luck. Before Pyrid changed his mind, Plyke climbed up and held tightly to the spike in front of him. Kora climbed up behind him, with Guiscard bringing up the rear.

"We're ready!" Plyke called down to Garnet. His heart lifted as Garnet rhythmically beat his wings against the ground. The crystal dragon rose into the cool night air and was off before any alarm could by anyone who may have noticed what had happened.

* * *

The snow storm raged all night. Eliséo watched it moodily.

"Can you fly through this?" he asked Hoarfrost. The crystal dragon moved his head to get a better look at the weather outside the mist bubble.

"I've never tried," Hoarfrost replied as quietly as he could. Luisella and Raeslin were still asleep. They were trying to let them rest as much as possible before the day ahead. "Loreli never let us fly in these conditions. She assumed that if the weather was bad enough to keep us grounded, we wouldn't have any trouble from attackers."

Eliséo nodded. "Could you walk us through it, if I keep up the mist?"

"I don't see why not, but you could just use your magic," Hoarfrost rumbled. "Isn't it all elemental? You could stop the snow storm."

Eliséo stared at the crystal dragon in shock. "I do not think any elf magic is great enough to stop a snow storm."

"Have you tried?"

Eliséo did not reply. Of course, he had not – it was a blatant manipulation of the elements that he would be a fool to try.

No worse than the blatant manipulation of lesser trees when you ask them to detach branches from themselves for your own personal use, Elessa reminded him. *No worse than asking the wind to speed you along when you run alone through the Outworld. You could try it.*

I would not even know where to begin, Eliséo pointed out. *Everything else I have done I was taught to do.*

Someone had to be the first. You could always be the first to try this.

It was a good point, but that did not make the decision any easier. Even if he wanted to try it, he did not know where to start.

"I would start by dispersing the clouds." Luisella sat up and yawned. "If there are no clouds, the snow cannot fall."

Eliséo looked up at the dark clouds above them. They stretched out as far as the eye could see in every direction. The wind whipped the snow around them in flurries so that it looked like the flakes were dancing.

"I can but try," he said half-heartedly.

"Stop your mist, then," Hoarfrost told him. "I will shelter your little elf with my wing."

Hoarfrost stretched his clear crystal wing out over Raeslin as Luisella rose to stand by Eliséo's side. Eliséo dissipated the mist. He had not realised how much it was protecting them until it was gone. The wind howled around them, knocking both Eliséo and Luisella to the ground.

Eliséo struggled to his feet and centred himself. It was not often he spoke to the skies. They were so far away, he had never really tried. He tried to disperse the clouds, but every time he had any success, the wind brought them back again. He tried to stop the wind, but it came rolling down from the Lesa Mountains with such force that he could not stop it.

"Try to calm the wind," Luisella yelled.

Calm the wind, he thought, *how do I do that?*

Try to disperse it around you, Silva suggested.

Eliséo closed his eyes and let the wind raise him up into the sky. He was buffeted from all sides, hair and clothes flicking his skin as snow bit into his face. He spoke to the wind, called out until it stilled in a small circle around him. He convinced that circle to grow wider until the wind no longer whipped around him. The snow now fell gently down in soft layers. Eliséo asked the wind to carry him back down to the snow-covered ground.

"I do not know how well this will work, but let us try it while we can," he told them.

Luisella woke Raeslin, who had somehow managed to sleep through the entire ordeal, safely tucked away under Hoarfrost's wing. Eliséo waited for them to climb aboard Hoarfrost before climbing up himself. If he had to do anything drastic with the weather, it would be easier to do it from behind the others.

Hoarfrost shook the snow from his wings and beat them against the white ground. Every beat created a flurry of snowflakes.

"You'll have to fly as low to the ground as you can," Luisella yelled just before he took off. "It will get too cold for us if you fly too high."

"I can fix that," Hoarfrost roared as he soared into the sky. Beneath him, Eliséo saw a ball of fire come together in Hoarfrost's belly. It warmed his crystal exterior to the touch. Grateful that at least part of his body would stay warm, Eliséo pressed himself against the crystal dragon and settled in for the flight. The fire would make them more visible from the ground, but at this point, speed was of the essence.

Lishe had certainly been to P5. If she was clever, she would have headed either straight up to P10 or to P9, closer to the Lesa Mountains. He could not guess how many days in front of them she was or if she had managed to reach the next Paradise before the blizzard hit.

* * *

Plyke walked quickly through the stables. He was torn between stopping to see Tika and going to make sure Rilla was safe.

"I'll get him," Kora told him. "You find Rilla and I'll bring Tika. Master Edric can deal with me if he's not happy about that."

Guiscard laughed quietly as Plyke dragged him along by the sleeve. "You two certainly know how to stir up trouble, don't you?"

"Look who's talking," retorted Plyke. "Imagine how furious Grandfather will be when he finds out *you* were the one to help us trick Pyrid!"

"Oh, Aaron has had plenty of practise getting angry with me. This will just be another line in a very long list," Guiscard waved aside Plyke's concern. "Now, let's find your cousin before anyone else stops us. She'll be able to tell Ensil that we've arrived, and all will be forgiven."

Plyke did not reply. He was not certain that Rilla would be in a fit state to talk with Ensil. The old weapons master had not been able to reach her the night before. If things had not changed, she may still not be able to converse with him.

Halfway up the twisting stairwell, Guiscard waved him ahead with a complaint that his old bones could not cope with such a pace. Plyke took the rest of the stairs two at a time.

He stopped at Rilla's door. It was wide open, and a cluster of people were in the common chamber.

"What's going on?" he asked worriedly.

Aislen turned to face him with a frown. "What are you doing here? Uncle Aaron didn't say you were returning."

Plyke went red. "He didn't want to disturb you at night. How's Rilla?"

"I'm ... fine." The answer was soft and uncertain. It came from the floor, in the middle of the huddle. Plyke was surprised to see Marilisa stand aside for him, without even a sneer. That was when he saw Rilla, pale and only just barely sitting up. He fell to his knees in front of her.

"What happened? Are you okay?"

The corners of Rilla's mouth twitched up into a half-smile.

"I ... don't really know. Kayte and Isis can tell you. I'm better now."

Mistress Kayte crossed her arms. "You'll survive now. I wouldn't go so far as to say you're better. You still need to rest. Your lessons will need to wait a while."

Aislen shook her head. "Her power has not finished peaking. She needs to continue her lessons, or *this* could happen again."

"Actually," Isis said as she held up a hand, "I agree with Kayte. Rilla's power peaking is not what caused this. She would do well to have a day or two of rest before she returns to her lessons."

Plyke tried to follow the conversation but found himself at a loss. He could not understand what they were talking about, but Rilla appeared to be safe enough and he was here now so he could return the favour and keep her safe as she had kept all of them safe.

"Plyke!" a familiar voice yelled behind him. Plyke barely had time to turn around before Tika bowled him over. "Why didn't you say you were coming back?"

Before Plyke could answer, he heard gasps behind him. He extricated himself from

Tika and turned to see Rilla's eyes glowing bright green. Their grandfather's voice boomed into his mind.

Plyke! I specifically forbade you from leaving! Kora, you bring him back here this instant!

"You tell *him*..." Kora started angrily.

"He can hear you," Rilla interrupted. Plyke realised Rilla must have sent her tendrils out to everyone in the room. "He can see you too unless you want him not to."

"I will *not* bring my son back to you. He told me his idea and you should have listened to him. Plyke may have discovered the key to everything, but you would not let him even try it. Are you so afraid of Rilla that you wanted to keep him well away from her? She is *not* her mother. She is a caring, intelligent and, well, stubborn girl. But so am I."

"Oh, Kora," Guiscard panted as he came into the room, doubled over from the stairs. "Don't be so harsh on your father. He's mostly angry with me for tricking Pyrid into letting us go."

Guiscard, I should have known! You and Kora always kept your secrets from me. Well, this is one that...

"Lord Aaron," Mistress Isis interrupted, "if you have nothing urgent to tell us about the state of the project or Lishe, then I must insist that you end this conversation. Plyke, Kora and Guiscard have arrived safely, and Rilla needs her rest."

There was a moment of silence before Rilla's eyes stopped glowing. She looked gratefully up at the fire mistress before leaning back against Shuut, who cradled her head gently.

"Kora, dear, why don't you help us get Rilla up into her bed?" Aislen asked. Kora instantly went to aid her niece. Plyke was surprised, yet again, when Marilisa bent to lend a hand.

"What did I miss?" he whispered to Umi and Ulf.

"The awesome and most magnificent transformation of Marilisa," Umi replied.

"The sudden self-realisation of a former spoilt brat," Ulf retorted.

Plyke and Tika exchanged a dubious look, uncertain whether they should believe the twins.

"Be off with you now," Mistress Kayte told the twins. "Clean yourselves up, have breakfast and get yourselves ready for lessons. You too."

Plyke nodded instinctively as the healing mistress turned to face him.

"I suppose you could be spared from your afternoon lesson. Rilla should be rested enough by then to talk sensibly. She will be well looked after until then."

"Plyke doesn't have lessons this morning," Umi piped up. "He only has classes with Mistress Isis this afternoon."

"Besides," said Plyke, "I didn't come all this way just to get back to my classes. I have an idea and I need Rilla's help."

"We'll need to go to Pér's house first," Kora said as she came back into the room. "You can demonstrate better if you have an instrument. Come, I'll take you there. It will give Rilla a chance to rest before you show her."

He could see Mistress Kayte was about to protest, but his mother's upraised hand stopped her. He smiled at the respect his mother commanded from others. Plyke and Tika held out their arms for her and they walked together from Rilla's chambers.

Chapter Fifty-One – Remembered tune

There was a snow storm ahead. It was gathering momentum. Leif had heard such storms could become blizzards. He had never seen one himself and did not wish to experience one from the skies. Snowcrest was waiting for them back on the other side of the Bramble River just as she had promised.

"How likely is that storm to come our way?" he asked her.

"They normally stay over the Lesa Mountains and over to the west. I've never seen one reach the Drakos Mountains – something about the heat from our fires."

"Do you think we will make it to Firechester?"

"I don't know," she replied doubtfully. "If we do not make it, I will shelter you with my wing. I may not be as large as Celtan or Pyrid, but I can certainly keep three people safe from a storm."

Leif did not like their options. He hated feeling trapped. He did not know where any of the others were, if they had found Lishe or if she was still out there somewhere. It irked him that he might be sending soldiers out to their death. He consoled himself that Lishe was likely not at any of the Paradises Baron Jayson was sending troops out to. If he were the rouge lintep, he would have gone north, where there were more Paradises close to each other.

"Let's be off then," he sighed. "Perhaps we'll get there before the storm hits and use the time stuck there to our advantage."

Wearily, he helped Talise up onto Snowcrest's back, then climbed up himself with Rownyn behind them. It was safer that way. If either of them fell, Rownyn could talk directly with Snowcrest to catch them before they hit the ground. He shivered involuntarily. The hazy memory of his fall still haunted him.

"Fly close to the ground, Snowcrest," Leif reminded her.

"Over the river so that if you fall, you won't be smashed on rocks – I know," Snowcrest grumbled.

"Can you swim?" Rownyn asked from behind.

"I don't intend to find out," Leif answered, holding tightly to the crystal spike in front of him.

* * *

Kora pushed open the door to Pér's house. *Her* house. Plyke and Tika stepped in after her. Plyke had barely spent any time here before they were whisked away to the Paradise. She knew he did not see it as his home. In truth, without Pér here, it hardly felt like her home either.

She wondered if Pér would be upset with her for commandeering one of his instruments. He had been teaching Plyke to play on his favourite lute, but she knew he had others in his stash.

"Come and choose one." She waved Plyke over once she had located them. "It's been so long since I played that I won't be much use to you."

"Did he teach you?" Plyke asked, sifting through the collection of instruments with Tika. "Or do all lintep learn to play?"

"All lintep whose parents can afford lessons learn to play," she informed him. "Mother and father were quite insistent about it for the five of us. Fredryck was the best of us. He played the flute. I think Pér has one here somewhere."

She found the wooden tube and tried it out, surprised at the fact that she still remembered how to make a sound. As Plyke strummed a few lutes to see which he preferred, Kora limbered up her fingers and began to play a tune she had learnt back when she was little. It was a short tune, meant to be played alongside a nursery rhyme. She smiled sadly. It had been Adina's favourite song. She remembered her little sister lisp her way through the song as Kora played her flute.

"I remember that tune." Plyke stood up, lute in hand and looked at her curiously. "Did they sing that to us in the dormitory in the Paradise when we were little?"

"I don't know," Tika replied, "but I remember the tune too."

Kora shook her head. "No, I used to hum it to your mind when I thought no one else would notice. You must have hummed it aloud for Tika to hear it."

Plyke looked at her oddly. "I wish you hadn't stopped."

"It wasn't intentional. Once I'd taught you to build your walls, you did such a magnificent job of keeping everyone out, including me, that I *couldn't* do it anymore."

There was an uncomfortable pause. They hadn't spoken about it since that first time in the castle. Kora knew she had neglected Plyke's lessons with his power, but there had been little she could do in the Paradise without Erton and his cronies finding out.

"Bring the flute along, Kora," Plyke told her. "You might play that better than I play the lute, even if you haven't played in a while."

They took their instruments and headed back to the castle. Kora exchanged pleasantries with the townsfolk as they passed through the markets. She expertly deflected queries about Pér's sudden and extended absence and her return without him.

As they reached the castle grounds, Kora turned to Tika. "You are free to stay with us today, Tika. I spoke with Master Edric and he agreed to spare you from your duties. It's up to you."

She saw the look pass between them, the immediate understanding without any words, and envied them that relationship.

"I'll go back to the stables now and come stay with you tonight if that's okay," Tika replied hopefully. They still had not discussed how things would work if Plyke came to live in Pér's house. Kora felt odd bringing the boys there without him.

"We'll stay in the castle tonight. Come and find us after you finish your duties for the day. If we aren't in the dining hall, we'll be in one of the royal chambers."

With a quick hug and a wave, Tika was gone. Plyke looked after him until he had rounded the corner to the stables.

"Maybe we can bring him with us next time," Kora suggested. "He might help you feel more deeply for the lintep song."

Plyke nodded. "I'd like that."

They walked arm in arm up the twisting stairwell towards their hope for the destruction of the Paradises.

Snowcrest roared and belched out a stream of fire. The heat all but singed the hair off Leif's face. He drew his cloak tighter to better cover his skin and, with his other hand, held on tightly to the spike in front of him. The dragon took no heed of the riders on her back but sped forward towards something only she could see.

"Make her stop!" Leif yelled back to Rownyn. He could not see the lintep properly over his shoulder but could just make out the shake of his head. He knew Rownyn would have had the same thought, but clearly the lintep could not get through to the clear crystal dragon. They were beginning to understand that she was a younger, more inexperienced dragon than the others. Perhaps that was why they had let her come on such a mission – to give her some experience in the Outworld, away from the watchful eye of Loreli.

In the distance, Leif spotted a return of fire shooting straight up in the air. As they drew closer, he recognised the creature as one of the other clear crystal dragons. They flew around each other in circles, in some strange kind of greeting before landing side by side on the riverbank.

"What are you doing here?" Snowcrest asked the other dragon. Leif dismounted alongside Talise and Rownyn. None of people on the other dragon, Shard as it turned out, looked familiar to Leif. That was not really surprising, considering two of them were elves. He had not met many elves before. There had been that unconscious one back in Illaria, who they had transported to Silvaren, and then the weapons master who had come with them to the Paradise – Leif recalled his name.

"Greetings young elves," Leif inclined his head towards them. "I have had the pleasure of making the acquaintance of your weapons master, Ensil."

The younger elf raised an eyebrow and looked at the older one. Her expression was studiously blank. Perhaps the weapons master was not such a popular elf.

"Forgive my fiancé," Talise said, stepping smoothly in front of him. "Duke Leif sometimes forgets his manner. I am Talise, soon to be his wife. We're travelling with Rownyn to the duchy fortresses to request they send out troops to the Paradises."

"Pleased to make your acquaintance, Lady Talise, Duke Leif," the female elf replied. "I am Liessa. This is Telon and Lord Braedan of Illaria."

"Lord Braedan!" Rownyn immediately bowed his head when he saw the man. "Why do you not travel with a lintep guard?"

The lintep lord scratched his stubbled chin. "Shard can only carry three people and it was agreed that even the royal family would be safe enough with two elves to negate the need for a lintep guard as well.

"Actually, though, you find us in a spot of trouble. We should have already reached P9 by now but were blown out of our way by a blizzard. Liessa was about to alert the others of our predicament."

The elf's eyes began to glow a bright silver. It reminded Leif of when Rilla's eyes had glowed bright green. They had not explained it to him, but perhaps she was somehow connected with the elves.

"Eliséo says they are already on their way to P9," she told them after a moment.

She shook her head almost angrily. "He says he managed to calm the storm around Hoarfrost so he can fly through it. We are to attempt to do the same. If we cannot, then we walk up to P9. It will take longer, but if we are slowed by the storm, the likelihood is that Lishe will be too."

Leif stepped closer to Liessa. "So, the rogue has not been found yet?" he asked softly. The elf shook her head.

"There is evidence that she was at P5, but she is no longer there," Liessa replied.

"Maybe one of the larger crystal dragons will be able to fly through the storm better than Shard. Groldor or Loreli would have more experience," Snowcrest suggested.

"We don't have time for that," Leif told her. "If Lishe has already started to destroy parts of the boundaries, those Paradises may already be exposed to the Outworld. We must continue with our mission to make sure troops are available as soon as they are needed."

Snowcrest gave a low groan but did not retort. She was a good dragon. She had a kind heart and showed some initiative but was clearly not used to time-sensitive matters.

"We should keep going," Leif insisted. "I would like to reach Firechester by nightfall or at least before the storm finds us."

Liessa's silver eyes glowed softly as she turned to him.

"King Lukys advises that he would like an elf to join you so that you can be in constant communication with the rest of us." She turned to the younger elf. "Telon, you may accompany Duke Leif and Lady Talise on their journey. Mind them well. Elves are not commonly seen in the Outworld, let alone in the large towns. Protect yourself if need be, but do not hurt any humans unless it is completely unavoidable."

Telon bounced excitedly on the balls of his feet. Leif regarded the young elf with some scepticism.

"Can you communicate with Snowcrest while she is flying?" Leif asked him.

"No," replied Telon with a shrug. "But I can communicate with almost anyone else involved in this mission."

"Rownyn, you'll have to come with us," Lord Braedan told the lintep guard. "These smaller crystal dragons can only carry three people each. It will be more dangerous for you, but I can't see a way around it."

Rownyn stood stiffly at attention. "It will be my utmost pleasure to be your guard, Lord Braedan. It is every guard's wish to be able to defend the royal family."

Lord Braedan shifted uncomfortably. "Yes, well, I would sooner have you back safely in Illaria away from this mess."

Rownyn looked crestfallen. Leif laid a hand on his shoulder.

"You have been invaluable to us, Rownyn. Talise and I would not have survived even the flight to Bryntown if not for you. I sincerely hope we meet again when this entire ordeal is over. If you ever find yourself in Deuterfoss, you will be treated as one of my most important guests."

"I, I ... thank you, Duke Leif," Rownyn stuttered. "Lady Talise, do not let him back out of his engagement, no matter how much he thinks you may not like his court."

Leif was about to protest when Talise threw her arms around Rownyn's neck and kissed him on the cheek. Before Leif could react, Lord Braedan took Rownyn by the arm and pulled him gently away.

"What do you mean you would not have survived the flight without Rownyn? What did he do?"

"Snowcrest flew too high at night and both Talise and I froze. I fell from the dragon's back and Talise would have but for Rownyn's quick thinking. He caught her arms, then spoke directly to Snowcrest's mind and he flew down to get me."

"Fire in the belly!" Telon cried out suddenly. Leif turned to see both elves' eyes glowing brightly. "Eliséo said the dragons can hold a ball of fire in their bellies to keep their passengers warm. Hoarfrost is doing that with them now."

Leif smiled. Perhaps it would not be so bad to trade a lintep for an elf. They quickly said their farewells and mounted their respective dragons. This time, Leif sat at the rear with Telon in the middle. He would not be able to forgive himself if anything happened to a child.

Chapter Fifty-Two – Strange recollections

Rilla lay in her bed, staring out of the window. The snow looked pretty as it fell. There had never been snow in the Paradise. It never got quite cold enough. She watched as the individual flakes were carried along on gusts of wind.

Isis had not let her light the fire herself. She had seemed worried that even such a small exertion would tire Rilla. In truth, Rilla wasn't sure she was wrong. She still did not quite remember what had happened, but she understood enough to know that she had lost a lot of energy somehow.

"Is she awake?" a voice whispered in the antechamber. Rilla strained to hear what was being said.

"She needs her rest," Mistress Kayte said firmly, but quietly.

"Playing some music to the poor girl is not going to tire her out," a louder voice insisted.

Is that Kora? What is she doing here?

Do you have no memory of it? a voice in her head asked. It took a moment for Rilla to place the voice.

Elessa! she embraced her tree with her mind. *Oh, how I've missed you!*

She was worse than I thought, Elessa said sourly. *You really should have let me keep a better eye on her.*

Not now, Eliséo said stiffly. *Rilla, are you well?*

Rilla tried to keep up with the conversation. There were so many things she could not remember. When was the last time she had properly spoken with Eliséo? It felt like weeks.

You are not far off there, Elessa advised her. *He has been rather absent of late. Something I have been trying to remedy.*

Enough! Eliséo shouted. Rilla cringed at his tone. Elessa said no more, but Rilla could feel her anger with him. *Rilla, are you well?*

I ... think so, Rilla replied uncertainly. *Something happened yesterday, or this morning – I'm not sure. I have such strange recollections of Marilisa being nice to me.*

"Rilla?" Plyke poked his head around the door.

What is Plyke doing here? she asked. *Isn't he meant to be with Lord Aaron at P3?*

He came back because he was worried about you, Eliséo replied softly. *We all were. Rilla, we could not contact you. Go, speak with your cousin, but I would like some of your time when you are done with him.*

Rilla could not help but notice his feelings – something akin to jealousy.

I promise, she told him. Rilla blinked and felt a dizzying sense of vertigo. She was suddenly thousands of feet in the air, flying on a crystal dragon. She blinked again and was back in her room, looking at a confused Plyke.

"Plyke!" she cried out. "It's so good to see you again!"

Before she could stop herself, she flung her arms out wide. Plyke ran over to her bed and held her tightly. All of his worries for her coursed through her mind – his relief that she was alive and awake, his happiness that she was so glad to see him.

What was wrong with her? She abhorred physical contact.

It is something you need right now, Elessa told her. Rilla wondered if her tree had somehow manipulated that exchange.

"Don't crush her, dear," Kora said as she lightly touched Plyke's shoulder. "Mistress Kayte will never forgive us if we hurt Rilla after we promised not to tire her out."

Rilla fell back on her bed as Plyke let her go. She felt so weak.

"I guess you'll be going now that you've seen I'm fine," Rilla mumbled, snuggling under her blankets.

"Don't be daft, Rilla," Plyke chided her. "I'm not leaving you now. I think I've figured out how to destroy the Paradises, but I need your help."

"Absolutely not!" Mistress Kayte called out from the doorway. "Rilla needs more care than we anticipated. She will *not* be joining you in the Outworld again."

Rilla did not have the strength, nor the desire, to argue. She turned her head to the side, away from her visitors.

"Kayte, you will kindly remember your place as a mistress, not as the girl's mother. You do not have a say in where she goes. All *you* can decide is which healing class she attends and don't think I'm not aware that you decided not to teach her yourself anymore.

"Plyke's plan is a good one and, if we teach her properly, it should not cost her any energy, so she will be no worse off than if she had stayed here under your ever-watchful eye."

Rilla did not want to listen but could not help but hear the conversation. She did not like people fighting over her. She never liked the attention. All she wanted to do was stay in the shadows.

"Both of you be quiet," Plyke told them. "Look what you're making her do. If you're going to fight, you can both leave. Otherwise, please be quiet."

There was a scuffling of shoes, then silence. Rilla waited a moment before turning over again. Plyke was sitting on the edge of her bed.

"There you are," he said as he reached out a hand to push the hair out of her face. "They're gone now. You don't need to disappear anymore."

Rilla frowned. She hadn't meant to fade from view. He pulled out a lute and began to strum the strings.

"I'm not very good yet. Pér is trying to teach me, but we've only been at it a few days. Can I play for you?"

She nodded, not quite certain why he wanted to play her a song so much. The words were familiar. She recognised them as the ones they said to make the crystal heart work.

"It doesn't work very well for me, but I think I know why. I don't *feel* enough," he told her. Rilla knew her mind was a little foggy, but Plyke was not making any sense at all.

"What do you mean?" she asked quietly, propping herself up onto an elbow.

"Well, it's like this. Pér can make his power work through music. It seems to be a rare skill, or just one that no one knew was possible until he came along. Anyway, his songs were always for Kora and he felt a great deal for her. That's when he really started to realise what he was doing. He managed to adapt his songs to any situation but always called on the depth of his emotions for Kora to do that.

"I don't have that well of emotions, so I can't seem to make it work properly. But *you* do. You always have had. I think a lot of people mistake it for a bad temper, but that's not what it is."

Plyke explained everything to her. He sounded so certain of himself, even when it came to her. No one had ever understood her like that.

"So ... you want to teach me a song?" Rilla asked in confusion.

"No." Plyke shook his head. "I want to teach you how Pér sings."

Rilla tried to raise herself up a bit and allowed Plyke to help her sit back against the headboard, eiderdown pillows fluffed up behind her.

"We'll pick a song you know – any song. Then I'll show you what he does."

"I ... don't really know any songs," Rilla replied softly, looking up at his confused eyes.

"Not a problem. I'll teach you Kora's lullaby. It's better on her flute though. Do you mind if I bring her back again?"

Rilla shrugged. Kora had only left the room because she and Mistress Kayte had quarrelled. Rilla didn't have any issues with her aunt, though it still felt strange to call her that.

Plyke called his mother in and, together, they taught Rilla the lullaby. It was a simple tune. Rilla bobbed her head as they sang it to her over and over again.

Willy wagtail sits up in the jacaranda tree.

Quiet willy wagtail. No rain today.

Willy wagtail sings a lullaby on the open field.

Noisy willy wagtail. Here comes the rain.

There were no jacarandas in their Paradise, but Rilla had seen the pretty purple flowers last summer in Illaria. They had covered the streets, turning to a brown mush as people, horses and carts trampled over them. She had been reminded of them recently in her mind lesson with Taddeo, Odille and Zefiro

The willy wagtail was a mystery to her.

"They're a small bird, about the same size as the fringa," Kora explained when Rilla asked about them. "People say they don't sing unless it's about to rain. It was my favourite lullaby growing up. Mother used to sing it to us when we were little. I sang it to Adina when mother wasn't around. It always helped her to sleep."

Rilla could feel the nostalgia flowing off Kora. That did not normally happen. She had not noticed that her power was swirling so far from her. Carefully, she gathered her power back around her, and the feeling disappeared.

"What now?" Rilla asked once she had learnt the tune.

"Now comes the important part," Plyke said as he waggled a finger at her. "We pour the emotion into it. Any emotion you can find. If you want to make someone happy, think of your happiest memory while you sing. If you want to make them sombre, think of a sad memory. Whatever it is you need them to feel, make yourself feel that first."

"So, you want us to manipulate their feelings, just like they tried to do to us when we first got here?" Rilla asked incredulously. Plyke started and stared at Kora. Rilla saw them both turn pale.

"That *is* what you're trying to teach me, isn't it?"

Kora nodded slowly. "I've never thought about it like that before. Pér always just made me feel better. He wanted me to be happy. He ... was the only one who ever could after my mother, brothers and little sister died."

"Does it work the same way, though?" Rilla asked, curious about why Kora was happy for them to learn this method when she actively instructed Plyke never to use touch to influence a human.

"Not *exactly*," admitted Kora. "The touch works instantaneously and is not often very subtle. Pér's song takes your feelings and works with them. It doesn't dismiss them out of hand."

Rilla thought back to the only time she had ever heard Pér sing. The concert where he had sung the ballad people now called "Pér's ballad" – the song about Kora. He didn't make everyone love Kora, he only expressed his love for her and allowed them to feel it too.

"Okay," Rilla replied. "Show me."

Plyke looked over to Kora. "You're probably better at it than I am. Will you show her?"

Kora gave him an odd look. "I've never tried it before, Plyke. Pér never had a need to teach me and, well, we tried to hide this particular skill from Uncle Lukys, so we rarely spoke about it. I can play the lullaby for you on my flute, but you'll have to show Rilla how it actually works through the words."

Plyke nodded eagerly and stood beside his mother. Rilla wondered what it must be like to have such a free and easy relationship with a parent. She had never experienced it and, now, she never would.

Willy wagtail sits up in the jacaranda tree.
Quiet willy wagtail. No rain today.
Willy wagtail sings a lullaby on the open field.
Noisy willy wagtail. Here comes the rain.

Rilla listened carefully to the words. She waited to feel something, but there was nothing. Plyke sang it over and over again and each time, she felt an expectation of something and then it was gone.

"Is it working?" Plyke asked. Rilla shook her head. Kora lowered her flute and laughed.

"Yes, dear, it's working," she said. "Rilla, could you feel an expectation of something? Were you waiting for it to happen?"

"Well of course," Rilla replied easily. "I was waiting to see how the power would work."

Kora nodded her head. "Those were the feelings Plyke amplified in you. He took your feelings and worked with them. Do you see now? He didn't change them, he just made you more aware of them."

Rilla looked from one to the other in surprise. It certainly had not been what she was expecting, but if she thought about it, her expectation grew only at certain parts of the song.

"Can you teach me?" she asked excitedly. "I don't think Mistress Kayte will object to me singing a bit."

Plyke sat back on the edge of her bed and sang the song with her over and over until Rilla did not have to think about the tune or the words. Next, he showed her how to pour her emotions, but not her power, into the song.

"It shouldn't take any energy to do it," Plyke told her. "Pér can sing like this for such a long time without getting tired."

At that point, Mistress Kayte walked in the room. Rilla realised she must have been eavesdropping the entire time. No one said anything as the healing mistress took a seat by the window – close enough to be of use if she was needed, far enough not to be intrusive.

Rilla ignored her as best she could and continued singing with Plyke. Bit by bit, she could feel her emotions pulling at her, wanting to be part of the music. She let go of her inhibitions and sang without a care.

"Stop!" cried Kora. Rilla immediately stopped singing. "Rilla, dear, you've done wonderfully well, but I think we should start a little slower."

Rilla looked at her in confusion. "I didn't do anything," she protested. "All I did was sing."

Kora glanced at Mistress Kayte who raised an eyebrow at her.

"Actually, you let your emotions flow through the music, which is exactly what you should have done, but I think you did it without thinking," Kora tried to explain. "You need to have a clear thought of what you want people to feel, otherwise you will only succeed in drowning them in your own emotions."

"Oh," replied Rilla in a small voice. "I don't think anyone needs that. I'll try harder next time."

Kora gave her a reassuring squeeze on her shoulder then began to play again. Rilla joined in when Plyke sang the lullaby. It was more difficult than it sounded to allow only certain emotions to flow through to the music. She concentrated on just one. It was something she wanted for herself but could never quite feel.

"Much better, Rilla!" Kora exclaimed, clapping her hands together against her flute. "You let your peacefulness flow into the music. That was a single and direct emotion."

Rilla said nothing. She did not feel the peace she had passed on. Why didn't it work that way? Why couldn't she influence her own feelings?

Rilla, I need to speak with Plyke, Eliséo said in her mind. *Can you find him for me?*

Rilla did not feel like talking – not with anyone. She understood that Eliséo needed to use her to communicate with others, but she did not have to actively participate. She stretched out a hand and placed it on Plyke's hand, letting him hear Eliséo directly.

Have you found a way to make the crystal heart work? Eliséo asked without preamble.

I'm working on it, he replied a little stiffly. *I won't be able to test it out without Rilla.*

You will need to hurry, the elf told him. *Lishe has begun stealing power from the Paradises and if we can't stop her soon, our only option will be to destroy the boundaries before she can get to them.*

Have you found her? Plyke asked, gripping Rilla's hand tightly.

Not yet. We think she may be at P9. Let Aislen know.

Without warning, Eliséo retreated from Rilla's mind. She shook her hand free from Plyke and sank down beneath the blankets on her bed. She did not want to be a part of this anymore. She did not want to go out into the Outworld, destroy Paradises and face Lishe. She was too tired. She felt empty, like someone had carved everything out of her and left only the shell of her.

"Rilla needs her rest." Rilla heard Mistress Kayte's muffled voice through the blankets. She heard them walk out of the room and leave her alone. It was what she wanted, but it made her feel even more empty.

Chapter Fifty-Three – Indecision

"There's nothing more we can do without Plyke," Kynon told him. Aaron listened to his cousin with half an ear. He was still furious with Kora and Guiscard for taking Plyke back to Illaria. Though, he had to admit the most frustrating part of that was that they were right. Plyke had made a good point, but Aaron simply did not trust Rilla enough to want that plan to go ahead.

"There is *one* thing we can do," Aaron said. He stood up and walked away from his cousin. There was little that they could achieve by complaining to each other. Now it was time for action. He wove his way through the soldiers' tents, out to where Pyrid lay.

The fire opal dragon lounged on a bed of scorched grass. Aaron remembered that the heat gave him strength. Pyrid lazily opened an eye as Aaron approached.

"Don't blame me," he growled. "Garnet was growing restless. If I hadn't let him take them back to Illaria, he would have been the death of me."

Aaron ignored the bad attempt at an apology. That was not what he was here for.

"We need another heart, Pyrid. Plyke is convinced that Rilla is the key to making it work now it's in his body, but that girl is too temperamental. She cannot be trusted."

Pyrid blew out a hot stream of smoke. "Aaron, we've been through this before. Celtan will not allow another heart to be given out. Not even to you. Imagine what would happen if people realised there were more to be had! The Drakos Mountains would be crawling with would-be scavengers."

"You don't see this as your problem, do you?" Aaron crossed his arms in front of his chest. "You think Lishe is a lintep problem and we should sort her out ourselves. Don't you think that a person like that will stop at nothing? If we cannot stop her and we cannot destroy the boundaries, she will grow stronger than you can possibly imagine.

"What then? You think she'll be satisfied at that point? Because I don't. I think she will be driven insane by all the different powers in her mind, if she isn't already. She will find out about the crystal heart and then she will seek you out. If you refuse to give her one, I doubt she would have any scruples about killing one of you to steal the heart from inside you."

Aaron stopped. This was not him. This was not how he normally behaved. He went to rub his temples with his fingers and was slightly startled to feel his power on his right temple.

"Stress is not your friend, old man," Pyrid rumbled. Aaron did not apologise. He felt too agitated. Pyrid pinned him with a fiery eye. "I am not afraid of this rogue lintep. She would not last long were she to invade the Drakos Mountains, no matter how powerful she has become. It is not so easy to kill a crystal dragon and take its heart as it may please you to think. We are in no danger from Lishe."

"Then do it for the rest of us," Aaron pleaded. "Do it for *me*."

Fire burned in Pyrid's belly, glowing through his crystal body. "You do not think of the consequences. You cannot see them. You think the crystal hearts are tools to help you destroy the Paradise boundaries. When used that way, it sets power free.

"You've heard that it freed your granddaughter from Lishe's mind snare, and you've seen it used yourself to free the powers that ensnared both your granddaughters.

"You have *never* seen their darker side. They hearts only limited by what the holder wishes to do with them. They can be used to trap people as much as they can be used to free them. I will not have people running around with these precious hearts, destroying the entire Outworld. A handful of people with crystal hearts could do more damage than your damned rogue lintep."

Pyrid fell silent and the fire in his belly dimmed, thought it did not go out. Aaron closed his mouth which he realised was hanging open. Pyrid was right – he had not realised what the hearts were truly capable of, the damage they could do.

"Forgive me, Pyrid," he whispered. "I ... forgive me."

The fire opal dragon growled softly. "Now, are you staying here or are we flying back to Illaria to see what plan that grandson of yours has come up with?"

Aaron leaned heavily against Pyrid's crystalline leg. "Back to Illaria," he sighed. "Kynon is right. There is nothing more we can do here without Plyke. Are you ready for another flight?"

"I will be by the time you get back," Pyrid told him. "Now let me sleep."

* * *

Hoarfrost laboured through the snowstorm. Eliséo had managed to lessen the intensity of it in a wide sphere around them, but that did not stop the wind from whipping around them in a frenzy, nor the snowflakes from encrusting their eyes. Despite their best efforts, Hoarfrost was flying off track. They needed to be flying a north-easterly course, but the wind was so powerful that, as much as Hoarfrost tried to maintain his heading, he kept being pushed further to the north.

Eliséo pressed himself against Hoarfrost's warm body. It must be costing the clear crystal dragon more strength than he let on to keep that fire burning in his belly.

We need to land soon, Luisella's voice was insistent in Eliséo's mind. *Hoarfrost is losing strength. He will be no use to us at all if he does not rest.*

Eliséo knew she was right, though it irked him that Lishe might have a long head start on them.

Tell him to fly close to the ground. According to Kora's map, there are four lintep villages between P5, P9 and P10. If he can get to one of them, we might even manage a hot meal tonight.

No sooner had he finished speaking than Hoarfrost began his descent. The intensity of the storm lessened as they drew nearer the ground. The fields and pockets of forests scattered over the land were covered in a rough white blanket with snow flurrying up in erratic streams.

"There!" Eliséo pointed and shouted, not knowing if anyone could hear him over the roar of the wind. The sheet of white was broken by brown and grey structures. They barely held their roofs up over the snow, but it was enough for Eliséo's sharp eyes to catch the anomaly.

Hoarfrost dived down too fast towards the buildings. Before anyone could warn him, he had sunk himself wing deep in a snowdrift. The fire in his belly melted a small circle around him, but that only made matters worse. The snow was already reforming in chunks around their feet. Eliséo, Luisella and Raeslin scrambled back up onto the dragon's back in an effort not to get their feet frozen in blocks of ice.

"Sorry," huffed Hoarfrost. "I was so tired, once I started going down, I couldn't stop myself."

Eliséo shook his head. "You did well to take us as far as you did today. Are you hurt?"

Hoarfrost stretched his wings and arched his neck. "I've been better. In a hot lake, I'd be fine in a day or so. Out here ..."

Eliséo understood what the dragon was not saying. He had hurt himself badly enough that they would be walking the rest of the way to the Paradise unless they could come up with another solution.

"Now what?" asked Raeslin.

"Now we walk, dear," Luisella told her in a motherly fashion.

Hoarfrost helped Eliséo to the top layer of snow, but as he set a foot down, he immediately sank through it to his thighs.

"Walking is not an option," he told them. "The snow is too deep. It will take us days to reach the village that way."

Use the mist platform, Elessa told him.

Eliséo considered the idea. It had merit, but he doubted Hoarfrost would fit on the platform. He created one anyway and helped Luisella and Raeslin onto it. They immediately noticed the problem.

"I could help," Raeslin suggested. "If I add my own mist platform to yours, it might fit Hoarfrost as well."

"We can but try," Eliséo agreed with a sigh. He explained what to do to Raeslin, who listened with eager anticipation. It took her a few tries, but eventually, she managed to create an adequate mist platform, half the size of Eliséo's one.

The three of them squished over to one side, leaving as much space for Hoarfrost as possible. The dragon jumped on and drove the mist platform into the snow.

Silva, is there any way to strengthen this platform? he asked without much hope. There was a long pause before Silva answered.

It is something I have rarely tried, but I can ask your mother to lend some of her power.

Eliséo knew what that would cost both of them. Eléna had been against this expedition in the first place. She would be less than impressed that they were in strife and asking for her assistance.

"Whatever it is, swallow your pride," Luisella told him sternly. "I do not wish to perish out here and we cannot leave Hoarfrost behind. Whatever your tree is telling you, we're trying it."

Eliséo was stunned by her forcefulness. She was right, of course, but he had not expected her to be quite so direct. Silva opened the connection between them and Eliséo sought her out gently.

Mother?

No. Her reply was short and sharp.

We cannot abandon Hoarfrost here, Eliséo pleaded. *He has served us well and is injured. I do not know how well crystal dragons do in the snow.*

Perhaps you ought to have thought of that before you asked him to fly through a blizzard.

Eliséo was silent. He foolishly had not realised that Silva might show her those things. The only way he could have prevented that was by blocking Silva out of his mind for the entire journey so she could not witness it herself. Now, there was no way to stop her from oversharing.

Mother, be reasonable. Liessa was suddenly in his mind. Her presence confused Eliséo. The only reason she could be there was if Silva had purposely brought her into the conversation. But why would Silva have shown Eléna everything if she really did want his mother's help.

I believe I am the only one of us being reasonable at the moment, Eléna replied stonily.

Eliséo was the closest to P9. Braedan and I were slowed by the blizzard. I would have done the same thing as my brother if I had his power at my disposal. As it is, I am even further from P9 than he is. We need your help.

Eléna's indecision was palpable. *Neither of you should be out there.*

However, we are, Eliséo reasoned with her. *Will you help me or would you rather I die from cold and starvation alongside Raeslin, Luisella and Hoarfrost?*

That is unfair, Eléna was heart-stricken.

Eliséo softened his approach. *We know you are worried about us, Mother, but Liessa and I may both need you during this expedition. Please do not allow your fear to paralyse you.*

He could feel her raw emotions flowing through Silva into both himself and his sister. His chest constricted as Eléna's fears broke down the walls to his own feelings and made him realise how scared he was himself.

Without warning, the mist platform holding Eliséo and his companions rose up out of the snow. He sighed deeply and silently thanked his mother before closing his connection with both Eléna and Liessa. Not wanting to discuss what had just happened with his companions, he steered the mist platform by manipulating the wind around them to flow from behind. With any luck, they would reach one of the villages in a short while.

* * *

Rilla paced her bedchamber restlessly. Unbeknownst to Eliséo, Elessa had kept her informed of his progress through the Outworld. It was a safe bet that Lishe was either heading towards P9 or p10. From Illaria, it was would take days to fly there. Rilla knew Lord Aaron had had no success in destroying the boundary at P2, with or without Plyke's help.

Plyke. Rilla thought about his idea to use the lintep song to destroy the boundary, but there was no time left to test it.

Making her decision, Rilla opened the door to the hallway and almost walked into Lord Aaron. She stepped back warily, the faintest memory of his anger clamouring for her attention. What in the Outworld was he doing here?

"Lord Aaron," she greeted him stiffly. He gave her a wounded expression, but she was uncertain what to make of it.

"Ah, yes, Rilla. I was ... looking for Plyke," he said as he rubbed his stubbly cheek. She looked at him coldly.

"Wrong door," she said as she pushed past him. "If you'll excuse me, I need to find Aislen."

"Has something happened?" he asked frantically. As he put out his hand to hold her back, Rilla flinched away.

"Rilla ... I'm sorry for my behaviour. It was unpardonable."

This was a man unaccustomed to apologising. She could see it in his very stance. Unable to forgive him, Rilla looked away.

"I need to find Aislen."

When Lord Aaron followed her down the hall, she did not stop him. On any other day,

Rilla would have sent out tendrils of her power to locate Aislen. Now, she was too scared. Especially if there was no one she trusted around her. The man following her was *not* counted among those few people.

Mistress Kayte had cleared her for lessons beginning tomorrow, but Rilla wished she hadn't. It was true, she was no longer exhausted, but her confidence had been shattered. A few days of near-isolation had not fixed that.

Rilla pulled up abruptly in front of Aislen's door and knocked. There was no answer. She turned to leave and noticed the curious look on Lord Aaron's face. He did not need an explanation. Not now.

"Aislen is in the library," he informed her. Rilla only nodded her thanks. Without waiting to see if he would follow, she descended the twisted stairs to the library.

"He found you, I see," Guiscard noted as Rilla walked through the double doors with Lord Aaron in tow. She frowned. It was not a discussion she wanted to have.

"Is Aislen here?"

Guiscard nodded down a long aisle. "She's been down there for a long time."

For a moment, Rilla pictured how this conversation would go if Aislen's mind was clouded by others.

"Lord Aaron was looking for Plyke. Can you help him?" she asked Guiscard, pointedly not looking at the old man. The librarian looked between the two of them in confusion.

"He'll be in his lessons. I'll send him up to see you when he's done," Guiscard told Lord Aaron. Rilla took a deep breath and counted to ten in her mind. There was no other way she could think of to effectively dismiss the old man. Ignoring him entirely, Rilla walked down the aisle where Aislen had closeted herself away. Her nose was buried in a book. She did not even glance up as Rilla approached.

"I think it's time," Rilla said quietly, but firmly. Aislen looked up from her book with her mouth open, about to speak until she saw Lord Aaron.

"Uncle Aaron! What are you doing here?" she exclaimed with a mixture of surprise and anger. "Why didn't Ensil tell us you were coming?"

"There was nothing else we could do without Plyke, so Kynon, Guiscard, Ensil, Pér and I returned today," Aaron replied, not actually answering her question. Rilla did not look at him and waited patiently until Aislen drew her attention back to the matter at hand.

"Are you sure?" she asked.

"If we delay any longer, we run the risk of others getting hurt when they have no chance at all of succeeding."

"What in the Outworld are you two talking about?" Aaron asked. Rilla took a guilty pleasure in his annoyance. Aislen glanced at him.

"Uncle, perhaps you should freshen up a bit before the evening meal. I'll invite our entire family to dine with me tonight."

Though Rilla did not want to share her plans with Lord Aaron, she understood that they could not keep him in the dark. He looked like he was about to protest, but Aislen must have spoken directly to his mind because he quickly glanced at Rilla and then bid them farewell.

"Sit with me, Rilla." Aislen patted a spot beside her. "Tell me everything."

Rilla told her as much as she knew of the progress in the Outworld. Lukys had not found anything out of the ordinary at P8 so everyone was now converging on P9 and P10, as best as they could through the snowstorm.

"I only wish I knew where Duke Leif was," Aislen sighed. "We need to keep the Paradisians safe after their boundary is destroyed, but I don't know if his soldiers will be there in time."

Rilla quickly spoke to Elessa, confirming her thoughts.

"Duke Leif is currently in Firechester, negotiating with the Duchess there for troops to be sent out to P9. She is being ... difficult about it."

Aislen looked at her oddly. "How do you know that?"

"Braedan, Liessa and Telon met up with them near Thistlehall. Apparently, the blizzard threw them quite far off course and Shard could not fly again until it was over. They decided it was more important to keep communication open than to have two elves with one lintep, so Telon is with Duke Leif and Talise now, while Rownyn flies with Braedan and Liessa."

Aislen grinned. "So, Talise is still with him, is she?"

"Telon just told me they're engaged," Rilla smirked. "There's quite a story behind it, but I've been promised to secrecy so Duke Leif can tell you himself."

The princess laughed. It was a pleasant sound. Rilla realised she had rarely heard it. She could not understand how she could find such pleasure in these things at such a time, but she knew Aislen had not had as difficult a life growing up here in the castle.

"So, what now? If Lord Aaron is back, I assume that means we have two crystal dragons at our disposal?"

"Yes, Pyrid and Garnet," Aislen rested her chin in the cup of her hand. "That makes a maximum of seven people. We'll need to send Ensil with you in case the dragons get separated. Plyke, of course."

"Do you think Kora and Pér will want to go this time?" Rilla asked.

Aislen nodded. "After the last time, they vowed they would not let Plyke go by himself. That's already five."

"I don't think Plyke will agree to go anywhere so far away without Tika," Rilla pointed out. "I think Tika was half the reason he came back without telling Lord Aaron."

Aislen sighed. "That only leaves room for one more person. I wish I could go, but it would be remiss of me to shirk my duties here. Besides, the twins will certainly wreak havoc if there's no one here to look out for them."

"Is it ... do you think Isis might come? I know Kayte is probably a better idea ... but I don't like her," Rilla finished lamely. Aislen raised her eyebrows at that but did not comment on it.

"They could both go with you if Ensil stays here with me," she suggested. "It *would* be helpful for me to know what is happening out there in the Outworld while I'm stuck here."

Keep Ensil in Illaria, Elessa told Rilla firmly. *We have learned that there is much he must account for and I do not want Eliséo distracted by him when so much is at stake.*

"I think that's the best idea," Rilla said. "If we meet up with any of the others on our way, we can always switch someone for an elf on whichever dragon needs, but I don't think we'll get separated."

"That's settled then. We'll sort out the rest of the details tonight. Would you be a dear and ask Cook Palmyra to ensure there is food ready for the seven of you tomorrow morning?" Aislen asked her. Rilla knew when she was being dismissed. She had barely stood up before Aislen had buried herself back in her book.

Chapter Fifty-Four – Head start

The blizzard hit after she had left P5. Lishe was pleased with the amount of power she had taken from that Paradise. She only hoped it was not enough for her pursuers to locate her. She had a good head start on them. They could not have tracked her directly from the prophecy child's Paradise, as she had stolen their map. That was her only saving grace. They would have had to fly back to Illaria on their crystal dragons to obtain another one, if they even had another one with the locations marked out.

Lishe peeked out through the hole she had created in the impromptu snow cave she had created. As the blizzard raged, she shaped the snow around herself and the mare to keep the brunt of the storm from killing them. They were effectively trapped now, but Lishe was not worried about that – she would find a way out.

She surveyed the land from the small opening. There was nothing to distinguish it from any other part of the Outworld. Before the snow fell, it had been flat, with tall yellow grass. The Lesa Mountains were faint peaks in the distance, with foothills increasing in density towards them, but she doubted they would slow her much.

"Come on, then," she said to herself. "Time to escape this prison."

She pushed a tendril of her power into the small hole, out into the air. It was certainly cold, but not freezing, which meant there was at least an iota of warmth in every part of it. She drew on that warmth and focused it in her snow cave to melt a tunnel. It was a tight squeeze, but she eventually managed to crawl through. Her mare was not so fortunate.

Lishe felt she was a reasonable person. She knew she could not find her way to any of the lintep settlements, let alone the Paradises, without a horse in all this snow. But right now, she stood with hands on her hips and glared furiously at the mare.

If she could think of any way of achieving her goal without the dumb beast, she would leave it to starve in that cave. Instead, she sent out tendrils in all directions around her, sucking the heat out of the air to create an even larger tunnel than that which already existed. It took a long time to create an exit large enough for the mare.

Lishe pulled the horse by the bridle. It resisted. She pulled harder and the horse flicked her head to snap the bridle out of Lishe's hand, prancing around to stop herself being caught again. Lishe struck the mare's rump with her fist. In that instant, she felt the horse's terror. A slow smile crept across her face. She could manipulate this horse as easily as any lintep or human she ever had before.

* * *

Aislen sighed. It had already been a long evening. Her decision was not a popular one with many of those gathered around the table, but their resources were limited. She could not persuade Plyke to leave without Tika any more than she could convince Kora to stay behind and leave her son's care to Pér alone.

"Uncle Aaron, my decision is made. Isis and Kayte will be the only mistresses in attendance. Kora and Pér will go out of necessity, as will Plyke, Tika and Rilla.

"If you will care to notice, not even the seer is joining them. If I had a choice, I would be sending more experienced masters and mistresses along with them, but I don't."

She rubbed her eyes tiredly. There had been too many late nights recently. She'd spent most of her free time in the library, researching anything she could about lintep stealing, borrowing or giving power. It surprised her to discover that Lishe was not the first lintep in written history to steal power. However, *that* lintep had been found out quickly and forced to relinquish the power back to its living owner.

Nor was Nyssa the first to give her power away. It appeared to be, if not a common occurrence, then an accepted one. Usually the transfer was by parents to their less gifted children when the parents were near death. It tended to happen among the poorer families where the parents had nothing else to give their children as an inheritance.

"Aislen, you are not being reasonable!" Aaron thumped the table with his fist, calling her back to the present. "Even if they reach P9 unharmed, what are they to do when they come across Lishe? Isis and Kayte may be well trained in their specialities, but I cannot vouch for their other skills."

"*I* can," Aislen told him firmly. "You cannot go with them."

"I am the only one who has successfully faced Lishe," Aaron implored her.

"But I would be better bait," Shuut said quietly. "She's always wanted Nyssa's power. She admitted that to me herself. What better way to distract her than to tempt her with that power again?"

Aislen grew very still. It was a valid point. Shuut and Rilla together would create a great distraction for Lishe. She shook her head.

"I cannot allow it," she said apologetically. "You have only recently become acquainted with Nyssa's power. It would be remiss of me to send you out as bait when I don't know you can defend yourself."

Aislen suddenly felt a suffocating force around her body, squeezing in around her.

"Is that enough proof for you?" Shuut asked, as she released her grip.

Aislen did not answer her question. There was no need for the others to know what Shuut was now capable of. "Plyke are you sure you won't leave Tika behind? He'll be safer here."

Tika looked over at his Partner questioningly, but Plyke only grasped his hand tightly. Aislen shook her head at the absurdity of it. If the heart was not in Plyke's body, he would not have a say in the matter – they *both* would be left behind.

"Isis?" Aislen looked over at the fire mistress hopefully, but it was Rilla who spoke.

"Not to cause any offence, but I trust Mistress Isis most to keep me safe."

"Mistress Kayte is more skilled at keeping you alive," Aislen reminded her.

Rilla kept her eyes firmly averted from the healing mistress.

"Yes, but Mistress Isis prevents most of the problems before they occur."

Much to Aislen's surprise, Kayte did not object.

"So, we are left with Plyke, Tika, Kora and Pér on Pyrid. Garnet will take Rilla, Shuut and Isis. Rilla, you are to report to the elves every step of the way. I will not be left in the dark."

"Would it be much of a detour for the dragons to fly through the Drakos Mountains first?" Marilisa asked. She and the twins had sat silently through dinner with their grandfather by their side. "It would help if you could ask for more crystal dragons so that a few of the more skilled lintep could follow in your wake."

Aislen took out her map and frowned as she tried to gauge distances. It did not look like it would take any longer. Either way should take about three days of flying.

"The second round of lintep would be at least two days behind the others. And there would not be any elves to spare for communication. Eliséo has made it clear that Ensil is to remain here until further notice."

Marilisa cleared her throat. "I should like to go with the second round. I am the most skilled in each of my classes and have more power than many. I ... would like to see the Outworld for myself and try to understand how difficult life is for everyone in the Paradises."

"Kynon, stop this foolishness." Aaron waved dismissively at Marilisa.

Kynon looked from Aaron to his grandchildren and then over to Aislen. "Aislen, would you mind watching the twins a while longer if I take Marilisa with me?"

"Kynon, you're not serious! You can't take her into the Outworld for *this*!" Aaron bellowed.

Kynon turned to him calmly. "Marilisa is more skilled than all three of your grandchildren. She has trained in every aspect of her power since she was a child. I find it heartening that she would like to be a part of this. Have no doubt, cousin, I will ask her father's permission first, but if he agrees, I see nothing wrong with it."

Aaron slammed his fist onto the table hard enough to make the plates rattle and a few glasses to topple before storming out of the room. Aislen sighed inwardly. Aaron was certainly more cautious of the Outworld since his accident, even though it had nothing to do with Lishe.

"Do not judge Uncle Aaron too harshly," Aislen told them with a half-hearted smile. "He cares very deeply for all of you."

Rilla huffed at that. Aislen could not blame her. He had treated the poor girl abominably. She watched as Rilla approached Kynon and Marilisa and placed a hand on each of their arms. Her eyes glowed bright green. Judging by their faces, they must have been talking to Daegan. Aislen had to admit it was very convenient to be able to communicate over such long distances with the elves. She idly wondered if Eliséo would consider allowing some of his elves to take up stations in Illaria, Goraburg and each of the duchies to keep communication open between them all. She put the thought aside for another day.

* * *

We'll be there in three days, Rilla told Eliséo as she mounted Garnet the next morning.

I hope to be there by tomorrow evening at the latest. Has Plyke figured out how to use the heart yet? Eliséo asked hopefully. Rilla explained their plan to him.

We can test it along the way at P6, if we manage to stop there overnight, Rilla suggested. Eliséo agreed it was probably their best option. However, if it worked, it would leave the Paradisians completely defenceless against the Outworld. Rilla suddenly smiled.

Garnet agreed to carry Anya as far as Goraburg. Perhaps she could ask Ilya to send up a troop of karliki to guard the Paradise until we have time to deal with it or until humans arrive from Firechester.

She felt pride flow through her from Eliséo and Elessa.

We'll make a strategist out of you yet, Eliséo proclaimed. *I'm sure Celtan won't mind, but please let the crystal dragons speak with him when you request more of them to fly to Illaria.*

Their conversation was over before everyone was mounted and settled. Rilla risked something she had not tried in over a week. Carefully, she pulled out a tiny sliver of power and edged slowly over to Aislen.

We're going to stop in P6 to try the lintep song there, she told the princess. *Eliséo thinks he'll reach P9 at least a day before us.*

It was a struggle to get the message to Aislen, not because she was not skilled enough or powerful enough, but because she was afraid to do anything with her power and so held on to it tightly. It began to struggle against her.

Isis laid a hand on her shoulder. Rilla marvelled at how well the fire mistress could read her. That simple gesture calmed Rilla enough for her to relax the grip on her power. It flowed back to her as easily and naturally as it always had.

"Don't doubt yourself," she whispered so that only Rilla could hear. "You are a clever, kind, skilful and powerful lintep. Your power is more a part of you than anyone else I have ever met. It would no sooner leave you than Elessa would break her bond with you."

Rilla did not reply – *could not* reply – with the lump in her throat. She only covered Isis' hand with her own until Garnet was ready to depart.

Chapter Fifty-Five – Gifted power

"No." The Duchess of Firechester shook her head. "You will not convince me to help you with your quest. No other duchy has as many Paradises as this one. Why should I be forced to send out troops to four – *four* – Paradises, when Duke Larse has only one Paradise to send troops to? He'll know that my fortress is weakened and will be poised to attack while my troops are gone."

"Forgive me, Duchess Gardena, but you're not being reasonable," Leif pointed out tactlessly. "It's no one's fault that your duchy has so many Paradises. I'm sure the lintep who created them had no idea where the duchy boundaries were. Besides, Rockford has *two* Paradises. One of them has already been destroyed."

"And has *lintep* guards stationed there," Duchess Gardena pointed out sourly. "He won't need to send any troops there."

"The lintep guards will not remain for long," he told her. "They only await Duke Larse's troops and then will return to Illaria."

Telon tugged at his sleeve. Leif tried to brush him aside. This was not a good time for him to interrupt. The elf tugged more insistently. Leif saw his eyes glowing bright silver from the corner of his vision.

"A moment, Duchess Gardena," Leif said, turning away from the bemused duchess.

"They're going to try to destroy the boundary at P6," Telon whispered. "Rilla and Plyke are on their way there now. Whether they succeed or not, they will meet Eliséo at P9. That's where they think Lishe is heading."

Leif felt a headache start to pound its way to his temples. He caught Talise's concerned look, but just shook his head.

"Duchess Gardena, may I speak plainly?"

She raised an eyebrow. "You weren't already?"

He ignored her jibe.

"We have just received confirmation that the rogue lintep is within your duchy. The likelihood is that she will attempt to destroy another Paradise here. All I ask is that you take care of the people within your own lands."

Duchess Gardena stared at him coldly. "I *do* take care of the people in my duchy. I'm not like Duke Ferris who lets his people starve and freeze to death while he gathers riches for himself."

Leif opened his mouth to retaliate when he felt Talise's hand on his arm. He looked over and saw the determination in her eye.

"Duchess Gardena, forgive Duke Leif his rather tactless remark. We have seen and are well impressed with the city of Firechester. It's given us many ideas to implement in our own duchy.

"Let's put aside the issue of the four Paradises and concentrate on one for now. If you would agree to send out troops to P9, I think that will suffice for the time being. P6 is closer to Goraburg than here. I'm certain the karliki will be more than willing to station some of their people there until other arrangements can be made."

"The karliki?" Duchess Gardena asked in surprise. "They will be of no use. I cannot remember the last time a karlik was seen outside the Lesa Mountains."

Talise smiled. "We had the good fortune to meet one when we were travelling with the lintep. She was quite a talented stonemason, from what I understand. In any case, their clan leader is a dear friend to the elf king. I am certain the two of them will be able to work together to find a solution for P6."

Leif watched Duchess Gardena's reaction closely. Talise had certainly made an impact. He only hoped it was enough.

"I will agree to send out troops to P9 if I get a written treaty with Duke Larse."

Before he had a chance to explode at the absurd request, Talise tightened her cool grip on his arm.

"I give you my word that Duke Larse will sign a treaty, but we do not have time for that treaty to reach you before you give your order. In the snow, it will take at least two or three days for your troops to reach P9," Talise explained calmly.

There was a spark in Duchess Gardena's eyes. "Yes, I think that will do nicely. His oldest child can bring me the treaty. My Esmerelda has always gotten along with Félicité. I'm certain they'll enjoy some together."

Leif swallowed down his outrage. He had no option but to accept, otherwise the people of P9 would be left defenceless in this bitter winter.

"I believe Duke Larse may be more likely to ask Félicité to bring you his treaty if you send Eddarn to play with Constantina," Talise said without pause. The light went out of Duchess Gardena's eyes. "I'm certain he would simply love to ride on a crystal dragon. What eleven-year-old child wouldn't?"

Leif closed his eyes briefly and thanked his lucky stars for Talise. With her quick wit, she had successfully negotiated a covert hostage swap. It was an awful way to ensure peace between the duchies, but he could not think of a better solution in the time they had available.

* * *

Twilight waned as they finally came upon a snow-covered village. Judging by Kora's map, it was Hazelston. Pér had insisted it was a lintep settlement, but there was no visible indication of that as the three of them walked the white streets. Hoarfrost had stopped when the streets became too narrow for him. Eliséo had left him with reassurances that they would return with whatever food they could scrounge up. He feared for the crystal dragon. There was no food to be seen for a creature his size and Hoarfrost had not eaten since before the blizzard.

"There won't be any food here," Luisella said softly, as snow crunched beneath their feet. "Not for Hoarfrost. Possibly not even for us."

Eliséo did not answer. He saw windows close quietly but quickly as they approached. A few curious children found ways to peek through the cracks and holes in wooden doors as their parents dragged them back. Raeslin drew closer to them, her usual good humour vanished.

"There must be a tavern somewhere. Every village in the Outworld has one," he told them. "Keep your eyes open for it."

They walked further into the village without seeing anything resembling a tavern or an inn. What they did see was a group of young men and women with large wooden brooms, sweeping away piles of snow to clear pathways. As Eliséo and his party approached, the villagers stopped sweeping and looked at them silently. There was no welcome in their eyes.

"Can we offer our assistance?" Eliséo asked them with a short nod. They all looked to one woman who stood straighter than the rest of them.

"We have no coin to pay you with," she replied warily.

"Would you happen to have a meal to share?" he asked hopefully. "We have not had a hot meal in longer than I care to remember."

The woman grinned. "*That* we can help you with. Brooms are over there. We can share a meal when our work is done."

Eliséo looked over to the shed the woman had indicated then over the streets. It would take them forever to sweep the snow from these streets with brooms, no matter how many hands were there to help.

"Allow me," he said as he motioned for them to lower their brooms. The villagers watched him curiously as his eyes, he knew, glowed bright silver.

Raeslin, you may as well practise, Eliséo told his charge. *Start with that street, I'll start here.*

In less time than it took to explain his idea to her, Eliséo had already begun to stir up the air into a strong enough wind to clear loose snow from the street, blowing it out past the last houses in the village. With a more concentrated effort, he shaped the air into a narrow wall and pushed it along the middle of the street, scraping the compacted snow out towards the sides.

Once he had cleared that small path, he then created similar paths from each building's doorway so that people could easily access the street. Raeslin took her cue from him and worked on her own side street.

Luisella did not attempt to use her powers to help, but simply took one of the brooms and began sweeping away snow from doorsteps in his wake. The ease with which the other villagers followed her example suggested that they were not human – if they were, there would have been an outcry at his blatant use of magic. Eliséo and Raeslin continued clearing pathways down the streets. Other villagers, seeing what Luisella and the small crew were doing with brooms, came out to help with the doorways.

In a remarkably short time, the task was complete. Every building had a clear doorway and access to the streets. Once the brooms were replaced in their shed, the woman who had promised them a meal walked over to the three of them, sweat dripping down the sides of her face despite the chill.

"Well, it wasn't quite how I expected you to help, but thank you." She held out a hand. Eliséo shook it gratefully and felt a flicker of power beneath her skin. Pér had not been mistaken when he claimed this was a lintep village. Eliséo saw the woman eye him closely. "Are you an elf?"

Raeslin laughed so hard that Luisella had to quieten her before Eliséo could answer. "Forgive Raeslin. This is her first time in the Outworld. The two of us are indeed elves. My name is Eliséo. Our companion, Luisella, is..."

He looked over at her, not entirely sure how she wanted to be introduced.

"I'm a lintep," she said in a quiet, confident voice.

The lady grinned broadly. "Then welcome to Hazelston, Luisella, Eliséo and

Raeslin. I am Marinelle. Come inside and tell us what brings you to these parts in such unkind weather."

"You mean to destroy the Paradises," Marinelle repeated a second time. "Really *destroy* them."

Eliséo nodded as took a bite of the pumpkin bread which had been laid out with the leek and radish soup.

"What will happen to all of the power within the boundary?"

Luisella gripped his arm tightly under the table.

How does she know? she asked directly to his mind. Eliséo was wondering the same thing himself.

"Ophélie asked for volunteers from this village to help create one of her Paradises. Will the power be returned to any of the lintep's descendants who are still alive?" Marinelle asked.

Eliséo replied cautiously. "I do not believe that has been done so far."

"Why not?" Marinelle threw her spoon into her bowl, careless of the splash as droplets of soup flew onto her shirt. "Who else should receive that power but the families who gave it up in the first place?"

Eliséo made to answer, but Luisella released her vice grip on his arm and patted it gently.

"As I understand it, the power was released – not given to anyone."

"Released how?" Marinelle asked curiously. "Power does not general simply disappear unless a lintep dies without gifting it to someone."

A wary silence settled over them. Eliséo had never heard of a lintep gifting their power to another until Nyssa had given hers to Shuut in an attempt to keep her daughter alive and her power away from Lishe. In this village, it appeared to be a regular occurrence.

He quickly relayed the information to all elves on this mission and asked them to check if any of the Illarian lintep knew of this practice. They sat in silence. Marinelle leaned back in her chair, arms crossed over her chest. A few of the others who had helped sweep the streets shared confused glances or indifferent shrugs.

Aislen has read of this practice in the library, Ensil finally told him, relaying the information to all elves concerned. *It seems to be quite common outside of Illaria. Generally, the power is transferred within families – the least powerful inheriting the power. If there are no family members to whom the power may be transferred, that appears to be the only situation where the power is lost.*

It becomes rather vague when the concept of children arises. There is no exact information on whether the children born from these lintep take a portion of that power or not. It is also unclear what happens when a lintep who has inherited power then gifts their power to another lintep – whether that lintep inherits both sets of power or only the one which originally belonged to the gifting lintep.

Eliséo listened closely, his hand brushing against Luisella's so that she could hear everything. She gasped, drawing looks from the other lintep in the room.

"Are we going to sit here in silence forever or are you going to answer my question? How was the power released?"

305

"In a way that is no longer possible," Eliséo replied evasively. He took his time eating a large spoon of soup, trying to decide what to tell this lintep.

Lukys says they are free to come to the Paradises, Kari told him, *but we cannot wait for them to arrive if we have a chance to destroy a Paradise before Lishe steals any more power.*

"Out of interest, which Paradise was the one your village helped with?"

Marinelle gestured vaguely south. "Over near the Bramble River."

Though Eliséo was the trained ambassador, it was Luisella who reacted first.

"We've just come from there. Some of the power has already been taken. As soon as you can safely ride through this snow, I would suggest whichever of you has a claim to that power should go there and protect it until we can return.

"The rogue lintep is surely heading to another Paradise. We intend to intercept and stop her there before she has the chance to steal anymore power."

It was not the way Eliséo would have done it, but it certainly had the desired effect. Marinelle was instantly gave instructions to her people to gather anyone who had a claim to that power. If they decided to take matters into their own hands and managed to destroy the Paradise themselves, at least it would mean that the power was out of Lishe's reach and not with any one single lintep.

Eliséo and Raeslin worked together to create an air platform for Hoarfrost. They transported him to the village square where there was just enough room for him to get airborne. The gasps of amazement and children squealing with joy at the sight of the clear crystal dragon brought a smile to Eliséo's face. If only life were always so simple and full of joy.

One day, Elessa told him. *Once this is all over, you will have the chance to give that simplicity and freedom to your people.*

He did not reply. There was nothing to say. At heart, they both knew it was never going to be as that simple.

Luisella was looking at him questioningly. He shook his head. This was not her problem, there was nothing she could do to help him.

With farewells to the villagers and many thanks for the warm meal, the three of them mounted the crystal dragon, to the delight of the lintep children. Hoarfrost beat his wings laboriously. It would still take a good day of flying to reach P9. Hoarfrost was visibly exhausted, but there would be no relief for him in a village like this. He needed a decent hunting ground and a warm place to rest.

With a great deal of effort, Hoarfrost took flight and turned towards P9. Eliséo hoped they would make it.

Chapter Fifty-Six – Dysfunctional family

Snowcrest landed in Rockford with a painstakingly drafted treaty and a delighted little boy who did not understand that he was to be taken hostage by Duke Larse in return for the duke's daughter, Félicité. Duchess Gardena had decided against explaining the real reason behind his departure to her son.

"Let him think it's because I thought he might enjoy a flight on a crystal dragon," she had told Leif before they left.

For the first time since they'd met, he found himself agreeing with her. It would not be in the poor boy's best interest to know that he was in danger should either of the duchies break the treaty.

Though Rockford was the most distant of all the duchies, Deuterfoss had always shared a close relationship with the dukes and duchesses of that region. Perhaps it was because they were not forced to see each other very often by reason of distance.

Leif found it odd that it was here, where he felt most at home, that he spent so little time. Duke Larse read through the treaty with a careful eye, every now and then looking up at Eddarn, who was already delighting Constantina with stories of his flight upon the crystal dragon. Félicité was listening closely, but not wanting to appear too interested. Their mother watched them with a serene smile as her husband continued to read.

"Duchess Gardena agreed to these terms?" he asked casually, clearly not wanting to alert his family of the delicate matter at hand.

"She penned the document herself," Leif told him seriously. "None of the clauses are negotiable, though I might add that myself and Lady Talise insisted on a number of changes in your favour before the document was finalised."

Duke Larse's laughter boomed throughout the room, earning him a few surprised looks. He ignored them all.

"Well then, if my wife agrees, I'll sign the papers now. Here Cassia. Read this and see if it meets with your approval while Duke Leif tells me more about these Paradises."

Leif heaved a sigh of relief. Duke Larse had certainly been the easiest of the rulers to deal with. Together with Talise and Telon, they walked over to a heavy wooden table. Leif laid out the map and pointed out the location of the two Paradises in Rockford.

"This one is already in desperate need of your troops. The boundary was destroyed some weeks ago and we left the inhabitants in tenuous circumstances. There is a small group of lintep guards still stationed there, awaiting the arrival of your troops.

"I would suggest sending out skilled tradesmen. These Paradises have little or no security. There are no locks or bars on their windows and doors. They have no guards of their own or, I daresay, effective weapons. As far as I understand, they have pottery enough to make some small trades to begin with however..." Leif looked at Duke Larse hesitantly. "They have no money."

Duke Larse took a pause. "I see. So, they're a bartering society then?"

"Not exactly," Talise answered when Leif stumbled. "They live as one big family. A dysfunctional one at the best of times, but a family, nonetheless. There is one kitchen which cooks for the entire village. They dine together in a large hall and freely share all goods in the village. No one asks for payment for services or wares. The very thought is unknown to them."

Duke Larse was at a loss for words. Leif found it laughable how similar his own reaction had been as Brynt took him for a tour around Bryntown when he had first arrived.

Eventually, Duke Larse found his voice. "So, what you're trying to tell me is to bring a skilled tradesman in *every* skill I can and pouches of money to trade with them so that they can begin to trade with other cities and villages."

Leif nodded. "That about sums it up. Yes. And the sooner the better. By the time you get there, you might need to implement some form of damage control. Some of the Paradisians have quite the temper and were not too well impressed that their way of life was effectively destroyed."

Duke Larse looked him in the eye. "It's a good thing I like you, Leif, or I wouldn't even consider it."

"That's a lie and we both know it." Leif smiled. "You care too much for the people in your duchy to do nothing when they need you. Now, we are needed elsewhere. As soon as Félicité is ready, we will escort her to Firechester and continue to deal with this mess that is the Paradises."

* * *

They landed in the crater of the Drakos Mountains at dusk. Pyrid and Garnet had flown almost all day. They stopped only once, at the Bramble River, for a long drink from the near freezing waters before resuming their journey.

Plyke looked at the resting dragons and drank in the sight. The last time they had been here, everything had been so tense. Shuut had still been mostly unconscious. Rilla had realised her mother was alive and Shuut was her half-sister. They had fled before any of the crystal dragons had a chance to realise who Rilla was for fear that they would manipulate her.

A wave of emotions hit him like a stone. Plyke almost doubled over at the intensity of it. Uncertainty, guilt, loss, hope, love, hurt – overwhelming hurt. He looked around to see who was giving off these emotions. Almost everyone looked excited to be here. Everyone except Shuut. She was staring blankly at the crater of dragons. If he didn't know any better, Plyke would have dismissed her as the source of the violent emotions, but he knew her. He knew the turbulent history she shared with these dragons.

Now that they were here, Garnet had flown off to find extra volunteers and Pyrid had scorched himself a bit of the earth to lie down on. The old dragon was clearly exhausted. He should not be making such trips himself anymore but would not listen to the other dragons who had tried to convince him to leave the adventure to them.

Plyke looked up as a lone clear crystal dragon approached them. He cumbersomely wove his way through the other dragons littered on the ground before him, eventually beating his wings just enough to skim over the tops of them. The dragon ignored the rest of them and landed in front of Shuut – a respectful distance away.

She glared at him coldly, obviously refusing to be the first to speak. The dragon hung his head, clearly unable to look her in the eye.

"Did Nyssa give you my message?" he asked in a low grumble.

"Nyssa is dead," Shuut informed him shortly.

"I ... They told me," he said quietly. "I'm sorry, Shuut. I never agreed with Celtan's plan. I did not want them to trick you and Nyssa."

"Then why did you let them?" Shuut asked, her voice cracking ever so slightly.

Groldor stretched out a paw and placed a talon gently on her shoulder. "I am not the head dragon. What Celtan says, goes. I had no choice in the matter, but I *never* agreed."

Shuut remained silent. Plyke felt all that hurt come flooding back to her. Nyssa abandoning Shuut to her banwep father for no reason other than the dragons convinced her to. Nyssa and Shuut both being told the other was dead so that Nyssa could more easily bear another child. The dragons sending Shuut on a fool's errand to find her sister in a Paradise because their mother had abandoned Rilla there.

Everything the dragons had ever done to her came flooding back, and Plyke could feel it crashing into her walls over, and over and over, again. Shuut could not hold out against it all. She fell to the ground in a sobbing heap.

Rilla was instantly by her side, an arm thrown lovingly around her shoulder. The two of them clung to each other as though nothing else in the world existed but the two of them. Plyke watched as Groldor slowly backed away, leaving the two of them to mend as well as they could. Upset for his cousins, Plyke walked over to comfort them. He placed his arms around them, pulling them in for a tight hug so that he could feel everything they did. Celtan had ruined both of their lives to manipulate the prophecy. It had never been a fair life for either of them.

"Pyrid, let me take your place," Groldor begged him. "I want to fly with Shuut, if she'll let me."

"Talk to Garnet. He's rounding up whichever other dragons want to help us. We need at least two to go back to Illaria. Some more of the lintep are insisting on coming along on this little adventure."

"Let Garnet take another dragon back with him. I'll come on with you, to wherever it is you're going," Groldor insisted.

Plyke had been listening to the entire exchange. All the dragons were ignoring everyone but Shuut. They barely knew any of the people. He walked up to the fire opal and the clear crystal dragon.

"We still need someone to take Anya to Goraburg," he told them, nodding over towards the karlik. "She needs to ask Ilya if he will send karliki to P6."

"P6?" Groldor looked over at him in confusion. "What are you talking about human?"

Plyke stared at him coldly. "I'm not a human. I happen to be Rilla and Shuut's cousin." Absurdly, he felt himself losing his temper. Within seconds, Tika was by his side, squeezing his hand. It instantly calmed him down. Plyke looked over at his Partner and smiled gratefully.

Plyke explained the plan to Groldor, as his other companions, including Rilla and Shuut, drew closer to them. By the time he was finished, Garnet had returned with a large clear crystal dragon and an even larger emerald one.

"Loreli has agreed to take Anya to Goraburg and then wait with a group of her scouts on the northern edge of the Lesa Mountains until the karliki are ready to be escorted to P6. Malachite," he said, flicking his snout towards the emerald dragon, "will fly to Illaria to gather some of the other lintep who wish to join us."

"Aye, that's a good idea," Pyrid agreed. "Malachite will be able to carry no less than five people herself. Do you know the way to Illaria?"

Malachite shook her head, her elongated neck swaying gently. "I've never been that far south."

"Garnet, will you go back with her? Show her the way?" Pyrid asked. "Then the two of you can meet us at P9."

Garnet reluctantly agreed. Plyke could tell that he really did not want to go back to Illaria again and miss out on the 'fun' the rest of them were going to have.

"That settles it then," Groldor announced. "I will take Garnet's place."

Plyke expected Shuut to object, but she remained oddly quiet.

* * *

By dusk, Eliséo could see the faint line of a stream on the horizon. On Kora's map, P9 was on this side of the river. Leaning as far over Raeslin as he could, he reached out a hand to touch Luisella's skin.

Can you ask Hoarfrost to find a place to land? I don't want us to be ambushed by Lishe during the night.

No sooner had he finished the thought than Hoarfrost had altered his flying pattern into a wide circle. Eliséo soon saw the problem as clearly as though he was reading Hoarfrost's mind. There was nowhere to land. The blizzard had covered everything in a thick layer of snow. They would not know how deep it was until they had landed and, by then, it would be too late.

Over by the stream, the snow will be thinner. Any snow on the bank will have fallen into the water and been carried away. Luisella translated Hoarfrost's thought to him. *We have no choice but to land there. It's our best hope.*

Eliséo did not like it but knew there was no point in arguing. They would simply have to hope that Lishe did not notice them as they swooped in for a landing.

Eliséo, is that you? Farrow's voice was in his mind. Eliséo scanned the skies in search of another dragon. In the distance, he saw a blur in the sky.

Any luck? Eliséo asked him.

Nothing. She must have gone straight to P9 from P5.

We assume so too, Eliséo told him. *Everyone is converging here. The lintep should be joining us within a day.*

The appearance of another dragon, two more elves and another lintep eased his mind. Lishe would not attack so many people at once. Even *she* could not be so irrational.

Rilla stared at the boundary of P6 feeling hopeless. It would all have been much easier if the crystal dragons had agreed to give them another heart, even just until the Paradises were destroyed. Grudgingly, she admitted that it would likely cause more problems if more people became aware of the power the hearts could channel.

"You ready to try now?" Plyke asked as he came up behind her. He and Pér had been teaching her the tune they had sung at P2. She already knew the words – they were using the same ones as they normally did with the heart.

Rilla shrugged. "Not really, but let's do it anyway."

"This time, I'm not asking you to keep your feelings bottled up like we did in the castle. We need you to let as much of those feelings into the song as you can. Got it?"

Rilla nodded, but looked over to make sure Isis was nearby. She did not trust herself to just let her feelings flow out through her power into her song. What if it was too much and her power tried to soar away with the rest of the Paradise boundary? What if it wasn't enough and it didn't work at all?

Without meaning to, she found herself backing away from the boundary, Plyke and Pér, straight into the fire mistress. Isis placed a firm hand on the small of her back and gently pushed her forward.

"No one has ever lost their power by singing," Isis reminded her. "Just try it, Rilla. They can't ask more of you than that."

Rilla closed her eyes for long seconds, taking ten deep breaths, calming herself as Master Bastienne had taught her. She couldn't believe how well it seemed to work but was secretly very relieved that it did.

She opened her eyes and saw where Plyke and Pér were waiting for her. Off to one side, Tika stood huddled in his travelling cloak, trying to ward off the cold. It only took her a moment to realise what was wrong with this. The entire reason Tika was with them was because Plyke insisted he come. They were Partners and should be allowed to do everything together, to strengthen their bond to the point where death could not separate them.

Smiling, Rilla held out a hand to him and led him over to his Partner. Tika beamed at her. It almost looked like he was glowing with happiness. If he had been a lintep, he would be infusing everyone with his happiness. It was such a shame he had been born without any magic.

The three of them, Rilla, Tika and Plyke, held hands with the two boys reaching out a hand each to rest on Pér's neck. Pér strummed a few notes on his lute before beginning the tune they had been practising over and over again. With a nod of his head, he led them into the song. All four of them sang the words, softly at first, then louder and louder growing more elated as they completed the phrase each time.

"*Be not afraid to fly alone. Fly free to the skies.*"

Rilla felt her heart soar. She felt a part of herself unlock. It did not frighten her that the wall she kept so closely guarded in her mind was now open to anyone who might wish to intrude. No one here would dare do that to her. She trusted them all. She was not afraid of them. She was *free* with them.

At a gasp behind her, Rilla opened eyes she had not realised she had closed. The boundary wall was wavering. It was not the same as with the other two Paradises, but something was definitely happening. Single wisps of power were escaping the boundary's hold on them and flying off into the sky, free for the first time in years.

She gripped Tika and Plyke's hands and motioned towards the Paradise. Their eyes grew wide with wonder. All three of them sang louder and louder as more and more bits of power detached from the boundary. It was working!

At least, she thought it was working, until she looked closer and saw that some of the wisps of power struggling to free themselves were being held back by other powers clinging to them.

It all made sense now – the powers had a sort of consciousness all of their own. They could act, even without a lintep to work with. These powers had lived together for years now. Clearly, some had become more dominant, clingier, than others, and refused to let everything end. Even with the song, they still were afraid to fly alone, to fly free to the skies. The song was not enough.

"Time to stop now." Kora's voice broke through the song. Rilla stopped and looked at her in surprise, as did the others. "You've been at it for a long time. Whichever of the powers that were going to leave have left now. There's nothing more we can do here. We need to keep going to P9. At least we know we're on the right track."

Chapter Fifty-Seven – The plan

Rilla thought she would hold herself back, that she wouldn't feel anything when she saw Eliséo. After all, she knew he was alive and well, and had done a marvellous job of ignoring her lately. She knew he had challenged his sister to the crown and won. She knew all of this ... but still she saw him in her mind as the unconscious lump they had returned to Silvaren, waking only long enough to panic at what they – *she* – had forced him into.

Instead, as soon as Groldor landed and Rilla spotted her elf, she ran headlong towards him, nearly bowling him over with the force of her embrace. She felt his surprise doubly through Elessa, and skin contact, but was elated when his surprise turned to happiness and relief as he hugged her tightly. He was just as pleased to see her alive and well as she was to see him.

Belatedly, Rilla noticed how many people and dragons were gathered in this one place and disentangled herself from her elf. She vaguely recognised some of the elves but was surprised to see Liessa standing by Eliséo's side looking at her with mild amusement. Without knowing why, it made Rilla blush and step away from Eliséo.

"I see being crowned king has not changed you," Liessa commented with a raised eyebrow.

"Not a bit!" Eliséo cried out to her as Tika and Plyke crashed into him with hugs. Rilla laughed as Kora gently pulled the boys away from Eliséo.

"Where do we stand?" she asked him. "Have you seen her? Has she been here yet?"

It was not Eliséo who answered. Luisella, held close by Braedan, spoke up.

"There is some small evidence that this Paradise has been tampered with, but not to the degree that P5 was. We have not found a shelter or her horse, which means she can't have been here for long."

Rilla thought on her words. If they had not found Lishe's shelter, either she didn't have one or it was so well hidden that looking for it would be pointless. From up in the sky, she had not noticed many trees or scrub for Lishe to hide in.

"She's in the Paradise," she said quietly. Eighteen sets of eyes turned on her. "There's nowhere else she could be hiding. But from within the Paradise, she could be safe from view and stealing power at the same time. That's what I would do if I was her anyway."

There was a stunned silence as everyone considered her words.

"Then we go in there and get her out," Shuut growled. "She can't hide from us forever."

Rilla shook her head. "That's just the point. She *can* hide from us forever. But we can draw her out. You and I."

Shuut grinned. "You read my mind."

"Absolutely not!" cried Lukys. "With your grandfather absent, *I* am responsible for the two of you. I will not allow you to offer yourselves as bait for a rogue lintep. Whatever would I say to Aaron if she captures you?"

Rilla crossed her arms. "Glad to see you're thinking of our safety first and Lord Aaron's opinion of you second."

"What's *your* plan then?" asked Shuut.

"We simply destroy the Paradise, so she will have nowhere to hide, and then capture her and relieve her of the powers she has stolen."

"As easy as that, is it?" asked Plyke indignantly. "Then why haven't you already done it?"

Lukys went red in the face and clenched his fists by his side. Rilla sighed. This was not going well for any of them.

"May I make a suggestion?" Isis asked timidly. Rilla crowded round with the others as Isis detailed her plan.

* * *

Lishe sat placidly inside the Paradise, back against a tree as she steadily drew out power after power from the boundary. She could hear her horse snuffling over the ground looking for whatever the blizzard left behind. After their initial dispute over the mare exiting the makeshift shelter and walking miles over blizzard-ruined fields, they had come to an understanding. Lishe was in charge and the mare would follow blindly or be given the biggest walloping of her life.

A blurred movement beyond the boundary caught her attention. Curious, she slipped the latest bit of power in with the others – they could coddle it until it felt secure – before a stern word to her mare had it hiding behind a nearby clump of trees. Lishe could not be bothered wasting energy on making both of them invisible as the mare could not be relied on to remain silent.

Lishe rose, stretched out her arms and arched her back like a cat. She could not remember how long she had been sitting there, siphoning off sliver after sliver of power. With barely a second thought, she wrapped power around herself to blend in with the background and stepped through the boundary into the Outworld.

The sight before her was a curious one. The little brat and two boys were off to one side, singing a rhyme about a bird or some such nonsense. She ignored them for the time being – a song could not do her any harm.

What caught her interest was the banwep. She was watching the others from a distance but was all alone. Lishe's lips curled in a triumphant smile. At last, she would have Nyssa's power. Lord Aaron was nowhere to be seen and no one else was capable of stopping her – of *that* she was quite certain.

Still wrapped in her power, she walked towards the banwep, sending tendrils out in front of her. With a burst of speed, she wrapped her power around the banwep's head, trapping Nyssa's power within.

The banwep turned to her with a mocking smile and attacked. Lishe flinched as Nyssa's power sparked out of the banwep's very skin. It clawed its way up to the banwep's neck, pushing and shoving until Lishe's power was thrown off.

"Looks like you underestimated me," the woman sneered at her.

Lishe did not bother to reply, but instead threw her power around the banwep's entire body. At least, she tried to. The banwep had some sort of barrier that stopped Lishe's power from entrapping her.

Around the banwep, people appeared out of thin air. She instantly recognised Lukys and Kora among them. Angrily, she threw tendrils of power out, quickly assessing which were lintep. There were six. Grinding her teeth, she trapped the weakest one

314

and struggled to trap the others. They created shields like the banwep so that she could not surround them easily. But they underestimated how much power she had.

Throwing caution to the wind, Lishe unleashed the full measure of her power, spreading it out as a dome to cover all those in front of her, even those whose pointed ears marked them out as elves.

Within the dome, she felt her powers acting on instinct. They knew what she wanted to do and rushed to please her. Soon, every elf and the weaker two lintep had a mind snare. Only the banwep, Kora, Lukys and the twins provided a challenge. She'd rarely had anything to do with Braedan and Daegan – not since she discovered they had less power than Lord Aaron's children. Her powers focused on the two of them and eventually overcame their struggles.

Lishe modified her dome to concentrate on the three remaining lintep. The others all lay motionless on the snow. Each of them did it in different ways, but their power was moulded around themselves in such a way that her power could not quite get a hold on them. She could not squeeze in, no matter how hard she tried.

She had time. She could wait until they ran out of energy. The thought gave her pause. Could she steal their energy with their power surrounding them? It was worth a try.

* * *

"Now!" Rilla yelled.

While they were singing Kora's lullaby, she had been surreptitiously watching Shuut and the others. It took a great deal of effort to stay where she was when Lishe attacked Shuut, but Rilla forced herself to remain seated. She watched for their cue. Once the rest of the group appeared from behind the elves' mist bubble, it was their turn.

Eliséo dissipated the mist bubble around Isis and Pér. Though Plyke and Rilla had insisted that everyone but Pér and Tika should help capture Lishe, Eliséo and Isis had refused to leave them unguarded when Lishe might turn her attention to them at any time.

Pér instantly began to play the Paradise-breaking song. Rilla, Plyke and Tika sang along with him. Even Eliséo and Isis joined in, everyone making skin contact. Rilla doubted that Eliséo or Tika could make much difference to the song's power, but she was willing to try anything to push them over that barrier they could not seem to surmount.

It was difficult to concentrate on the Paradise while the others were under attack, but Rilla knew it was their best chance. She focused all her emotions into the song and sang as loudly as she could, not knowing if the volume made any difference.

Just as with P6, slivers of the power making up the boundary began to detach and fly off into the sky. Encouraged by the sight, Rilla squeezed Eliséo and Tika's hands. They returned her grip and sang ever louder. With a sudden burst, Rilla realised she could harness their feelings as well.

Careful not to touch anything but Eliséo and Tika's feelings, she drew on them and added them to her own. It appeared to magnify the effect of her song. With a quick thought to Plyke, Pér and Isis, they soon emulated what she was doing. The song's power grew with such intensity that ever more slivers of power began to drift away from the Paradise.

* * *

"*No!*"

Tika heard the anguished scream and turned to see that Lishe had finally realised what they were doing. He continued to sing with the others with ever-growing urgency. If they were going to make this work and defeat Lishe, it would be now. It *had* to be now. If they couldn't beat her with so many lintep, elves and crystal dragons helping, they never would.

He shifted his stance, allowing him to watch Lishe. Tika knew he was powerless against her. Plyke was his only protection and even *he* was not yet well enough trained to defeat the rogue lintep. He squeezed his Partner's hand tightly.

Something was wrong. Lishe did not abandon the others to come and stop them. This was the moment when she should have been so overcome with anger that she recklessly turned her back on the skilled lintep she effectively had trapped and come after *them*. But she wasn't. Instead, after that single scream, Lishe ignored the six singers, the elves and lintep lying in the snow at her feet, and Shuut, Kora and Lukys who seemed transfixed in place.

Lishe was looking at something *inside* the Paradise. By the time Tika figured out what she was doing, it was already too late. A horse was galloping towards them with wild eyes. It skittered and reared up not twenty yards from them. Tika felt Plyke send a tendril of power through his mind and over towards the horse. He felt the battle within the horse between Lishe and Plyke. The poor mare zigzagged onwards, sometimes haltingly prancing on the spot, clearly torn between the two powers.

Talk to it, Tika. Plyke pleaded. *Calm it down.*

When the tendril reached the horse, Tika murmured soft noises to it, trying his best to calm the frantic mare, but there was only so much he could do with Lishe still in her mind. He could sense that she was coming over to trample them all, but he couldn't do anything from where he was.

Tika shook his hands free and walked slowly forward, arms outstretched. He could feel Plyke's tendril still coursing through his mind and out towards the horse. He continued to talk calmly and softly to it as he approached the distraught horse. She skittered to the side and Tika managed to lay one hand on her neck and place the other in front of her nose. He felt her pulse racing. The whites of her eyes were showing, and her nostrils flared. She pranced on the spot as Tika stroked her neck.

He could feel the mare struggle against Lishe's commands to trample them. With one hand, he unclipped his cloak and draped it over the horse like a rope. Careful to keep murmuring soothing sounds to the horse, Tika began to slowly lead the mare to his friends, who continued to sing.

Everything was going to be fine. He could feel it. He kept his hand on the horse as he gently led it forwards.

Tika sensed it too late. Lishe's thoughts broke through to the horse again. Tika watched helplessly as the mare reared up and knocked him to the ground. He felt the crushing weight of her sharp hooves on top of him.

Chapter Fifty-Eight – Traumatised

Arishen sat at his workbench, heart pounding as he helplessly watched Tika being crushed by a frenzied horse. His scarred hands tightly gripped his tools. It hurt, but he would rather focus on that pain than the one in his mind, in his heart. He couldn't help it – a tear rolled down his cheek.

"Crying about your hands again?" Narseo taunted him.

Arishen wiped the tear away with the back of his hand. Narseo was not a bad person but he, like every other apprentice in Master Timothée's workshop, did not think Arishen belonged.

"Leave me alone," Arishen mumbled. He did not bother looking up but focused on his project. It was a simple shelf – one he should have been able to make by himself by now. The problem was that he had spent so much away from the workshop that he was falling behind in his work and the other apprentices were noticing.

"Why won't you just tell us what happened?" Narseo asked.

Arishen could feel Narseo's breath as the apprentice leaned over his workbench. They had asked him every day since his return. Mistress Kayte had healed the burns only enough so that he could return to his post as an apprentice – not enough so that the others wouldn't notice.

"Because it's none of your business," Arishen replied as he always did.

He waited for Narseo to move away and leave him to his grief. He needed to be alone. He wanted to play back his vision – to see if there was any way a lintep could heal Tika. Maybe it was possible. Maybe.

Narseo wasn't moving away. Arishen looked up to see why not. Narseo's eyes were on something over his shoulder. Arishen turned to see what it was. Fear gripped him as he watched Master Timotheé leave the workshop.

The apprentices barely waited until the door had closed behind their master before attacking. Five of them dove into Arishen's mind, searching for his memory of burning his hands.

They didn't find it.

What they *did* find was Arishen's vision of Tika being trampled by a horse, his bones crushed against the ground. Arishen felt one of them retreat, screaming, from his mind.

If that was what it took to get them out of his mind, then that's what he would do. Arishen thought of the worst visions he'd ever had. One by one, he showed them the murders in the Paradise. The apprentices were seemingly mesmerised, unable to retreat. He would make them pay for their intrusion.

Blood rushed in ears, making him deaf to the screams around him. He brought forth one final vision – the children burning in the isolation hut.

"Stop!" Narseo screamed. "Stop it!"

Arishen smiled grimly. He would give them cause never to hurt him again – never to jump into his mind again.

He shoved the memory of Erton's burning house to the front of his mind. Focused on every detail – the smell of smoke, of fire burning his hands, the screams of Erton, Torak and Belial, the knowledge that he, Arishen, had caused it all.

With a suddenness that shocked him, Arishen was free of the apprentices. There was no one in his mind, no one trying to hurt him.

Arishen opened his eyes. He didn't remember closing them.

He looked around trying to understand what had just happened. Most of the apprentices were staring at him warily. Only the few who had been in his mind at the end were sprawled on the ground, whimpering.

Master Timotheé was standing in the doorway. Arishen watched as the master carpenter stood there for a long moment, his eyes darting to each apprentice.

"What happened here?"

One of the apprentices pointed at Arishen.

"*He* did this."

Arishen clenched his fists through the pain of his scars. He stood up, noticing with grim satisfaction that the apprentices all took a step away from him.

"*They* jumped into my mind the moment you were gone. They wanted to find out what happened to my hands … so I showed them."

Narseo sat up, avoiding Arishen's gaze.

"He's a murderer, Master Timotheé. He doesn't belong here."

Arishen couldn't deny it and had no wish to. No matter what his friends tried to tell him, humans didn't belong here. At least now these apprentices feared him enough to hopefully leave him alone.

Master Timotheé gave him an odd look. Arishen thought it looked strangely like pity. He didn't really care right now. He just wanted to be away from here, to be somewhere safe … and find out if his vision of Tika had actually happened.

"Come, Arishen," Master Timotheé said. "I'm taking you to the castle."

Arishen followed him wordlessly. He noticed the master carpenter was careful not to touch his skin the entire walk to the castle, right up until they had to cross the bridge. Arishen could sense his hesitation.

"Don't worry. I'll keep my mind clear if you keep out of my thoughts."

Again, there was that odd look. Master Timotheé said nothing but nodded. Together, they crossed the bridge. As soon as they were past the barrier, the master carpenter let go of his hand. He was strangely silent the entire way to a classroom with a snake wrapped around a sceptre carved into the door.

"Wait here," Master Timotheé said.

He knocked on the door and entered, leaving Arishen in the hallway. The hallway was empty. Arishen sat on one of the windowsills facing the inner courtyard. There were a handful of students practising with their white stones, just as on the first day he had arrived in Illaria. That had been so many months ago now. He didn't think much had changed in that time.

Humans, most of them anyway, still did not appear to be very welcome in the town of Illaria, despite a lot of the royal family having close ties to them. He wondered if any of them knew or could understand what it had been like for him living in the town, away from them all. Did they know he had to be escorted to and from the workshop every day by Master Reuben to ensure no one attacked him? Did they know he felt under threat every time he was around the other apprentices? He wasn't free here. He couldn't visit his friends whenever he wanted to – not without a lintep to escort him into the castle. He was isolated, and scared.

The door opened. Arishen looked up. Master Timotheé and Mistress Kayte walked over to him.

"I'm sorry, Arishen, but your apprenticeship isn't working," Master Timotheé told him. "You're a good worker, and you have skill, but…"

"I don't fit in with your other apprentices," Arishen finished his sentence. "Don't worry, I'd be saying the same thing if I were you."

Master Timotheé looked like he was going to say something else. Instead, he patted Arishen's shoulder and walked away, leaving Arishen with Mistress Kayte.

"Until further notice, you will be under my protection. I will speak to Princess Aislen about it. You will be given quarters somewhere safe in the castle. In return, I expect you not to traumatise anyone else."

Arishen narrowed his eyes at her. "As long as everyone stays out of my head, I won't try to *traumatise* them."

"Agreed."

Arishen noticed that Kayte did not hold out her hand to shake on their agreement. In truth, he did not blame her.

A thought occurred to him.

"Is Mistress Emeline in the castle? I had a vision I need to show her."

Kayte looked for a moment as though she would deny him. Instead, she took him down the hall to another room. This one had a tri-wave symbol on it. She knocked and waited until the door was opened.

"Kayte, Arishen, what a pleasant surprise."

Mistress Emeline looked genuinely pleased to see him. That confused Arishen. Most lintep just barely tolerated his presence.

"Emeline, the boy wants to show you a vision. It can wait until after class. Do not let him out of your sight until he is returned to me. He will not be returning to his apprenticeship in the town."

Arishen smouldered inside. It was no wonder Rilla didn't get along with this teacher. She was rude and dismissive. Emeline smiled sweetly.

"Arishen is welcome to stay in my class all day if you are otherwise occupied."

Kayte looked surprised, and well she should if she thought so little of him. Arishen let out a breath he hadn't realised he was holding. Emeline ushered him into her classroom.

"Class, you are graced by the presence of Illaria's only human seer. Please be respectful towards him and do not attempt to jump into his mind without his consent. Any who do so will be severely punished. Am I understood?"

The class chorused with a round of "Yes, Mistress Emeline."

Arishen found it strange that he felt more comfortable here, around students that were learning to use their mind skills, than in a workshop where they were only meant to be using their powers to help with their carpentry.

"Please continue on with your work while I attend to Arishen's latest vision."

Emeline led him over to a set of chairs at the front of the room. Tears prickled his eyes as he prepared to show her.

"It isn't a nice one," he told her through a voice thick with emotion. "I ... I think one of my friends has died."

Suddenly, Emeline's arms were wrapped around him. Arishen stiffened in shock until he realised she was hugging him. When was the last time anyone had hugged him? Tears flooded down his face, soaking the shoulder of Emeline's shirt.

"You poor dear," she said, pulling him gently away from her. "Show me your vision. We'll see if there is anything to be done."

Arishen nodded and gathered his courage to show her his vision of Tika's death.

Chapter Fifty-Nine – Partners

Tika opened his eyes and looked around. Plyke was crouched over him, tears falling down his cheeks and through the air.

"Help him! Someone help him!" Plyke's voice cracked. Rilla and Pér knelt by his side with Isis and Eliséo behind them.

They looked down at him helplessly. Tika sat up, not understanding why they had to help him. What was wrong with him?

"Plyke, I'm fine," he said, standing up.

No one replied. They weren't looking at him anymore – they were still looking down. Tika followed their gaze and saw himself lying there, skull kicked in and thick, sticky blood covering his entire crushed body.

"Plyke, I'm here," he said. "Can't you see me?"

Plyke did not reply. Instead, he roared out a blood-curdling sound. Guilt and sorrow flowed out of him. Tika could feel it as if it was part of himself. Apparently, so could everyone else. They all fell to the ground, moaning.

In the distance, Tika could see Lishe had also fallen to the ground. Her power must have retreated into itself because he could now see Shuut, Kora and King Lukys lying on the ground, also moaning in sadness.

Tika reached out and tried to grip Plyke's shoulder but his fingers passed straight through him.

"Plyke, *please*!" Tika cried out mournfully. "I'm *here*. Just use our Partner bond and you'll see me."

Plyke did not react. He kept crying, and apologising, over and over and over again. Was it true then? Would their Partnership really not work because Plyke was a lintep?

Tika could not and would not believe that. If he was still here, there must be a reason. He would *make* Plyke see him if it was the last thing he did. But how?

* * *

Pér fought against the guilty, sorrowful stupor. He had struggled against such crushing waves of feeling with Kora, when she had returned from the Outworld with her mother, brothers and little sister dead. It was not a pleasant thing to do, nor was it easy, but it was something he knew he could do because he had done it before, many times.

He stretched out his fingers towards his lute. It had fallen from his grasp when Plyke's feelings had overwhelmed him. Sluggishly, he curled his fingers around the wood and laboriously dragged it to himself. It took all the strength he had to roll onto his back – he did not have the will to sit. Pér heaved the lute onto his chest and tried to strum a few strings. He could not manage more than one. It was not enough.

* * *

Tika watched as Pér tried to play his lute. He knew there was magic involved with it somehow. He understood that Pér was trying to help his son. But Plyke's grief was clearly overwhelming him. Tika had to do something to help. Otherwise all the elves and lintep would die from exposure in the snow.

Desperately, Tika looked around to see if anyone else had managed to save themselves from Plyke's outpouring of emotion. Even the dragons were lying motionless. Tika stubbornly strode over to Pér and tried to lift the muscular lintep, but his hands slipped right through him. He even tried to pick up the lute but could not grasp it.

There was a sudden tug in his head as he walked further away from Plyke. Tika turned and looked back towards his Partner. Between them was a thin, silvery thread. Tika threw back his head and laughed long and hard. He had died with part of Plyke's power going through him. It looked like in death that power had stuck with him.

Tika turned back to Pér, who was still struggling to play his lute, and thought back on everything he had every overheard about using lintep powers. He sat by Pér's side, reached out and gently drew part of the silver thread over Pér's head. He focused on every pleasant memory he could think of, trying to dislodge Plyke's guilt and sorrow from Pér's mind.

There was a flicker of relief on the minstrel's face. Tika renewed his efforts. He thought of his Partnership with Plyke, his first meeting with the elves, his arrival in Illaria, Plyke's acceptance of his powers, his own appointment as stablehand in Illaria, destroying their Paradise and ending Erton's oppression, helping all the people in their Paradise reunite with each other.

Pér moved his hands over his lute, without attempting to sit up. From where he lay on the ground, he strummed a gentle tune. Tika recognised it as Pér's ballad – the song he had sung for Kora. There was little in it about Plyke or Tika, but it was a song of love and hope. It was a song which might pull others out of their stupor.

* * *

Kora lay on her stomach in the freezing snow. Lishe's power had retreated, quite suddenly, and a crushing weight of sadness had pushed Kora over – wave after wave of guilt kept her down. It made her remember every other time she had felt this way.

Finding her Fredryck and little Adina lying dead in the grass, their mother dying while trying to save Vaughn. She had felt guilty about that, even though she was not the one who had killed them. She remembered how she had wished it was herself lying there instead of her little sister. She knew Adina was everyone's favourite – had always been her father's favourite.

Vaughn wasn't far behind. He had been younger than Kora, but he had already grown into such a responsible young boy. Their father had loved him for that, but Kora had loved him for bringing her laughter. No matter how she felt, if lessons had gone badly, or she'd fought with another student in class, Vaughn had always made her feel better. She had been devastated when he died, especially knowing that he had died trying to save their little brother.

Fredryck had been the quiet one. He was usually overlooked because of it, but Kora knew the depth of feeling inside him. Too often had she found him curled up in a ball on his bed, crying softly into his pillows. He was the only person Vaughn couldn't ever help. Vaughn had always come to get Kora when Fredryck was upset. Fredryck had not wanted cheering up. He only wanted someone to sit with him until the tears dried up. Kora was the one who did that for him, running her fingers through his tangled hair and singing softly to him.

It took her a moment to realise it, but that was what their mother had done. Graesyn had been a gentle spirit. Gentle and quiet. She had not needed many words. Her gift was listening. She listened to their problems but rarely offered solutions. Somehow, she was able to make her children figure out the answer to problems by themselves. How she missed her mother!

Another wave of sorrow tried to smother her.

That was when she heard it. Pér's ballad drifting on the wind. *Her* song! Kora's heart lifted at the sound – the love and happiness it brought her. She felt snow on her face and sat up, trying to rub warmth back into her cheek. She looked around to see all the lintep and elves lying motionless on the ground – including Lishe.

Lishe was still a problem. Her stolen power had engulfed everyone before they were all knocked down together. If she somehow recovered before the rest of them, they were all lost. Much as she disliked Lishe, they had known each other for years, studied together, discovered things about their power and experimented with things that they shouldn't have. Lishe was a link to Nyssa, no matter how bad. Kora knew what she had to do, though it cut her deeply.

Shaking away the thought, Kora let out a large ball of power, shaped it into an open bubble and slipped it over Lishe, closing it tightly over the fallen lintep's body. No matter how strong she was now, Lishe was trapped unless Kora fell again.

* * *

His songs never worked on himself. Pér had understood that long ago. He could work wonders for others, but they made not a pinch of difference to him. So, it was very odd that he could muster the spirit to play now. Something was making him feel lighter than he had, to think of the good things about Tika rather than the soul crushing knowledge that he was dead. He was seeing things in his mind that he himself had never seen, things he hadn't even known about. Events in the Paradise that had made Tika smile, little victories, stories of magic. Their Partnership. *That* was the best thing in Tika's life. His way to keep Plyke safe in the Paradise. His one claim to magic. His hope that it would work in the end.

Pér felt all these things as he played. Soon, he was simply humming a tune as he strummed his lute. Eventually, he began to put words to the tune. It was a patchwork of Tika's life.

In a Paradise, lived a human boy.
He was born with a wish for magic.
He found a boy unlike the others,

A boy with a special secret.
He asked this boy to be his Partner,
In the hopes that his life would change.
Along came a stranger to take them away,
Led by a girl who kept all their secrets.
She led them through the Outworld
to wondrous places of magic.
Elves, karliki, crystal dragons and lintep.
His wish for magic was coming true.
Together, they lived among the lintep,
finding ways to destroy Paradises.
They freed their friends and reunited families.
Together, they changed the world.
Now Tika's life is at an end,
but his Partnership can live on.
His wish for magic can finally come true.

* * *

Rilla listened to Pér's ballad. She tried to focus on that instead of the guilt that overwhelmed her. Guilt over Rhanya's death and the fact that she had failed to keep her promise to him – to keep the boys safe. Guilt over every other death in the Paradise that she could have prevented by standing up to her father, just as Arishen said she should have all those months ago. Guilt over her bond with Elessa that had eventually forced Eliséo to reveal his secret and lose his freedom by becoming king.

There was even a sense of guilt over Nyssa's death. Had she not been so afraid of the crystal dragons that she hid herself from them, Nyssa would never have been tricked into leaving and Lishe would never have had the chance to capture and torture her, leaving Nyssa with no choice but to gift her power to Shuut.

And, finally, guilt over Shuut. No matter how much good had come of their relationship, there were so many things Rilla had forced her sister to do. Shuut's entire life had been shaped and ruined because of Rilla's very existence.

Pér's ballad ended. Rilla noticed only because his head was right next to hers and the sound had changed into wordless humming. She felt empty inside, like there was nothing left to live for, and no one would care if she died. It would certainly make things easier for a lot of people. She struggled to think of anyone who would be even remotely upset if she were to die right here, on this carpet of snow. Tika's death meant more to Plyke than her death would mean to ... anyone.

The wordless hum eased into words. There was such hope and wonder in this new song. Pér stumbled and caught himself in many places, but it barely detracted from the song at all. Rilla finally noticed how cold she was, lying in the snow. She pulled her knees up under her stomach and pushed herself up into a kneeling crouch.

She looked around and saw the only other person who was sitting was Kora, all the way over where Shuut had laid the trap for Lishe. Everyone else in that group was still lying motionless in the snow. Beside her, Pér was singing and playing while lying on his back. Plyke was still hunched over Tika, shaking through heart wrenching sobs. It was clear his feelings were overwhelming everyone and even Pér's song was having no effect on him.

She shuffled over to her cousin and wrapped her arms around him. Touching his skin, she could feel something was terribly wrong. Tika's death was more than just that. It had somehow ripped away a part of Plyke and made him no longer whole. She leaned her head down over his to pull him closer, but something stopped her. She went to brush the obstacle aside with her hand, only to realise she couldn't see anything there.

Tentatively, she sent out a tendril of her power. It searched around Plyke's head until it found a tendril of Plyke's own power flowing from his head and off towards Pér. Curiously, Rilla's tendril followed the path of Plyke's tendril. It went into Pér and back out again to hover just above the minstrel. She gently touched Plyke's tendril on both sides of Pér and marvelled at what she felt.

It was Tika. Or at least the essence of Tika. She followed that tendril to the end and could have sworn she saw something there for just a moment, a ripple in the air, like with the Paradise boundaries. If it was truly him, she wondered how long Tika's spirit could stay if Plyke did not see him.

"Plyke, Tika is still here," she whispered, still holding him close. Plyke angrily pushed her aside and kept rocking himself back and forth next to Tika's mangled body. "Plyke, just *look*."

Pér stopped playing and turned his head on the snow towards her. "So, I wasn't imagining it then?" Rilla looked at him questioningly. "I've been seeing things from their past that I could not possibly know and thought it might be Tika trying to get through to us."

Rilla laughed sadly and shook her head. "It *had* to be this way. Plyke was always the one who thought it wouldn't work and now we're going to have to convince him it really did before all of this can be fixed." She gestured to the other people lying on the snow.

Pér heaved himself up into a sitting position and looked hard at Rilla. "I'll need your help for this. Much as I want to be close to my son, I don't know him well enough. I don't know what will help him see Tika. Or even what will stop him sending out these waves of raw emotion keeping the others down."

"Not *everyone*," Rilla told him, pointing over to Kora. Pér smiled briefly.

"Kora has always been more sensitive to my songs than anyone else. I've never been able to figure out why."

"Maybe it's because you love her so much," Rilla suggested shyly. Pér looked at her with a bemused expression. "Well, isn't it?"

"I ... had never thought about it like that," he admitted, but Rilla was barely listening. She was already thinking about Plyke and what might help him. He and Tika had had so many arguments over their Partnership since leaving their Paradise. It all came down to guilt. Plyke felt guilty about agreeing to the Partnership with Tika when he did not believe it could work between a human and a lintep. Unfortunately, if they did not change his mind, he would be right and Tika would be lost forever.

"Well, sing to him," Rilla told Pér. "Just do the same thing you do with Kora but try to convince Plyke to look at Tika. He must be right beside you if you can feel his memories pouring into you."

Pér plucked a few strings on his lute as he shuffled over to Plyke. Rilla knelt beside him, willing to help in any way that she could. As Pér began to sing Tika's song to Plyke, she began to hum along as the tune became familiar to her. She noticed that the words of the song were popping into her head just before Pér sang them. Deciding that she couldn't possibly make matters worse, she began to sing along with him. Rilla pictured Tika in her mind, grasping for his essence and threw it into her song, sending wave after wave of his spirit towards Plyke.

Eventually, she noticed that what she was sending towards Plyke wasn't the essence of Tika anymore – it was freedom. Tika's sense of freedom now that he finally had a meaningful link to magic. It made her want to soar into the sky like a bird or a crystal dragon, high above the mountains and the clouds, up where no one could touch her, and she could truly be free.

"The Paradise!" Eliséo called out from behind her. Rilla turned to see that both her elf and Mistress Isis had finally picked themselves up off the snow. Eliséo was pointing at the boundary. Rilla turned back towards it and saw that so many more portions of power were struggling free of the others to fly free into the sky.

"I don't care about the Paradise!" Plyke shouted from the ground. Pér's music faltered and stopped. "I don't care about any of it! Tika is dead because of these stupid creations! I want nothing, *nothing* to do with them anymore."

Rilla could not bear it. This was the nearest they had come to destroying a Paradise since she had stolen the crystal heart to save Plyke's life and he was throwing it all away because he could not see that his Partnership bond was working.

"Tika cares about the Paradise," Rilla told Plyke angrily. "*Tika* is the one who changed Pér's song enough to detach power from the boundary. Tika is there, waiting for you to stop being so blind and *see* him!"

"Don't you *dare* talk to me about my Partner!" Plyke yelled at her as he got to his feet. "You never had a Partner. You will *never* be able to understand what I did to him. I took away Tika's only chance at a proper Partnership when we were both too young to understand it!"

Normally, that sort of rebuke would have made Rilla blush bright red and storm away from him. But today. She walked right up to Plyke and slapped him, hard, across the face. She did not shy from the shocked and angry glare he threw at her.

"You're right," she growled. "I never had a Partner because no one in our Paradise cared for me as much as Tika cared for you. I never had someone so excited to be part of my life as Tika was to be part of yours. Even if it started because he suspected you had magic and it was the only way he could think to get magic in his own life. Even if you accepted it to blend in with everyone else in our awful Paradise. That is *not* the way it ended.

"You two became the envy of all other Partners in our Paradise. Everyone said that if anyone could make the Partnership bond work properly, it would be the two of you."

Rilla was breathing hard, trying so hard to keep her temper with Plyke. She pointed over towards Pér without breaking her stare.

"Tika is right over there, waiting for you to see him. Hoping that you will finally put aside your stupid notion that lintep and humans can't be Partners. I can feel him there. Pér can feel him there. Tika is trying *so hard* to get through to you. All you have to do is look for him and believe."

Plyke looked past her towards Pér, a hint of hope in his eyes but it soon turned to anger.

"There's no one there," he said stonily.

"Use your eyes, Plyke!" Rilla shouted at him. "I can *feel* him." It was true. She could feel him now without her tendril of power around Pér. It felt like Tika was trying to get through to her now. She had an idea.

"Ask me a question," she told Plyke. "Something that I have no way of knowing the answer to. Something special between you and Tika. Anything."

Plyke opened his mouth then shook his head and knelt down beside Tika's crushed body. Pér walked over and sat by his side.

"What's the worst that could happen, Plyke?" he asked softly. "If she tells you the answer, you know Tika is there. If she doesn't, well, you're no worse off than you are right now."

Rilla watched as Pér put an arm around his son's shoulder. Plyke buried his head into his father's shoulder for a long moment.

"Whose idea was it to leave our Paradise?" he asked, still nestled in his father's shoulder.

Rilla instantly saw the image of the two boys sitting by the river at the mill, discussing their options regarding the Outworlder.

"Tika's," Rilla replied. "After Kora had her chat with you and after Tika went to speak with Rhanya about Shuut, he decided you were both going to choose her and visit the elves."

Plyke stiffened but did not turn towards her.

"What did we used to call you, before we left the Paradise?"

Again, Rilla's mind was filled with memory after memory. This time of the two of them talking about her.

"*The girl*," she replied uncomfortably. "I didn't realise the two of you spoke about me quite so often."

Plyke sniffed and wiped his nose on his sleeve. "Tika never dared talk to you, but he was always fascinated by you. He..."

"I know," Rilla replied. "He showed me."

Plyke finally turned towards her. "He really did, didn't he?"

Rilla nodded and pointed in front of herself. "He's throwing all of his memories into me, trying his hardest to get you to believe. I can almost see him myself, but the image keeps slipping.

"In front of you?" Plyke asked hesitantly. Rilla nodded. "You mean, a ripple, like the Paradise boundaries?"

"Yes, exactly!" Rilla replied as the ripple began to move closer to Plyke. "Can you see him?"

Plyke hesitantly reached out a hand into the air and curled his fingers around a part of the ripple. Relief flooded out from him as Tika's spirit appeared before their eyes.

"You took your time," Tika laughed as his spirit danced around, dragging Plyke with him. "I always told you it would work!"

"How?" Plyke asked, happy tears leaving streaks through the dirt on his face.

"I don't know," Tika continued to laugh. "But I have magic now! *Real* magic!"

Eliséo touched Rilla on her shoulder. She turned to him with a smile but frowned when she saw his expression.

"What's wrong?" she asked him worriedly.

"What is happening?" he asked, looking pointedly at Plyke.

Rilla jostled him in the rib with her elbow, thinking it a poor joke. Eliséo only stared at her blankly.

"You can't see him?"

"See who?" he asked confused.

"Tika," Rilla replied hesitantly. "He's right over there, with Plyke."

"There is no one there, Rilla," Eliséo told her. "Plyke is behaving quite oddly."

Rilla looked over to Isis who appeared just as confused as Eliséo. "You can't see him either?"

Isis shook her head. Rilla looked back over to Plyke and Tika. Her friend's spirit was as clear to her eyes as his lintep Partner.

"Pér, you can see him, can't you?" Rilla asked. The minstrel nodded with a bemused expression. "Then why can't Eliséo and Isis?"

"Beats me," Pér replied. "I can barely believe my own eyes."

"Tika?" Kora called out from a distance away. Rilla turned to see Kora with a floating Lishe behind her. Shuut and Lukys were following, but they both looked at Kora oddly when she said Tika's name.

"I don't understand," Rilla said to no one in particular. "Why can the four of us see Tika, but no one else can?"

"That's not important right now," Isis told her, though her tone indicated that she was also curious about it. "We need to finish destroying that boundary and deal with Lishe before she gets free again."

"We'll have to figure out a way to get the mind snares off the elves and lintep over there," Kora said, pointing to the rest of her group who were still lying motionless on the snow.

"Tika's song," Rilla said, turning to Pér. "That was working so well. Now maybe Tika and Plyke can help us too. Let's try it."

Together, the four of them sang Tika's song, pouring in all their hopes and desires for freedom. It worked just as well as before. They were almost done when Kora cried out and fell to her knees.

"What's wrong?" Pér asked, putting his lute under his arm and running to her. "What happened?"

Kora put a hand to her forehead. "It's stopped now," she whispered. "When you were playing, it felt like I was holding a storm in there with Lishe. But it's stopped now."

Rilla listened to Kora's explanation and wondered if what she was thinking could possibly be happening.

"Mistress Isis, if we all protect ourselves with our own power and Eliséo protects himself with his mist, will Lishe be able to put a mind snare on us?"

Isis turned pale, clearly understanding Rilla's plan. "I ... I don't know, Rilla. It's quite a risk to take."

"Her mind snare cannot hurt anyone within my mist," Eliséo reassured them.

Isis shook her head. "It's still quite a risk. She could incapacitate every lintep here. Then what?"

"Kora can't do *that* forever," Rilla pointed to the fallen lintep. "You know yourself how tiring it is to have to use your power for an extended period of time without being able to rest."

"I won't allow such a big risk," Isis told her firmly. "I must insist that every other lintep than yourselves and Kora must be kept safe within Eliséo's mist in case something goes wrong."

"Agreed!"

Rilla quickly detailed her plan to Kora, Plyke, Pér and Tika. Everyone except Pér readily agreed.

"You're placing an awful lot of faith in this plan, Rilla." Pér's voice was low with worry. "If Kora retrieves her power from Lishe, she will be the first victim. Lishe was not only jealous of Nyssa's power you know."

Rilla looked to Eliséo pleadingly. Her elf stepped forward.

"If I see Kora fall, I will instantly bring her within my mist. Lishe will not be able to permanently harm her."

Pér reluctantly agreed to the plan. Eliséo created his mist around Isis, Lukys and Shuut. Through their bond, Rilla looked through his eyes to make sure that he would be able to see if Kora needed help. Once she was satisfied, she turned her attention to the others.

"Kora, once we begin, hold onto Lishe as long as you can," she advised her. For a brief moment, Rilla thought it strange that all these adults were taking orders from her and listening to her plans. She wondered what would have happened if Lukys had taken charge of the situation instead, but he looked completely drained of energy.

Before she had time to dwell on it, Pér started playing his lute. Rilla stood apart from the others and hugged her arms tightly around herself. If this went wrong, she knew Lord Aaron would never forgive her for putting his only remaining child in danger.

As Pér's music grew louder, Rilla joined in the song. She cringed as she felt a swirl of doubt running away from her and into the song. It wasn't going to work, and everyone would blame her. Her doubt grew and fed into the song. Just as she was about to tell Pér to stop playing, she felt a hand tug her fingers from their vice-like grip around her arm. Plyke entwined his fingers around hers and squeezed gently. He looked at her and smiled reassuringly.

Don't doubt yourself, he told her directly to her mind. *You brought Tika back to me, Rilla. Together, we can do anything.*

I get to use lintep magic now! Tika told her excitedly. *Anything is possible!*

Rilla smiled despite herself. Together, Tika and Plyke had turned her doubt into hope. The power in Tika's song flowed all around them. At the excitement in Tika's voice, Rilla saw that the song was working again, much more quickly than the last time.

One by one, powers flew as shimmering lines through the sky. The Paradise boundary was unravelling faster than she'd anticipated. Rilla could already see the tiny forest before them and off to the left. Beyond that, were trade buildings just like in her own Paradise. She could hear shouts of alarm as some of the Paradisians began to realise something was wrong.

A grunt of effort tore Rilla away from the Paradisians. She turned to Kora to see her brow deeply furrowed.

"I can't hold on," she cried out.

Rilla placed a shield of her own power in front of Plyke and Pér as Kora disappeared from view. Beyond where she had been, Rilla saw the fallen elves and lintep slowly get to their feet.

In front of her, Lishe lay on the snow-packed ground screaming and writhing as though in pain. Rilla peered at her as she sang as loudly as she could. Slivers of power were floating away from Lishe in shimmering strands. Some of them were being pulled back, presumably by Lishe's own meagre power, but the lure of the song was too strong. One by one, they fought free from the screaming wreck on the ground.

The sight was horrifying. There was no love lost between Rilla and Lishe, but still she could not help feeling the depth of Lishe's loss. The powers had been stolen, but many of them had been part of her for years. It must have felt like her own power abandoning her. It was enough to drive the lintep crazy.

When the last power had left her and Lishe was powerless to do anything against the much more powerful lintep around her, she continued crying and screaming in turns. She looked up at Rilla with a crazy glint in her eyes.

Rilla felt a tiny tendril snake around her forehead. Angrily, she protected herself with her own power and walked towards Lishe. She bent down and slapped Lishe.

"Don't *ever* try that again," she said in a low and dangerous voice. Lishe cringed back from her, tears streaming down her face, screaming out in rage.

Pér stopped playing his song and Rilla turned to see that the Paradise boundary was now completely gone. It had worked!

Eliséo, we're done, she told her elf. Within seconds their other companions appeared before her eyes.

Chapter Sixty – Prophecy untangled

It was snowing outside the tavern. Not a wild blizzard like Eliséo's memories showed her, but a soft sort of flurry of snowflakes. Rilla stared at it through the open door, mesmerised by the sight. She still couldn't get used to snow.

Tika and Plyke waved, catching her attention. Everyone else had gone ahead but the three of them. It was strange to think they were going to Tika's cremation. She couldn't get her mind around the absurdity of it. Yes, Tika's body was no longer functioning, but he wasn't dead. Not really.

The three of them walked toward the funeral pyre in silence. What was there to say? Thankfully, the older lintep had taken over the arrangements. It had been clear that neither Tika nor Plyke wanted to deal with Tika's crushed body. Rilla felt sick at the thought of it.

His death seemed such a waste. Lishe had purposely taken his life with a horse – a horse of all things! Tika's love of horses had been one of the most important things in his life.

She felt grief welling up inside her, but this time she knew what to do. She sent a tendril of her power over to Tika. Physically, she could not touch him, hug him, but her power could. The feel of him made her smile and swallow the lump in her throat.

Everything was going to be okay. Lishe was defeated and they knew how to destroy the other Paradises. Though she wondered how many they would actually destroy with their song now that Eliséo had told them about the lintep from Hazelston. Perhaps others would want to reclaim their family's power. It was an interesting idea, but she had no time to think about it now.

At the funeral pyre, she noticed with great relief that Tika's body had been placed under the wood so that they could not see it. Rilla watched as Plyke stepped forward. Usually it was the Paradise leader who spoke at cremations, but Eshkin didn't know Tika at all.

"Today should not be a sad day," Plyke began in a soft voice. "I know only a few of us can see Tika's spirit, so for the rest of you it must seem strange that we are not as sad as you."

"This is weird," Tika said, looking out at the gathered people and over to his own body on the funeral pyre.

Rilla stifled a laugh, which caused people to look at her strangely. She noticed Plyke was grinning and couldn't help but laugh aloud.

"Rilla, be respectful!" Lukys chided her.

Rilla turned to retort but was beaten to it by Kora.

"Uncle, she was only laughing at Tika. He said something funny."

"Oh," Lukys replied uncomfortably. "Well then, let's just carry on."

"This feels wrong," Plyke said. "I can't talk about Tika as though he isn't here anymore. He *is* here – right beside me."

"I'll do it," Shuut volunteered. "I can't see him."

Plyke smiled his thanks to her and came to stand beside Rilla. She held his hand for only a moment – this was not a time when they should have to worry about guarding their thoughts and feelings from each other.

"I've known Tika longer than most of you and to be honest, he was a bit of a pain to start with. He had this cheerful insistence that he could follow me into the Outworld and I would somehow keep all of them safe."

"I was right!" Tika shouted.

Rilla struggled to contain her laughter and could see Plyke's shoulders shaking beside her.

"Don't laugh," she mumbled. He burst out laughing. Shuut glared at them.

"Tika, dear, if you could refrain from commenting, this might go along a little easier," Kora said in a patient voice.

"But this is ridiculous! Can't you just tell them I'm sorry they can't speak to me properly anymore, but I'm not really gone. Then just get on with it. I don't want to think of my body lying on that pyre any longer than it needs to."

"Me neither," Rilla said at the same time as Plyke.

"If no one objects, perhaps I can take the three of them back to the tavern," Eliséo offered. Rilla smiled her thanks at him. He was in an interesting position. Rilla knew if he looked through her eyes, using their bond, that he could see Tika, but he couldn't see him with his own eyes.

"That may be for the best," Lukys replied. "This Partner bond is a human thing. It might help if you could find someone in this Paradise who has some experience with it."

"I wonder if there are any," Rilla said as they walked away from the funeral. "I don't think anyone in our Paradise made their Partnership work."

"Ours could be different because I'm a lintep," Plyke suggested. "I mean, I wonder if we'd be able to see Tika if my power wasn't going through him when..."

"When I was crushed," Tika finished the sentence.

There was an awkward silence. Rilla shared a looked with Eliséo. Their bond was very different to a Partnership.

"What happens when elves die? Do their spirits stay with their trees?"

"No," he replied quietly, not looking at her.

"So, that's it then, when you die there's nothing left?"

"Believe it or not, that's what happens when *most* creatures die, human or otherwise," Eliséo told her. "When Plyke dies, hopefully many, many years from now, you likely won't see Tika any more. That will be the end of it."

It was a chilling thought.

"What if the same thing happens though?" Rilla asked. "What if Plyke dies while another lintep's power is going through him? Will both he and Tika still be there?"

"No."

Rilla stopped and looked around to see where the voice had come from. There was an old man standing in the doorway of a building, huddled against the cold. She hadn't realised they were already back in the main part of the Paradise.

"Were you talking to us?" Plyke asked him.

"That I was. I've been watching you." He pointed to Plyke. "You're the one with a dead Partner, ain't you?"

Rilla felt Plyke tense up beside her. He nodded.

"And you can see him too, plus two other lintep, right?"

Rilla nodded, gripping Eliséo's hand. This man felt oddly threatening.

"That's *unnatural*."

The way he said it made Rilla's skin crawl.

"Partnerships are a sacred thing shared between two humans. You've gone and bastardised it with your lintep blood. Your Partner should only be visible to you, not anyone else. It should be a private thing that you don't share with anyone else. And you'll both be gone when you die. There ain't no two ways around that."

"By your own admission, it's different with lintep." Eliséo spoke to the man with a calm voice. Rilla envied him being able to control his emotions so well in this situation. "Unless you have known this exact situation to occur before, then I would suggest you have no more knowledge than the rest of us."

"I *have* experience, you pointy-eared freak," the man snarled. "My sister's Partner turned out to be a lintep and their bond didn't work. Same with everyone else in our Paradise who made that stupid decision."

"Were there a lot of lintep in your Paradise then?" Rilla asked, trying to keep her voice from trembling. She couldn't tell if it was from anger or fear.

The man turned his glare to her. "There *were*. We found them and fixed that. Then the Partnerships started to work again, the way they were meant to."

"You didn't fix it quite as well as you thought you did," Rilla retorted. It was definitely anger rising up in her now. "But now I understand why the lintep who were living here wanted to leave."

"All but that kid, the one your lintep took under their wing. They don't belong here and neither do you."

Rilla shifted her weight and heard a splash as her boots moved in the puddle at her feet. She didn't realise how hot she was getting until she saw the melted snow. She closed her eyes.

Breathe. One, two, three, four, five, six, seven, eight, nine, ten. Breathe.

Rilla opened her eyes and saw the man stare at her in a mixture of disgust and horror. Not allowing him to affect her any further, Rilla turned to her friends.

"Let's go to the tavern. I'm sure the others will meet us there later."

They walked back in silence. Only when they were behind closed doors did she trust herself to speak.

"Did you hear him? He made it sound like they murdered every lintep they could find!"

"Well, yes. So did Erton," Tika pointed out. "Even people who weren't lintep."

"But Erton must have felt some sort of shame for doing it. This sounds like the entire population went out of their way to find all the lintep they could and kill them all!"

Plyke put a hand on her shoulder. "Rilla, it's really no different. Maybe they were more open about it here, but it doesn't sound any more dangerous than our Paradise. Not really."

"But it's ... it's..." She didn't know how to finish her own thoughts.

"It's abominable," Eliséo said pulling her in for a hug. "It's the reason we can't leave any of the Paradises intact, even now that Lishe is no longer a threat. And we can only do that thanks to the three of you. Only together is your song powerful enough to do it. Turns out the prophecy wasn't talking about any one child from a Paradise, but all three of you."

Rilla looked at Eliséo in confusion. She had barely thought about the prophecy since she'd stolen the crystal heart to save Plyke's life. Everyone, including herself, assumed that she had somehow ruined the prophecy. The way Eliséo put it made it sound like this was the way it was meant to happen all along.

Chapter Sixty-One – New arrivals

"They're here," Rilla told Lukys. It was two days after the destruction of the Paradise and the incapacitation of Lishe, and a quiet sort of calm had descended. Even the Paradisians who had newly been exposed to the Outworld were not all as angry or distraught as had been the case with the other broken Paradises. It seemed only the older generation truly hated lintep and everything to do with magic.

After explaining to the Paradise leader, Eshkin, how things had developed in Bryntown, and that Duchess Gardena was already sending people up to help them here, things had calmed down considerably.

Eshkinville had almost unanimously been chosen as the village's new name, following in the tradition that had started in Bryntown. A few lintep had been identified and given the option to stay in Eshkinville or move to one of the many lintep settlements they now knew were scattered throughout the Outworld. All but one had quickly decided to move to the nearest lintep town and were currently being escorted there by a few of the clear crystal dragons. Apparently, they had not felt quite safe enough in their homes once their secrets were exposed.

"I can't say I'll be sorry to leave," Lukys replied wearily. "There are so many more Paradises to destroy. I wish we could somehow do it all in one go, but I know that's not possible."

Rilla studied the king. He did not even have the energy to look up at her, let alone stand. This last trip into the Outworld had not done him any good – nor had his struggle against Lishe.

"You could always take Lishe back to Illaria with Lord Aaron," she suggested. "One last flight and then you would be home. The rest of us can deal with this now that she's ... no longer a problem."

Rilla was being polite. The fact was that Lishe had become a rambling idiot since her stolen powers had fled. There was not a coherent thought going through her brain and she had neither the power nor the will to struggle against them anymore.

Lukys finally looked at up Rilla with a wry smile. "Would you, by any chance, be trying to get rid of me and your grandfather in one fell swoop?"

Rilla did not answer. It was true she was not looking forward to her grandfather's arrival. Oddly enough, she was more excited about seeing Marilisa and Lord Kynon than Lord Aaron.

"He loves you, Rilla," Lukys said as he reached out a hand to her. She took it gingerly. "He is so scared of losing more of his family that he sometimes acts irrationally and says things I know he regrets."

"He didn't seem to regret anything he said to me the last few times we spoke," Rilla growled and clenched her other hand into a fist. Lukys squeezed her hand.

"I know I've said some harsh words to you as well and I am sorry. I am sorry for all the times I got angry with you for trying to think creatively and come up with ideas that would never have occurred to me in my entire life.

"Indeed, it was for that very reason that I was angry. Not that you had dared make those suggestions, but because I knew they were good and I was humbled into accepting them. You are still a child, Rilla, but that should not stop us from listening to you. I'm sorry you spent so much of your time being invisible to everyone around you. I never want that for you again. I want so much *more* for you than that."

Rilla stared at him in disbelief. She had always assumed he disliked her intensely because she was Nyssa's outspoken daughter. It had never occurred to her that it was because he wished he could come up with the ideas she did, even if they were rash and sometimes just outright dangerous.

Before she had a chance to reply, the dragons which she had seen in the distance finally arrived. She and Lukys walked very sedately over to the clearing to greet them. Garnet and Malachite carried Lord Aaron, Lord Kynon, Marilisa, Mistress Kayte, Séverin and Maéva, and surprisingly, Arishen.

"What are you doing here?" Rilla asked him with a bemused smile, only belatedly noticing his forlorn expression. She wished she had kept her mouth shut until they were alone.

"Arishen thought it would be good idea to see through this project of destroying the Paradises," Mistress Kayte replied smoothly. "I thought it was more fitting to his skills than apprenticing with Master Timothée."

Rilla refrained from commenting. She could see that was far from the truth. Plyke, with Tika floating beside him, came running up to them.

"Arishen! Look! Our Partnership worked!" Plyke was yelling at him from a distance. Rilla was certain she was not the only one to see Arishen cringe. His own Partner had threatened to expose him in their Paradise and then ordered him killed the last time they met. Any mention of successful Partnerships was bound to be difficult for him to hear now.

When Arishen did not answer him, Plyke looked enquiringly over at Rilla. She pursed her lips and shook her head.

Not now, she spoke directly to his mind.

"Where's my Kora?" Lord Aaron asked, once Plyke's outburst was over. Rilla noticed that he seemed as dismissive of Plyke as he was of herself. She glanced at Lukys, but his shoulders were already stooped over in weariness again.

"Marilisa, good to see you again." Rilla dismissed her grandfather and walked over to her cousin. "Let me show you around this Paradise. Then you can see what kind of world we grew up in."

Much to her surprise, Marilisa took her arm and strode off from the older lintep. Plyke joined them, tugging Arishen along behind him. Rilla tried not to think of what must have befallen the seer to make Mistress Kayte bring him out here again.

* * *

Shuut watched her family from a distance. Marilisa had changed quite a bit since they had first met. The spoilt little brat who thought she was better than everyone had vanished. Here she was walking arm in arm with Rilla, talking animatedly and looking at everything with such keen curiosity.

Her gaze drifted to Rilla. The half-sister she had not known existed until a few months ago, but who had been the greatest cause of trouble in her life without even knowing it. Shuut thought back to the moment of that revelation – had her mother not been there and treated Rilla so harshly, Shuut knew she probably would have been too angry with Rilla to ever speak to her again. Instead, she had turned her fury towards the mother who should have treated *both* of them better.

Then there was Plyke. Now an heir to the throne by default. He would never be allowed to stray too far from Illaria, but his Partnership with Tika might help to strengthen ties between humans and lintep. Shuut wondered if Aislen had considered that before making her decision about Kora.

A crunching of snow nearby stole her attention and Shuut turned, hand on the hilt of her sword. Séverin held up his hands in mock defeat.

"I'll never be able to surprise you," he laughed. Shuut blushed at the praise and relaxed her hand. Séverin walked confidently to her, wrapped his arms around her waist and pulled her close. Without a moment of hesitation, he kissed her softly. Still amazed that he felt anything for her, Shuut flung her arms around his neck, pulling him even closer and returned his kiss not quite so softly.

"So, have you made a decision yet?" Séverin asked between kisses. "Are you going to live in Illaria or am I going to spend my life following you around the Outworld?"

Shuut was taken aback by his question. She could tell he felt her confusion, but he melted away her fears and doubts with ever more kisses.

* * *

Kora found her father in the tavern late that afternoon. She had heard that he'd arrived but had not had time to spare for him until now. The one lintep who had decided to remain in the Eshkinville was dire need of training. Kora, Pér and Isis had spent all day with the boy, trying to make sure he did not lose his power. It made her desire for a school all the greater. He would not be able to stay in a place this hostile to his kind for long.

"Father." She greeted him with a kiss on the cheek. That brief skin contact told her something was amiss, but her father's control over his power was too great for her to glimpse what it was. "Are you here to shadow Rilla and Plyke as they destroy the rest of the Paradises?"

"Don't be absurd!" he scolded her harshly. "I'm here to take them back to Illaria so they can continue their lessons and not put themselves in any more danger."

"Uh," Kora replied slowly. She looked over to Uncle Lukys for his insistence that they would not return, only to find him sleeping, head resting on his crossed arms at a table of the tavern.

"I also expect *you* to return home with us," Aaron continued as though Kora had agreed enthusiastically. Kora looked at her father closely as she sat across the table from him.

"Father, you know that is not possible," she told him cautiously. "Not for any of us."

"Of course, it is," Aaron replied with a dismissive wave. "If you insist on Pér returning with us, he can teach the other lintep who are to remain in the Outworld, and they can destroy the rest of the Paradises themselves."

Kora placed a hand on his arm.

"Father. Stop."

He looked up at her almost as though seeing her for the first time.

"We cannot return now. *None* of us. You know very well that Pér is unique in his ability with music. It has taken him a great deal of time and effort to teach Rilla and Plyke and neither of them can do it well without him.

"Then, after the Paradises are destroyed, there will be lintep who need my help out here. Bastienne has agreed to travel with me to Statera when I bring Abelin and Lorella there. He is certain they will be willingly adopted into his old village.

"I'm already helping to teach a lintep right here. Pér has decided to join me, and it is very likely Plyke will also when he has completed his training in Illaria. You cannot expect things to remain the same."

Aaron put his head in his hands and sucked in deep breaths. Kora suspected he was trying to hold back tears.

"You can't do this to me," he told her quietly. "I missed so much of your life. You can't leave me again and take my grandson with you."

Kora felt a well of guilt open up inside her. She stoppered it quickly. She'd lived through a lifetime of guilt. She would *not* succumb to it again.

"We won't be gone forever, Father. We will return several times each year. But I will not remain in Illaria simply because you miss me. I *need* to do this. I will never be content otherwise." Kora realised how true the words were as she said them. "Aislen has made sure that I will end my days in Illaria, as *queen* of all things, but until the time when I am needed, I will not be held back by anyone. Not anymore."

* * *

Eliséo slept through the first half of the night. He had pushed himself too far and it was beginning to wear on him. He remembered, with a twinge of sadness, that Tika had once reminded him that elves needed to sleep sometimes too. In the darkness of the tavern, he looked over at Plyke. The boy looked quite serene, almost as though Tika had not died. In a way, he supposed that was true. Tika would never leave Plyke now. It did not matter that few could see him – all that mattered was that Plyke could.

Much as he tried to stop himself, his gaze wandered until he found Rilla. She was curled up in a corner, Shuut's arms wrapped protectively around her. It made him happy that she had found at least some family who was good to her.

"You watch her often," Liessa commented from behind him. Eliséo did not answer. He did not know how. "You know you cannot stay with her forever. I do not think the elves will mind if you remain with her while the Paradises are being destroyed, if you can give them even a tenuous excuse for doing so. However, once she returns to Illaria, you cannot remain with her."

"I cannot ..." His voice broke. He swallowed the lump in his throat and tried again. "I had not realised quite how much I had missed her presence until I saw her again."

Liessa shuffled to sit beside him.

"She will not live in Illaria her entire life. With her lifespan extended through her bond with Elessa, she will grow bored there, if the lintep do not turn on her first for having such an unnaturally long life."

"It may take a long time for *that* to happen," Eliséo sighed.

Chapter Sixty-Two – A Choice

Troops from Firechester arrived the next day, along with Duke Leif, Talise and Telon atop Snowcrest. The other crystal dragons were quick to melt more snow to create a grassy patch for her to rest on. They had quickly discovered that they did not enjoy sleeping on snow. Though the blizzard had stopped days ago, a white blanket still covered everything in sight.

Rilla watched the proceedings from a distant hill. Duke Leif introduced King Lukys to a lady rugged up in a voluminous red coat. She must have been Duchess Gardena. Rilla had heard from Telon that the duchess had decided she needed to see at least one broken Paradise with her own eyes before fully agreeing to commit her troops to the operation. The group quickly disappeared into Eshkin's private hut, presumably to discuss important matters.

She gazed over the rest of Eshkinville. It was a fractured village. The sudden exposure and departure of the resident lintep had left a sour taste in Rilla's mouth. Lintep were clearly not welcome in this village, though the humans were currently forced to work with them.

Rilla's thoughts drifted to Arishen. She wished he would tell her what had happened.

You could ask him, Eliséo spoke directly to her through their bond.

I tried, Rilla replied sullenly. She watched Eliséo walk up the hill to join her.

"Do you know anything of what transpired?"

"Mistress Kayte told us he isn't apprenticed anymore and isn't safe in the town. She's been sharing the care of him with Mistress Emeline but couldn't leave him with her while she was gone, so brought him out here because it was safer for him. No one knows what to do with him."

"I daresay the masters and mistresses in Illaria will find good use for him in the castle if he agrees to work with them."

Rilla doubted Arishen's willingness to work with them. He'd had such a violent reaction the last time students had worked with him. Still, he could not stay in Illaria without earning his keep somehow. Rilla knew that even *she* would need to choose a trade at some point or find a way to be useful in Illaria.

She still did not know what she wanted to do, but she was more than skilled enough to attempt to become a mistress if they would ever let her pass the tests given her tendency to "reckless" behaviour. Rilla smiled to herself at that. It was no wonder some of them were so wary of her – in many ways, she could potentially be just as dangerous as Lishc. The real difference was that she would never stoop to hurt anyone intentionally with her power.

Rilla mulled over that thought. She would never intentionally hurt anyone with her power. But could she protect someone with it?

"What are you thinking?" Eliséo asked, looking down at her. "You have that little light in your eye that sparks every time you have an idea."

"You said the lintep in Hazelston give each other their power, right?"

Eliséo nodded.

"And the Paradises were created when lintep gave *some* of their power to create it. So, would it be possible to give someone just a small portion of your power, without it becoming a mind snare?"

Rilla looked at Eliséo with so much hope that she could barely breathe. Had she just found a way to protect Arishen – forever?

Together, they ran down the hill. Rilla sent tendrils of her power out in every direction searching for Arishen. She found him shadowing Mistress Kayte in the healers' house. That would not do.

Kora, Isis, I need you. Meet me outside the healers' house.

By the time Rilla and Eliséo reached the healers' house, Isis was already there. They waited a few moments for Kora to arrive, Rilla refusing to explain herself twice.

"I need your help," Rilla told them. "Arishen needs protection. I can't be there all the time and I really don't want to be. He won't tell us what happened to him in Illaria, but it must have been awful for Mistress Kayte to bring him out here again.

"I want to do something so that he doesn't have to live in fear of lintep anymore. I want to give him some of my power."

Kora and Isis stared wide-eyed at her. Rilla looked at Eliséo for help.

"It should be possible, from everything we have learned recently," he told them. "We learned in Hazelston that the gifting of lintep power is a common occurrence in the Outworld and we know the splitting of power is possible from the very creations we have been destroying."

Isis recovered first. "It *should* be possible, but I would wager it was often done by much more experienced lintep."

"I want to try it," Rilla insisted. "I *need* to try it. I trust you both to keep me and Arishen safe while I try it. Will you help me?"

"Yes," Kora answered quietly.

"Lady Kora!" Isis turned to her in surprise.

Kora glanced at Isis then back at Rilla. "We'll help you. It's a marvellous idea. And you're the only lintep Arishen would trust enough to do this with."

Rilla smiled her thanks and turned her attention to Mistress Isis. She kept her tendrils well away from the fire mistress, not wanting to accidentally intrude on her thoughts. Eventually, Isis nodded.

"Thank you."

Rilla pushed the door to the healers' house open and searched through the rooms until she found Mistress Kayte and Arishen. Instead of barging in there herself, she waited outside with Eliséo while Mistress Isis and Kora explained her idea.

"She is not skilled enough," Kayte said. "She will likely hurt herself or the seer."

Rilla tapped her teeth together. She knew she would only make things worse if walked in and argued.

"Let her try," Arishen said quietly. "It can't be worse than doing nothing. I can't live in the Outworld – I don't belong here – and I can't live in Illaria as a human seer. I have no protection from anyone.

"Master Timotheé terminated my apprenticeship because his apprentices kept jumping into my mind whenever I refused to answer their questions. I don't want to live in fear the rest of my life. *Please* let her try."

Rilla squeezed Eliséo's hand tightly as she listened to Arishen. She knew she hadn't been given a choice, but she would never be able to forgive herself for leaving him in Illaria at the mercy of any lintep who wanted to abuse their power over him.

Mistress Kayte sighed loudly. "Come in, Rilla. If you're going to try this, I suppose there's no safer environment to do it."

Rilla squeezed Eliséo's hand and pulled him into the room with her. She had spent so much time away from him that she didn't want to be separated from him now.

She looked around the room. Her breath caught in her throat. It was so similar to Rhanya's old room that she had to look closely to find the differences. Instinctively, she felt for Rhanya's letter in her pocket and closed her fingers tightly around it.

Arishen looked at her with a frown. "You still carry Rhanya's letter with you?"

"Everywhere," Rilla replied quietly.

"Is that why you're doing this?" he asked bitterly. "Because of your promise to him?"

From his voice, Rilla would have thought he was angry that it took a promise for her to offer this help, but that wasn't it. She could feel hopelessness cascading off him. Hopelessness and a fear that he was a burden to everyone.

"No, not really," she answered slowly. "It's true, that's how everything started out, back when we first met Shuut. But that's not why I'm offering this. Your gift is *yours* and no one should be able to manipulate you to use it. If this works, you'll have control over your own life. You'll be able to do anything, live anywhere. The choice will be yours. We all deserve that choice, don't you think?"

Arishen's hopelessness stopped crashing into her. A smile spread hesitantly across his face.

"A choice would be nice."

Mistress Kayte stepped between them and stared at Rilla with hard eyes.

"This is no parlour trick. If any of us feel that things are getting out of control, you must stop. Do you understand?"

Rilla breathed slowly. "I understand. But I want *you* to understand that I didn't come to you for help. If Arishen hadn't been with you, I would only have asked Kora and Isis for help."

Mistress Kayte's face turned red. Kora walked slowly over to her.

"Mistress Kayte, I do believe your area of expertise lies in healing. If your skills are required, we will alert you. Until then, you will kindly keep your hands, and your powers, off my niece. Is *that* understood?"

Rilla struggled to keep the smirk off her face as Mistress Kayte moved to a corner of the room. This was not the time to goad the healing mistress.

"Now, does anyone have the slightest idea how to begin this?" Kora asked.

Rilla looked around at everyone. Her heart sank.

Ensil, find Master Bastienne and Princess Aislen. Rilla heard Eliséo's voice in her mind. She looked over to see his eyes shining bright silver.

"I believe Master Bastienne's father helped to create a Paradise. If anyone has information on how to split their power, it would be him."

Rilla sat beside Arishen on the floor while they waited for Ensil to reply.

"What will you do if this works?"

"I honestly don't know," Arishen replied. "I still wouldn't belong in the Outworld."

"You could belong if you found an apprenticeship."

Arishen huffed. "I doubt it. I expect a lot of people out here would react the same way as Parthak did. Humans don't see this as a gift."

"So, Illaria then? Or one of the smaller lintep settlements?"

Arishen didn't answer for a moment. "I don't know. It might be nice to work with Mistress Emeline, if I knew her students couldn't just dive in whenever they wanted to."

Rilla squeezed his hand gently. It was nice to know there was at least one lintep Arishen liked working with.

They're here. Ensil's voice was in her mind.

Eliséo motioned the older lintep to gather around him. They each placed a hand on his arm. Rilla held out her hand for Arishen to hold then explained her idea to Aislen and Master Bastienne.

Rilla, I really don't think you've thought this through. Aislen sounded worried.

Bah, you're just afraid of her idea because it isn't common practice here, Bastienne scoffed. *Don't forget it was one of your own princesses who approached hundreds of lintep asking for a portion of their power to create the Paradises.*

Rilla could feel Aislen's tension.

The idea has merit, Aislen. The voice was not one Rilla recognised. *We spoke to a number of lintep in Hazelston where the procedure is quite commonplace. In fact, they were furious that the Paradises were being destroyed without a chance for families to reclaim power that was rightfully theirs.*

The door opened and Luisella walked in with Raeslin by her side – the elf's eyes were glowing brightly. Rilla looked up in surprise. She'd had very little to do with Umi and Ulf's mother since arriving in Illaria.

"Rilla, dear, it seems what you need to do is take a portion of your power and attempt to detach it from the rest. If you can do that, we can help you figure out the rest," Luisella said as she sat by Rilla's side. "By all accounts, you're quite the clever girl. I believe you will find a way."

Inexpressibly buoyed by Luisella's faith in her, Rilla concentrated on her power. She knew there was a lot of it but had no idea what would be necessary to help Arishen. With a shrug, she selected an amount and held it in front of Luisella.

"Is this enough?"

Rilla could feel Luisella's power fluttering gently around her own. Luisella laughed lightly.

"No, dear, that's too much. Something like this would be sufficient."

Rilla felt around with her power until she found the tiny amount Luisella held out before her.

"That's all?" she asked in surprise. "How can that be enough?"

"For what you wish to achieve, you only need enough to shield his mind. Now, try to detach that portion of your power."

Rilla focused on the tiniest portion of her power, held it in front of her face and tried to pull it apart from the rest of her power. Over, and over, again, she tried to detach it but to no avail.

Do not forget to talk to your power, Eliséo told her directly. *You could try to explain what you intend for it.*

Rilla smiled. She had been so focused on what others had been telling her, she forgot to do what she did best.

She turned to Arishen and looked into his eyes. They were so full of fear.

"Hold out your hands," she told him.

Hesitantly, he did as she requested. Rilla placed the selected portion of power into his hands. It hovered above them, not touching them.

I need you to stay with Arishen now. You will belong to him now. Protect him from anyone who wishes to jump into his mind.

Rilla waited patiently. Eventually, she felt the power detach and fall into Arishen's hands.

"Can you feel it?"

Arishen closed his hands gently around the power and brought it up to his face, looking closer, trying to see it.

"I can feel something, but I can't see it."

"No, dear, you won't ever be able to see it," Luisella told him gently. "However, if you will allow me, I will assist Kora and Isis in teaching you how to use it. Would you like that?"

Arishen looked from Luisella to Rilla. Rilla nodded eagerly. A slow smile crawled onto Arishen's face.

"That would be ... nice."

Rilla sat back with Eliséo by her side. Together, they watched as Luisella, Kora and Isis showed Arishen how to take her power and use it to protect himself from lintep who did not respect his privacy. Rilla was mildly surprised that Mistress Kayte had not attempted to intervene since Kora had spoken to her. Perhaps Kora had more authority than Rilla had realised.

"That's all we can do for now," Luisella said after a long while. "This shield will prevent anyone from entering your mind. However, should you choose to live in a lintep community, I would suggest you take further lessons on how to effectively use this power.

"You may not realise it, but Rilla has given you as much power as a part-lintep. It is not enough to do great feats of magic, but it is enough for you to learn simple skills should you wish it."

Rilla looked up in surprise. It had been such a tiny portion of her power that she did not think she would ever miss it. How could it possibly be useful for anything?

Luisella laughed. "My dear, you were quite generous. Now all that remains is for Arishen to decide where he would like to live and how he would like to use his gift in the future. But there is no rush. It can be decided once the Paradises are all destroyed."

Rilla saw the look of indecision in Arishen's eyes. They had both grown up in a place they didn't belong. Rilla felt at home in Illaria. She wondered if Arishen ever would.

Rilla excused herself and left Eliséo with the older lintep. It was a brisk day. Snow fell in a light flurry as she walked aimlessly through Eshkinville.

"Rilla, wait for me," Arishen called out.

Rilla turned to see him jogging through the snow.

"I just wanted to ... I don't know how to say ..." Arishen took a deep breath. "Thank you."

"Thank her for what?" Plyke asked as he and Tika approached them from the eating hall.

"For giving me some of her power," Arishen answered.

Plyke's mouth dropped open.

"All of us!" Tika squealed. "We all have lintep power now. How amazing!"

Arishen nodded. "All of us."

Rilla turned to Arishen in surprise. "You can hear Tika now?"

"You can't?" he asked.

"Well, yes, but so few of us can. I didn't realise you could too."

"Maybe it's just the people I like the most who can see me," Tika suggested.

"No, then Eliséo would definitely be able to see you," Rilla pointed out. "It's only the three of us, Kora and Pér as far as I can tell."

"We've known Tika the longest," Arishen pointed out.

"But you couldn't see him before I gave you some of my power."

"We're all family now," Plyke said.

Rilla frowned at him. "No, we're not."

"Yes, we really are. My power goes through Tika, which basically makes Tika my family. Kora is my mother, so she can see him. You're my cousin, so you can see him. Now Arishen has some of your power, so he can see Tika too."

"Then why can't Shuut see him?" Rilla asked, unconvinced.

"Maybe Arishen's right," Tika suggested. "The four of you have known me the longest. If anyone was going to be able to see me, it would be you and Plyke's parents. I've never heard of anyone other than the living Partner being able to see the spirit one. So, it's probably only because I died with Plyke's power in me that more people can see me."

Rilla didn't bother arguing the matter any further. It was an unprecedented event she had no chance of understanding. All she really cared about was that the four of them could now stay together as long as they wanted.

* * *

Decisions had to be made and Lukys wished, for the first time, that it was not all up to him. He was too tired for all of this. The arguments with his cousin were not helping matters.

"Aaron, I cannot force her to return to Illaria any more than you can," he sighed heavily. "Kora will do as she pleases. She always has, and I don't see that as a bad thing. If she had not left Illaria, we would never have known where to find the Paradises, and your grandchildren would not exist. Don't be so hard on her."

Aaron crossed his arms and huffed angrily.

"Now, I'm taking Lishe back to Illaria tomorrow morning. You can choose to come with me or stay with the others. I understand everyone else has decided to remain in the Outworld until all the Paradises are destroyed. If you choose to return to Illaria with me, I will ask you to take on some classes as we are severely shorthanded."

"I never took the tests, Lukys," Aaron reminded him.

Lukys waved his protest aside. "A mere technicality. Most of the masters and mistresses defer to your judgment when it come to their powers. I have appreciated your help over the years in running Illaria, but I rather think your talents were wasted. When things have settled down a bit, I would like to see you take on more classes – possibly those special skills which are granted by Isis' council."

Aaron drew in a deep breath. Lukys knew Aaron would not be happy about that decision, as he had been the one to argue against such lessons, but at least it meant he would be cautious in the teaching and make sure the students knew all sides to the skills being taught.

Lukys sat back and closed his eyes. He was so very tired.

* * *

Aislen was wrapping up the last petitioners of the day when she saw Ensil's eyes glow bright blue. She nodded to herself. Her father would now be on his way home. In all honesty, she was glad he had gone to the Outworld himself. These audiences were exhausting, and her father had looked so tired of late. When the audience was at last at an end, she walked over to Ensil whose eyes were still glowing.

"What news, Ensil? Is my father returning?"

Ensil did not avoid her gaze, but he was certainly uncomfortable.

"King Lukys is dead," he told her bluntly.

Aislen took a step back and shook her head. She must have heard wrong.

"Impossible!"

The elf reached out and took her hand. In her mind, Aislen saw Aaron sitting by her father's side, weeping bitterly. Her father looked like he was sleeping, and he no longer looked tired.

I'm sorry, Aislen. It was Rilla's anguished voice in her mind. *Lord Aaron said they were talking and Lukys closed his eyes but never opened them again. He was going to come home tomorrow with Lishe. Lord Aaron says he will escort them both back to Illaria and help you plan your coronation. He has warned it will take a few months to get everything in order.*

Aislen took her hand back from Ensil. *My ... coronation.* The thought seemed absurd to her. Surely it was a jest, a bad one.

"It is no jest," Ensil told her as he gently led her to her throne. "I have seen the end of many monarchs in my time. The heir almost always wishes for their turn not to come, but it always does. I've watched you closely these past weeks, Aislen. You will make a good queen. Your people love and trust you – that is a good start."

Aislen looked up at him in disbelief. How could it all change so quickly? It was a new world. She must endeavour to make it better than the old one. She had already promised Leif as much, though she had failed miserably with Arishen. Aislen gritted her teeth. She would find a way for humans and lintep to live in peace, *without* letting Rilla give more of her power in that pursuit.

* * *

With a growing numbness inside of her, Rilla scanned the Paradise from her favourite hill. The younger elves mingled easily with the younger lintep and children of Eshkinville. The older elves mostly kept to themselves or spoke only with the oldest of the lintep.

Tika and Plyke were happily testing the limits of their bond and the powers that had been bestowed upon Tika. Nearby, Kora and Pér were instructing Arishen and the only remaining lintep resident of Eshkinville. It made her oddly happy to know that she had given Arishen enough power not only to shield his mind, but to actually use in a practical way.

She knew they would all be leaving soon. With the arrival of Duchess Gardena and her troops, there was no reason for any of them to stay. Aislen had already decreed, in a conversation with Lord Aaron through Rilla and Ensil, that any lintep who wished to return to Illaria could now do so.

There was little chance of any harm coming to the rest of them now that Lishe was

343

incapacitated. That also meant there was no real reason for the elves to stay with them. The very thought made her chest ache.

My heart will always be torn in two, Rilla told Elessa in confidence. *One part will always belong with my family and friends in Illaria. The other part will always belong with you and Eliséo in Silvaren. Wherever I am, I won't be happy.*

Elessa embraced her mind as only a tree could. *We'll always be with you,* she told Rilla. *Even if you stay in Illaria for years at a time, we will be there too.*

It's not the same, Rilla sobbed. *I thought it was, but when I saw Eliséo, I ... couldn't hug him tightly enough. When I'm not with you, it's like you both become a dream that might not be real. I start to think that I'm imagining my bond or that it will weaken over time or that you'll get used to not having me around and discard it altogether.*

Eliséo was suddenly in her mind. *That will never happen.* His answer was strong and certain. *I gave up my freedom to keep you in our lives. We will not discard you so lightly as you think possible.*

Rilla did not realise she had closed her eyes until she felt an arm around her shoulder pulling her close. She opened her eyes to see Eliséo. He did not look at her. It felt as though he couldn't, or he would break down.

"Most of my elves will be returning to Silvaren this afternoon. A few of the younger ones have requested leave to travel the Outworld for a while before returning. With our new method of communicating across distances, I have granted their request, with Liessa chaperoning them."

"What will *you* be doing?" Rilla asked, barely trusting her voice.

He did not reply for a long while. Rilla knew better than to push him for an answer and did not attempt to pry through their bond. Eventually, he turned to face her.

"I would like to help strengthen ties between humans, lintep, elves and karliki. I think it would be a good idea for at least one elf to be stationed in all major human cities as well as Goraburg and Illaria. I will need to ask permission of their leaders, but I don't think many will object."

"You're avoiding my question," Rilla pointed out.

Eliséo shifted his weight.

"Before I travel to each of these places, I would like your permission to accompany you to the remainder of the Paradises."

Rilla smiled. "You don't need my permission, but I'll give it anyway. Besides, I'd like *your* permission to visit Silvaren as often as I choose between my studies, and perhaps bring a friend or two each time."

"Granted," Eliséo said with a mock bow. "I should like to meet some of your friends, most especially Kalydron and Miette. Not to mention that as king, I should like to be present at Aislen's coronation. By that time, the humans should have come to some sort of agreement between themselves about how to proceed with other races."

Rilla looked up at him and grinned.

"You're going to make a brilliant king, you know. Even though you never wanted to be one. Eléna must have known she was training you for it your entire life."

Eliséo's eyes sparkled, but he remained silent.